Born in Paris in 1947, Christian Jacq first visited Egypt when he was seventeen, went on to study Egyptology and archaeology at the Sorbonne, and is now one of the world's leading Egyptologists. He is the author of the internationally bestselling RAMSES series, THE QUEEN OF FREEDOM trilogy and several other novels on Ancient Egypt. Christian Jacq lives in Switzerland.

Also by Christian Jacq:

The Ramses Series
Volume 1: The Son of the Light
Volume 2: The Temple of a Million Years
Volume 3: The Battle of Kadesh
Volume 4: The Lady of Abu Simbel
Volume 5: Under the Western Acacia

The Stone of Light Series
Volume 1: Nefer the Silent
Volume 2: The Wise Woman
Volume 3: Paneb the Ardent
Volume 4: The Place of Truth

The Queen of Freedom Trilogy
Volume 1: The Empire of Darkness
Volume 2: The War of the Crowns
Volume 3: The Flaming Sword

The Judge of Egypt Trilogy
Volume 1: Beneath the Pyramid
Volume 2: Secrets of the Desert
Volume 3: Shadow of the Sphinx

The Black Pharaoh
The Tutankhamun Affair
For the Love of Philae
Champollion the Egyptian
Master Hiram & King Solomon
The Living Wisdom of Ancient Egypt

About the translator

Sue Dyson is a prolific author of both fiction
and non-fiction, including over thirty novels both
contemporary and historical. She has also translated
a wide variety of French fiction.

The Judge of Egypt Trilogy

Secrets of the Desert

Christian Jacq

Translated by Sue Dyson

POCKET
BOOKS

LONDON • SYDNEY • NEW YORK • TORONTO

First published in France by Plon under the title
La Loi du Désert, 1993
First published in Great Britain by Simon & Schuster UK
Ltd, 2004
This edition first published by Pocket Books, 2004
An imprint of Simon & Schuster UK Ltd
A Viacom company

1 3 5 7 9 10 8 6 4 2

Simon & Schuster UK Ltd
Africa House
64–78 Kingsway
London WC2B 6AH

www.simonsays.co.uk

Simon & Schuster Australia
Sydney

A CIP catalogue record for this book is available
from the British Library

ISBN 0-671-01799-3
EAN 9780671017996

Typeset in Times by SX Composing DTP, Rayleigh, Essex
Printed and bound in Great Britain by
Cox & Wyman Ltd, Reading, Berkshire

Great is the Rule, and lasting its effect; it has not been disrupted since the time of Osiris.

Iniquity is capable of gaining possession of the many, but evil shall never bring its undertakings to fruition.

Have no part in any plot against the human race, for God punishes such actions . . .

If you have listened to the maxims I have just told you, all your plans will proceed well.

The teachings of the sage Ptah-hotep: extracts from maxims 5 and 38

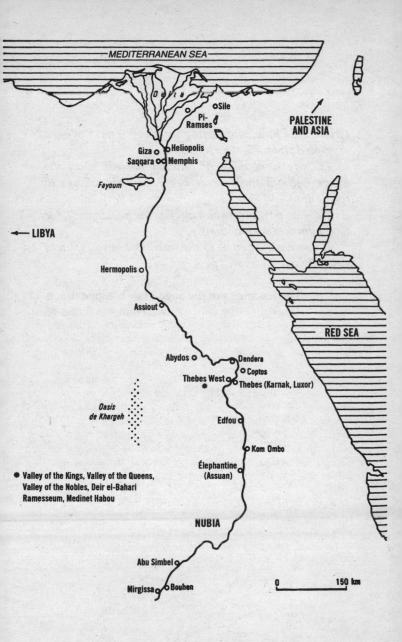

1

The heat was so overpowering that the only creature to venture out into the sand-covered prison yard was a black scorpion. Deep in the desert between the Nile Valley and the Khargeh oasis, a week's march west of the holy city of Karnak, the prison housed persistent offenders who had been sentenced to back-breaking hard labour. When the temperature allowed, they maintained the track linking the valley to the oasis, along which caravans of donkeys travelled, laden with supplies.

For the tenth time, Judge Pazair presented his request to the camp's governor, a giant of a man who was quick to lash out at anyone who breached his iron discipline.

'I cannot go on getting preferential treatment like this,' said Pazair. 'I want to work like all the others.'

Pazair was a lean man, quite tall, with chestnut hair, a broad, high forehead and green eyes flecked with brown. Although his prison ordeal had banished all traces of his youthful energy, he still had a nobility which commanded respect.

'You aren't like the others,' said the governor.

'I'm a prisoner, too.'

'You haven't been sentenced, you're just being held secretly. For me, you don't even exist. No name in the register, no identification number.'

'That doesn't mean I can't break rocks.'

'Go back and sit down.'

The governor was wary of Pazair. The judge had astonished Egypt by organizing the trial of the famous General Asher. Asher had been accused by Pazair's best friend, Lieutenant Suti, of the torture and murder of an Egyptian scout, and of collaborating with the sand-travellers and with the Libyans, who were Egypt's hereditary enemies.

The unfortunate scout's body had not been found at the place Suti had indicated. So the jurors, who were unable to convict the general, had confined themselves to demanding an additional investigation. An investigation which was swiftly aborted, since Pazair had fallen into an ambush, and had been accused of murdering his spiritual father, the sage Branir, the designated High Priest of Karnak. Caught red-handed, he had been arrested and deported, with no regard for the law.

Pazair sat down on the burning sand. He thought constantly of his wife, Neferet. For a long time, he had believed that she would never love him; then happiness had come along, as blazing as a summer sun. A happiness which had been brutally shattered, a paradise from which he had been driven, without any hope of ever returning.

A hot wind began to blow. It turned the grains of sand into whirlwinds that whipped the skin. Pazair sat with a white cloth over his head and paid it no heed; he was reliving the stages of his investigation.

He had come from the provinces as a junior judge, quite lost in the great city of Memphis, and had made the mistake of being too conscientious, by studying a strange case in detail. He had uncovered the murders of five former soldiers who had been the honour-guard of the Great Sphinx at Giza, murders which had been made to look like an accident. He had also discovered the theft of a large quantity of sky-iron, which was strictly reserved for use in the temples, and a conspiracy involving important and influential people. But he had been unable to find conclusive proof of General Asher's guilt, or his intention to overthrow Egypt's great king, Ramses II.

Just when Pazair had obtained the full powers he needed to link these diverse elements together, disaster struck.

Pazair recalled every second of that terrible night: the anonymous message telling him Branir was in danger, his mad dash through the streets of the town, his discovery of Branir's body, a mother-of-pearl needle driven into the old man's neck. The arrival of the commander of the city guards, Mentmose, who had instantly treated the judge as a murderer, the sordid complicity of the Judge of the Porch, the most senior magistrate in Memphis. Pazair had been seized and held in absolute secrecy, and all he had to look forward to now was a lonely death. He had not even been able to make the truth known.

The plot had been very cleverly staged. With Branir's support, Pazair could have investigated within the temples and identified the people who had stolen the sky-iron. But his master had been killed, like the soldiers of the honour-guard, by mysterious attackers whose aims were still unknown. Pazair had learnt that a woman and men of foreign origin were among their number; consequently his suspicions had fallen upon Sheshi the inventor, Qadash the tooth-doctor, and the wife of Denes the ship-owner, a rich, influential and dishonest man; but he had not established anything for certain.

Pazair withstood the heat, the sandstorms and the bad food, because he wanted to survive, to hold Neferet in his arms and see justice blossom again.

What story had his superior, the Judge of the Porch, made up to explain Pazair's disappearance? What lies were people spreading about him?

Escape was an impossible dream, even though the camp

opened on to the neighbouring hills. On foot, he would not get far. He had been imprisoned here so that he would die. When he was worn out, eaten away, when he had lost all hope, he would lose his mind, babbling incoherently like a poor madman.

Neither Neferet nor Suti would abandon him. They would not listen to lies or slander; they would search for him all over Egypt. He must hold fast, let time flow through his veins.

The five conspirators met once again at the abandoned farm. The atmosphere was joyful, for their plan was unfolding exactly as they had envisaged.

First, they had violated the Great Pyramid of Khufu and stolen the all-important insignia of power – the gold cubit and the Testament of the Gods, without which Ramses the Great was deprived of his rightful claim to the throne. Now they were getting closer to their goal with each day that passed.

From the Great Sphinx ran an underground passageway, enabling the conspirators to enter the pyramid. The murder of the honour-guard and the elimination of Judge Pazair were minor incidents which they had all but forgotten.

'The most important thing is still to be done,' declared one of the conspirators. 'Ramses is holding firm.'

'We mustn't be impatient.'

'Speak for yourself.'

'I speak for everyone; we need more time to consolidate the foundations of our future empire. The more tightly Ramses is bound hand and foot, powerless to act, knowing that he is heading for his own downfall, the easier our victory will be. He cannot tell anyone that the Great Pyramid has been desecrated and that the centre of spiritual energy, for which he alone is responsible, no longer functions.

'Soon his powers will be exhausted, and he will be forced to go through the regeneration ritual.'

'What will force him to do so?'

'Tradition, priests and himself. It is impossible for him to avoid that duty.'

'At the end of the festival, he must show the people the Testament of the Gods.'

'And the testament is in our hands.'

'Then Ramses will abdicate, and offer the throne to his successor.'

'The very successor we have designated.'

The conspirators were already relishing their victory. They would leave Ramses no choice, and he would be reduced to the status of a slave. Each member of the conspiracy would be rewarded according to his or her merits, and soon they would all occupy privileged positions. The greatest country in the world would belong to them; they would alter its structures, the way its government operated, and reshape it according to their own vision, which was radically opposed to that of Ramses, a prisoner of outdated values.

While the fruit was ripening, they would develop their network of contacts, sympathizers and allies. Crimes, corruption, violence . . . None of the conspirators regretted them. Such things were the price of power.

2

The setting sun was turning the hills a rosy hue. At this time of day Pazair's dog, Brave, and his donkey, Way-Finder, would be enjoying the food Neferet had prepared for them, after a long day's work. How many sick people had she healed? Was she still living in the little house in Memphis, where he had had his office on the ground floor, or had she returned to her village in the Theban region, to continue her work as a doctor far from the bustle of the city?

The judge's courage was weakening. He had dedicated his whole life to justice, but he knew now that it would never be meted out to him. No court would recognize his innocence. Besides, even if he did get out of prison, what future could he offer Neferet?

An old man, thin, toothless and with deeply lined skin, came over and sat down beside him. 'It's over for me,' he said with a sigh of relief. 'I'm too old. The governor's letting me off carrying stones. I'm going to do the cooking. Good news, isn't it?'

Pazair nodded.

'Why aren't you working?' asked the old man.

'They won't let me.'

'Who did you steal from?'

'Nobody.'

'Everyone's a hardened thief here – they've all committed

lots of crimes. They'll never get out of this prison, because they broke their oath not to steal again. The courts take a dim view of people who don't keep their word.'

'Do you think they're wrong?'

The old man spat in the sand. 'That's a strange question! Are you on the side of the judges?'

'I am one.'

The old fellow could not have been more astounded if he had been told he was about to be set free. 'You're joking.'

'Do you really think I'd want to do that?'

'Good heavens . . . A judge, a real judge!' He stared at Pazair with a mixture of fear and respect. 'What did you do?'

'I was carrying out a major investigation, and people wanted to shut my mouth.'

'You must be mixed up in something very peculiar. As for me, I'm innocent. A disloyal colleague accused me of stealing some honey which actually belonged to me.'

'You're a bee-keeper?'

'I had hives in the desert – my bees gave me the best honey in Egypt. My competitors were jealous; they laid a trap and I fell into it. At the trial, I got angry. I rejected the verdict against me, asked for a second judgement and prepared my defence with a scribe. I was sure I'd win.'

'But you were convicted?'

'My competitors hid some things they'd stolen from a workshop in my house, and said it was proof that I'd stolen again. The judge didn't look any further.'

'He was wrong. In his place, I'd have examined the accusers' motives.'

'And what if you really were in his place? What if you showed that the so-called proof was false?'

'I'd have to get out of here first.'

The bee-keeper spat in the sand again. 'When a judge betrays his office, they don't keep him secretly in a camp like this one. They haven't even cut your nose off. You must be a spy, or something like that.'

'Whatever you say.'

The old man got up and walked away.

Pazair did not touch his daily ration of soup. He had lost the will to fight. What did he have to offer Neferet, other than disappointment and shame? It was better that she should never see him again, that she should forget him. She would retain the memory of a magistrate with an unshakeable faith, a man who was madly in love, a dreamer who had believed in justice.

He stretched out on his back and gazed up at the lapis-lazuli sky. Tomorrow, he would die.

White sails travelled up and down the Nile. At nightfall, the sailors liked to jump from one boat to another, as the north wind increased the boats' speed. Men were falling into the water, laughing, calling to each other.

A young woman was sitting on the riverbank, deaf to the rivals' shouts. Neferet had fair hair, a face of great purity and tenderness, summer-blue eyes, and was as beautiful as a lotus in bloom. She was calling upon the soul of Branir, her murdered master, and imploring him to protect Pazair, whom she loved with all her being. Pazair, whose death she could not accept, even though it had been officially proclaimed.

'May I speak with you for a moment?'

She turned her head. Close by stood Nebamon, the most senior doctor at Pharaoh's court. He was still a fine figure of a man at fifty. He was also her bitterest enemy – he had tried several times to destroy her career. Neferet loathed him. He was greedy for wealth and women, and used medicine to gain power over other people and as a means of making his fortune.

Nebamon's hot gaze roamed over Neferet, whose perfect,

enticing curves could be glimpsed through her linen dress. Firm, high breasts, long, slender legs and delicate hands and feet were a delight for the eyes. Neferet was radiantly beautiful.

She said coldly, 'Be good enough to leave me alone.'

'You should be more friendly. I know something that will be of great interest to you.'

'Your intrigues are of no interest to me.'

'It's about Pazair.'

She could not hide her emotion. 'Pazair is dead.'

'That's not true, my dear.'

'You're lying!'

'I assure you I'm telling the truth.'

'What do you want from me? Must I beg for the truth?'

'Beg? No. I prefer you unbending and proud. What I have to tell you is this: Pazair is alive, but has been accused of murdering Branir.'

'That's . . . that's absurd! I don't believe you.'

'You should,' said Nebamon. 'Mentmose, commander of the city guards, has arrested him and is holding him secretly.'

'Pazair would never have killed Bramir.'

'Mentmose is convinced that he did.'

'People want to destroy him, ruin his reputation and stop him carrying on with his investigation.'

'That doesn't matter to me.'

'Why are you telling me this?'

'Because I am the only person who can prove Pazair's innocence.'

A shiver ran through Neferet's flesh, mingling hope and anguish.

'If you want me to take the proof to the Judge of the Porch, you must become my wife, Neferet, and forget your little judge. That is the price of his freedom. By my side, you will be in your rightful place. Now you are mistress of the game. Either you free Pazair or you condemn him to death.'

3

The thought of giving herself to Nebamon appalled Neferet, but if she refused his proposition she would become Pazair's torturer. Where was he being held, and what torments was he suffering? If she delayed too long, imprisonment would destroy him. Neferet had not confided in Suti, Pazair's loyal friend and spiritual brother: he would have killed Nebamon on the spot.

She decided to give in to his demand, on condition that she saw Pazair once more. Sullied and in despair, she would confess all to him before poisoning herself.

She looked up and saw Kem, a Nubian guard who had worked for Pazair, coming towards her. In Pazair's absence, he had continued to patrol Memphis with Killer, his formidable baboon, who specialized in arresting thieves by sinking his teeth into their legs.

Kem had had his nose cut off for being implicated in the murder of an officer who was guilty of trafficking in gold; but once his innocence and good faith had been recognized, he had become a guard officer. A false nose made of painted wood lessened the effect of the mutilation. Kem admired Pazair. Although he had no confidence in justice, he believed in the young judge's probity, which had been the cause of his death.

'I have a chance to find out where Pazair is,' Neferet told him gravely.

'In the kingdom of the dead, from which no one returns. Didn't General Asher send you his report, saying that Pazair had died in Asia, searching for proof?'

'That report was false. Pazair is alive.'

'Do you mean they lied to you?'

'Pazair has been accused of murdering Branir, but Nebamon has proof of his innocence.'

Kem took Neferet by the shoulders. 'Then he is saved!'

'On condition that I become Nebamon's wife.'

In rage, the Nubian drove his fist into the palm of his other hand. 'Suppose he's just playing games with you?'

'I want to see Pazair again.'

Kem tapped his wooden nose. 'You won't regret confiding in me.'

After the cooks and kitchen workers had left, Pazair slipped into the kitchen, a wooden frame covered with cloth. He would steal one of the pieces of flint used to light the fire, and cut his wrists. Death would be slow, but sure; in the full sunlight, he would slip gently into a pleasant stupor. In the evening, a passing guard would kick him and his corpse would roll over on the burning sand. During these last hours, he would live with the soul of Neferet, in the hope that its invisible presence would help him on his final journey.

Just as he was grasping the sharp stone, something hit him hard on the back of the neck and he fell to the ground, next to a cooking-pot.

The old bee-keeper was standing over him with a wooden club in his hand and a sarcastic smile on his face.

'So the judge becomes a thief!' he said loudly. 'What were you planning to do with that flint? Don't move, or I'll hit you! Shed your blood and leave this accursed place by the road of bad death! This is stupid of you, and unworthy of a good man.'

Then he lowered his voice to a whisper and said, 'Listen to

11

me, Judge. I know a way out of here. I wouldn't have the strength to cross the desert, but you're young. I'll tell you, if you agree to fight my case for me and get my sentence overturned.'

Pazair came to his senses. 'It wouldn't be any use.'

'Are you refusing?'

'Even if I escape, I won't be a judge any more.'

'Become one again for me.'

'That's not possible. I'm accused of having committed a serious crime.'

'You? Never!'

Pazair rubbed his neck.

The old man helped him to his feet, and told him, still whispering, 'Tomorrow is the last day of the month. A cart drawn by oxen will come from the oasis, bringing food, and it'll go away again empty. Take your water-skin and get into the cart and hide while it drives off. When you see the first dry river-bed on your right, get out of the cart and climb up the river-bed until you reach the foot of the hill. You'll find a spring at the centre of a thicket of palm-trees there. Fill your water-skin, then walk towards the valley and try to meet up with the nomads. At least you'll have tried.'

For the second time, Nebamon had removed the rolls of fat from the lady Silkis, the young wife of Bel-Tran, a wealthy papyrus-maker and high official whose influence was steadily growing. For making women more beautiful in such ways, Nebamon charged enormous fees, which his patients paid without a murmur. Precious stones, fabrics, foodstuffs, furniture, tools, oxen, donkeys and goats had swollen his fortune, which now lacked only one priceless treasure: Neferet. Other women were equally beautiful, but she was the embodiment of a unique harmony in which intelligence was allied to charm, giving birth to an incomparable radiance.

How could she have fallen in love with a fool like Pazair?

It was a piece of youthful madness, which she would have regretted all her life if Nebamon had not intervened.

Sometimes he felt as powerful as Pharaoh. After all, he knew secrets which saved or prolonged lives, he held sway over many doctors and remedy-makers, and it was he whom the highest men in the land begged for help to recover their health. His assistants might work in the shadows to produce the best treatments for him, but it was Nebamon, and no other, who would reap all the glory. And Neferet had a genius for medicine, which he was determined to exploit.

After the operation on Silkis, Nebamon was enjoying a week's rest at his house in the country, south of Memphis, where an army of servants satisfied his every wish. Abandoning lesser tasks to his medical team, which he controlled with a firm hand, he would prepare the list of forthcoming promotions on board his new pleasure-boat. He was eager to sample a white wine from the Delta, which came from his own vines, and his cook's latest dishes.

His steward came in, bowed, and informed him that he had a young and pretty visitor.

Intrigued, Nebamon went out to the gate of his estate. 'Neferet! What a delightful surprise. Will you have lunch with me?'

'I'm in a hurry.'

'You'll soon have a chance to visit my home, I'm sure. Have you by any chance brought me your reply?'

Neferet bowed her head.

Nebamon's heart leapt. 'I knew you'd see reason.'

'Give me time.'

'Since you've come here, you must have made your decision.'

'Will you grant me the privilege of seeing Pazair again?

Nebamon frowned. 'You are submitting yourself to a pointless ordeal. Save Pazair, but forget him.'

'I owe him one last meeting.'

'As you wish. But my conditions have not changed. First, you must prove your love to me. Then, and only then, I shall take action. Are we fully agreed?'

'I'm in no position to bargain.'

'I admire your intelligence, Neferet; it is equalled only by your beauty.'

He took her tenderly by the hand.

'No,' she said quickly, 'not here, not now.'

'Where and when, then?'

'In the big palm-grove by the well.'

'Is that place dear to you?'

'I often go there to think.'

Nebamon smiled. 'Nature and love make good bedfellows. Like you, I enjoy the poetry of the palm-trees. When?'

'Tomorrow evening, after sunset.'

'Very well. I accept that our first union will take place in darkness, but afterwards we shall be united in the full light of day.'

4

Pazair slid out of the cart as soon as he saw the dry river-bed winding up through the sand-dunes and rocks towards a steep, wind-ravaged hill. He dropped soundlessly out on to the sand, and the cart continued its journey through the dust and heat. The driver had fallen asleep, leaving the oxen to find their own way.

No one would bother to come after the fugitive, because he would have no chance of survival without water in the furnace-like heat of the desert. In due course, a passing patrol would bring back his bones. Barefoot and wearing only a threadbare kilt, he forced himself to walk slowly and to conserve his breath. Here and there, squiggles on the ground marked the passage of a sand viper, a fierce creature with a deadly bite.

Pazair imagined that he was walking with Neferet through verdant countryside, filled with birdsong and criss-crossed by canals; it made the landscape seem less hostile, his step lighter. He followed the dry river-bed to the foot of the hill, where he was greeted by the incongruous sight of three palm-trees.

He knelt down and began to scoop out a hole. A handspan beneath the cracked crust, the earth was damp: the old bee-keeper had told the truth. After an hour's digging, punctuated by a few brief pauses, he reached the water. He slaked his

thirst, then took off his kilt, cleaned it with sand and used it
to rub himself down. Then he filled the goatskin water-bag he
had brought with him.

At nightfall, he set off eastwards. He could hear hissing all
around him; the snakes emerged when the sun went down. If
he stepped on one by accident, there would be no escape from
a horrible death. Only a very learned doctor – like Neferet –
knew how to cure their bite. The judge resolutely ignored the
danger and went on, under the moon's protection. He revelled
in the relative coolness of the night air. When dawn broke, he
drank a little water, dug a hollow in the sand, covered himself
with the loose sand and went to sleep, curled up in a ball.

When he awoke, the sun was beginning to sink. With his
muscles aching and his head burning, he continued in the
direction of the valley, so far away, so inaccessible. His
reserves of water were exhausted, and he would have to rely
on finding a well, surrounded by a circle of stones. In the
immense space, sometimes flat, sometimes bumpy, he began
to stagger. His lips were dry, his tongue swollen, and he was
at the end of his strength. What was there left to hope for,
save the intervention of a benevolent god?

Nebamon ordered his chair-bearers to set him down within
earshot of the big palm-grove, and then sent them away. He
was already savouring this marvellous night when Neferet
would give herself to him. He would have preferred more
spontaneity, but the methods used were of little importance.
He had obtained what he desired, as usual.

The guards of the palm-grove were leaning against the
tree-trunks, playing the flute, drinking cool water and talking.
Nebamon set off along a wide path which forked to the left
and led to the ancient well. The place was lonely and quiet.

She seemed to emerge from the sunset's glow, which
turned her long linen dress orange.

Neferet was yielding to him. She, who was so proud, who

had defied him, would obey him like a slave. When he had conquered her, she would become attached to him and would forget the past. She would acknowledge that only Nebamon could offer her the life she had dreamt of without realizing it. She loved medicine too much to hide any longer in a subsidiary role; becoming the wife of the highest doctor in the land was the most enviable destiny imaginable.

She did not move. He went forward.

'Will I see Pazair again?' she asked.

'You have my word.'

'You must have him set free.'

'That is my intention, if you agree to be mine.'

'Why are you so cruel? Be merciful, I beg of you.'

'Are you mocking me?'

'I'm appealing to your conscience.'

'You shall be my wife, Neferet, because that is what I have decided.'

'Give up that idea.'

He moved closer, stopping a single pace from his prey. 'I enjoy looking at you, but I want other pleasures, too.'

'Is destroying me part of those pleasures?'

'Freeing you from an illusory love and a second-rate existence.'

'One last time, please change your mind.'

'You belong to me, Neferet.' He reached out to seize her.

The moment he touched her, he was brutally dragged backwards and thrown to the ground. He looked up and saw a terrifying attacker: an enormous baboon with a wide-open mouth and foam-flecked lips. Its powerful left hand encircled the doctor's throat while its right grabbed his testicles and pulled. Nebamon let out a howl.

Kem set his foot on Nebamon's forehead. The baboon froze, but did not slacken its grip.

'If you refuse to help us, my baboon will castrate you. I won't have seen anything, and he won't feel the slightest remorse.'

17

'What do you want?' quavered Nebamon.

'The proof that Pazair is innocent.'

'No, I—'

The baboon gave a low growl, and its grip tightened.

'All right, all right!'

'Go on,' said Kem.

Nebamon panted, 'When I examined Branir's body, I saw that he'd died several hours or even a whole day earlier. The state of the eyes, the appearance of the skin, the mouth, the wound – the signs were unmistakeable. I wrote down my observations on a papyrus. Pazair wasn't caught in the act of committing murder; he was nothing but a witness. No serious charges could be brought against him.'

'Why did you suppress the truth?'

'It was too good an opportunity to miss – I could have Neferet at last.'

'Where is Pazair?'

'I . . . I don't know.'

'Oh yes you do.'

The baboon growled again. In fear for his life, Nebamon gave in.

'I bribed Mentmose not to kill Pazair – he had to be kept alive, if my plan was to succeed. The judge is being held secretly, but I don't know where.'

'Do you know who the real murderer is?'

'No, I swear I don't!'

Kem did not doubt the honesty of his answer. When the baboon carried out an interrogation, suspects did not lie.

Neferet closed her eyes and prayed, giving thanks to Branir's soul. The master had protected his pupil.

The Judge of the Porch dined frugally on figs and cheese. He had not slept well and had lost his appetite, and he had sent his servant away because he could no longer bear anyone near him. Why should he blame himself? All he had wanted was to save Egypt from turmoil. And yet his conscience did not rest easy. Never in all his long career had he departed from the Rule in this way.

Sickened, he pushed away the wooden bowl.

He could hear what sounded like someone moaning outside; according to magicians, ghosts came to torture unworthy souls. The judge swallowed hard and went out to see what it was.

To his astonishment he saw Kem dragging Nebamon along by the ear. The baboon was at his side.

Kem bowed and said, 'Nebamon wants to make a confession, Judge.'

The judge disliked Kem. He knew the big Nubian's violent past, disapproved of his methods and deplored the fact that he had been recruited into the guards. He said coldly, 'Nebamon is not acting of his own free will. His statement will be worthless.'

'I'm talking about a confession, not a statement.'

Nebamon tried to pull free. The baboon bit him in the leg, but did not sink its teeth right in.

'Be careful,' advised Kem. 'If you annoy him, he won't hold back.'

'Leave my house!' ordered the infuriated judge.

Kem pushed the doctor towards him. 'Hurry up, Nebamon. Baboons aren't patient creatures.'

'I have evidence relating to the Pazair case,' said Nebamon.

'Not evidence,' Kem corrected him. 'Proof of his innocence.'

The Judge of the Porch went pale. 'Are you trying to make fun of me?'

'The doctor is a serious and respectable man.'

Nebamon reached into his tunic and took out a rolled and sealed papyrus. 'This contains my written conclusions about Branir's body. The arrest of Pazair was a . . . miscalculation. I . . . forgot to send you this report.'

The judge took the document with no great enthusiasm. It felt like putting his hand into hot coals.

'We were wrong,' he lamented, 'and now for Pazair it is too late.'

'Perhaps not,' objected Kem.

'What do you mean? He's dead.'

The Nubian smiled. 'Another miscalculation, no doubt. Your good faith has been abused.'

Kem gestured to Killer to let go of Nebamon.

'Am I free to go?'

'Yes, go – quickly.'

Nebamon fled, limping. His leg bore the imprint of Killer's teeth, and he thought he could still see the animal's eyes shining red in the darkness.

The Judge of the Porch coughed. 'If you agree to forget these deplorable events, I can offer you a quiet, easy posting.'

'Don't do anything of the sort, Judge, or I won't restrain Killer. Soon the truth must be told – the whole truth.'

5

Pazair had dragged himself into the shade of an enormous rock, which had become detached from a natural pyramid. He was at the end of his strength: without water, he could go no further.

A cloud of dust rose up in the midst of the landscape of pale sand and black-and-white mountains. Looking out from his shelter, he saw two men on horseback.

They must be either desert guards or sand-travellers – except for caravans, no one ventured into these desert wastes. If they were desert guards, they would take him back to prison. If they were sand-travellers, they would do whatever they felt like at that moment: either torture him or enslave him. At the worst, Pazair would exchange prison for slavery. But perhaps . . . As the men rode nearer, he staggered out from behind the rock and collapsed on the sand.

They were sand-travellers: they wore brightly striped robes and had long hair and short beards. When they saw him, they stopped and stared in amazement.

'Who are you?' asked one of them.

'I escaped from the thieves' prison.'

The younger man dismounted and stared narrowly at Pazair. 'You don't look very strong.'

'I'm thirsty. Will you give me some water?'

'Water has to be earned. Get up and fight.'

'I can't, I'm not strong enough.'

The sand-traveller unsheathed a dagger. 'If you can't fight, you'll die.'

'I'm a judge, not a soldier.'

'A judge! Then you can't have come from the thieves' prison.'

'I was wrongfully accused. Someone wants to destroy me.'

The sand-traveller laughed. 'The sun's driven you mad.'

'If you kill me, you will be cursed in the afterlife. The judges of hell will cut your soul into pieces.'

'Nonsense!'

The older man stayed the younger man's hand. 'The Egyptians' magic is formidable. Let's get him back on his feet, and then we can make use of him as a slave.'

Panther was furious. The beautiful, bright-eyed Libyan girl was a sworn enemy of Egypt; she had fallen into the hands of the young chariot officer, who had become a hero following his first campaign in Asia. On a whim, he had given her back her freedom – not that it benefited her much, because she thoroughly enjoyed making love with him.

Panther lived for love. Deprived of Suti's, she was wasting away. Suti was tall and well-built, with a long face, a direct and honest gaze, and long black hair; ordinarily, his every move was invested with strength, elegance and seductive power. But her usually passionate and inventive lover had turned into a gloomy, wretched creature.

Suti had seen General Asher murdering one of his own scouts, but the court had been unable to convict the killer because the body had disappeared before witnesses could be brought to see it. Even when he was expelled from the army – for trying to strangle Asher – Suti had not lost his buoyant energy. But since the death of his friend Pazair he had withdrawn into silence, had stopped eating, and hardly even looked at her.

'When are you going to come back to life?' demanded Panther.

'When Pazair returns.'

'Pazair, always Pazair! Don't you understand? His enemies killed him.'

'We aren't in Libya. Killing is such a serious act that it condemns the perpetrator to utter destruction. A murderer doesn't come back to life.'

Panther shrugged impatiently. 'Forget all that nonsense. There's only one life, and it's here and now.'

'Forget a friend?'

'I'm a free woman and I won't live with a stone. If you stay like this, I shall leave.'

'Very well, go.'

She knelt down and put her arms round his waist. 'You don't know what you're saying.'

'If Pazair suffers, I suffer. If he's in danger, I feel his fear. You won't change that.'

Panther unfastened Suti's kilt; he didn't protest. She had never seen such a handsome, powerful, well-coordinated body. Since the age of thirteen, Panther had had many lovers; but none of them had satisfied her desires like this Egyptian, the sworn enemy of her people. She stroked his chest gently, then his shoulders, his nipples, his navel. Her light, sensual fingers contained the very essence of pleasure.

At last he reacted. Suddenly, almost sneeringly, he tore away the straps of her short dress. Naked now, she stretched out beside him, pressing her body against his.

'Just feeling you,' she said, 'being one with you, that's enough for me.'

'It isn't for me.'

He threw her on to her belly and took her. Triumphantly sensual, she accepted his desire as though it were the elixir of life, smooth and fiery.

From outside, someone called to Suti in a serious, commanding voice. Suti rushed to the window.

'Come with me,' said Kem. 'I know where Pazair is.'

The Judge of the Porch was laboriously watering the little flower-bed at the entrance to his house. As he got older, he found it more and more difficult to bend down.

'Can you help me?' asked a voice behind him.

The Judge turned round and recognized Suti: the former chariot officer had lost none of his impressiveness.

'Where is my friend Pazair?' demanded Suti.

'He is dead.'

'That's a lie.'

'An official report has been produced.'

'I don't give a curse for that.'

'You may not like the truth, but nothing can alter it.'

'The truth is that Nebamon has bought your conscience, and Mentmose's, too.'

The Judge of the Porch drew himself up. 'No, not mine.'

'Then tell me.'

The judge hesitated. He could have Suti arrested for insulting a judge and for verbal violence. But he was ashamed of his own behaviour. True, Judge Pazair frightened him: he was too determined, too passionate, set too much store by justice. But surely he, the old judge, broken by all the intrigues, had betrayed his youthful faith? The fate of his young colleague haunted him. Perhaps Pazair was already dead, having been unable to withstand the ordeal of prison.

'He's in the thieves' prison, near Khargeh oasis,' he whispered.

'Give me a warrant.'

'You ask a great deal.'

'Do it quickly – I haven't much time.'

Suti left his horse at the last staging-post, near the track that led to the oasis; only a donkey would be able to bear the heat, dust and wind. Armed with his bow, fifty arrows, a sword and two daggers, Suti felt sufficiently well armed to face the enemy, whoever that might be. The Judge of the Porch had given him a wooden tablet stating that he was under orders to bring Judge Pazair back to Memphis.

Kem had, very reluctantly, stayed with Neferet. Once Nebamon had recovered from his fright he would retaliate, and only Killer and his master could defend her properly. The big Nubian, although he badly wanted to take part in rescuing Pazair, had to admit that it was his duty to protect her against attack.

When her lover had said he was leaving, Panther flew into a rage. If he stayed away for more than a week, she hissed, she would deceive him with the first man she met and tell everyone how unfortunate she was. Suti had promised nothing, except that he would return with his friend.

The donkey carried water-skins and baskets filled with dried meat and fish, fruit and loaves which would keep for several days. The man and the animal would allow themselves little rest, for Suti was in a great hurry to reach his goal.

Within sight of the camp, a collection of miserable hovels scattered over the desert, Suti called upon the god Min, patron of caravan-leaders and explorers. Although he considered the gods beyond men's reach, in certain circumstances it was better to ensure their cooperation.

Suti woke the camp governor, who was asleep in the shade of a cloth awning and grumbled about being disturbed.

Suti ignored his protests and said, 'You are holding Judge Pazair here.'

'Don't know the name.'

'He isn't registered, I know.'

'I told you, I don't know him.'

Suti showed him the tablet. It brought no reaction at all.

'No Pazair here,' said the governor. 'Persistent thieves, no judge.'

'My mission is an official one.'

'Wait for the prisoners to come back, and see for yourself.' The governor went back to sleep.

Suti wondered if the Judge of the Porch had sent him up a blind alley, while having Pazair killed in Asia. Had he, Suti, been naive again?

He went over to the kitchen, to refill his water-bags.

The cook, a toothless old man, awoke with a start and asked, 'Who are you?'

'I've come to rescue a friend. Unfortunately, you don't look like Pazair.'

'What name did you say?'

'Judge Pazair.'

'What do you want with him?'

'To free him.'

'Really? Well, you're too late.'

'What do you mean?' demanded Suti.

The old bee-keeper explained in a low voice. 'With my help, he's escaped.'

'Him, in the middle of the desert? He won't last two days. What route did he take?'

'The first dried-up riverbed, the hill, the thicket of palm-trees, the spring, the rocky plateau, and then due east towards the valley. If he has a strong will to live, he'll succeed.'

'Pazair isn't very strong.'

'Then hurry up and find him – he's promised to prove me innocent.'

'But you're a thief, aren't you?'

'Not much of one, and a lot less than others. I just want to tend my bee-hives. Get your judge to send me back home.'

6

Commander Mentmose received the Judge of the Porch in his armoury, where he exhibited shields, swords and hunting trophies. The commander had a pointed nose, a nasal voice, and a bald, red scalp which often itched. Rather overweight, he followed a diet in order to keep a reasonable figure. Mentmose was cautious and cunning. He attended all the big receptions and had a large network of friends; he reigned unchallenged over all the different city guards companies in the kingdom. No one had ever been able to criticize him for making a mistake; he paid close attention to keeping up his reputation as an impeccable official.

He asked, 'Is this a private visit, my dear Judge?'

'A discreet one, as you alway prefer.'

'That's how to ensure a long and peaceful career, isn't it?'

'When I had Pazair secretly detained, I set a condition,' said the judge.

'My memory must be going . . .'

'You were to discover the motive for Branir's murder.'

'Don't forget I caught Pazair red-handed.'

'Why should he have killed his master? The old man had been summoned to become High Priest of Karnak, and was therefore his most valuable supporter.'

Mentmose shrugged. 'Jealousy – or madness.'

'Don't treat me like a fool.'

'What does the motive matter to you? We've got rid of Pazair – that's the important thing.'

'Are you absolutely certain he's guilty?'

'As I told you, he was bending over Branir's body when I caught him. In my place, what conclusion would you have come to?'

'Yes, but the motive?'

'You admitted it yourself: a trial would have been very damaging – the country must respect its judges and have confidence in them. Pazair has a taste for scandal. Branir no doubt tried to calm him, and he lost his temper and stabbed the old man. Any jury would have condemned him to death. You and I were generous to him: we've kept his reputation intact. Officially, he died while on a mission. Isn't that the most satisfactory solution for him as well as for us?'

'Suti knows the truth.'

'How . . . ?'

'Kem made Nebamon talk. Suti knows Pazair is alive, and I told him where his friend is being held.'

To the judge's astonishment, Mentmose, who was generally regarded as a cool-headed man, reacted with fury.

'That's madness, utter madness! You, the most senior judge in the city, giving in to a disgraced ex-soldier! Kem and Suti can do nothing against us.'

'You're forgetting Nebamon's written statement.'

'A confession obtained under torture is invalid.'

'It was made well before that, and it's dated and signed.'

'Destroy it!'

'Kem made Nebamon write out a copy and have it witnessed by two servants on his estate. Pazair's innocence has been proven. During the hours leading up to the crime, he was working in his office. Witnesses will testify to that – I've checked.'

'Very well, but . . . Why on earth did you say where we're hiding him? There was no hurry.'

'To be at peace with my conscience.'

'With your experience, and at your age, you—'

'Exactly: at my age. The judge of the dead may call me at any moment. In the case of Pazair, I betrayed the spirit of the law.'

'You chose to further Egypt's interests, rather than concern yourself with the privileges of one person.'

'Your words don't deceive me, Mentmose.'

'Surely you aren't abandoning me?'

'If Pazair comes back . . .'

'People often die in the thieves' prison.'

For a long time, Suti had heard the sound of galloping horses. They were coming from the east, two of them, and they were approaching rapidly. Sand-travellers on a raid, on the lookout for easy prey.

Suti waited until they were within range, then drew his bow. He went down on one knee, took aim at the man on the left, and fired. Hit in the shoulder, the man toppled backwards. His comrade galloped towards the attacker. Suti adjusted his aim. The arrow sank into the top of the man's thigh. Roaring with pain, the sand-traveller lost control of his mount, fell off and knocked himself out on a rock. The two horses ran in aimless circles.

Suti laid the point of his sword against the throat of the first man, who was now back on his feet and staggering about.

'Where are you from?' he asked sternly.

'The tribe of sand-travellers.'

'Where are they camping?'

'Behind the black rocks.'

'Did you capture an Egyptian a few days ago?'

'Yes, a man who was lost in the desert – he claimed to be a judge.'

'What did you do with him?'

'Our leader's questioning him.'

29

Suti leapt on to the back of the sturdier horse, and held the other by the rudimentary reins the sand-travellers used. He left the two wounded men to fend for themselves.

He set off along a track bordered by stones. It got steeper and steeper, and the horses were blowing hard and bathed in sweat by the time they reached the summit of a hill, covered with a random scattering of stone blocks.

It was a sinister place. Between the burnt, blackish rocks were hollows where the sand swirled; they reminded him of the cauldrons of hell in which the damned were consumed, upside down.

At the foot of the hill was the nomads' camp. It was not very big, so there would be only comparatively few people there. The tallest and most brightly coloured tent, in the middle, must belong to the chief. Horses and goats were penned in an enclosure. Two sentries, one at the south and the other at the north, were keeping watch.

Suti waited for night to fall. It was against the rules of warfare to attack at night, but he reckoned that, since sand-travellers constantly criss-crossed the desert in search of victims to loot and pillage, they didn't deserve any respect. As soon as it was dark enough, he crawled forward silently, little by little, rising to his feet only when he was very close to the southern sentry, whom he felled with a blow to the back of the neck. Suti slunk through the darkness to the chief's tent, and slipped into it through an oval hole which served as a door. Tense and focused, he felt ready to unleash all his violence.

A totally unexpected sight met his eyes.

The chief was lying on a pile of cushions, listening to Pazair, who was sitting on the floor, apparently under no restraint.

The sand-traveller sat up and Suti pounced on him.

'Don't kill him,' cried Pazair. 'We were just beginning to understand each other.'

Suti flattened his adversary against the cushions.

'I asked the chief about his way of life,' explained Pazair, 'and tried to show him that he was doing wrong. My refusal to become a slave, even when threatened with death, astonished him. He wanted to know how our legal system works, and—'

'When you no longer amuse him, he'll tie you to a horse's tail and drag you across sharp stones until you're cut to pieces.'

'How did you find me?'

'How could I ever lose you?' Suti began binding and gagging the sand-traveller. 'Let's get out of here quickly. Two horses are waiting for us at the top of the hill.'

'What's the point? I can't go back to Egypt.'

'Follow me, instead of talking rubbish.'

'I haven't the strength '

'You'll find it when you realize that you've been proved innocent and that Neferet is waiting impatiently for you.'

7

The Judge of the Porch did not dare look at Judge Pazair. 'You are free,' he declared in a broken voice.

The Judge of the Porch was expecting bitter reproaches, perhaps even a formal accusation. But Pazair simply stared at him.

'The charges have been dropped, of course. As to the rest, I beg you to be patient for a little while. I am working to resolve your situation as quickly as possible.'

'What about Mentmose?'

'He sends his apologies. He and I were both deceived . . . '

'And Nebamon?'

'He is not really guilty. It was a matter of simple administrative negligence. You were the victim of an unfortunate conjunction of circumstances, my dear Pazair. If you wish to lodge a complaint . . . ?'

'I shall think about it.'

'Sometimes it is important to know how to forgive.'

'Give me back my official status without any more delay.'

Neferet's blue eyes were like two precious stones, born at the heart of the golden mountains, in the land of the gods; at her throat hung a turquoise, protecting her from evil. A long white linen dress with straps accentuated her slender waist.

As he drew near her, Judge Pazair breathed in her perfume.

Lotus and jasmine wafted from her satin skin. He took her in his arms, and they remained locked in an embrace for a long time, unable to speak.

'So you do love me a little bit?' he asked.

She pushed him away to look at him. He was proud, passionate, a bit mad at times, thorough, young and old at the same time, lacking superficial physical beauty, fragile but energetic. Those who thought him weak and easily defeated were very much mistaken. Despite his stern face, his high, austere forehead and his demanding nature, he had a taste for happiness.

'I don't ever want to be separated from you again,' she said.

He held her tightly for a moment, then released her. Life had a new energy, as powerful as the young Nile. And yet it was a life so close to death, in this immense burial ground at Saqqara where Pazair and Neferet were walking slowly along, hand in hand. They wanted to visit the tomb of their murdered master, Branir, straight away, to meditate there. For he had passed on the secrets of medicine to Neferet and encouraged Pazair to turn his vocation into reality.

Because of his occupation, the embalmer Djui lived apart from ordinary men. When they entered his workshop they found him sitting on the floor, his back against a whitewashed wall. He had a long face, thick black eyebrows joined above his nose, thin, bloodless lips, extraordinarily long hands and skinny legs. He was eating pork with lentils, even though this meat was forbidden during hot periods: he was uncircumcised and had no time for religious rules and regulations.

On the embalming table lay the mummy of an old man whose flank he had just cut into with an obsidian knife.

'I know you,' Djui said, looking up at Pazair. 'You're the judge who's investigating the deaths of the honour-guard.'

'Did you mummify Branir?' asked the judge.

'That's my job.'

'Did you notice anything unusual?'

'No, nothing.'

'Has anybody come to visit his tomb?'

'Not since the burial ceremony. Only the priest in charge of the funeral service has entered the shrine.'

Pazair was disappointed. He had hoped that the murderer, in the grip of remorse, might have come to beg his victim's forgiveness, in order to escape the punishments of the afterlife. But it seemed even that threat did not frighten the killer.

'Have you found out what you wanted to know?' asked Djui.

'I will.'

Shrugging indifferently, the embalmer sank his teeth into a slice of pork.

The stepped pyramid of King Djoser dominated the eternal landscape. Many tombs faced it, in order to share the immortality of the king, whose immense shade travelled up and down the gigantic stone staircase each day.

Usually, sculptors, hieroglyphic engravers and painters were to be found working on countless sites. Here, they were excavating a rock-tomb; there, another was being restored. Long lines of workmen hauled wooden sledges laden with blocks of limestone or granite, while water-carriers were on hand to slake the workers' thirst.

Today the site was deserted, for it was the day when people paid their respects to Imhotep, the master craftsman of the Step Pyramid. Pazair and Neferet walked between lines of tombs dating from the days of the first pharaohs, which were carefully maintained by one of Ramses' sons. Whenever someone's gaze alit on the names of the dead written in hieroglyphs, it brought them to life, shattering the obstacle of time. The power of the word was greater even than the power of death.

Branir's tomb was close to the Step Pyramid. It was built of fine white limestone brought from the quarries at Tura. The head of the funerary well, which gave access to the underground chambers where the mummy lay, had been blocked by an enormous stone slab, while the shrine remained open to the living, who could come to feast in company with the statue and pictures of the dead man, which had been endowed with his immortal energy.

The sculptor had created a magnificent image of Branir, immortalizing him as an old but sturdily built man with a serene expression. The main text, written in horizontal lines, hoped that the reborn Branir would be welcomed into the beautiful West; at the end of a tremendous journey he would arrive among his own people, his brothers the gods, would feed upon stars and be purified with water from the primordial ocean. Guided by his heart, he would walk along the perfect paths of eternity.

Pazair read out the words addressed to visitors to the tomb: *'You who live upon the earth and pass by this tomb, you who love life and hate death, speak my name that I may live, pronounce the offertory words for my sake.'*

'I shall find the murderer, master,' he promised.

Neferet had dreamt of a quiet happiness, far from quarrels and the demands of men's ambition. But her love had been born in the whirlwind, and neither she nor Pazair would ever know peace until the truth had been discovered.

When the darkness had been vanquished, the earth grew light. Trees and grass became green once more, birds flew from their nests, fish leapt out of the water, and boats sailed up and down the river. Pazair and Neferet emerged from the shrine, whose carved panels welcomed the first light of dawn. They had spent the night with the soul of Branir, whom they had sensed close by, vibrant and warm.

They would never be separated from him.

Now that the festival was over, the craftsmen were returning to the site. Priests were celebrating the morning rites, so as to perpetuate the memory of the dead. Pazair and Neferet walked along King Unas's long covered roadway, which led to a temple below, at the edge of the fields. A little laughing girl brought them dates, fresh bread and milk.

'We could just stay here and forget about crimes, the law and men,' said Pazair wistfully.

'You aren't becoming a dreamer, are you?'

'Someone wanted to get rid of me in the vilest way and he won't give up. Is it wise to embark on a war which is lost before it begins?'

'For Branir, the man we revere, we have a duty to fight without thinking of ourselves.'

'I'm only a junior judge. The powers that be will transfer me to a distant corner of some far-off province. They'll break me easily.'

'Surely you aren't afraid?'

'I've not much courage left. Prison was a terrible ordeal.'

She laid her head on his shoulder. 'We're together now. You have lost none of your strength – I know it, I can sense it.'

A gentle warmth washed over Pazair. The pain faded, his exhaustion ebbed away. Neferet was a sorceress.

'Each day for a month,' she said, 'you must drink water from a copper vessel. It is an effective remedy against weariness and despair.'

'Whoever laid that trap for me must have been someone who knew Branir would soon become High Priest of Karnak and would therefore be our most powerful supporter.'

'Who did you tell?'

'Only Nebamon – to impress him.'

'Nebamon? The man who held the proof of your innocence and was trying to force me to marry him!'

'I know. I made a terrible mistake. When he learnt of

36

Branir's appointment, he must have decided on a double blow: kill Branir and have me accused of the crime.' A furrow appeared across Pazair's brow. 'But he isn't the only suspect. When Mentmose arrested me, it was obvious he had an understanding with the Judge of the Porch.'

'So the city's guards and magistrates were partners in crime.'

'A conspiracy, Neferet, a conspiracy bringing together men of power and influence. Branir and I were becoming inconvenient, because I had collected irrefutable evidence and he would have enabled me to carry my investigation to its conclusion. Why was the Great Sphinx's honour-guard wiped out? That's the question to which I must find the answer.'

'Don't forget the inventor Sheshi, the theft of the sky-iron, and that murderer General Asher.'

'I haven't. But I can't find a way of linking the suspects and their crimes.'

'Let us concern ourselves above all with Branir's memory.'

Suti insisted on celebrating his friend Pazair's return properly, by inviting the judge and his wife to a respectable Memphis tavern, where they enjoyed mature red wine, fine grilled lamb, vegetables in sauce, and unforgettable cakes. The life and soul of the party, he tried to make them forget Branir's murder for a few hours.

When he stumbled unsteadily back into his house, his head spinning, he bumped into Panther.

She grabbed him by the hair. 'Where have you been?'

'The prison.'

'Half drunk?

'No, completely drunk, but Pazair's safe and sound.'

'And what about me? Don't I get any attention?'

He seized her round the waist, lifted her off the ground and held her above his head. 'I've come back – isn't that a miracle?'

'I don't need you.'

'You're lying. Our bodies haven't finished exploring each other yet.'

He carried her into the bedchamber, laid her down gently on the bed, took off her short dress with the delicacy of an old lover, and entered her with the wild enthusiasm of a youth. She cried out in pleasure, unable to resist this longed-for attack.

When they were resting side by side, panting and sated, she laid her hand on Suti's chest. 'I said I'd be unfaithful to you while you were away.'

'And were you?'

'You'll never know. The doubt will make you suffer.'

'Don't deceive yourself. For me, the only things that matter are pleasure and the moment.'

'You're a monster!'

'Are you complaining?'

'Are you going to go on helping Judge Pazair?'

'We're blood-brothers.'

'Is he going to take his revenge?'

'He's a judge first and a man second. The truth matters more to him than his own feelings.'

'For once, listen to me. Don't encourage him and, if he persists, keep away.'

'Why do you say that?'

'He's attacking an enemy who's too strong for him.'

'What do you know about it?'

'I had a premonition.'

'What are you hiding from me?'

'Nothing – no woman could deceive you.'

Mentmose's office was like a buzzing bee-hive. He was rushing about, issuing orders which sometimes contradicted each other, urging his scribes to hurry up and transport the papyrus scrolls, wooden tablets and every small record accumulated since he took up his post. His eyes darting all over the place, he kept scratching his head and cursing his staff's slowness.

As he stepped out into the street to check that a cart had been loaded correctly, he bumped into Judge Pazair.

'My dear Judge,' he almost stammered.

'You're looking at me as if I were a ghost.'

'What an idea! I hope your health . . . '

'Prison life damaged it, but my wife will soon get me fit again.' Pazair looked at the bustle around him. 'Are you moving?'

'The Irrigation secretariat has predicted a very high annual flood. I must take precautions.'

'This district isn't vulnerable to flooding, surely?'

'It pays to be cautious.'

'Where are you moving to?'

'Er . . . my own house. It's only temporary, of course.'

'That is illegal. Has the Judge of the Porch been informed?'

'The dear judge is very tired – disturbing him would have been very inconsiderate.'

'I think you should stop this transfer of files until he has been informed.'

Mentmose's voice became nasal and shrill. 'You may be innocent of the crime you were accused of, but your position is still uncertain and it doesn't grant you authority to give me orders.'

'That's true, but yours obliges you to help me.'

The commander's eyes narrowed. 'What do you want?'

'To examine closely the mother-of-pearl needle that killed Branir.'

Mentmose scratched his head. 'In the middle of moving—'

'It is a piece of evidence, not an item from your archives. It must be held in a file, with the message that deceived me: "Branir is in danger, come quickly." '

'My men didn't find it.'

'And what about the needle?'

'Just a moment.'

Mentmose disappeared inside the office. Gradually, the hustle and bustle calmed down. Bearers carrying papyri laid their burdens in the carts and got their breath back.

Mentmose reappeared ten minutes later, looking sombre. 'The needle has disappeared.'

8

As soon as Pazair drank the healing water from a copper cup, Brave demanded his share. He had long legs and a curly tail, big floppy ears which pricked up at mealtimes, and a fine pink and white leather collar inscribed with the words '*Brave, companion of Pazair*' The dog lapped up a cupful of the water, and so in turn did the judge's donkey, Way-Finder. Mischief, Neferet's green monkey, sprang on to the donkey's back, pulled the dog's tail and then hid behind her mistress.

'How can I possibly work in these conditions?'

'Don't complain, Judge. You have the privilege of being constantly cared for at home by a conscientious doctor.'

He planted a kiss on her neck, in the place where it made her shiver.

Neferet summoned up enough resolve to push him away. 'The letter,' she said firmly.

Pazair sat down on the ground, and unrolled a fine papyrus scroll. Given the importance of the message, he would write on only one side. To the left was the portion he had unrolled; to the right was the part on which he was going to write. In order to give additional formality to the text, he would write in vertical lines, separated by a straight line drawn in his best ink, with a reed pen whose point had been sharpened to perfection.

His hand was perfectly steady.

To Tjaty Bagey, from Judge Pazair.

May the gods protect the tjaty: may Ra illuminate him with his rays, Amon preserve his integrity, Ptah grant him coherence. I hope that your health is excellent, and that you continue to prosper. I am appealing to you in my capacity as a magistrate, in order to keep you informed regarding facts of exceptional gravity. Not only was I wrongly accused of murdering the sage Branir and deported to a thieves' prison, but the murderer's weapon has disappeared while in the possession of Mentmose, commander of the city guards.

I am a district judge, and believe I have brought to light the suspicious behaviour of General Asher and shown that the five former soldiers who formed the Great Sphinx's honour-guard were murdered.

The attack on me was an attack upon the entire legal system. Someone attempted to get rid of me, with the active cooperation of the commander of the guards and of the Judge of the Porch, in order to suppress my inquiry and protect conspirators who are pursuing an unknown goal.

My personal fate is of little importance, but I wish to identify the guilty party or parties who killed my master. May I also be permitted to state my anxieties as regards the country: if so many atrocious deaths remain unpunished, surely crime and falsehood will soon be the people's new guides? Only the tjaty has the ability to tear up this evil by the roots. That is why I am begging him to act, in the sight of the gods, and swearing upon the Rule that what I say is true.

Pazair dated the document, placed his seal upon it, rolled it up and fastened it with a clay seal. He wrote his name and that of the recipient. In less than an hour, he would hand it to a messenger who would deliver it to the tjaty's office that same day.

When he had finished, he got to his feet and said worriedly, 'This letter might mean exile for us.'

'Have faith. Tjaty Bagey's reputation has never been called into question.'

'If we're wrong, we'll be parted for ever.'

'No, we won't, because I shall go with you.'

There was no one in Suti and Panther's little garden. The door of the small white house was open, so Pazair went inside. Neither of them was there, though it was late. It was almost sunset, so perhaps the lovers had gone to take the air in the palm-grove by the old well?

Pazair crossed the main room to sit down and wait. As he did, he heard a few sounds. They came not from the bedroom but from the open-air kitchen, which was behind the house. It was clear that Panther and Suti were working.

The Libyan was making butter, mixed with fenugreek and caraway, which she would keep in the coolest part of the cellar. No water or salt would be added, to prevent it turning brown.

Suti was making beer. Using barley flour, he had made a dough which he kneaded and partly cooked in dishes arranged around the hearth. The loaves would then be soaked in water sweetened with dates; after fermentation, the liquid must be brewed and filtered, then transferred into a jar covered with clay, which was vital in order to keep it fresh.

Three jars had been placed in holes in a raised plank, and stoppers had been made from dried river-silt.

'Are you starting your own workshop?' asked Pazair.

Suti spun round. 'I didn't hear you! Yes, Panther and I have decided to make our fortune. She's going to make butter, and I shall brew beer.'

In irritation, Panther pushed away the greasy mass, wiped her hands on a brown cloth and disappeared without saying a word to the judge.

'Don't hold it against her – she's in a bad mood. Let's forget the butter. Fortunately there's the beer! Taste this for me.'

Suti lifted the largest jar out of its hole, removed the stopper, and put in place the pipe linked to a filter that would allow only liquid to pass through and would hold the pieces of dough in suspension.

Pazair took a mouthful, and almost choked. 'It's sour!'

'What do you mean, sour? I followed the recipe to the letter.' Suti took a sip, and spat it out at once. 'That's vile! I'm giving up making beer – it's no job for me. What have you been up to?'

'I've written to the tjaty.'

'A bit risky, isn't it?'

'It's essential.'

'You won't survive the next prison.'

'Justice will prevail.'

'Your gullibility is touching.'

'Tjaty Bagey will take action.'

'What makes you think he isn't corrupt and compromised like Mentmose and the Judge of the Porch?'

'Because he is Tjaty Bagey.'

'That old lump of wood is impervious to all feeling.'

'Perhaps, but he'll put Egypt's interests first.'

'May the gods hear you!'

'Tonight, I relived the horrible moment when I saw the needle sticking out of Branir's neck. It was a precious, expensive thing, which could be wielded only by an expert hand.'

'Have you got a new lead?'

'No, just an idea – and perhaps a futile one, at that. Would you mind paying a visit to the main weavers' workshop in Memphis?'

'Are you sending me on a mission?'

Pazair smiled. 'They say the women there are very beautiful.'

'Why don't you go yourself?'

'The workshop doesn't come under my jurisdiction. If I make the smallest mistake, Mentmose will pounce.'

Weaving was a royal monopoly, employing a large number of men and women. They worked at looms with low rails, comprising two rollers on which the threads were wound, and high rails, made up of a rectangular frame arranged vertically. The threads were wound round the upper roller, and the woven cloth round the lower one. Some pieces of fabric were more than forty cubits long.

Suti watched a man finishing off a length of braid for a noble's tunic, his knees drawn up to his chest, but paid closer attention to the young girls who were rolling linen fibres into balls. Their colleagues, who were no less charming, were arranging the warp threads on the upper roller of a loom which had been laid down flat, before interlacing the two sets of taut threads. Nearby, a spinner was shaping fibres into a thin, strong thread, using a stick with a wooden disc on the end, which she handled with stunning dexterity.

Suti did not pass unnoticed. Few women were indifferent to his lean face, direct gaze, long black hair, and blend of elegance and strength.

'What do you want?' asked the spinner.

'I'd like to speak to the overseer of the workshop.'

'The lady Tapeni only receives visitors who have been recommended by the palace.'

'Aren't there any exceptions?' whispered Suti.

Somewhat smitten, the spinner put down her staff. 'I'll go and see.'

The workshop was large, airy and clean, as the inspectors demanded. Light entered through rectangular skylights set below the flat roof, and air circulated by means of carefully placed oblong windows. The place was warm in winter and cool in summer. After an apprenticeship lasting several years, qualified weavers could command high pay, and there was no discrimination between men and women.

As Suti was smiling at a weaving-woman, the spinner reappeared and beckoned to him.

'Please follow me.'

The lady Tapeni, whose name meant 'mouse', was sitting in an immense room containing looms, bobbins, needles, spinning-staffs and other equipment needed for the practice of her craft. She was small and lively, with black hair, green eyes, and brown skin, and directed the workforce with military precision. Her apparent gentleness concealed an often tiresome authoritarianism. But the fabrics and clothes that emerged from her workshop were so beautiful that no one could criticize her methods. At the age of thirty, Tapeni was still unmarried and thought only of her profession. She viewed a family and children as obstacles to the pursuit of a career.

As soon as she saw Suti, she was afraid: afraid of falling stupidly in love with a man who had only to look at a woman to seduce her. But her fear was instantly transformed into another feeling, as exciting as she could wish for: the irresistible attraction of a huntress for her quarry.

She said in her most beguiling voice, 'How may I help you?'

'It's a . . . private matter.'

Tapeni dismissed her assistants. The scent of mystery increased her curiosity tenfold. 'We're alone now.'

Suti walked around the room and halted in front of a row of mother-of-pearl needles laid on a cloth-covered plank.

'These are superb. Who has permission to use them?'

'Are you interested in the secrets of our craft?'

'Passionately.'

'Are you an inspector from the palace?'

'No, don't worry. I'm simply looking for someone who used this type of needle.'

'A runaway mistress?'

Suti smiled. 'Not necessarily.'

'Men use them, too. I hope you aren't . . . ?'

'I can soon lay your fears to rest.'

'What's your name?' asked Tapeni, blushing.

'Suti.'

'And your profession?'

'I travel a great deal.'

'A merchant with a touch of the spy . . . You're very handsome.'

'And you're very attractive.'

'Really?' Tapeni drew the wooden bolt across the office door.

'Are these needles found in every weaving-workshop?'

'Only the largest ones.'

'So the number of people who use them is limited.'

'Indeed.'

She went closer, walked round him, touched his shoulders. 'You're very strong. You must know how to fight.'

'I'm a real hero. Will you give me some names?'

'Perhaps. Are you in a hurry?'

'Yes, to identify the owner of a needle like these.'

'Be quiet for a moment – we can talk about it later. I'll help you, provided you're loving, very loving . . .' Her lips touched Suti's.

After a moment's hesitation, he was obliged to respond to the invitation. Politeness was, after all, one of the intangible values of civilization. Not refusing a gift was one of Suti's moral imperatives.

Tapeni smoothed a pomade made from crushed acacia-seeds and honey over her lover's penis. Now that his sperm had been sterilized, she could enjoy his magnificent body without fear, forgetting the sound of the looms and the workers' complaints.

'Investigating on behalf of Pazair,' mused Suti to himself, 'brings nothing but danger.'

9

When Pazair reached his office he found Kem waiting for him outside, and the two men embraced warmly. The big Nubian was accompanied, as always, by Killer, whose gaze was so fierce that it frightened passers-by. Kem was moved to tears, which he tried to hide by rubbing his wooden nose.

'Neferet told me everything,' said Pazair. 'I know it's you I have to thank for my freedom.'

Kem cleared his throat. 'Killer was very persuasive.'

Pazair led the way inside. When they were seated in his office, he asked, 'Is there any news of Nebamon?'

'He's "resting" at home.'

'He'll attack again, I'm sure of it.'

'So am I. You must be more careful.'

'I will, so long as it doesn't stop me carrying out my duties as a judge. I've written to the tjaty: either he'll take charge of the enquiry and confirm me in my office, or he'll think my request impertinent and unacceptable.'

Red-faced, breathless and weighed down with armfuls of papyri, Pazair's scribe, Iarrot, came in. 'These are all the matters I dealt with while you weren't here. Am I to start work again?'

'I don't know what the future holds, but I detest leaving cases to wait. For as long as I'm not forbidden to do so, I shall set my seal on them. How is your daughter?'

'She is coming down with measles, and she has had a fight with an odious little boy who scratched her face. I've lodged a complaint against the parents. Fortunately, she's dancing better and better. But my wife . . . What a vicious woman!' Iarrot went on grumbling as he put the papyri into the right cases.

'I shan't leave my office until I have an answer from the tjaty,' said Pazair.

'I'll go and prowl around outside Nebamon's house,' said the Nubian.

Neferet and Pazair had decided never to live in Branir's house. No one should live in that place, where misfortune had struck. They would be content with the little official residence, half of which was taken up with the judge's files. If they were driven out, they would return to the Theban region.

Neferet rose earlier than Pazair, who liked to work late. After washing and putting on her face-paint, she fed the dog, the donkey and the monkey. Brave, who had a slight infection in his paw, was treated with Nile mud, which had antiseptic qualities and worked fast.

She placed her medical equipment on Way-Finder's back; the donkey had an instinctive sense of direction, and guided her through the narrow streets of the district where sick people required her services. They paid her by piling various types of food into the panniers that the donkey carried with obvious satisfaction. Rich and poor did not live in separate districts; leafy terraces rose above little houses of dried brick, huge houses surrounded by gardens stood alongside narrow alleyways crowded with animals and people. People called to each other, haggled and laughed, but Neferet had no time to participate in the discussions and celebrations.

After three days of hard struggle, she was at last succeeding in driving a bad fever from the body of a little girl, which had been invaded by the demons of the night. The patient could now drink milk from a wet-nurse, which was kept in a vase shaped like a hippopotamus; her heart was beating properly, and her pulse was regular. Neferet put a necklace of flowers round the child's neck and light earrings on her ears; her patient's smile was the best reward of all.

When she returned home, exhausted, she found Suti and Pazair there, deep in discussion. She greeted them, then went to wash and to put on fresh perfume.

'I saw the lady Tapeni, who oversees the main weaving-workshop in Memphis.'

'Did you learn anything?'

'A bit, and she's agreed to help me.'

'Have you found a promising line of investigation?'

'Not yet. A lot of people use that type of needle.'

Pazair looked down at his feet. 'Tell me, Suti, is Tapeni pretty?'

'She's not unattractive.'

'And was this first contact purely . . . friendly?'

'Tapeni's independent and affectionate.'

Neferet came back into the room, and poured drinks for them.

'This beer is safe,' said Pazair, 'which may not be true of your liaison with Tapeni.'

'Are you thinking of Panther? She'll understand that it's purely in the interests of the inquiry.' Suti kissed Neferet on both cheeks. 'Don't forget, you two: I'm a hero.'

Denes, a wealthy and famous ship-owner, loved to rest in the living room of his sumptuous Memphis house. The walls were painted with lotus-flowers, while the coloured tiles on the floor depicted fish frolicking in a pond. On small tables stood baskets of pomegranates and grapes. When he returned from the docks, where he oversaw the departure and arrival of his boats, he liked to eat salted curds and drink water which had been kept cool in a terracotta ewer. Stretched out on cushions, he was massaged by a servant-girl and shaved by his personal barber, who carefully trimmed the narrow white beard fringing his square, heavy face.

Denes stopped issuing orders when his wife, Nenophar, appeared, a striking figure dressed in the latest fashions. She owned three-quarters of the couple's fortune, so, during their frequent arguments, Denes felt it wise to give in.

That particular afternoon, there was no argument. Denes wore a glum expression and did not even listen to Nenophar as she angrily cursed the tax authorities, the heat and the flies.

When a servant showed in the tooth-doctor Qadash, Denes rose to greet him warmly.

Qadash was moist-eyed, with a low brow and jutting cheekbones. His nose bore a tracery of little purple veins looking fit to burst, and he constantly rubbed his hands, which were red because of poor circulation. Pazair had suspected him and his friend Denes of wrongdoing, and had investigated their activities, although he had not been able to prove their guilt.

Qadash's white hair was ruffled, and he was obviously in a state of great agitation. 'Pazair has come back,' he said, his voice shaking. 'What can have gone wrong? There was an official report saying he was dead!'

'Calm down,' urged Denes. 'He may be back, but he won't dare do anything against us. His imprisonment has broken him.'

'What do you know about it?' protested Nenophar, who was putting on her face-paint. 'That little judge is a determined man. He'll take his revenge.'

'I'm not afraid of him,' said Denes.

'Because you're blind – as usual!'

'Not at all. Now that you've been made steward of fabrics and a Treasury scrutineer, your court connections mean we can always keep track of what Pazair's doing.'

'Legal matters are kept quite separate from trade and

finances,' she objected. 'And supposing he takes his case to the tjaty?'

'Bagey's as uncompromising as he is awkward. He won't let himself be manipulated by an ambitious judge who only wants to cause a scandal and thereby become better known.'

They fell silent as the steward announced Sheshi the inventor and showed him in. Sheshi was a small man with a black moustache, and a manner so withdrawn that he spent entire days in complete silence. He moved about like a shadow.

'I apologize for being late,' he said.

'Judge Pazair's alive and here in Memphis!' stammered Qadash.

'I know.'

'What does General Asher think about it?'

'He's surprised as we are. We were delighted when the judge's death was announced.'

'Who freed him?'

'Asher doesn't know.'

'What's he going to do?'

'He doesn't confide in me.'

'What about your new weapons?' asked Denes.

'Their development is continuing.'

'Is a military expedition planned?

'That Libyan warlord Adafi caused trouble near Gubla – a couple of villages rose in rebellion – but the appearance of a detachment of troops was enough to put a stop to it.'

'So Pharaoh still trusts Asher?'

'So long as Asher's guilt isn't proven, Ramses can hardly dismiss a hero whom he decorated himself and appointed chief instructor to the Asian army.'

Nenophar stroked her amethyst necklace. 'War and trade often make good bedfellows. If Asher says there's to be a campaign against Syria or Libya, let me know straight away so that I can change my trading-routes. You won't find me ungrateful.'

Sheshi bowed.

'You're all forgetting Pazair!' protested Qadash.

'He's just one man trying to fight forces which will soon crush him,' sneered Denes. 'We shall continue as planned.'

'But suppose he finds out?'

'We'll leave Nebamon to deal with him. After all, our brilliant doctor is the main person involved.'

Nebamon took ten hot baths a day in a large pink granite pool, which his servants filled with scented water. Then he smoothed a soothing ointment over his testicles; little by little, it took away the pain.

Kem's damned baboon had come close to castrating him. Two days after the attack, a crop of spots had afflicted the delicate skin on his testicles. Fearing that they would ooze pus, Nebamon had shut himself away in his most beautiful house, cancelling the operations he had promised to carry out to restore the ageing beauties of the court.

The more he hated Pazair, the more he loved Neferet. She had mocked him, it was true, but he did not bear her a grudge. Had it not been for that insignificant, obstinate little judge, she would undoubtedly have yielded and become his wife. Nebamon had never failed before, and this intolerable insult caused him actual physical pain.

His most valuable ally was still Mentmose. The position of the guards commander, who had destroyed the message that lured Pazair to Branir's house, was becoming very delicate. A detailed inquiry would show, at the very least, that he was incompetent. Mentmose, who had plotted throughout his career to obtain his current post, would not be able to bear being dismissed. So all was not lost.

With Mentmose in attendance, General Asher was himself directing exercises involving the elite soldiers, who would leave for Asia as soon as they received the order. He was short, with a ratlike face, close-cropped hair, a wiry black pelt covering his shoulders and his short legs, and a scar across his chest. Asher took real pleasure in seeing men suffer as they crawled through the sand and dust, laden with sacks filled with stones, and had to defend themselves against knife-wielding attackers. Those who failed, he killed without pity. Nor were the officers spared: they, too, had to demonstrate their physical prowess.

Asher turned to Mentmose. 'What do you think of these future heroes?'

The commander was wrapped up a woollen cloak; he could not bear the dawn chill. 'I congratulate you on them, General.'

'Half of these fools are unfit for service,' spat Asher, 'and the others are hardly better! Our army is too rich and too lazy. We have lost the taste for victory.'

Mentmose sneezed.

'Have you caught a chill?'

''No, I'm just tired – and worried.'

'About Judge Pazair?'

'Your help in the matter would be invaluable, General.'

'In Egypt, no one can attack the legal system. In other countries, we'd have more freedom of action.'

'It was officially reported that he'd died in Asia.'

'A stupid administrative error, for which I am not responsible. The court case Pazair brought against me came to nothing, and as you see I've kept my command. The rest doesn't interest me.'

'You should be more careful.'

'Why? The little judge has been disqualified, hasn't he?'

'The charges against him have been dropped. Couldn't the two of us come up with . . . a solution?'

'You're commander of the city guards, I'm a soldier. We shouldn't mix the two occupations.'

'But in both our interests—'

'My interests lie in keeping as far away from Pazair as possible. I must leave you now, Mentmose. My officers are waiting for me.'

10

The hyena crossed the southern outskirts of the city, gave its sinister cry, climbed down the riverbank and drank from the Nile. Children howled in fear. Their mothers hurried them inside and slammed their front doors. No one dared attack the animal, because it was so big and fierce – not even experienced hunters dared go near it. Once its thirst was slaked, the hyena went back into the desert.

Everyone knew the ancient prophecy: 'When wild beasts drink from the river, injustice will reign and happiness will flee the land.'

The people whispered, and their words spread from place to place until they reached the ears of Pharaoh Ramses. The Invisible One was beginning to speak: by manifesting himself in the form of a hyena, he was disowning the king in the eyes of all Egypt. In every province, people worried about the evil omen, and wondered about the legitimacy of the king's reign. Soon, Pharaoh would have to take action.

Neferet was sweeping the bedroom with a short-handled broom. Kneeling, she held it firmly and nimbly flicked the long tufts of reed fibres back and forth.

'There's been no answer from the tjaty,' said Pazair, who was sitting on a low chair, sorting out papyri for that day's work.

Neferet laid her head on his knee. 'Why do you torment yourself like this? Worry is eating away at you, sapping your strength.'

'I worry about what Nebamon may try to do to harm you.'

'Whatever he does, you'll protect me, won't you?'

He stroked her hair. 'In you, I have found everything I could ever desire. How beautiful this time is! When I sleep beside you, an eternity of happiness washes over me. By loving me, you have lifted up my heart. You are within it, you fill it with your presence. Never go far away from me. When I look at you, my eyes no longer need any other light.'

Their lips met as tenderly as if it were their first kiss.

Pazair was very late for work.

Neferet had loaded her remedies and equipment on to Way-Finder, and was about to set off on her rounds of the city, when a breathless young woman came running up to her.

'Wait! Please wait!' cried Silkis, wife of Bel-Tran.

Neferet drew the donkey to a halt.

'My husband wants to see Judge Pazair on a matter of great urgency.'

Bel-Tran, a maker and seller of papyrus, had come to prominence because of his abilities as a manager and had been raised to the rank of head overseer of granaries, then deputy director of the Treasury. Pazair had helped him during a difficult period, and in return he had offered gratitude and friendship. Silkis, who was much younger than he, had been to see Nebamon, who had succeeded in making her face and her plump thighs slimmer. Bel-Tran set great store by displaying a wife comparable to the most beautiful women in Egypt, even at Nebamon's prices. Silkis had clear skin, and now that her features were more delicate she looked like a curvaceous adolescent.

'If he'll come with me now, I'll take him to the Treasury,

where Bel-Tran will receive him before leaving for the Delta. But, first, I'd very much like to consult you yourself.'

'What's the matter?'

'I keep getting terrible headaches.'

'What do you eat?'

'A lot of sweet things, I have to admit. I adore fig-juice and pomegranate-juice, and I dip my pastries in carob-juice.'

'What about vegetables?'

'I don't like them so much.'

'Eat more vegetables and fewer sweetmeats, and your headaches should improve. And you must rub this into your forehead.'

Neferet handed her a jar of ointment made from reed-stems, juniper, pine-sap, laurel-leaves and terebinth resin, all crushed and reduced to a compacted mass to which fat had been added.

Silkis thanked her and said, 'My husband will pay you handsomely.'

'As he wishes.'

'Would you agree to become my doctor?'

'If you're happy with my treatment, why not?'

'My husband and I will both be very happy. May I take the judge to him now?'

'As long as you don't lose him.'

Bel-Tran had jet-black hair, which he smoothed down with scented pomade, and a round head. He was heavily built, with plump hands and feet. He spoke quickly and never stopped moving. He seemed unable to enjoy even a short rest, torn between ten different projects and a thousand cares.

The faster he worked, the more he was entrusted with thorny, complex cases. His prodigious memory for figures and his ability to add up at incredible speed made him indispensable. Only a few weeks after taking up office among the senior officials at the Treasury, he had been promoted and become one of the closest colleagues of the director of the House of Gold and Silver, in charge of the kingdom's finances. Everyone spoke of him in glowing terms; he was accurate, quick, methodical and a hard worker; he never seemed to sleep, and was always the first to arrive at the Treasury offices and the last to leave. People were predicting a dazzling career for him.

When his wife showed Pazair in, Bel-Tran was flanked by three scribes, to whom he was dictating administrative orders. He greeted the judge warmly, finished what he was doing, sent away the scribes and asked his wife to prepare an especially good midday meal.

'We have a cook, of course, Judge, but Silkis won't use any but the best foodstuffs and ingredients – she's fussy about that.'

'You seem very busy,' said Pazair.

'I hadn't realized my new duties would be so enthralling. But never mind that. Let's talk about you. You've been through a terrible ordeal. I wasn't told about it until so late that there was nothing I could do to help.'

'I don't hold it against you. Suti was the only person who could have got me out of that dreadful situation.'

'Who do you think are the guilty parties?'

'The Judge of the Porch, Mentmose and Nebamon.'

'The judge ought to resign,' said Bel-Tran angrily. 'Mentmose's case is more difficult because he'll swear he was deceived. Nebamon's gone to earth on his estate, but he's not a man to give up. And don't forget General Asher – he really hates you because during the trial you almost destroyed his reputation. He's still as powerful and influential as ever ... Mightn't he be the one hiding in the shadows, pulling the strings?'

'I've written to the tjaty, asking him to pursue the inquiry.'

Bel-Tran nodded approvingly. 'A good idea.'

'He hasn't replied yet.'

'I'm sure Bagey won't see justice scorned like this. If your enemies attack you, they'll come up against him, too.'

'Even if he removes me from the case, even if I am no longer a judge, I shall find out who murdered Branir. I consider myself responsible for his death.'

'Whatever do you mean?'

Pazair shook his head. 'I've already said too much.'

'Don't torture yourself like this, my friend.'

'Accusing me of murdering him was the cruellest blow anyone could have dealt me.'

'But they failed, Pazair, and will again. I wanted to see you to assure you of my support. Whatever trials you may face in the future, I'm with you. Now tell me, wouldn't you like to move house, to somewhere a bit more spacious?'

'I'm waiting for the tjaty's answer.'

Even in his sleep, Kem stayed on the alert. He still had the hunter's instinct he had acquired during his youth in far-off Nubia. Many of his comrades had been over-confident and had died there in the grasslands, torn to shreds by a lion's claws.

He awoke with a start and felt for his wooden nose; sometimes he dreamt that the inert material had turned into living flesh. But this was no time for illusions; men were climbing the stairs. Killer was awake, too.

Kem lived surrounded by bows, swords, daggers and shields; so he armed himself in a moment, just as two guards broke down the door of his lodgings. He knocked out the first and Killer dealt with the second, but twenty more attackers followed them.

'Run away, Killer!' Kem shouted.

The baboon gave him a look which mingled bitter disappointment with the promise of vengeance. Then he escaped from the crowd, slipped through the window, jumped on to the roof of the house next door and vanished.

Kem struggled with every last bit of his strength, and the

guards had great difficulty overcoming him. But at last they succeeded in throwing him down on his back, binding him tightly, and putting a rope round his neck.

At that point Mentmose came into the room. The commander himself put manacles on Kem's bound wrists.

'At last,' he said with a smile, 'we have the murderer.'

Panther crushed fragments of sapphire, emerald, topaz and haematite, sifted the powder through a fine sieve made of reeds, then poured it into a cooking-pot under which she had lit a fire of sycamore wood. She added a little terebinth resin to produce a luxurious unguent, which she shaped into a cone; she would use it to grease wigs, head-dresses and hair, and to perfume her whole body.

She was bending over her mixture when Suti came in.

'You cost me dear, you she-devil, and I still haven't found the way to make my fortune. I can't even sell you as a slave.'

'You've slept with an Egyptian woman.'

'How do you know that?'

'I can smell it. Her scent has soiled you.'

'Pazair entrusted me with a delicate investigation.'

'Pazair, always Pazair! Did he order you to betray me?'

'I had a conversation with a remarkable woman, who runs the largest weaving-workshop in the city.'

'What's so . . . remarkable about her? Her backside, her sex, her breasts, her—'

'Don't be coarse.'

Panther threw herself on her lover with such force that she flattened him against the wall and he could barely breathe.

'In your country it's illegal to be unfaithful, isn't it?'

'We aren't married.'

'Of course we are, because we're living under the same roof.'

'You're a foreigner, so we'd need a contract. I hate formalities like that.'

'If you don't finish with her at once, I'll kill you.'

Suti reversed the situation: it was her turn to be flattened against the wall.

'Listen to me carefully, Panther. No one has ever told me how to behave. If I have to marry another woman to fulfil my duties as a friend, I'll do it. Either you understand that, or you leave.'

Her eyes widened, but she did not shed a tear. She would kill him; that much was certain.

In his best script, Judge Pazair was preparing to write another message to the tjaty, further emphasizing the gravity of the facts and requesting urgent action on the part of Egypt's most senior judge.

At that moment, Mentmose entered his office, looking thoroughly pleased with himself. 'Judge Pazair, I deserve your congratulations!'

'Why? What have you done?'

'I have arrested Branir's murderer.'

Pazair looked at Mentmose, but did not move a muscle. 'The matter is too serious for joking,' he said coldly.

'I'm not joking.'

'What is his name?'

'Kem.'

'That's ludicrous!'

'The man's nothing but a brute. And remember his past: this isn't the first time he's killed.'

'Your accusation is extremely serious. On what evidence do you base it?'

'We have an eye-witness.'

'He must appear before me.'

Mentmose looked sheepish. 'Unfortunately, that's impossible – and pointless.'

'Pointless? What do you mean?'

'The trial has already been held and sentence pronounced.'

Pazair rose to his feet, speechless.

'I have here the relevant document, signed by the Judge of the Porch.'

Pazair read it quickly: Kem had been condemned to death, and thrown into a cell in the great prison. 'The witness's name isn't given,' he protested.

'It doesn't matter. He saw Kem kill Branir, and has declared so under oath.'

'Who is he?'

'Forget about him. The murderer will be punished, that's the important thing.'

'You must be losing your mental balance, Mentmose, or you wouldn't dare show me such a miserable document.'

The commander gaped at him. 'I don't understand.'

'The accused was not present when the judgement was handed down. That is illegal, and annuls the verdict.'

'I bring you the head of the guilty party, and you talk to me about legal quibbles!'

'No, about justice,' Pazair corrected him.

'Be reasonable for once! Some scruples are futile.'

'Kem's guilt has not been proven.'

'That matters little. Who'll regret the loss of one mutilated Nubian with a criminal background?'

If Pazair had not been bound by his dignity as a judge, he could not have contained the anger burning inside him.

'I have more experience of life than you,' Mentmose continued. 'Certain sacrifices have to be made. Your office obliges you to think first and foremost of Egypt, its well-being and security.'

'How did Kem pose a threat to those things?'

'Neither you nor I have any interest in lifting certain veils. Osiris will welcome Branir into the paradise of just souls, and the criminal will have been punished. What more could you want?'

'The truth,' snapped Pazair.

'That's just an illusion.'

'Without it, Egypt would die.'

'If you aren't careful it's you who'll die, Judge.'

Kem had no fear of death, but he missed Killer very much. After so many years working together, he regarded the animal as a brother, and now he could no longer exchange meaningful looks with it or take account of its intuition. Nevertheless, he consoled himself with the knowledge that Killer was still free. Kem was locked up in a low-ceilinged room like a cellar, in stifling heat. No proper trial, an immediate sentence, and a summary execution: this time he wouldn't escape from his enemies. Pazair wouldn't have time to intervene, and would be able only to mourn the Nubian's death, which Mentmose would portray as an accident.

Kem felt no warmth towards the human race. He regarded it as corrupt, vile and sly, fit only to serve as fodder for the monster who sat beside the scales of the last judgement, waiting to devour the damned. One of his few joys had been to know Pazair, whose conduct had affirmed the existence of a justice Kem had long since ceased to believe in. With Neferet, his companion for all eternity, the young judge had embarked on a battle that was lost before it began, without caring about his own fate. Kem would have liked to help him right to the end, until the final disaster, when falsehood would bear him away, as it always did.

The cell door opened.

Kem sat up and stuck out his chest: he wasn't going to present the torturer a picture of a broken man. Heaving himself up, he emerged from his prison into the sunlight, pushing away the arm reaching out to him.

Dazzled by the light, he thought his eyes were deceiving him. 'It's can't be . . . '

Pazair cut the rope binding Kem's wrists. 'I overturned the charges, because many of the procedures followed were illegal. You are free, my friend.'

The big Nubian picked the judge up and hugged him, almost suffocating him. 'Haven't you got have enough troubles of your own, Pazair? You should have left me there in that dungeon.'

'Imprisonment seems to have weakened your mind.'

Kem looked around. 'Where's Killer?'

'He's run away.'

'He'll come back.'

'He was acquitted, too. The Judge of the Porch acknowledged that my protests were well founded, and disowned what Mentmose had done.'

'I shall wring Mentmose's neck.'

'Then you really would be guilty of murder. Besides, we've got better things to do – especially identifying the mysterious eye-witness who was the cause of your arrest.'

The Nubian raised his clenched fists to heaven. 'Leave that one to me!'

Pazair didn't reply. Instead, he handed Kem his weapons.

Kem felt a savage joy enter him as he was reunited with his bow, arrows, club and ox-hide-covered wooden shield.

'Killer isn't called that for nothing,' he added with a laugh. 'No guards will ever arrest him.'

Pharaoh Ramses stood before Khufu's looted sarcophagus and gathered his composure. His throat was tight and his chest ached, for the most powerful man in the world had become the slave of a band of murderers and thieves. By seizing the sacred emblems of kingship, and depriving him of the great state magic willed by the gods, they had rendered his power illegitimate and condemned him to abdicate, sooner or later, in favour of a plotter who would destroy the work that had been carried out over so many dynasties.

What the criminals were attacking was not just Pharaoh but the very ideal of government and the traditional values he embodied. If Egyptians were among the culprits, they had not acted alone; Libyans, Hittites or Syrians had almost certainly prompted them to this most evil of plans, so as to topple Egypt from its pedestal and open the country up to foreign influences, so much so that it would be dependent on on them.

The Testament of the Gods had been passed on and preserved intact from one pharaoh to the next. Today, impure hands held it and demon-like minds were manipulating it. For a long time Ramses had hoped that heaven would protect him and that the people would remain ignorant of what had happened – at least until he could think of a solution.

But the great king's star was beginning to wane.

The next Nile flood would be a poor one. Of course, the reserves in the royal granaries would feed the worst-affected provinces and no one would starve. But farmers would be forced to leave their fields, and people would whisper that the king could no longer ward off misfortune, unless he celebrated a festival of regeneration, during which the gods and goddesses would endow him with new energy, an energy reserved for the man who possessed the Testament legitimizing his reign.

Ramses pleaded for help from the Light that had given him birth; he would not give in without a fight.

11

Keeping a firm grip on the wooden handle of his razor, the barber drew the copper blade across Judge Pazair's cheeks, chin and neck. Pazair was sitting on a stool outside his house, next to Way-Finder, who watched the scene placidly, while Brave slept between the donkey's hooves and Neferet watched from the doorway.

Like all barbers, this one was talkative. 'If you're making yourself so handsome, you must have been summoned to the palace.'

'I see I can't hide anything from you.'

Pazair did not explain that he had just received an extremely brief response from the tjaty, summoning him without delay on this beautiful summer's morning.

'Promotion, is it?'

'I think that's unlikely.'

'May the gods look favourably upon you. After all, a good judge is their ally.'

'Yes, indeed he should be.'

The barber dipped his blade in a cup containing water mixed with natron. He drew back from his client, contemplated his work and delicately shaved a few rebellious hairs from underneath his chin.

'Ramses' officials have handed down some strange decrees these past few days. Why is he so set on re-affirming that he's our only defence against bad luck and disasters? No one in the land doubts that – well, almost no one. But there are rumours that his power is failing. The hyena drinking from the river, the poor flood, rain in the Delta at this time of year: all those things are tangible signs of the gods' disfavour. Some people think Pharaoh should celebrate a festival of regeneration so as to regain his full magical powers. What a splendid thing that would be! A fortnight's rest, free food, as much beer as anyone could want, dancing-girls in the streets. While the king was locked away in the temple with the gods, we'd have a fine old time!'

The royal decrees had puzzled Pazair: what secret enemy was Ramses afraid of? He had the feeling that the king was on the defensive, albeit the visible or invisible foe he was fighting remained unidentified. And yet Egypt was calm, and the only sign of instability was the mysterious conspiracy Pazair had dismantled, at least in part. But how could the theft of the sky-iron endanger Pharaoh's throne?

Of course, there was still General Asher, who Suti had sworn was a traitor and a secret ally of the Asians, and they were always on the alert for a chance to invade Egypt, the source of all wealth. But Asher held one of the highest military posts in the country, so would he really want to raise troops and rebel against the king? The idea seemed most unlikely. What the general cared about was his own career and privileges, not the burden of ruling, which he was wholly incapable of taking on.

Since Branir's murder, Pazair felt as if the ground under his feet was no longer solid. He was groping for answers in a void, felt jolted around like a load on a donkey's back. Although he had established a solid case against Asher and his probable accomplices, he could not see clearly, so obsessed was he with the martyred face of the man whom he had revered and whose life had been so brutally cut short.

'That's perfect,' pronounced the barber. 'You might

mention my name at the palace – I'd love to shave a few of those courtiers.'

It was Neferet's turn to look Pazair over. His hair was combed, his body washed, perfumed, his white kilt was spotless. She could find no fault at all.

'Are you ready?' she asked.

'I shall have to be. Do I look nervous?'

'Not on the outside.'

'The tjaty's letter wasn't encouraging.'

'Don't expect any goodwill, and you won't be disappointed.'

'If he dismisses me, I shall demand that the investigation continues.'

'We shan't let Branir's murderer go unpunished.'

He was reassured by her smile, which expressed her inflexible will. 'I'm afraid, Neferet.'

'So am I. But we shan't draw back.'

The nine Friends of Pharaoh were dressed in heavy black wigs and long, white, pleated robes, belted at the waist. They had met during the morning, summoned by Tjaty Bagey. After a somewhat heated debate, they had reached a unanimous decision. Following detailed exchanges of views, the bearer of the Rule, the overseer of the white Double House, the official in charge of canals and director of water-dwellings, the overseer of writings, the overseer of fields, the head of secret missions, the scribe of the land registry and the king's steward had all adopted the tjaty's surprising proposal, which they had at first thought unrealistic or even dangerous. But the urgency of the situation and its dramatic nature justified a quick and unusual decision.

When Pazair was announced, the nine Friends filed into the great audience chamber, with its bare white walls, and took their seats on stone benches on either side of Bagey, who was sitting on a low-backed chair.

At his throat the tjaty wore an imposing copper heart, the

only ritual jewel he allowed himself. Beneath his feet, a panther-skin symbolized the savagery that had been tamed.

Judge Pazair bowed before the august assembly, and kissed the ground. The icy expressions of the nine Friends did not bode well.

'Stand up,' ordered Bagey.

Pazair got to his feet, facing the tjaty. Bearing the weight of nine relentless pairs of eyes was a formidable ordeal.

'Judge Pazair, do you agree that only the practice of justice maintains the prosperity of our land?'

'That is my most profound belief.'

'If we do not act in accordance with justice, if it is considered to be a falsehood, rebels will lift up their heads, famine will strike and demons will roar. Is that also your conviction?'

'Your words express the truth as I live it.'

'I received your two letters, Judge Pazair, and handed them to this council so that each of its members might judge your conduct. Do you consider that you have been faithful to your mission?'

'I do not believe I have betrayed it. I have suffered in my flesh, and I have had the taste of despair and death in my mouth, but these sufferings are insignificant compared to the outrage inflicted upon the office of judge. It has been sullied and trampled underfoot.'

'When I tell you that the commander of the city guards, Mentmose, and the Judge of the Porch were appointed by this assembly, and with my approval, will you persist in your accusations?'

Pazair swallowed hard. He had gone too far. Even with strong evidence, irrefutable proofs, a junior judge ought not to attack leading citizens. The tjaty and his council would take the side of their close colleagues.

Summoning all his courage, he said, 'Whatever it may cost me, I shall uphold my accusations. I was unjustly deported,

Mentmose made no serious attempt to find out what had really happened, and the Judge of the Porch rejected the truth in favour of lies. They wanted to get rid of me, so that the investigation into Branir's murder, the mysterious deaths of the Great Sphinx's honour-guard and the disappearance of the sky-iron would not be pursued. You, the nine Friends of Pharaoh, have heard this truth and will not forget it. Corruption has emerged from its lair and infected part of the state. If the sick limbs are not cut off, it will infect the entire body.'

Pazair did not lower his eyes; he met the tjaty's gaze, something few men had dared to do.

'Haste and intransigence lead even the best of judges astray,' observed Bagey. 'Which of these two paths would you follow: making a success of your life, or serving justice?'

'Why must they be opposed to each other?'

'Because the life of a man is rarely in accordance with the law of Ma'at.'

'Mine was dedicated to her under oath.'

The tjaty was silent for a long time. Pazair knew he was about to pronounce a sentence against which there could be no appeal.

At last Bagey spoke again. 'The bearer of the Rule, the king's steward and myself have examined the facts, asked questions and reached the same conclusions. The Judge of the Porch has indeed made serious mistakes. Because of his age, his experience, and the service he has given to the law, we sentence him to exile in the Khargeh oasis, where he will end his days in solitude and meditation. He will never return to the valley. Are you satisfied?'

'Tjaty, I cannot find satisfaction in a judge's misfortune.'

'Sentencing him is a duty.'

'The continuance of the investigation is another.'

'I am entrusting it to the new Judge of the Porch. You, Pazair.'

The judge went pale. 'But I am too young.'

'The office of Judge of the Porch does not require great age, but it does require the skill that this assembly recognizes in you. Do you fear the weight of this burden so much that you would refuse it?'

'I had not expected . . .'

'Destiny strikes in a moment, as swiftly as the crocodile that dives into the water. What is your answer?'

Pazair raised his clasped hands as a sign of respect and acceptance, and bowed very deeply.

'Judge of the Porch,' declared Bagey, 'you have no rights. All that counts is your duties. May Thoth guide your thoughts and direct your judgement, for only a god can save man from his baseness. Know your rank, be proud of it, but do not boast of it. Place your honour above the crowd, be silent and useful to others. Do not let go of the tiller-rope, be as a solid pillar in your office, love goodness, and hate evil. Offer no falsehood, be neither flippant nor confused, have no greed in your heart. Explore the depths of those you judge, by means of the eye of Ra, the celestial light. Hold out your right hand with the fingers spread.'

Pazair obeyed.

'Here is your ring, bearing your seal. It will authenticate the documents on which you place it. Henceforth, you will sit at the gates of the temple to dispense justice, and to protect the weak. You will ensure that order is respected throughout Memphis, and you will see that taxes are paid on time, fields are properly worked, and foodstuffs delivered. If necessary, you will sit in Egypt's highest court of justice. In all circumstances, do not be content with what you hear, and look deep into the secret depths of men's hearts.'

'Since you desire justice, who will deal with Mentmose, whose deceitfulness is unforgivable?' asked Pazair.

'Your investigation must set out his offences.'

'I promise you that I shall not yield to any passion, and that I shall take all the time necessary.'

The bearer of the Rule got to his feet. 'I confirm the tjaty's decision in the name of the council. From this moment on, Judge of the Porch Pazair will be recognized as such throughout Egypt. He will be granted a house, material goods, servants, offices and administrative staff.'

The overseer of the Double House also stood up. 'In accordance with the law, the Judge of the Porch will be responsible, on peril of losing all his possessions, for all unjust decisions. If reparations are due to someone who brings a charge, he will pay them himself, without recourse to public finances.'

The tjaty gave a sudden gasp of pain, and everyone turned to look at him. Bagey clasped his hand to his right side, gripped the back of his chair, tried in vain to hold himself upright, and fell to the ground, where he lay very still.

When Neferet saw Pazair running towards her, with his brow covered in sweat and anguish in his eyes, she thought he had fled from the palace.

'The tjaty has been taken ill.'

'Is Nebamon with him?'

'Nebamon isn't well, and none of his assistants dares do anything without his permission.'

The young woman fixed her portable clock to her wrist, and quickly loaded her remedies and equipment on to Way-Finder's back. The donkey set off along the right road.

When she reached the palace, she was shown into a private chamber where Bagey was lying on a cushioned couch. Neferet sounded him, listened to the voice of the heart in his chest, in his veins and in his arteries. She identified two currents, one heating up the right side of the body, the other chilling the left side. The illness was deep-seated and involved the whole body. Using her timepiece, she calculated the rhythm of his heart and the reaction times of his main organs.

Secrets of the Desert

The members of the court anxiously awaited her diagnosis.

'I know and can treat this illness,' she said. 'The liver is affected, the portal vein obstructed. The hepatic arteries and the bile duct, which link the heart to the liver, are in bad condition. They are no longer giving enough air and water and are sending out blood which is too thick.'

Neferet gave the patient an infusion of chicory to drink. This plant, with its large blue flowers which closed at noon, was grown in temple gardens. It had many curative powers; mixed with a little old wine, it was used to treat several afflictions of the liver and gall bladder. She magnetized the obstructed organ; before long, the tjaty sat up, looking very pale, and vomited.

Neferet told him to drink several cups of the chicory infusion, to keep doing so until he was able to keep the drink down; at last the patient's body was refreshed.

'His liver has been opened up and washed out,' she announced.

'Who are you?' asked Bagey.

'My name is Neferet, Tjaty, and I am a doctor and Judge Pazair's wife. You must be careful what you eat,' she added calmly, 'and drink chicory every day. To avoid another serious blockage, which would completely incapacitate you, you are to take a potion made from figs, grapes, sycamore fruit, bryony seeds, persea fruit, gum and resin. I shall prepare this mixture for you myself and it must be exposed to the dew and filtered in the early morning.'

'You have saved my life.'

'I did my duty, and we were fortunate.'

'Where do you practise?'

'In Memphis.'

The tjaty got to his feet. Although his legs felt heavy and he had a bad headache, he managed a few steps.

'It's vital that you rest,' said Neferet, helping him to sit down. 'Nebamon will—'

'You are the one who will treat me.'

Just one week later, Tjaty Bagey had entirely recovered. He gave the new Judge of the Porch a limestone stele, on which were engraved three pairs of ears, one pair coloured dark blue, one yellow, and the third pale green. This evoked the lapis-blue sky where the stars of the sages dwelt on high, the gold from which the gods' flesh was made, and the turquoise of love. In this way the duties of the most senior judge in Memphis were set out: to listen to plaintiffs, respect the will of the gods, and be benevolent but without weakness.

Listening was the basis of a child's upbringing, and the ability to listen remained a magistrate's most important quality. Serious and intensely focused, Pazair took the stele, and raised the limestone block to his eyes before all the judges of the great city, who had met to congratulate the new Judge of the Porch.

Neferet wept with joy.

12

The house allocated to the Judge of the Porch was situated at the heart of a modest district, made up of small two-storey white dwellings housing craftsmen and junior officials. The young couple marvelled at it: it had only just been finished, and no one had ever lived in it before. It had originally been meant for another official, but he would lose nothing by the change. It was a long building with a flat roof, and was made up of eight rooms whose walls were decorated with paintings of many-coloured birds frolicking in the papyrus forest.

At first, Pazair didn't dare go in. He lingered in the poultry-yard, where an employee was force-feeding geese; ducks were quacking in a pond dotted with blue lotus-flowers. In the shade of a hut, two boys who were supposed to be throwing grain for the poultry were fast asleep. The new master of the estate did not wake them. Neferet, too, was delighted to have such riches. She gazed at the fertile earth, aerated by worms whose casts made excellent manure for cereal crops. No peasant would kill worms, knowing that they ensured the fertility of the soil.

Brave was the first to scamper into the splendid garden, followed immediately by Way-Finder. The donkey lay down under a pomegranate-tree, whose beauty was the most lasting of all, since whenever a flower fell a new one opened. The dog preferred a sycamore-tree, whose rustling leaves evoked the sweetness of honey. Neferet caressed the slender branches and the ripe fruit, some red, some turquoise, and drew her husband towards her in the shadow of the tree, shelter of the sky goddess. In delight they gazed upon a path bordered by fig-trees imported from Syria, and a shelter built of reeds, from which they could watch the splendid sunsets.

Their peace did not last long; Mischief, Neferet's little green monkey, let out a cry of pain and leapt into her mistress's arms. Sheepishly she held out her paw, in which an acacia thorn was embedded. The wound must not be taken lightly; if the foreign body remained under the skin, it would eventually cause internal bleeding which defied many doctors. Without needing to be told, Way-Finder got to his feet and came over to them. Neferet took a scalpel from her medical kit, took out the thorn with infinite gentleness, and smeared the wound with an ointment made from honey, colocynth, ground cuttlefish-bone and powdered sycamore-bark. If infection did develop, she would treat it with sulphur of arsenic. But Mischief's life hardly seemed in any danger; as soon as she was free of the thorn, she climbed up into a date-palm in search of ripe fruit.

'Shall we go inside?' suggested Neferet.

'Things are becoming serious.'

'What do you mean?'

'We got married, it's true, but neither of us owned anything then. The situation has changed.'

'Surely you aren't tiring of it already?'

'Never forget, Doctor, that I was the one who came along and tore you away from your peaceful life.'

'My memories are rather different; didn't I notice you first?'

'We should have been seated side by side, surrounded by a crowd of relatives and friends, and have chairs, clothing-chests, vases, toilet articles, sandals and goodness knows what else paraded in front of us. You would have been brought in a litter, dressed in ceremonial clothes, to the sound of flutes and tambourines.'

'I prefer it like this: the two of us alone together, without any noise or fuss.'

'As soon as we cross the threshold of this house we shall become responsible for it. The authorities would rebuke me if I didn't draw up a contract safeguarding your future.'

'Is that an honest proposition?'

'I'm conforming with the law. I, Pazair, bring all my possessions to you, Neferet, who will retain your name. Since we have decided to live together under the same roof, and so to be married, I will owe you reparation if we should ever separate. A third of all that we have acquired, from this day onwards, shall come to you as of right, and I must feed and clothe you. In all other matters, the court will judge.'

'I must confess to the Judge of the Porch that I am madly in love with a man and that I have the firm intention of remaining bound to him until my last breath.'

'Perhaps, but the law—'

'Hush! Let's go inside.'

'Before we do, one correction: it's I who am madly in love with you.'

Arm in arm, they crossed the threshold of their new life.

The first room, which was small and low-ceilinged, was reserved for the veneration of the ancestors. They meditated there for a long time, venerating the soul of Branir, their murdered master. Then they explored the reception chamber, the bedchambers, the kitchen, the washing areas with their terracotta pipes and a toilet equipped with a limestone seat.

They were hugely impressed by the bathing-room. On the limestone flagged floor, set in a corner were two brick benches on which serving-men and -girls stood to pour water on anyone who wanted a shower. Square tiles of limestone covered the brick walls, so that they were not exposed to the damp. A slight incline, leading to the opening of a deep-buried earthenware pipe, enabled the water to run away.

In the airy bedchamber a mosquito-net hung over a bed made of solid ebony, with feet in the shape of a lion's paws. On the sides was the jovial face of the god Bes, whose task was to guard people while they slept and give them happy dreams. Wide-eyed, Pazair lingered over the sleeping-frame, which was made from plaited ropes of vegetable fibres and was of an exceptional quality. The many cross-pieces had been positioned with perfect precision to support a heavy weight for many years.

At the head of the bed was a robe of the finest white linen, the bride's garment which would also be her winding-sheet.

Pazair said, 'I'd never have imagined sleeping in a bed like this, not even for a single night.'

'Why wait?' asked Neferet teasingly.

She laid out the precious robe on the sleeping-frame, took off her dress, and stretched out naked, happy to welcome Pazair's body on top of hers.

'This moment is so sweet,' he said, 'that I shall never forget it. By the way you look at me, you make it eternal. Don't ever leave me. I belong to you like a garden which you shall enrich with flowers and scents. When we form a single being, death no longer exists.'

But the very next morning, Pazair began to miss the little house he had lived in as a junior judge and to realize why Tjaty Bagey was content with a modest dwelling in the centre of city. True, there were plenty of reed brushes and besoms with which to clean the place thoroughly, but you still needed hands to wield them. Neither he nor Neferet had the time to do this work, and it was out of the question to ask the gardener or poultryman, who stuck strictly to their own jobs. No one had thought to employ a cleaning-woman.

Neferet and Way-Finder left early for the palace; the tjaty

wished for a consultation before his first audience. Without a clerk, without a proper office, without servants, the Judge of the Porch felt completely lost, in charge of a domain which was too big for him. The sages had been quite right when they called the wife 'mistress of the house'.

The gardener recommended a woman in her fifties, who hired out her services to householders in distress; for six days' work, she demanded no less than eight goats and two new dresses! Bled white, certain that he was endangering the couple's financial stability, the Judge of the Porch was obliged to accept. Until Neferet returned, he would live in straitened circumstances.

Suti gazed at the new house in wonder, and prodded the walls. 'They feel real.'

'The building's new, but it's of good quality.'

'I thought I was the greatest practical joker in Egypt, but you've outdone me by a thousand cubits. Who lent you this house?'

'The state,' replied Pazair.

'Surely you're not going to keep on claiming you're the new Judge of the Porch?'

'If you don't believe me, ask Neferet.'

'Ha! She's your accomplice.'

'Then go to the palace.'

Suti was shaken. 'Who appointed you?'

'The nine Friends of Pharaoh, led by the tjaty.'

'You mean that cold fish Bagey actually dismissed your predecessor, one of his esteemed colleagues, a man with a spotless reputation?'

'He had his faults. Bagey and the High Council acted according to the law.'

'It's like a miracle, a dream . . .'

'My request was heard by the full council.'

'But why appoint you to such an important post?'

'I've been thinking about that.'

'And what have you concluded?

'Suppose half of the High Council is convinced of Asher's guilt, and the other half isn't. Wouldn't it be a clever move to entrust an increasingly dangerous investigation to the judge who lifted the first veil? When the case is settled, one way or the other, it will be easy either to disown me or to congratulate me.'

'You aren't as stupid as you look,' said Suti, grinning.

'I'm not surprised or shocked by their decision; it's in accordance with Egyptian law. I began the matter, so it's up to me to finish it – if I didn't I'd be nothing more than an agitator. Besides, why should I complain? I've been given resources beyond my wildest hopes. Branir's soul is protecting me.'

'Don't rely on the dead. Kem and I will protect you much more effectively.'

'Do you think I'm in danger?'

'You're getting more and more exposed. The Judge of the Porch is usually an old, cautious man, determined not to take risks and to enjoy his privileged life to the full – in short, the complete opposite of you.'

'What can I do? Destiny has made its choice.'

'I may not be as mad as you are, but I'm pleased to hear that. You'll arrest Branir's murderer, and I shall enjoy removing Asher's head.'

Pazair smiled and then changed the subject. 'And how is the lady Tapeni?'

'She's a splendid mistress – no match for Panther, but what imagination! Yesterday afternoon, we fell out of bed at the crucial moment. An ordinary woman would have paused for a moment, but not her. I had to show I was her equal, even though I was underneath.'

'You have my admiration. On a less convivial note, what have you learnt from her?'

'It's obvious that you aren't an expert in seduction. If I ask too many direct questions, she'll close up like a night-flower at noon. We've begun to talk about the illustrious women who practise the art of weaving. Some are incredibly skilled with the needle. You and I are on the right track, I can feel it.'

Neferet came back at last, led by Way-Finder. Brave greeted the donkey with joyful barking, and the two companions ate together; one had a chunk of beef and the other had fresh fodder. Mischief wasn't hungry any more; her belly was so full of fruit she had stolen from the orchard that she was indulging in a long nap.

Neferet was radiant. Neither tiredness nor cares had any hold over her. Often, Pazair felt unworthy of his wife.

'How is the tjaty?' he asked.

'Much better, but he'll have to go on having treatment for the rest of his life. His liver and his bile duct are in a dreadful state, and I'm not sure I can prevent his legs and feet from swelling when he's tired. He ought to do a lot of walking and get some country air, not stay seated for whole days at a time.'

'You're asking the impossible. Did he say anything about Nebamon?'

'He's ill. Killer seems to have left his mark.'

'Ought we to feel sorry for him?'

A loud bray from Way-Finder interrupted them: he hadn't had enough to eat.

'I'm overwhelmed,' confessed Pazair. I did manage to take on a temporary cleaning-woman – at an extortionate rate – but I feel lost in this big house. We haven't got a cook, the gardener does only what he feels like, and I don't understand the first thing about all these different brushes. My files are all untouched, I haven't got a clerk, and I—'

Neferet kissed him.

13

Dressed in a kilt with a weighted panel at the front and a fine pleated shirt with long sleeves, Bel-Tran came to visit Pazair and Neferet in their new home.

He began by congratulating them both warmly. Then he said, 'This time, Pazair, I definitely am going to help you, and in the most direct way. I've been charged with reorganizing the central government offices. As Judge of the Porch, you are a priority.'

'That's very kind of you, but I can't accept any favours at all, no matter how small.'

'This isn't a favour. It's merely an arrangement, in accordance with the rules, which will enable you to have all your files to hand. We shall work side by side, in large, spacious premises. Please don't stop me pleading the cause of our common efficiency!'

Bel-Tran's rapid rise to power had amazed even the most world-weary members of the court, but no one criticized it. He would blow the dust off secretariats which had become mired in routine, get rid of lazy or incompetent officials, and face up to the thousand and one problems that arose from one day to the next. Endowed with infectious enthusiasm, he happily bullied his subordinates. Sons of noble families deplored his modest origins, but accepted that they must obey him or be sent back home. No obstacle daunted Bel-Tran: he took its measure, attacked it with an inexhaustible energy, and eventually overcame it. Whenever an insoluble difficulty presented itself, Bel-Tran was its inevitable recipient. To his great credit, he had even managed to sort out the wood tax, which large landowners – ignoring the public good – had for a long time escaped paying. On this occasion, Bel-Tran had not omitted to call on Pazair's judicious intervention once again.

Pazair saw that he had a powerful ally. Thanks to Bel-Tran, he would avoid many pitfalls and snares.

Bel-Tran turned to Neferet. 'Silkis is feeling much better. She's very grateful to you and considers you a friend.'

'How are her headaches?'

'Much less frequent. When they start, we apply your salve and it's remarkably effective. I'm afraid, though, that despite your warnings and those of the interpreter of dreams – like you, he told her not to eat too much sugar – she's still greedy. I hide the pomegranate juice and the honey but she secretly obtains carob-juice, or figs.'

'No medicine can replace willpower.'

Bel-Tran grimaced. 'May I consult you, too? For the last week, my ankles have been painful. I'm even finding it difficult to get my sandals on.'

Neferet examined his small, plump feet. 'Boil beef-fat and acacia-leaves, pound them into a paste and apply it to the sensitive areas. If that doesn't help, let me know.'

They paused for a moment as the cleaning-woman came to ask Neferet which room should be cleaned next. Neferet was adapting marvellously to her role as mistress of the house, and would soon set up her consulting-room in one of the ground-floor rooms.

At the palace her reputation was growing: curing the tjaty had brought her glowing praise which provoked envy among the court doctors, who were still paralysed by Nebamon's absence.

"This house is delightful,' observed Bel-Tran, nibbling a slice of watermelon.

Pazair smiled. 'Without Neferet, I'd have run away.'

'Don't be so unambitious, my dear Pazair! Your wife is an exceptional person. No doubt many people will be jealous of you.'

'Nebamon's jealousy is quite enough for me,' said Pazair.

'He won't stay quiet for long. You and Neferet humiliated him, and he'll be thinking of nothing but getting his revenge – though, admittedly, your new position will make that more difficult.'

'Let's talk of something else,' said Pazair. 'What do you think of the recent royal decrees?'

'They're very puzzling. Why does the king need to reaffirm a power which nobody's challenging?'

'The last annual flood was very low, a hyena came and drank from the river, several woman have given birth to malformed children . . .'

Bel-Tran snorted. 'Those are just the common folk's superstitions.'

'Perhaps, but superstitions can sometimes be very powerful.'

'It is up to the servants of the state to prove they're groundless. Now, tell me, are you going to resume your case against Asher and the investigation into the killing of the honour-guard?'

'Of course. They're the main reasons for my appointment.'

'A lot of people at the palace were hoping those unfortunate events would be forgotten. I'm delighted to see that they won't be – mind you, it's no more than I expected of you, with your courage.'

'Ma'at is a smiling but implacable goddess. The source of all happiness is within her, so long as she isn't betrayed. If I didn't seek the truth, I'd be unable to breathe.'

In a darker tone, Bel-Tran said, 'Asher's calmness worries

me, too. He's a violent man, a doer of brutal deeds. Once he knew of your promotion, he ought to have reacted in some visible way.'

'Surely he has less room to manoeuvre now?'

'That's true, but don't celebrate too soon.'

'It isn't in my nature to do that.'

'You're no longer alone now, but your enemies have by no means vanished. Everything I learn, I shall tell you.'

For two weeks Pazair lived in a whirlwind. He consulted the Judge of the Porch's enormous archives, oversaw the separate filing of tablets made from clay, limestone and wood, draft legal documents, furniture inventories, official mail, sealed rolls of papyrus and scribes' materials. He consulted the list of his staff, summoned each scribe, oversaw the payment and adjustment of salaries, examined delayed complaints and corrected a host of administrative mistakes. Although he was surprised by the size of the task, he did not balk at it and quickly built up good relationships with his subordinates. Each morning, he conferred with Bel-Tran, whose advice was very valuable.

Pazair was sorting out a delicate land-registry problem when a scribe with a red face and thick features arrived.

'Iarrot!' exclaimed the judge. 'Where on earth have you been?'

'My daughter's going to become a professional dancer, that's definite. But my wife won't agree to it, so I'm having to get divorced.'

'When will you be coming back to work?'

'I don't belong here.'

'You couldn't be more wrong! A good scribe—'

'You're too important now. In these offices, scribes have to work set hours – and stick to them. That wouldn't suit me. I'd sooner take charge of my daughter's career. We'll travel from province to province and take part in village festivals, then obtain a contract with a well-established troupe. The poor little thing must be protected.'

'Is that your final decision?'

'You work too hard. You'll come up against interests which are too powerful for you. I'd rather give up my staff, official kilt and funerary stele while I still can, and live at a safe distance from dramas and quarrels.'

'Are you sure you really will escape them?'

'My daughter worships me and will always listen to me. I shall make her happy.'

Denes was enjoying his cherished victory. The fight had been taxing, and his wife had had to enlist all her relations to drive away their countless competitors, who were extremely bitter at their defeat. But it would be Denes and Nenophar who organized the banquet in honour of the new Judge of the Porch. The ship-owner's know-how and his wife's strength of belief had once more gained them the title of Master of Ceremonies for the whole of Memphis. Pazair's appointment had been such a surprise that it deserved a true celebration, at which the members of high society would vie with each other in elegance.

Pazair got ready without enthusiasm. 'I know this reception is going to bore me,' he complained to Neferet.

'But you're the honoured guest, my darling.'

'I'd rather spend the evening with you. My office doesn't mean I have to be involved in this kind of worldly activity.'

'We've refused all the purely social invitations from Memphis's leading citizens, but this one has an official aspect.'

'That man Denes doesn't miss a thing. He knows I suspect him of being part of the conspiracy, and he's playing the delighted host.'

'It's a good idea. He hopes to put you off your guard.'

'Do you think he'll succeed?'

Neferet's laughter enchanted him. How beautiful she was in that clinging dress, which left her breasts bare. Her black wig, with highlights of lapis-lazuli, set off her slender face, which bore hardly a trace of paint. She was the embodiment of youth, grace and love.

He took her in his arms. 'I wish I could lock you away.'

'Are you jealous?'

'If anyone so much as looks at you, I'll strangle him.'

'Judge of the Porch! How dare you suggest such a horrible thing?'

Pazair encircled Neferet's waist with a belt of amethyst beads, incorporating worked gold in the form of a panther's head. 'We're ruined, but you're the most beautiful woman in all the world.'

'This seems remarkably like an attempt at seduction.'

'You've unmasked me.' Pazair slid down the left strap of her dress.

'But we're already late,' she protested.

Before dressing for the banquet, Nenophar went to the kitchens, where her butchers had cut up an ox and were preparing the pieces, which they hung on a beam held up by forked posts. She picked out the joints to be grilled and those to be stewed, tasted the sauces, and made sure that several dozen roasted geese would be ready in time. Then she went down to the cellar, where her cellar-keeper showed her the chosen wines and beers. Reassured about the quality of the food and drink, Nenophar inspected the banqueting-hall, where serving-men and -women were setting out gold cups, silver salvers and alabaster plates on low tables. The whole house was full of the delectable scent of jasmine and lotuses. The reception would be a memorable one.

An hour before the first guests were due to arrive, the gardeners picked fruit, which would be served fresh and full of flavour; a scribe noted down the number of jars of wine placed in the banqueting-hall, so as to prevent fraud. The head gardener checked that all the pathways were clean, while the gate-keeper tugged at his kilt and adjusted his wig. The latter was the estate's unbending guardian and would not allow in anyone whom he did not know or who did not have an invitation tablet.

As the sun got lower in the sky, preparing to sink behind the Peak of the West, the first couple presented themselves to the gate-keeper. He identified them as a royal scribe and his wife, and they were soon followed by the great city's elite. The guests strolled in the garden, which was planted with pomegranate-, fig- and sycamore-trees, and chatted as they stood around the ornamental lakes, under the pergolas or wooden canopies, or admired the flowers arranged at the junctions of the pathways. The presence of Tjaty Bagey, who never attended parties, and of all the Friends of Pharaoh impressed everyone: it was going to be an unforgettable evening.

At the precise moment when the sun's disc vanished, the servants lit lamps which filled the garden and the villa with light. Nenophar and Denes appeared on the threshold of the house. She wore a heavy wig, a white dress bordered with gold, a necklace of ten strings of pearls, gazelle-shaped earrings and golden sandals, while he sported a layered wig, a long pleated robe with a cape, and leather sandals ornamented with silver. They were the perfect fashionable hosts, happy to display their wealth in the avowed hope of arousing envy.

In accordance with protocol, the tjaty was the first to walk towards them. His legs were heavy, and he had confined himself to worn-out sandals, a full, inelegant kilt and a short-sleeved overshirt.

Nenophar and Denes knelt in delight.

'How hot it is,' grumbled the tjaty. 'Only the winter is bearable. A few moments in the sun, and my skin burns.'

'One of our lakes is at your disposal, should you wish to cool down before the banquet,' offered Denes.

'I can't swim and I loathe the water.'

Denes led the tjaty to the place of honour. The Friends of Pharaoh came in turn, then the senior officials, other royal scribes and assorted people who had had the good fortune to be invited to the year's most prestigious celebration. Bel-Tran and Silkis were among these last; Nenophar greeted them distractedly.

'Is General Asher coming?' Denes whispered in his wife's ear.

'He's just sent his apologies – demands of work.'

'What about Mentmose?'

'He's ill.'

In the banqueting-hall, with its vine-decorated ceiling, the guests sat in comfortable armchairs padded with cushions. In front of them were pedestal tables bearing cups, plates and salvers. Three female musicians – a flautist, a harpist and a lute-player – played light, cheerful tunes.

Naked young Nubian girls moved about among the guests and placed little cones of perfumed pomade upon their wigs; as the cones melted, they gave off sweet smells and drove away insects. Each person was given a lotus-flower. A priest poured water on to an offertory table in the centre of the room, in order to purify the food.

Suddenly, Nenophar realised that the very people being celebrated weren't there. 'It's unbelievable that they should be so late!' she exclaimed to her husband.

'Don't worry about it. Pazair's no doubt working late on a case – he's obsessed with his work.'

'On an evening like this? Our guests are getting impatient. We must begin to serve the food.'

'Don't be so fretful.'

Hiding her anger, Nenophar asked the best professional dancing-girl in Memphis to perform earlier than planned.

Twenty years old, and a pupil of Sababu, owner of the most respectable ale-house in the city, she wore only a belt of shells, which clinked together delightfully at each step. On her left thigh were tattoos of the god Bes, the laughing dwarf, guarantor of joy in all its forms. The dancer easily held the guests' attention; she would execute the most acrobatic moves until Pazair and Neferet arrived.

While the guests were nibbling grapes and thin slices of melon to stimulate their appetites, and Nenophar was getting more and more angry, she noticed a certain amount of activity around the gates of the estate. It was them – at last!

'Come in, quickly.'

'I'm extremely sorry,' apologized Pazair.

He could hardly explain that he'd been unable to resist the urge to undress Neferet, that his ardour had led him to tear one of the straps of her dress, that he'd managed to make her forget all about the banquet, and that their love was worth more than the most brilliant of invitations. Her hair in a mess, Neferet had had to choose a new dress in haste and almost drag Pazair out of their bed of pleasure.

The dancing-girl withdrew and the musicians stopped playing when the young couple crossed the threshold of the banqueting-hall. In a second, they were judged by dozens of pairs of eyes, without indulgence.

Pazair had not bothered about elegance: his short wig, bare torso and short kilt made him look like an austere scribe from the time of the pyramids. His only concession to his own time was a pleated front panel in his kilt, which slightly relieved his sober dress. The man, thought the guests, was living up to his reputation for thoroughness. Inveterate gamblers wagered on the date when he would, like everyone else, yield to corruption. Others, less enjoyably, contemplated the extensive powers of a Judge of the Porch, whose somewhat incongruous youth would inevitably lead him to fatal excess. And people criticized the decision of the old tjaty, who was increasingly absent-minded and too quick to delegate parts of his authority: many courtiers were urging Ramses to replace him with an experienced, active administrator.

Neferet did not provoke the same debates. A simple band of flowers round her hair, a broad necklace hiding her breasts, light earrings in the form of lotus-flowers, bracelets at wrist and ankle, a long dress of transparent linen which revealed more of her figure than it hid: the sight of her enchanted the most world-weary and sweetened the most bitter. To her youth and beauty were added the brilliance of an intelligence so lively that it was expressed, without the least haughtiness, in her laughing eyes. They were right: her charm did not exclude a strength of character which few people would ever succeed in shaking.

Why, the guests wondered, had she bound herself to a junior judge whose stern appearance promised nothing for the future? True, he had obtained an eminent post, but he would not be able to hold it for very long. The love-affair would die, and Neferet would choose a more glittering partner. Where the unfortunate Nebamon had failed, another would succeed. A few grand ladies in their middle years deplored such daring clothes being worn by the wife of a senior magistrate, unaware that she had no other dress to put on.

The Judge of the Porch and his wife took their places beside the tjaty. Servants hurried to bring them slices of grilled beef and smooth red wine.

'But I see your wife isn't with you, Tjaty,' said Neferet. 'I hope she isn't unwell.'

'No, it's simply that she never goes out. Her kitchen, her children and her home in the city are enough for her.'

'I'm almost ashamed to have accepted such a grand house,' confessed Pazair.

'You shouldn't feel that way. I refused the estate Pharaoh grants to the tjaty, but that's because I detest the countryside. I've lived in the same place for forty years, and I have no intention of moving. I love the city. Wide-open spaces, insects, fields as far as the eye can see – they leave me cold or drive me mad.'

'All the same,' Neferet told him, 'as a doctor I advise you to walk as much as possible.'

'I walk to and from my office.'

'You need more rest, too.'

'As soon as my children's futures are settled, I shall start working shorter hours.'

'Are you worried about them?'

'Not about my daughter, though I am disappointed. She entered the Temple of Hathor as an apprentice weaver, but she didn't like the life because the whole structure of the day is governed by ritual. She's now been taken on as accounting-scribe of grain for a farm and will make a career of that. My son is more difficult to handle. He's a brick-checker, but he loves gambling and loses half his pay at the gaming-board. Fortunately, he lives at home and his mother feeds him. If he's hoping I'll use my position to improve his own, he's going to be disappointed: I have neither the right nor the wish so to do. But don't let my tedious difficulties discourage you; having children is the greatest happiness of all.'

The excellent food and wines delighted the guests, who exchanged small-talk until the Judge of the Porch's short speech, whose tone surprised everyone.

'All that matters is my office, not the individual who occupies it for a time. My only guide will be Ma'at, goddess of justice, who lays out the path for this country's magi-strates. If mistakes have been made recently, I feel respon-sible for them. So long as the tjaty grants me his trust, I shall fulfil my duties without regard for anyone's interests. Current cases will not remain secret, even if leading citizens are involved. Justice is Egypt's most precious treasure. I hope that each of my decisions will enrich it.'

Pazair's voice was strong, clear and trenchant. Anyone

who still doubted his authority was enlightened. The judge's apparent youth would not be a handicap; on the contrary, it would give him indispensable energy, placed at the service of impressive maturity. Many changed their opinions; perhaps the reign of the new Judge of the Porch would not be so brief, after all.

Late in the night, the guests dispersed; Tjaty Bagey, who liked to retire early, was the first to leave. Everyone wished to greet Pazair and Neferet, and to congratulate them.

When they were free at last, they went out into the garden. The sound of voices caught their attention. As they drew near a thicket of tamarisks, they came upon Bel-Tran and Nenophar, locked in a fierce argument.

'I hope never to see you again in this house,' said Nenophar.

'Then you shouldn't have invited me.'

'Politeness obliged me to.'

'In that case, why are you so angry?'

'Not only are you persecuting my husband with a tax demand, but you have also abolished my post as scrutineer of the Treasury.'

'It was only an honorary one. The state paid you at a rate out of all proportion to the real work. I am setting to rights all government departments which were too free with their money, and I shall never permit such extravagance again. Be sure that the new Judge of the Porch will agree with my course of action, and that he would have done the same thing – with a punishment thrown in. Be grateful that you have escaped that.'

Nenophar scowled at him. 'A fine way to justify yourself! You're more ferocious than a crocodile.'

'Crocodiles clean the Nile and keep the numbers of hippos down. Denes ought to beware of them.'

'Your threats don't impress me. Cleverer plotters than you have come to grief.'

'Then I wish you good luck.'

Nenophar stormed away from Bel-Tran, who hurried to rejoin his impatient wife.

Pazair and Neferet greeted the dawn on the roof of their house. They thought of the happy day that was breaking and would light them with a love as sweet as a festival perfume. On earth as in the afterlife, when generations had been wiped away, he would deck his beloved wife with flowers and plant sycamores near the cool lake, where they would never tire of gazing at each other. Their unified soul would come to drink in the shade, nourished by the song of the leaves as they rippled in the wind.

14

Pazair was obsessed by the urgent need to put together a case which would prove Kem's innocence once and for all and give him back his dignity. In so doing, Pazair would identify Mentmose's secret witness and find the commander guilty of producing false evidence.

As soon as she arose, and before even kissing him, Neferet made him drink two big gulps of copper-water; an obstinate cold proved that the Judge of the Porch's lymph was still infected and fragile, following his imprisonment.

Pazair ate his breakfast too quickly and rushed to his office, where he was immediately besieged by an army of scribes brandishing a series of strident complaints from twenty small villages. Because of the refusal by an overseer of the royal granaries, oils and cereals – which were vital to the well-being of the inhabitants because the flood had been so meagre – had not been delivered. Using an obsolete ruling to justify himself, the petty official was mocking the hungry peasants.

With help from Bel-Tran, the Judge of the Porch devoted two long days to resolving this apparently simple matter without making any administrative errors. The overseer of granaries was transferred to control the canal serving one of the villages that he was refusing to feed.

Then another difficulty arose, a conflict between some fruit-growers and the Treasury scribes whose task was to assess their profits; to avoid an interminable case, Pazair himself went to the orchards, punished the individuals behind the fraud and rejected the unjustified accusations made by the taxation scribes. He understood ever more clearly the extent to which the country's financial equilibrium, which allied private individuals and business with state planning, was a miracle, ceaselessly renewed. It was up to the individual to work as he chose and, beyond a certain threshold, to harvest the rewards of his labour; it was up to the state to take care of irrigation, the safety of property and persons, the storage and distribution of food when the flood was inadequate, and all other tasks in the community's interests.

Realizing that he would be in difficulties if he did not regulate the use of his time, Pazair scheduled the 'Kem case' for the following week. As soon as the day was announced, a priest from the Temple of Ptah opposed it: it was an ill-omened date, the anniversary of the cosmic battle between Horus, the celestial light, and his brother Set, the storm.* On such a day it was better not to leave one's house and not to undertake a journey; of course, Mentmose would use the argument so as not to appear.

Pazair was annoyed with himself, and almost gave up when an obscure customs matter was submitted to him, implicating foreign traders. Once his momentary discouragement had passed, he began to read the file, then pushed it away. How could he forget the distress of the big Nubian, who was searching for Killer in the most obscure corners of the city?

On his way home that evening, Pazair stopped to buy some red Nubian flowers to make an infusion Brave enjoyed.† As he turned away from the flower-seller's stall, he was accosted by Mentmose.

*Papyri provide us with lists of 'auspicious days' and 'days of ill omen', which correspond to mythological events.
†It was karkade, which is still drunk in modern Egypt. The flowers are those of the hibiscus.

The commander was clearly ill at ease, and his voice was unctuous as he said, 'I was badly deceived. But, deep inside, I always believed in your innocence.'

'Yet you still sent me to prison.'

'In my place, wouldn't you have done the same thing? The law must be pitiless towards judges, otherwise it will lose all credibility.'

'But in my case the judgement had not even been handed down.'

'An unfortunate combination of circumstances, my dear Pazair. Today destiny favours you, and we all rejoice at that. I have heard that you are planning to hold a trial, under the porch, concerning that regrettable Kem affair.'

'You're well informed, Commander. It only remains for me to set a date which, this time, will not be a day of ill omen.'

'Shouldn't we forget those regrettable incidents and put them behind us?'

'Forgetting is the beginning of injustice. The porch is the place where I must protect the weak and save them from the powerful.'

'Your Nubian is hardly weak.'

'But you are powerful, and you are trying to destroy him by accusing him of a crime he did not commit.'

'Would you accept an arrangement which would prevent a great deal of unpleasantness?'

'What sort of arrangement?'

'Certain names might be mentioned . . . And leading citizens set great store by their respectability.'

'What would an innocent man have to fear?'

'Rumours, tittle-tattle, ill-will, things like that.'

'Those things will hold no sway beneath the porch. You committed a serious offence, Commander.'

'I am the active arm of the law. Cutting yourself off from me would be a grave mistake.'

'I want the name of the eye-witness who accused Kem of having murdered Branir.'

Mentmose looked down. 'I made him up.'

'You certainly did not. You would not have put forward that argument if the person did not exist. I consider false testimony a criminal act, with the power to ruin a life. The trial will take place. It will shed light on your role as a manipulator, and will enable me to interrogate your famous eye-witness in Kem's presence. What is his name?'

'I refuse to give it to you.'

'Is he so highly placed?'

'I promised to tell no one. He took a lot of risks and doesn't wish his identity to be made public.'

'You refuse to cooperate in an investigation? You know the punishment for that.'

'You're mad! I'm not just a nobody, I'm the commander of the city guards.'

'And I am the Judge of the Porch.'

Suddenly Mentmose, whose face had turned brick-red and whose voice had grown very shrill, realized that he was no longer up against a junior provincial judge with a thirst for integrity, but was facing the highest judge in the city, who was moving, neither hastily nor slowly, towards his goal.

'Judge,' he said, 'I need time to think.'

'I shall expect you tomorrow morning, at my office. You will then reveal the name of your false witness.'

Although the banquet in honour of the Judge of the Porch had been a great success, and had much increased his prestige, Denes had stopped thinking about that lavish celebration. He was preoccupied with calming his friend Qadash, who was so agitated that he had begun to stutter. Pacing up and down, the tooth-doctor constantly fiddled with the wayward strands of his white hair. An influx of blood had turned his hands red, and the small veins in his nose looked ready to burst.

The two men had taken refuge in the furthest part of the pleasure-garden, well away from indiscreet ears. The inventor Sheshi, who joined them there, checked that no one could hear them, then sat down at the foot of a date-palm. Although the little man with the black moustache deplored Qadash's agitation, he shared his anxieties.

'Denes, your plan is a disaster,' said Qadash accusingly.

'All three of us agreed to use Mentmose, have Kem accused, and thus cool Judge Pazair's hot head,' Denes reminded him.

'And we failed – lamentably! I can't practise my profession because my hands are shaking so badly, and you have refused to let me use the sky-iron! When I agreed to join you, you promised me a post at the very pinnacle of the state.'

'First the post of principal doctor, in place of Nebamon,' said Denes reassuringly, 'then even greater things.'

'Farewell, beautiful dreams!'

'Not at all.'

'Have you forgotten that Pazair is Judge of the Porch, that he wants to stage a trial to clear Kem of all suspicion and force the eye-witness – namely, me – to appear?'

'Mentmose won't reveal your name.'

'I'm not so sure about that.'

'He's schemed his whole life long to get his present job. If he betrays us, he'll condemn himself.'

Sheshi nodded in agreement. Reassured, Qadash accepted a cup of beer.

Denes, who had eaten too much at the banquet, massaged his swollen belly. 'This commander of the guards is a useless idiot,' he groused. 'When we take power, we must get rid of him.'

'Too much haste would be dangerous,' said Sheshi, in a small, barely audible voice. 'General Asher is working away in the shadows, and I'm not unhappy with my latest results. Soon we'll have access to excellent weapons, and we'll also have control of the main weapons stores. Above all, we must not show our hand. Pazair is convinced that Qadash wanted to steal the sky-iron from me, and that we are enemies. He knows nothing about the links between us, and if we're careful he'll never find out. Thanks to Denes's public declarations, he believes that the army's aim is to make unbreakable weapons. Let us encourage him in that idea.'

'Can he really be that naive?' worried Qadash.

'Far from it. But a project of this size will draw his attention. What could be more important than a sword which can cut through helmets, armour and shields without breaking? With its aid, Asher will foment a conspiracy to seize power. That is the truth which will impose itself on the judge's mind.'

'It implies your complicity,' Denes pointed out.

'My obedience, as an expert, clears me of responsibility.'

'All the same I'm worried,' insisted Qadash, who had started pacing up and down again. 'Ever since he crossed our path, we've underestimated Pazair. And now he's Judge of the Porch!'

'The next storm will sweep him away,' prophesied Denes.

'And every day that passes is in our favour,' said Sheshi. 'Pharaoh's power is weakening, being eroded like a stone.'

None of the three conspirators noticed the presence of a witness who had not missed one word of the conversation. Perched high in a palm-tree, Killer was gazing fixedly at them with his red-rimmed eyes.

Appalled by Bel-Tran's bigoted, hostile attitude, Nenophar took immediate action. She summoned to her house the scribes who oversaw the financial affairs of the fifty wealthiest families in Memphis. Like herself, their patrons enjoyed a number of honorary positions which did not oblige them to do any work but which gave them access to confidential information and afforded them privileged contact with the highest levels of government. Nenophar explained the situation clearly to the scribes. In his frenzy of reorganization, Bel-Tran was abolishing these posts one after another. Since the beginning of its history, Egypt had always rejected the authoritarian excesses of this kind of jumped-up official, who was as dangerous as a sand viper. Everyone thoroughly approved of this passionate speech. One man was obliged to take the side of reason and justice: Pazair, the Judge of the Porch. So a delegation, made up of Nenophar and ten eminent representatives of the nobility, obtained an audience the very next morning.

No one arrived empty-handed: at the judge's feet they laid vases of ointment, precious fabrics and a chest full of jewels.

'Receive this homage to your office,' said the eldest man.

'Your generosity touches me, but I am obliged to refuse your gifts.'

The old scribe was highly indignant. 'Why is that?'

'Attempted corruption.'

'Nothing could not be further from our thoughts. I pray you, do us the honour of accepting them.'

'Take these gifts away and give them to your most deserving servants.'

Nenophar decided it was time she intervened. 'Judge of the Porch, we seek proper respect for Egypt's traditional society and values.'

'In that, you will find an ally in me.'

Reassured, she spoke warmly. 'Without any proper cause, Bel-Tran has abolished my honorary post as scrutineer of the Treasury, and is preparing to do similar harm to many members of the most respected families in Memphis. He is attacking our customs and our ancient privileges. We ask you to take action to stop this persecution.'

Pazair read out a passage from the Rule:

101

'*You who judge, make no distinction between a rich man and a man of the people. Pay no attention to fine clothes, and do not disdain those who dress simply because of their modest resources. Accept no gifts from the man who possesses much, and be not prejudiced against the weak man or in his favour. Thus the country will have a solid foundation if you concern yourself only with the laws when handing down your sentence.*'

Although everyone knew these precepts, they still caused a stir.

'What does this reminder mean?' asked Nenophar in surprise.

'That I am fully aware of the situation and that I approve of what Bel-Tran is doing. Your "privileges" are hardly ancient, since they date only from the first years of Ramses' reign.'

'Are you daring to criticize what the king did?'

'He would urge you, as nobles, to take on new duties, not to derive profit from a title. The tjaty has made no objections to Bel-Tran's reorganization of the government secretariats. The early results are encouraging.'

'Surely you aren't hoping to impoverish the nobility?'

'No, I hope to give it back its true greatness, so that it may serve as an example to others.'

Bagey the rigorous, Bel-Tran the ambitious, Pazair the idealistic: Nenophar shuddered at the thought that these three were allies. Fortunately, the old tjaty would soon retire, the ambitious jackal would break his long teeth on a stone, and the honest judge would sooner or later succumb to temptation.

'Enough of this preaching,' she said. 'Which side are you taking?'

'Have I not made that clear?'

'No senior official has ever built a successful career without our cooperation.'

'Then I must resign myself to being the exception.'
'You will fail.'

Tapeni was insatiable. She did not have Panther's inimitable fervour, but she showed splendid imagination both in positions and in caresses. So as not to disappoint her, Suti was obliged to follow – and even anticipate – her initiatives. Tapeni felt a deep affection for the young man, for whom she reserved treasures of love. Brown-skinned, small, and highly excitable, she practised the art of the kiss, sometimes with refinement, sometimes with violence.

Fortunately, she was equally occupied with her work. Suti was grateful for the resulting periods of rest, which he used to reassure Panther and prove to her that his passion was undimmed.

After their latest bout of love-making, Tapeni put on her dress, and Suti adjusted his kilt.

'You're a very handsome man and a lusty stallion,' she purred.

'"Leaping gazelle" would suit you.'

'Poetry bores me, but your virility fascinates me.'

'And you know how to speak to it persuasively. But we've rather lost sight of the reason for my first visit.'

'The mother-of-pearl needle?'

'The very same.'

'Something as beautiful, rare and precious as that would only be handled by women of quality: the most highly skilled weavers.'

'Do you have a list of them?'

'Of course.'

'Will you let me have it?'

'Those women are my rivals. You're asking too much.'

Suti had been afraid she'd say something like that. 'How can I persuade you?'

'You're the man I've always wanted. In the evening, and

at night, I miss you. I have to make love to myself while I think of you. This pain is becoming unbearable.'

'I could let you have one night, from time to time.'

'I want all your nights.'

'You mean you want—'

'Marriage, my darling.'

'I'm rather against the idea, on principle.'

'You'll have to give up your mistresses, get rich, live with me, wait for me, always be ready to satisfy my wildest desires.'

'There are more painful duties.'

'We shall make our union official next week.'

Suti did not protest; he would find a way of escaping this slavery. 'What about the weavers?'

Tapeni simpered. 'Have I your word?'

'I have only one.'

'Is this information really so important?'

'For me, yes. But if you refuse . . . '

She gripped his arm. 'Don't be angry.'

'You're torturing me.'

'I'm teasing you. Few noble ladies know how to use those types of needle perfectly and steadily, with the nimbleness and precision required. I have seen only three: the wife of the former overseer of canals is the best.'

'Where can I find her?'

'She is eighty years old, and she lives on the island of Elephantine, near Egypt's southern border.'

Suti frowned. 'What about the other two?'

'The widow of the director of granaries is small and frail. She used to be incredibly strong, but she broke her arm two years ago, and—'

'And the third?'

'Her favourite pupil who, despite her wealth, continues to make most of her dresses herself: the lady Nenophar.'

15

The hearing was due to begin halfway through the morning. Although he had still not found Killer, Kem had agreed to attend.

At daybreak, Pazair inspected the porch to which destiny had called him. Confronting Mentmose would not be easy: the commander might have been pushed into a corner, but he would not let himself be trussed up like a frightened hen. The judge was anxious that he might have to deal with a vicious reaction, typical of a high official who was ready to trample others underfoot to maintain his standing.

Pazair left the porch and gazed at the temple it backed on to. Behind the high walls experts in divine energy were working; although aware of human weaknesses, they refused to accept them as inevitable. Man was clay and straw; God alone built houses of eternity where the forces of creation dwelt, inaccessible for ever and yet present in the humblest flint. Without the temple, justice would have been no more than petty annoyances, the settling of accounts, domination by one caste; thanks to it, Ma'at held the tiller of the ship and watched over the weighing-scales. No individual could own the justice system; only Ma'at, whose body was as light as an ostrich-feather, knew the weight of deeds. It was the judges' task to serve her with all the love a child feels for its mother.

Mentmose suddenly loomed out of the fading darkness.

Pazair, chilly despite the time of year, had thrown a woollen cape round his shoulders; the commander was content with a heavy robe, which he wore haughtily. At his belt hung a short-handled dagger with a slender blade. His eyes were cold.

Pazair said, 'You are up and about very early.'

'I have no intention of playing the role of the accused.'

'I have called you solely as a witness.'

'Your plan is simple: to crush me beneath more or less imaginary misdeeds. I remind you that, like you, I apply the law.'

'While forgetting to apply it to yourself.'

'An investigation cannot always be carried out with absolute virtue. Sometimes one has to get one's hands dirty.'

'Have you perhaps forgotten to wash them?'

'The time for moralizing is past. I warn you, do not choose a dangerous Nubian criminal over the commander of the guards.'

'There is no inequality in the eyes of the law: I have sworn an oath to that effect.'

'Who do you think you are, Pazair?'

'An Egyptian judge.'

Those words were spoken with such power and gravity that they shook Mentmose. He had had the misfortune to come up against a judge from ancient times, one of those men depicted on carved panels dating from the golden age of the pyramids, with their upright stance, respect for righteousness, love of truth and imperviousness to blame and praise alike. After so many years spent in the labyrinthine ways of high government, Mentmose had been convinced that that race of men would die once and for all with Tjaty Bagey. Alas, like a weed once thought destroyed, it had been reborn with Pazair.

'Why are you persecuting me?' he asked.

'You are not an innocent victim.'

'I was used and manipulated.'

'By whom?'

'I don't know.'

'Well, Mentmose! You're the best-informed man in Egypt, and you're trying to tell me that someone even more cunning than yourself wove the web that entrapped you?'

'If you want the truth, yes, that's it. You can see that it doesn't make me look good.'

'I'm still not convinced.'

'You should be. I know nothing about the reason for the honour-guard's deaths or about the theft of the sky-iron. Branir's murder gave me an opportunity – through that anonymous accusation – to get rid of you. I didn't hesitate, because I hate you. I hate your intelligence, your will to win through whatever the cost, your refusal to compromise. One day you would have attacked me. My last chance was Kem; if you'd accepted him as a scapegoat, we could have reached a truce.'

'Is your false eye-witness not the puppet-master, then?'

Mentmose scratched his head. 'There's certainly a conspiracy, and General Asher is the brains behind it, but I haven't been able to disentangle the threads. You and I have common enemies. Why don't we become allies?'

Pazair's silence seemed to augur well.

'Your obstinacy won't last long,' declared Mentmose. 'It has enabled you to climb high in the legal establishment, but don't play on it any more. I know life; take my advice, and you'll do well.'

'I'm thinking.'

'About time! I am prepared to put aside my hatred and regard you as a friend.'

'If you aren't at the centre of the conspiracy,' said Pazair pensively, 'it's much more serious than I realized.'

Mentmose was taken aback. He had hoped for a very different reaction.

'The name of your false witness is becoming an absolutely vital piece of evidence.'

Christian Jacq

'Don't insist on knowing it.'

'Then you will fall alone, Mentmose.'

'Would you dare accuse me—'

'Of conspiring against the safety of the state.'

'The jurors will never follow you!'

'We shall see. There are enough grievances to alert them.'

'If I give you the name, will you leave me in peace?'

'No.'

'You're mad!'

'I shall not give in to blackmail.'

'In that case, I have no further interest in talking to you.'

'As you wish. I shall see you later, in court.'

Mentmose's fingers tightened round the hilt of his dagger. For the first time in his career, he felt caught in a hunter's net. 'What future have you in mind for me?'

'The one you have chosen for yourself.'

'You are an excellent judge, I am a good officer. A mistake can be set right.'

'What is the false witness's name?'

Mentmose was not prepared to be disgraced alone. 'Qadash the tooth-doctor.' He watched for Pazair's reaction, but the judge said nothing so Mentmose was reluctant to leave. 'Qadash,' he repeated.

He turned on his heel, hoping the revelation would save him. He had not noticed an attentive witness, whose red eyes had not left him for a moment. Killer, perched on the roof of the porch, looked like a statue of the god Thoth. Seated, with his hands laid flat on his knees, he seemed to be meditating.

Pazair knew Mentmose had not lied. If he had, the baboon would have hurled itself on him.

The judge called to Killer. The baboon hesitated, then slid down the length of a column, landed in front of Pazair and held out its hand.

108

When it was reunited with Kem, the animal flung its arms round his neck and the man wept for joy.

Pazair could not help brooding. Surely Mentmose's confession proved that, since the very first days of his investigation in Memphis, Pazair had been drawn to one of the damned souls in the conspiracy? Qadash had not hesitated to bribe Mentmose in order to send the judge to prison. Caught in a dizzy spiral, the Judge of the Porch asked himself whether he might not be the instrument of a superior will, which was carving out its own path and forcing him to follow it, whatever happened.

Qadash's guilt led him to ask himself questions he must not answer hurriedly or without proof. A strange, sometimes unbearable, fire tormented him; in his haste to discover the truth, was he risking destroying it by burning his bridges?

Neferet decided to drag him away from his office and his cases. Paying no heed to his protests, she took him into the smiling solitude of the countryside.

A flock of quail flew over the fields and came down in the corn. Tired after a long migration, the leading bird had not seen the danger. Lying flat on their bellies on the ground, a group of hunters deployed a net with small mesh, while their assistants shook pieces of cloth to frighten the birds. They succeeded: the birds were captured in great numbers, to be roasted and enjoyed on the very best dinner-tables.

Pazair did not enjoy the sight. To see a creature, even a simple quail, deprived of liberty caused him real pain.

Neferet, who could sense every change in his mood, led him further into the countryside. They walked to a lake with calm waters, surrounded by sycamores and tamarisks, which a Theban king had created for his Great Royal Wife. According to legend, the goddess Hathor came to bathe there at sunset. Neferet hoped the sight of this paradise would bring the judge peace.

Her hopes were not realized.

'I'm wasting precious time,' complained Pazair.

'Is my company such a burden?'

'No, of course not. Forgive me.'

'You need some rest.'

'Qadash gives us the link to Sheshi and so to General Asher, hence to the murder of the honour-guard, and doubtless to Denes and his wife. The conspirators are among the highest dignitaries in the country. They want to seize power by creating a military plot and ensuring that only they have use of the new weapons. That's why they killed Branir, who would have allowed me to investigate the theft of the sky-iron from the temples. That's why they tried to kill me by accusing me of my master's murder. The affair is enormous, Neferet. And yet . . . I'm not sure that I'm right. I sometimes doubt my own words.'

She guided him along a path beside the lake. It was the middle of the afternoon, and the heat was overwhelming, so the peasants were dozing in the shade of the trees or huts.

Neferet knelt down on the bank and picked a lotus-bud, which she put in her hair. A silvery fish with a plump belly leapt out of the water and vanished in a shower of sparkling droplets. She waded into the water; once wet, her linen dress stuck to her and revealed her shapely form. She dived and swam with lithe grace, laughing as her hands followed the zigzag movement of a carp swimming ahead of her. When she emerged, her scent was intoxicating, heightened by her bathe.

'Won't you join me?' she asked.

Looking at her was so wonderful that Pazair had forgotten to move. He slipped out of his kilt while she took off her robe. Naked and entwined, they slid into a papyrus thicket, where they made love, aglow with happiness.

Neferet received a summons from Nebamon, and decided to obey it. Pazair was strongly opposed to her going: why should

Nebamon summon her, if not to spring a trap and take his revenge? But she was adamant, and the best he could do was tell Kem and Killer to follow her, to ensure her safety. The baboon would slip into Nebamon's garden; if there was any threat to Neferet, it would take instant action.

Neferet was not in the least afraid. On the contrary, she was glad to know her worst enemy's intentions. Despite Pazair's misgivings, she had accepted Nebamon's condition that it be a private conversation between the two of them.

Nebamon's gate-keeper allowed the young woman to pass, and she set off along an avenue of tamarisks, whose many intertwined branches touched the ground; their fruit, with its long, sugary hairs, had to be gathered in the dew and dried in the sun. With the wood, valuable coffins could be made, similar to Osiris's, as well as staves to drive away the enemies of light. Surprised by the abnormal silence reigning over the vast estate, Neferet suddenly regretted not arming herself with such a stave.

Not a single gardener, not one water-bearer or servant . . . The surroundings of the sumptuous house were deserted. Hesitating, Neferet crossed the threshold. The vast room reserved for visitors was cool, well ventilated, dimly lit by a few rays of light.

'Nebamon? I am here,' she called.

There was no answer. The house seemed abandoned. Had Nebamon returned to the city, forgetting his meeting? Uneasily, she began to look around the private apartments.

She found Nebamon lying asleep on his back in his large bed. The bedchamber's walls were decorated with ducks in flight and egrets at rest. His face was hollow-cheeked, his breathing shallow and irregular.

'I am here,' she repeated softly.

Nebamon awoke. Incredulous, he rubbed his eyes and sat up. 'You dared . . . I would never have believed it.'

'Are you really so formidable?'

He gazed at her slender form. 'I used to be. I longed for Pazair's death and your ruin. Knowing you were happy together tortured me; I wanted you at my feet, poor, begging for mercy. Your happiness destroyed mine. Why hadn't I been able to seduce you? So many others gave in – but you aren't like them.'

Nebamon looked much older, and his voice, once famous for its languorous inflexions, was halting.

'What is wrong with you? Are you ill?' asked Neferet.

'I am a wretched host. Would you like to try my pyramid-cakes stuffed with date preserve?'

'Thank you, but I'm not hungry.'

'And yet you love life and give yourself to it unstintingly. We would have made a splendid couple. Pazair is no match for you – you know that. He won't be Judge of the Porch for long, and you will seek a wealthy man instead.'

'Wealth isn't essential.'

'It is: a poor doctor cannot have a successful career.'

'And do your riches protect you from illness and pain?'

'I have a growth in one of my veins.'

'That isn't incurable. To ease the pain, I prescribe applications of sycamore-juice, extracted from the tree in early spring, before it bears its fruit.'

Nebamon nodded. 'An excellent prescription. You know the remedies for many infirmities, don't you?'

'But, in addition, you must have an operation. I shall create an incision with a sharpened reed, remove the tumour by heating it with fire, and cauterize the wound.'

'You'd be right so to do, if I were strong enough to withstand the operation.'

'Have you grown so very weak?'

'My days are numbered. That's why I have sent away those close to me and my servants. They all bore me. There must be turmoil at the palace. No one will take any decisions in my absence – the dolts who obey me so slavishly won't know which foot to put forward first. What a miserable farce! But seeing you again brightens my last days.'

'May I sound you?'

'Please do as you wish.'

She listened to the voice of his heart, which was weak and irregular. Nebamon was not lying: he was gravely ill. He remained motionless, breathing in Neferet's scent, savouring the gentleness of her hand on his skin, the softness of her ear on his chest. He would have traded his eternal life if only these moments could never end. But he no longer possessed such a treasure; the soul-eater was waiting for him at the foot of the scales of judgement.

Neferet straightened up and stepped back. 'Who is treating you?'

'I'm treating myself. I am, after all, the most respected doctor in the kingdom of Egypt.'

'What method are you using?'

'Contempt. I hate and despise myself because I am cannot make you love me. My life was a series of successes – and of lies and shameful behaviour. I miss your face, the passion that should have brought you to me. I am dying from the lack of you.'

'I cannot leave you here alone.'

'Don't hesitate for a moment. Make the most of your good fortune. If I recovered, I'd become a brute again, and would never stop trying to kill Pazair and possess you.'

'A sick man deserves to be treated.'

'Will you do it?'

'There are other doctors in Memphis.'

'It must be you, no one else.'

'Don't be childish,' said Neferet firmly.

'Would you have loved me, if it hadn't been for Pazair?'

'You know the answer to that.'

'Lie to me, please!'

'I'll see that your servants come back this very evening. For now, I prescribe a light diet.'

Nebamon sat up. 'I swear to you that I took no part in any of the conspiracies your husband is investigating. I know nothing about the murder of Branir, the deaths of the honour-guard or General Asher's machinations. All I wanted was to send Pazair to prison and force you to become my wife. As long as I live, I shall have no other ambition.'

'You ought to give up chasing the impossible.'

'The wind will change, I'm sure of it.'

16

Panther was radiant as she caressed Suti's chest. He had made love to her with all the energy of a rising flood so potent that its tide sought to drown the mountains.

'Why are you so gloomy?' she asked.

'Oh, it's nothing important.'

'There are a lot of rumours flying round the town.'

'What about?'

'Ramses' luck. Some people claim it has turned. Last month there was a fire at the docks, there have been several accidents on the river, and some acacia trees were split in two by lightning.'

'Those are just trivial things.'

'Not for your fellow-countrymen,' said Panther. 'They're convinced that Pharaoh's magical power has run out.'

'So what? He'll celebrate a festival of regeneration, and the people will shout for joy.'

'What is he waiting for?'

'Ramses has an instinct for doing the right thing at the right time.'

'And what about your worries?'

'I told you, they aren't important.'

'It's to do with a woman, isn't it?'

'No, my investigation.'

'What does she want?'

'I've got to—'

'Marry her, with a proper contract! In other words, you're casting me off!' Hysterical, Panther leapt off the bed. She vented her rage by smashing several terracotta bowls and tearing apart a straw-seated chair.

'What's she like?' she demanded. 'Tall, short, young, old?'

'Small, with very dark hair – she isn't nearly as beautiful as you.'

'Is she rich?'

'Of course.'

'I'm not good enough for you – I have no money. You don't enjoy your Libyan whore any more, so you're turning respectable with your rich brunette!'

'I have to get some information out of her,' said Suti.

'And that means you have to get married?'

'It's only a formality.'

'And what about me?'

'Be patient for a little while. As soon as I've got what I want, I shall get a divorce.'

'And how will she take that?'

'For her this marriage is merely a whim. She'll soon forget me.'

'Don't do it, Suti. You're making a huge mistake.'

'I've got to do it.'

'Stop doing what Pazair wants!'

'The marriage contract has already been signed.'

Pazair, Judge of the Porch, the most senior judge in Memphis, whose moral authority was incontestable, was sulking like a thwarted child. He could not accept the efforts Neferet had made to help Nebamon. She had asked help from several other doctors, who had gone to the sick man's bedside, brought back his servants to the estate, and ensured that he was cared for and had people around him.

Pazair furiously resented all this. 'We shouldn't help our enemies,' he growled.

'How can a judge say such a thing?'

'He must.'

'I'm a doctor.'

'That monster tried to destroy both of us.'

'But he failed,' said Neferet. 'And now he's destroying himself, from the inside.'

'His illness does not wipe out his crimes.'

'You're right: it doesn't.'

'If you admit that, have nothing more to do with him.'

'I don't think about him at all, but I had to do my duty as a doctor.'

Pazair's grim expression relaxed a little.

'Surely you're not jealous?' she asked, smiling.

He drew her towards him. 'No one in the world is more jealous than I am.'

'Will you give me permission to treat a patient other than my husband?'

'If the law allowed me to, I'd forbid it.'

Brave, who had been watching them anxiously – any disagreement between his master and mistress made him unhappy – sat up on his haunches and offered his right paw to Neferet and his left to Pazair. His acrobatic pose made them burst out laughing, and, reassured, the dog joined in with joyful barking.

In a towering rage, Suti pushed his way between two scribes, their arms full of papyri, barged into a clerk, and flung open the door of Pazair's office. He found the judge drinking a cup of copper-water.

Pazair took one look at his friend's dishevelled long black hair and asked, 'Is something wrong?'

'Yes, you!'

The judge got up and closed the door; there were fierce

storms ahead. He said, 'Perhaps we should discuss this somewhere else.'

'Absolutely not! This place is precisely the reason I'm angry.'

'Why? Has it done you an injustice?'

'You've been sucked into the system, Pazair! You've swallowed the bait of titles and respectability. Look around you: petty scribes, narrow-minded officials, little minds preoccupied with their own advancement. You've forgotten our friendship, you're neglecting the investigation into General Asher, you've given up trying to find the truth – you're acting as though you don't believe me any more. But I tell you again, I saw Asher torture and kill an Egyptian, I know he's a traitor – and here you are, parading around like a courtier!'

'You've been drinking.'

'Bad beer, and far too much of it. I needed it. No one dares talk to you the way I do.'

'Subtlety isn't your strong point,' said Pazair, 'but I never thought you were stupid.'

'Don't insult me as well! Deny it if you can.'

'Sit down.'

'I won't be patronized!'

'Let's at least call a truce.'

Swaying slightly, Suti managed to sit down without losing his balance. 'It's no use trying to sweet-talk me. I've seen right through your game.'

'Then you're lucky. I've lost my way.'

Astonished, Suti blinked at him. 'What do you mean?'

'Take a closer look: I'm overwhelmed with work. In my district of Memphis, as a junior judge, I had a little time for investigation. Here, I have to answer a hundred pleas, deal with hordes of cases, calm the anger of some people and the impatience of others.'

'There you are, that's it, the trap. Resign, and follow me.'

'What are you planning to do?'

'To wring Asher's neck and cure Egypt of the sickness eating away at her.'

'You won't manage to cure Egypt.'

'Of course I will! If you kill the head of the conspiracy, there'll be no more sedition.'

'And what about Branir's murderer?'

Suti smiled ferociously. 'I was a good investigator, but I had to marry Tapeni.'

'I'm grateful for your sacrifice.'

'If I hadn't, she wouldn't have told me anything.'

'So now you're rich.'

'Panther's taken it badly.'

'A seducer like you should be able to cope with that.'

'Me, married! It's worse than a prison. As soon as possible, I'm getting a divorce.'

'Did the ceremony go well?'

'It took place in the strictest privacy – she didn't want anyone there at all. In bed she's uncontrollable, treats me like an inexhaustible sweetmeat.'

'And what about your investigation?'

'Only a few high-born weavers use the type of needle that killed Branir. Of them, the most skilled and the most remarkable is Nenophar. Her post as Treasury scrutineer may have been only honorary, but she's still steward of fabrics and she knows the craft extremely well.'

Nenophar. She was married to Denes the ship-owner, the bitterest enemy of Bel-Tran, Pazair's greatest supporter. And yet, as a member of the jury during the Asher case, she had not censured Pazair. Once again, the judge felt wrong-footed. Her guilt seemed evident, but his belief was not strengthened.

'Arrest her at once,' advised Suti.

'I can't. We've no proof.'

'The same as with Asher! Why do you always refuse to accept the evidence?'

'I don't, but the court would. To recognize a person as guilty of murder, the jurors require a flawless case.'

'But I married Tapeni to get you this information!'

'Try to get more.'

'You're getting more and more demanding, and you're losing yourself in a maze of laws which stop you facing reality. You won't accept the truth: that Asher is a traitor and a criminal who's trying to gain control of the Asian army, and that Nenophar murdered your master.'

'If that's true, why hasn't Asher made his move?'

'Because he's still stationing his men in the protectorates and in Egypt itself. As instructor to the Asian officers, he's creating a clan of scribes and soldiers who are devoted to him. Soon, with the help of his friend Sheshi, he'll have access to unbreakable weapons, and they'll enable him to face any army in the world without fear of defeat. Whoever controls those weapons will be able to govern the country.'

Pazair still wasn't convinced. 'If Asher tried to seize the throne, he'd never succeed.'

'This isn't the golden age, it's the reign of Ramses II. In our provinces, there are thousands of foreigners, and our dear compatriots think more about getting rich than about pleasing the gods. The old morality is dead.'

'Perhaps, but the person of Pharaoh is still sacred. Asher does not have that stature. No clan would support him – the whole country would reject him.'

That argument won the day. Suti admitted that his reasoning, although cogent for an Asian country, did not work for the Egypt of Ramses. A faction, even one with invincible weapons, could not force the temples – still less the people – to accept it. To govern the Two Lands, force was not enough. It required a magical being who could make a pact with the gods and cause a love of the afterlife to shine forth on earth. Laughable words to the ears of a Greek, a Libyan or a Syrian, but essential to those of an Egyptian; whatever his abilities as a strategist and plotter, Asher did not have those particular qualities.

'It's strange,' observed Pazair. 'We had three suspects in the murder of Branir: the exiled Judge of the Porch, who is dying of starvation; Nebamon, who has been struck down by a serious illness; and Mentmose, who's standing right at the edge of the abyss. Any one of them could have written the message summoning me to my master, and then set up the charade intended to incriminate me. And now you've added Nenophar to the list. The old judge seems unlikely: his behaviour was that of a worn-out, weak man, broken by his own compromises. Nebamon swore to Neferet that he was not involved in a conspiracy. And Mentmose, who's usually so skilful and sure of himself, now seems like a puppet, rather than the puppet-master. If we've been so utterly deceived by those three, surely we shouldn't be too hasty when it comes to Nenophar?'

'There it is, your conspiracy! Asher isn't content with his chosen soldiers. He needs support from the nobility and the rich, and he's got it from Nenophar and Denes, the wealthiest traders in Memphis. With their fortune, he'll be able to buy silence, consciences and cooperation. There are two brains behind this affair.'

'But Denes organized the banquet to celebrate my investiture.'

'Maybe so, but didn't he once try to buy you, too? When he failed, he fabricated a story which suited him. You became Branir's murderer, and Qadash became a witness to the murder so as to get rid of your faithful guard, Kem, once and for all.'

This time, despite Suti's drunkenness, Pazair found his reasoning persuasive. 'If you're right,' he said thoughtfully, 'our enemies are even more numerous and more powerful than we thought. Could Denes ever attain the stature of a pharaoh?'

'Of course not! He's much too full of himself, and he

doesn't care in the least about other people. He's also too short-sighted: he can't see beyond his money and his own interests. Nenophar, on the other hand, is much more formidable than she seems. I think she might well be capable of establishing a regency. We aren't dreaming, Judge of the Porch! Five dead ex-soldiers, Branir's murder, several other murder attempts – Egypt hasn't known disruption like this for a lifespan. Your investigation is alarming people. You've got power, so use it. Your administrative chores can wait.'

'No, because they guarantee the country's stability and the people's daily happiness.'

'If the conspiracy succeeds, how much of all that will be left?'

Pazair grew tense as he thought about it. He stood up. 'Inactivity weighs you down, doesn't it?'

'A hero needs to do brave deeds.'

'Are you ready to face danger?'

'As ready as you are. I want to be there when Asher gets the punishment he deserves.'

Silkis's colic had reached alarming proportions. Fearing it might be dysentery, Bel-Tran had himself fetched Neferet to her in the middle of the night. The doctor gave the sick woman fragrant dill seeds; their sedative and digestive properties would ease the spasms. Used in an ointment, added to bryony and coriander, they relieved migraines. The fine umbelliferous plant with the yellow flowers would not be enough on its own, so painful was the diarrhoea; every quarter of an hour, therefore, Neferet made Silkis drink a full cup of carob-beer, made from the pods mixed with oil and honey. After only an hour of this treatment, Silkis's symptoms began to ease.

'You're a marvel,' she breathed.

Neferet smiled. 'Don't worry. You'll be better by tomorrow. Drink carob-beer for one week.'

'Are there likely to be any complications?'

'No. It was a simple case of food poisoning, though it might have become serious if not properly treated. For a few days, you must eat only cereals.'

Bel-Tran thanked Neferet warmly, then led her to one side. 'Is that true, or were you just reassuring her?'

'Don't worry, it's true.'

He thanked her again, and said, 'You must be tired. Won't you sit down and have something to eat?'

Neferet was glad of this short rest before another long day spent visiting more patients, both rich and poor. It would soon be dawn, so there was no point trying to go back to sleep.

'Since I entered the Treasury,' said Bel-Tran, 'I've suffered from terrible insomnia. While Silkis is asleep I work on the next day's files. Sometimes such a painful lump forms in the pit of my stomach that I'm almost paralyzed.'

'You're wearing yourself out with nervous strain.'

'The Double House never lets me rest. I accept what you say, Neferet, but isn't the same thing true of you? You run from one place to another, all over town, and you never refuse a request for help. You really belong elsewhere. The palace has no doctors of your skill and quality. By surrounding himself with second-rate ones, Nebamon created a void around himself. He drove you out of the doctors' organization because he was jealous of your skill.'

'The court's principal doctor decides on appointments — neither you nor I can do anything about them.'

'You cured the tjaty and several other important people. I shall gather their statements and present them to the doctors in charge of maintaining discipline. Even the stupidest of them will have to recognize your talent.'

'I have no stomach for a fight like that.'

'Pazair, as Judge of the Porch, can't intervene in your favour because he'd be accused of partiality. But I can. And I shall — I'll fight for you.'

*

123

Thebes was in uproar. The greatest city of southern Egypt, guardian of the country's most ancient traditions, was hostile to innovations which its northern rival, Memphis, accepted with too much readiness. Now Thebes was impatiently awaiting the announcement of the name of the new High Priest of Amon. He would reign over more than eighty thousand employees, sixty-five towns and villages, a million men and women working more or less directly for the temple, four hundred head of livestock, four hundred and fifty vineyards and orchards, and ninety ships. It was Pharaoh's task to supply the ritual objects – food, oil, incense, precious ointments and clothing – and to bestow gifts of land whose ownership would be marked with large stelae set at the edges of the fields, one at each corner. It was the High Priest's task to levy taxes on merchandise and on fishermen.

The High Priest ruled a state within a state; so the king must appoint a man whose fidelity and obedience to him were absolute, yet who was by no means an empty-headed person who lacked authority. Branir would have been a man of that stamp; his murder had put Ramses in a quandary. The day before the new High Priest's enthronement was due, his choice was still not known.

Pazair and Suti had gone to the temple at Karnak out of both curiosity and necessity. The High Priest of Ptah in Memphis had been consulted, but could provide no information about the theft of the sky-iron. The precious metal must originally have come from a Southern temple; only the High Priest of Amon could set the investigators on the right track. But what kind of person would Pazair be facing?

As Judge of the Porch, Pazair was admitted to the landing-stage, along with Suti, whom he presented as his assistant. A host of boats occupied the lake that had been created between the Nile and the temple; rows of trees kept the air cool.

The two friends, led by a priest, walked past the human-headed sphinx, whose eyes drove away unbelievers. Before each of these watchful guards, an irrigation channel carried the water to a ditch, about a cubit deep, where flowers grew. So the sacred way, leading from the outside world to the temple, was adorned with the most vivid, shimmering colours.

Pazair and Suti were allowed into the first great courtyard, where shaven-headed priests in linen robes were garlanding the altars with flowers. Whatever else might happen, worship must continue. The pure ones, the divine fathers, the servants of the god, the masters of the secrets, the enacters of rituals, the star-watchers and musicians were all attending to their occupations, which had been fixed by the Rule that had been in operation since the time of the pyramids. Only a few of these people lived permanently within the temple complex; the others officiated there for periods ranging from a week to three months. Twice a day and twice a night they carried out their ablutions, believing that inner purity must be accompanied by impeccable physical cleanliness.

The two friends sat down on a stone bench. The calm majesty of the place, the profound peace inscribed within the stones of eternity, made them forget their cares and questions. Here, life – delivered from the erosion of time – took on a different taste. Even Suti, who did not believe in the gods, felt his soul fulfilled.

The new High Priest of Amon received the insignia of his office from the king: a gold cane and two rings. Henceforth in charge of the wealthiest and largest of all Egypt's temples, he would see that its treasures were preserved. Each morning, he would open the double doors of the secret shrine, the region of light where Amon regenerated in the mystery of the East. He had taken an oath to observe the ritual, to ensure that offerings were replenished, and to take care of the divine dwelling where the creation of the first moments was kept in balance. Tomorrow, he would think about his many staff, including the head of his household, a head steward, scribes, secretaries and team-leaders; tomorrow, he would regret losing the tranquil life from which Pharaoh's decision had torn him away. In this most intense of moments, he thought about the main precept of the Rule:

> *Do not raise your voice in the temple: God detests shouting. May your heart be loving. Do not question God wrongly or indirectly, for he loves silence. The silent one is like the tree that grows in the orchard; its fruits are sweet, its shade is agreeable, it grows green and ends its days in the orchard where it was born.*

The High Priest meditated for a long time in the holy of holies, alone facing the innermost shrine which contained the god's statue. Never had he hoped to experience such an emotion, reducing to nothing his aspirations of yesterday and his derisory hopes. The robe of the First Servant of Amon stripped him of his humanity and made him a stranger to his own eyes. That mattered little, since he would no longer have the leisure to wonder about his own tastes or doubts.

The High Priest withdrew, walking backwards and wiping away his footprints. As soon as he had left the holy of holies, he would return to confront the universe of the temple.

Cheers greeted the appearance of the new High Priest on the threshold of the immense pillared hall built by Ramses. From now on, it would fall to him to open the way with his gold staff and to lead a peaceful army, devoted to the glory of Amon.

Pazair stared. 'That's incredible.'

'Do you know him?' asked Suti.

'It's Kani, the gardener.'

17

When the dignitaries paid him homage in the great courtyard, Kani halted for a long time in front of Pazair. The judge bowed. As their eyes met, the two men shared the same profound joy.

'I should like to consult you at the earliest opportunity,' said Pazair.

'You may come to see me this evening,' promised Kani.

The High Priest's palace, which stood close to the temple entrance, was an architectural and decorative marvel. The beauty of the paintings enchanted the eye, glorifying the presence of the gods in nature. Kani received Pazair in his private study, which was already full to overflowing with papyri.

They greeted each other with a warm embrace.

'I am very happy for Egypt,' said Pazair.

'I pray that you're right to be. The office I now hold was meant for Branir. He was a sage among sages – who can equal him? I shall honour his memory each morning, and offerings will be made to his statue, which has been erected inside the temple.'

'Ramses has chosen well.'

'I love this place, it is true, as if I'd always lived here. It's thanks to you that I'm here.'

'I did very little.'

'Perhaps,' said Kani, 'but your influence was decisive. However, I can tell that you're worried.'

'My investigation is proving to be extremely difficult.'

'How can I help you?'

'I should like to make inquiries in the temple at Kebet, to try to discover the origin of the sky-iron that was delivered to Sheshi the inventor, General Asher's accomplice. To implicate the first and prove the second's guilt, I must follow the trail back. Without your permission, that would be impossible.'

'Might priests be the criminals' accomplices?'

'It cannot be ruled out.'

'We shall not shirk our responsibilities. Give me one week.'

Pazair stayed in a little house beside the sacred lake of Karnak, and took part in the rites as a 'pure priest', his entire body shaven. Each day he wrote to Neferet, praising the splendour and peace of the temple. Suti, who would not sacrifice his long hair, took refuge with a lady friend he had encountered at a naval tournament. She was not yet married, and dreamt of Memphis; he devoted body and soul to entertaining her.

On the agreed day, the High Priest received the two friends in his audience chamber. Kani had already changed. Although his features were still those of the former gardener who specialized in medicinal plants, his face sunburnt and deeply lined, his bearing had become regal. In choosing him, Ramses had detected the humble man's great authority. He would need little time to adapt; already, in just a few days, Kani had become imbued with the majesty of his office.

Pazair introduced Suti, who was ill at ease in this austere place.

'It is indeed at Kebet that you must investigate,' said Kani.

'The experts in precious metals and rare minerals are answerable to the High Priest of the temple there. He was a miner before becoming a desert guard and then a priest, and if anyone can enlighten you as to the origin of this sky-iron, he can. Kebet is the departure-point for all the great expeditions to the mines and quarries, and he also has special responsibility for the gold road.'

'Is it possible that he himself might be implicated?' asked Pazair.

'According to the reports I've received, no. He both oversees and is overseen, and takes charge of deliveries of precious metals to all the temples in Egypt. Not once has he acted incorrectly in twenty years. Nevertheless, I have drawn up a written order which will give you access to the temple archives. To my mind, the fraud is taking place elsewhere. Perhaps you should look among the miners and prospectors.'

A strong wind tousled Suti's black hair as he stood at the prow of the boat, sailing towards Memphis. He was still furious, and indignant at Pazair's calm demeanour.

'Kebet, the desert, the treasures of the sands – it's crazy!'

'With the document Kani gave me, I can search the temple at Kebet from top to bottom.'

'That's ridiculous. The thieves aren't stupid enough to have left traces of their crime.'

'Your point of view seems reasonable. So—'

'So we ought to act like heroes and set off on an adventure, along with some fearless fellows who wouldn't hesitate to kill their grandmothers for a pittance! A while ago the experience might have tempted me, but I'm married, and—'

Pazair laughed. 'You, a staid middle-class husband!'

'Well, yes, I'd like to enjoy the benefits of Tapeni's wealth for a little while, in exchange for my good and loyal services. Besides, didn't you ask me to get more information out of her while I hold her in my arms?'

129

'It's not like you to live at a woman's expense.'

'Send your Nubian friend, Kem.'

'He'd be identified straight away. I shall follow the trail myself.'

'You're mad! You wouldn't last two days.'

'I survived the prison camp.'

'The men who search for minerals are used to almost dying from thirst, to enduring the burning sun, and to fighting scorpions, snakes and wild animals. Forget this idiocy.'

'The truth is my profession, Suti.'

Neferet was called urgently to Nebamon's bedside. Although three doctors were permanently in attendance, the sick man had lapsed into a coma, after calling for her. Way-Finder agreed to act as her mount; he set off at a good pace for Nebamon's house.

As soon as Neferet arrived, Nebamon recovered consciousness. He had pains in his stomach, arms and chest. 'A heart attack,' Neferet diagnosed. She laid her hand on his chest, and magnetized him until the pain eased. She heated a root of bryony in oil and completed the potion with acacia-leaves, figs and honey.

'You must drink this four times a day,' she told him.

'How long do I have left to live?'

'Your case is serious.'

'You cannot lie, Neferet. How long?'

'Only God is master of our destiny.'

'I'm not interested in fine words. I'm afraid of dying, and I want to know how many days I have left, so I can have whores brought to me, and can drink my wine.'

'That is your choice.'

Nebamon grasped her arm. 'I'm still lying, Neferet. It is you I want. Kiss me, I beg you. Once, just once.'

She freed herself, as gently as possible.

His face was dripping with sweat, his complexion waxy.

'The judgment of the afterlife will be a severe one. My life was second-rate, but I was happy to be leader of the most illustrious doctors in Egypt. All I lacked was a woman, a real woman, who could have made me less evil. Before meeting Osiris, I shall help Pazair, the man who defeated me. Tell him that Qadash bought my testimony with amulets, exceptional pieces which his former steward deals in. To pay such a price, the matter must be enormous. Enormous.'

That was Nebamon's last word. He died drinking in Neferet with his eyes.

Pazair remembered Qadash's corrupt steward, who had in fact already been implicated in trafficking in the precious objects of which his employer was so fond. A fine lapis-lazuli amulet could be exchanged for a whole basket of fresh fish. All people, the living and the dead alike, wanted this magical protection against the forces of darkness. Amulets – in the shape of an eye, a leg, a hand, a staircase to the heavens, tools, a lotus-flower or papyrus-stem, or bearing images of the gods – were receptacles for positive energy. Many Egyptians, irrespective of age or social class, gladly wore them round their necks, in direct contact with the skin.

Qadash was beginning to look more and more important, so Pazair instructed his staff to track down the tooth-doctor's former steward. The investigations soon brought results: the steward had obtained a similar post on a large estate in Middle Egypt. An estate which belonged to a close friend of Qadash, Denes the ship-owner.

At the weekly audience the tjaty granted to his close colleagues, many subjects were debated. Bagey liked concise comments and detested people who rambled; his own conclusions were brief and not open to discussion. One scribe wrote them down, while another transformed them into administrative decisions to which the tjaty added his seal.

131

'Have you anything further to say, Judge Pazair?' asked Bagey.

'Only that we need a new commander of the city guards. Mentmose is unworthy of his office. His misdeeds are too serious to be pardoned.'

The tjaty's secretary was highly indignant. 'But Mentmose has given great service to the country. He has always been extremely conscientious about maintaining law and order in the city.'

'The tjaty knows my reasons,' replied Pazair. 'Mentmose has lied, falsified evidence and made a mockery of the law. Only the former Judge of the Porch has been punished. Why should his accomplice go free?'

'The commander can hardly be expected to be an innocent little lamb!'

'That is enough,' cut in Bagey. 'The facts are known and established, and there are no ambiguities in the case. Read the charges, scribe.'

They were overwhelming. Without exaggerating them, Pazair had brought all Mentmose's crimes out into the light.

'Does anyone still wish Mentmose to remain in his post?' inquired the tjaty, when the scribe had finished.

Not one voice was raised in Mentmose's favour.

'Mentmose is dismissed,' decided Bagey. 'If he wishes to appeal he shall appear before me, and if he is again found guilty he will be sent to prison. Let us proceed immediately to the appointment of his successor. Whom do you propose?'

'Kem,' said Pazair in a steady voice.

'That's outrageous!' protested one of the scribes, and others followed his lead.

'Kem has a great deal of experience,' Pazair went on. 'He has suffered what he regards as injustice, but he has always remained on the side of law and order. True, he is not fond of the human race, but he carries out his duties as rigorously as a priest.'

'A Nubian of low birth, a—'

'A man with practical experience, and with no illusions. No one will ever corrupt him.'

The tjaty put an end to the argument: 'Kem is appointed commander of the city guards of Memphis. If anyone objects, he may present his arguments to my court. If I consider them inadmissible, he will be sentenced for slander. The audience is at an end.'

In the presence of the Judge of the Porch, Mentmose handed Kem the official seal of the guards' commander, the ivory staff, crowned with a hand and known as the 'Hand of Justice', that symbolized his authority, and a crescent-moon-shaped amulet engraved with an eye and a lion, emblems of vigilance. Despite his appointment, the Nubian had refused to trade his bow, arrows, sword and club for the garb of a leading citizen.

Kem did not thank Mentmose, who was on the verge of apoplexy. No speeches were made. The wary Nubian tested the seal immediately, in case his predecessor had falsified it.

'Are you satisfied?' demanded Mentmose, almost choking.

'I bear witness that the tjaty's decree has been observed,' replied Pazair serenely. 'As Judge of the Porch, I hereby register the transfer of offices.'

'It was you who persuaded Bagey to dismiss me!'

'The tjaty acted in accordance with his duty. It is your own misdeeds which condemn you.'

'You . . . I should have . . . ' Before Mentmose dared utter the word searing his lips, Kem's glare silenced him.

'Making a death threat is a crime,' said Kem sternly.

'I haven't made anything of the sort.'

'Don't try to do anything against Judge Pazair. If you do, I shall deal with you.'

'Mentmose, your new duties await you,' said Pazair. 'You would do well to leave Memphis as soon as possible.'

Mentmose had been appointed overseer of the Delta fisheries. From now on he would live in a small coastal town where the only plots he could hatch would be to do with calculating the price of fish, according to size and weight.

He tried to think of a stinging retort, but the sight of the imposing Nubian took his breath away.

Kem put away the 'Hand of Justice' and his official amulet at the bottom of a wooden chest, underneath his collection of Asian daggers. Delegating the administrative tasks to scribes who were accustomed to such fastidious work, he closed the door of Mentmose's office behind him, resolutely determined to make only brief appearances there. The streets, the fields and nature were and would remain his preferred workplace: you couldn't arrest criminals by reading papyrus scrolls. Then, taking Killer with him, he left the office and joined Pazair at the Nile landing-stage, delighted to be travelling with him. Their boat sailed as soon as they were aboard.

They disembarked at Khmun, city of the god Thoth, master of sacred language. Riding donkeys bred specially to carry important people, they passed through beautiful, peaceful countryside. It was sowing time. After the flood had abated, the earth, enriched with fertile silt, was given over to the ploughs and hoes, which broke up the lumps of earth; sometimes the ploughman would find a fish trapped in a small pool left by the receding floodwaters.

The seed-sowers, their necks and heads garlanded with flowers, cast seeds on to the soil from little papyrus-fibre bags. Sheep, oxen and pigs then trampled on the seeds, pushing them down into the soil. The rams led their flocks on to firm ground; the shepherds wielded leather thongs, which they cracked occasionally to bring stragglers back to the flock. Once covered over, the seed would make Egypt into a fertile, rich land, by means of an alchemical process which mirrored the death and resurrection of Osiris.

Denes's estate was absolutely enormous: no fewer than three villages served it. In the largest one, Pazair and Kem drank goats' milk and sampled creamy fermented milk, salted and preserved in jars. They spread it on slices of bread, and then added fine herbs. The peasants used alum from the Khargeh oasis to curdle the milk without making it sour and for making very popular cheeses.

Their appetites satisfied, the two men walked to Denes's huge farm, which was made up of several groups of buildings: grain-stores, a cellar, wine-press, stables, sheds for livestock, poultry yard, bakery, butchery and workshops. After washing their feet and hands, they asked to see the steward of the estate. A groom went to fetch him from the stable.

As soon as the steward spotted Pazair, he tried to run for it. Kem did not move, but Killer leapt forward and brought the fugitive down in the dust. He sank his teeth into the steward's back, and the steward at once stopped struggling. Kem decided that this position was quite suitable for a detailed interrogation.

'I'm glad to see you again,' said Pazair. 'But you seem frightened to see us.'

'Get that monkey off me!'

'Who engaged you?'

'Denes the ship-owner.'

'On Qadash's recommendation?'

The steward hesitated, and Killer's jaws tightened. 'Yes – *yes!*'

'So he didn't hold it against you that you'd stolen from him,' said Pazair thoughtfully. 'Of course, there may be a simple explanation for that: Denes, Qadash and you are accomplices. Perhaps you tried to run away because you're hiding incriminating evidence here on the farm. I have drawn up a search warrant, which takes immediate effect. Will you help us?'

'Judge,' gasped the steward, 'you're making a mistake.'

Kem would happily have let Killer make the steward talk, but Pazair preferred a less rough, more methodical solution. The steward was pulled to his feet, tied up and placed under the guard of several peasants. They hated him because he had been a tyrant to them, and were more than happy to cooperate with the judge. They told him the steward had forbidden them to go into one particular storehouse, which was always kept locked by several wooden bolts. Kem forced them open with his dagger.

Inside were many ornate wooden chests of different sizes, some with flat lids, others with curved or triangular. The lids were all held in place by cords wound round two pegs, one on the side and the other on top. Taken together, this collection of furniture was worth a great deal. Kem cut the cords and they began to inspect the contents. In several sycamore-wood chests they found pieces of the very finest linen, robes and bedsheets.

'Lady Nenophar's treasure?' suggested Kem.

'We'll ask her for the scrolls recording when they left the workshops.'

The two men next opened some softwood chests veneered with ebony and decorated with panels in different kinds of valuable wood. Inside were hundreds of lapis-lazuli amulets.

'These are worth an absolute fortune!' exclaimed Kem.

'The work is so fine that it should be easy to find out where they were made.'

'I'll see to it.'

'Denes and his accomplices sell them for high prices in Libya, Syria, Canaan and other countries where Egyptian magic is valued. They may even offer them to the sand-travellers to make them invulnerable.'

'Isn't that tantamount to attacking the safety of the state?'

'Denes will deny it and accuse the steward.'

'Are you saying that, even though you're Judge of the Porch, you doubt the legal system can cope with all this?'

'Don't be so pessimistic, Kem. After all, we're here in an official capacity.'

Hidden under three flat-lidded chests, they found something unexpected which astounded them: a massive, gilded acacia-wood chest, about one cubit tall and a little less wide and deep. On its ebony lid were two ivory pegs, carved to perfection.

'This is worthy of a pharaoh,' murmured Kem.

'Anyone would think it was meant for a tomb.'

'In that case, we have no right to touch it.'

'I must make a list of the contents,' said Pazair.

'But wouldn't that be committing sacrilege?'

'No. There's no inscription on the chest.'

Kem allowed the judge to remove the string binding the ivory pegs to the ones on the sides. Pazair raised the lid slowly.

The flash of gold dazzled him. It was an enormous scarab made of solid gold. Beside it were a miniature sculptor's chisel made from sky-iron, and a lapis-lazuli eye.

'The eye of the Risen One,' he whispered, 'the chisel used to open his mouth in the otherworld, and the scarab laid in the place of his heart so that his metamorphoses may be eternal.'

On the belly of the scarab there had been a hieroglyphic inscription, but it had been so throughly hammered away that he could not decipher it.

'These things *were* made for a pharaoh,' said Kem, appalled, 'a pharaoh whose tomb has been looted.'

In the era of Ramses II, such a crime seemed impossible. Several centuries earlier sand-travellers had invaded the Delta and looted the burial-grounds, so, ever since Egypt's liberation from the Hyksos, pharaohs had been buried in the Valley of the Kings and their tombs were guarded night and day.

'Only a foreigner could have conceived such a monstrous plan,' Kem went on, his voice shaking.

Deeply troubled, Pazair closed the chest. 'We must take this treasure to Kani. It will be safe at Karnak.'

18

The High Priest of Karnak ordered the temple craftsmen to examine the chest and its contents. As soon as he had their findings, he summoned Pazair. The two men strolled together beneath a portico, shaded from the sun.

'I regret to say,' said Kani, 'that we cannot identify the owner of these marvels.'

'Was he a king?'

'The size of the scarab is worrying, but that on its own isn't enough to tell for certain.'

'Kem thinks a tomb has been looted.'

'That's most unlikely. The break-in would have been discovered – how could such a thing, the most hideous of all crimes, go unnoticed? It is more than five hundred years since it was committed. Nobody could possibly have suppressed the scandal. Ramses would have condemned the crime as beyond all hope of pardon, and the names of the guilty parties would have been destroyed in full view of the entire population.'

Kani was right, thought Pazair, and Kem's fears were unjustified.

'It's likely,' Kani went on, 'that these wonderful things were stolen from the workshops. Either Denes planned to sell them, or else he intended them for his own tomb.'

Knowing the ship-owner's vanity, Pazair was inclined towards the second solution.

'Have you investigated at Kebet yet?' asked Kani.

'I haven't had time, and I'm not sure what methods I should use.'

'Be very careful.'

'Have you learnt something new?'

'The goldsmiths of Karnak are certain that the scarab's gold comes from the mine at Kebet.'

Kebet, which lay a little to the north of Thebes, was a strange town. The streets were thronged with miners, quarrymen and desert explorers, some on the eve of departure, others back from a season in the hell of the burning, rocky wastes. Every man always promised himself that, next time, he would discover the richest vein. Caravan traders sold their wares, which they had brought all the way from Nubia, hunters brought back game to the temple and the nobles, and nomads tried to integrate into Egyptian society.

Everyone was waiting for the next royal decree, which would urge volunteers to take one of the many tracks leading to the quarries of jasper, granite or porphyry; to the port of Kosseir, on the Red Sea; or indeed to the turquoise deposits of Sinai. Men dreamt of gold, of secret or unexploited mines, of that flesh of the gods which the temple reserved for the gods and the pharaohs. The miners were closely watched, and had no chance of spiriting away large quantities of the precious metal. A thousand times, plots had been hatched to seize it; a thousand times, they had failed, because of the omnipresent special guards known as 'the All-Seeing Ones' and their ferocious, tireless dogs.

These were rough and pitiless men, who knew every last track, even the smallest dried-up riverbed, and who could find their way without difficulty in a hostile world where outsiders did not survive for long. Hunters of animals and men, they killed ibex, wild goats and gazelles, and recaptured fugitives who had escaped from prison. Their favourite prey was the sand-travellers who tried to attack caravans and rob travellers. Although the sand-travellers were numerous and well trained, the All-Seeing Ones gave them little opportunity to succeed in their cowardly attacks. If, by some misfortune, a group of more cunning sand-travellers did succeed, the desert patrols took on the assignment of catching them and wiping them out. It was many years since a looter had survived to boast of his exploits.

On his way to the great temple at Kebet, where the priests guarded age-old maps showing the locations of Egypt's mineral wealth, Pazair met a group of All-Seeeing Ones and their dogs. They were herding along some prisoners, who had been mauled by the dogs.

He felt impatient and uneasy. Impatient to make progress and to know if Kebet would yield useful information; uneasy because he was afraid the temple's High Priest might be in league with the conspirators. Before doing anything, he must either banish this doubt or confirm it.

Kani's scroll of authorization was highly effective: as soon as it was read the gates opened one after another, and the High Priest received Pazair within the hour. The priest was elderly, stout and sure of himself; the dignity of his office had not wiped out his past as a man of action.

'What honours and attentions!' he said with irony, his harsh voice making his subordinates tremble. 'A Judge of the Porch authorized to search my modest temple? There is a mark of esteem I was not expecting. Is your detachment of guards about to invade this place?'

'I have come alone,' said Pazair.

The priest knitted his bushy eyebrows. 'I don't understand.'

'I wish for your help.'

'Here, as elsewhere, people have talked a great deal about the case you brought against General Asher.'

'What do they say?'

'The general has more supporters than opponents.'

'In which camp do you stand?'

'He's a villain!'

Pazair hid his relief. If the priest meant what he said, things were looking brighter. 'What makes you say that?'

'I'm a former miner and officer of the desert guards. For a year Asher has been trying to take control of the All-Seeing Ones – but as long as I live he won't do it.'

Pazair was sure the priest's anger was genuine. Relieved, he said, 'You are the only person who can perhaps help me regarding the theft of a large quantity of sky-iron. It was found in Memphis in the workshop of an inventor called Sheshi. Of course, he says that he didn't know it was there and that he was an innocent victim. But he is trying to make unbreakable weapons, probably on Asher's behalf, so he would need that special iron.'

'Whoever told you that was making fun of you.'

'Why?'

'Because sky-iron isn't unbreakable. It comes from rocks which fall from the sky.'

'Not unbreakable?'

'That story's spread far and wide, but a story's all it is.'

'Are the locations of these rocks known?'

'They fall all over the country, but I have a map. Only an official expedition, under the control of the desert guards, is allowed to collect sky-iron and bring it to Kebet.'

'A whole block of sky-iron has been stolen.'

'That's not very surprising. A band of looters probably stumbled on a rock whose position hadn't been mapped.'

'Would Asher use it?'

'What for? He knows sky-iron is reserved for ritual uses. By making weapons from it he'd lay himself open to serious trouble. On the other hand, selling it abroad – especially to the Hittites, who value it extremely highly – would earn him a fortune.'

Selling, speculating, trading . . . Those were the specialities not of Asher but of Denes, with his insatiable greed for money and possessions. In the process, Sheshi would get his commission. Pazair had been wrong: the inventor was only playing the role of go-between, in Denes's schemes. However, Asher wanted to gain control of the desert guards.

'Have there been any thefts of precious metals from your stores?'

The High Priest smiled. 'I'm watched by an army of guards, priests and scribes, and I watch them – we watch each other. Did you by any chance suspect me?'

'Yes, I must confess I did.'

'I appreciate your honesty. Stay here a few days, and you'll see that theft is impossible.'

Pazair decided to trust him. 'Among the treasures acquired by a trafficker in amulets, I found a very large scarab made of solid gold – and the gold came from the mine at Kebet.'

The High Priest looked troubled. 'Who says so?'

'The goldsmiths of Karnak.'

'Then it's true.'

'I suppose such a precious piece would be listed in your archives?'

'What's the owner's name?'

'The inscription has been removed.'

'That's a pity. Since the most ancient times, each consignment of gold from the mine has been meticulously registered, and you'll find all the records in the archives. Its destination is given: which temple, which pharaoh, which goldsmith. Without a name, you won't be able to find out anything.'

'Do craftsmen work at the mine itself?'

'Not often, but from time to time goldsmiths have made things on the site of the mine. This temple is open to you; search it from top to bottom.'

'That won't be necessary.'

'I wish you good luck. And rid Egypt of that man Asher. He brings bad luck.'

*

If the High Priest of Kebet was innocent – and Pazair was convinced he was – Pazair would probably have to give up trying to find out where the sky-iron had come from. It must be at the heart of a new illegal trade by Denes, whose abilities in the field seemed unlimited. But it might be that the miners, goldsmiths or desert guards were stealing precious stones or metals on behalf of either Denes or Asher, or perhaps even for both of them. After all, the two allies were amassing a huge fortune which they intended using to fund an attack on Egypt's security. But Pazair still did not know what form that attack would take.

If he could prove that Asher was the head of a gang of gold thieves, the general would receive the most severe penalty the system permitted. The only way to get proof, he thought, would be if someone were to mingle with the prospectors and pretend to be one of them. Finding a man brave enough to do that would be difficult, if not impossible, because it would be very dangerous – he had only suggested it to Suti to provoke him.

The only solution was to get taken on himself, after persuading Neferet that he was justified in doing so.

Brave's barking gladdened his heart. The dog came charging madly towards him and stopped, panting, at the feet of his master, who lavished caresses on him. Knowing his donkey's tetchy nature, Pazair went to him immediately to prove his affection. Way-Finder's smiling eyes were his reward.

As soon as he took Neferet in his arms, Pazair could tell that she was tired and careworn. He asked her what had happened.

'It's serious,' she said. 'Suti's taken refuge in our house. For the last week, he has gone to ground in a bedchamber and he refuses to come out.'

'What's he done?'

'He won't speak to anyone but you. This evening he drank an awful lot.'

Sighing, Pazair went into Suti's room; Neferet followed silently.

'Here you are at last!' exclaimed Suti with great relief.

'Kem and I have unearthed vital clues,' said Pazair.

'If Neferet hadn't hidden me, I'd have been exiled to Asia.'

'Why? What crime have you committed?'

'Asher has accused me of desertion, insulting a superior officer, abandoning my post, losing official weapons, cowardice in the face of the enemy and slanderous denunciation.'

'You'll certainly win the case.'

'I certainly won't.'

'What do you mean?'

'When I left the army, I didn't complete the documents that freed me from further army service. The period for doing so has expired, and Asher – he's within his rights – has pounced on my negligence. Effectively, I'm a deserter and can be sent to a military prison.'

'That's annoying.'

'Annoying? I'm facing a year in a labour camp. Can you imagine how the general's scribes would treat me? I wouldn't get out alive.'

'I'll see what I can do.'

'No, Pazair, you mustn't,' said Suti. 'It's my own fault. You're Judge of the Porch – you can't go against the law.'

'We're blood brothers, aren't we?'

'But you mustn't suffer because of me. The trap was cleverly laid. There's only one thing to do: as you suggested, I'll become a prospector and vanish into the desert. I'll escape from Tapeni and Panther as well as Asher, and I might even make my fortune. The gold road! There's no finer dream.'

'Nor, as you said yourself, is there a more dangerous one.'

'I wasn't made for a sedentary life. The women will miss me, but I'm trusting in my luck.'

'We don't want to lose you,' objected Neferet.

Moved, he gazed at her. 'I'll come back – and I'll be rich,

powerful and honoured. All the Ashers in the world will tremble at the sight of me and crawl at my feet, but I shall be merciless and trample them underfoot. I shall come and kiss you on both cheeks and gorge myself on the food and drink you'll have ready for me.'

'To my mind,' said Pazair, 'it would be better to have the feast straight away and give up your plan to be a drunkard.'

'I've never been so clear-headed. If I stay here, I'll be found guilty. And I'll take you down with me, because you're so stubborn that you'll insist on defending me and fighting for a lost cause. Then all our efforts will have been in vain.'

'Is it really necessary to take such a huge risk?' asked Neferet.

'Without drastic action, how can I get myself out of this mess? From now on the army is forbidden to me, and all that's left is the damned profession of gold-seeker. No, I haven't gone mad. This time I shall make my fortune. I can sense it, in my head, my fingers, my belly.'

'Is that your final decision?'

'I've been going round in circles for a week; I've had plenty of time to think. Even you won't change my mind.'

Pazair and Neferet looked at each other; he wasn't joking.

'In that case,' said Pazair, 'I've some important information for you.'

'About Asher?' asked Suti.

'Kem and I have uncovered an illegal trade in amulets, involving Denes and Qadash, and it's possible that Asher is involved in stealing gold. In other words, the conspirators are amassing money.'

'Asher a gold thief? Wonderful! That carries the death penalty, doesn't it?'

'If it can be proved.'

'You really are my brother, Pazair.' Suti hugged his friend warmly. 'I'll bring you that proof. Not only am I going to I get rich, but I'll knock that murderer off his pedestal.'

'Don't get too excited. It's only a theory.'

'No, it's the truth, I'm sure it is.'

'If you insist on going ahead, I'm going to make your mission official.'

'In what way?'

'With Kem's agreement, you enlisted in the desert guards a fortnight ago. You'll be paid a wage.'

'A fortnight ago? You mean before Asher made his accusation?'

'Kem takes little notice of administrative formalities. Matters will be in order, that's the vital thing.'

'Let's have a drink,' demanded Suti.

'Get yourself a job with the miners,' advised Pazair, 'and don't tell anyone at all that you're a guard, unless you need to in order to save yourself from immediate danger.'

'Do you suspect anyone in particular?'

'Asher would like to take control of the desert guards, so he must have infiltrated spies or bought a few consciences – probably even among the miners. We'll communicate either by the official message service or by any other means that doesn't endanger you. We must keep each other informed as to the progress of our respective inquiries. My code-name will be . . . Way-Finder.'

'If you admit you're a donkey, the path to wisdom isn't yet out of your reach.'

'I want a promise from you.'

'You have it.'

'Don't force your famous good luck. If danger becomes pressing, come back.'

'You know me.'

'Yes,' said Pazair drily, 'I do.'

'I'll be acting in secret, but you'll be an exposed target.'

'Are you trying to say I'll be running bigger risks than you?'

'If judges are becoming intelligent, this country may yet have a future.'

19

In the garden of his estate, Denes counted the dried figs and then counted them again. After checking several times, he came to the conclusion that some had been stolen. Eight were missing, according to the list prepared by the scribe in charge of his fruit trees. Furious, he summoned his staff and threatened them with terrible punishments if the guilty party did not confess. An old cook who valued her quiet life pushed forward a ten-year-old boy, the fruit-tree scribe's own son. The scribe was sentenced to ten strokes of the rod, and the boy to fifteen. Denes demanded strict absolute honesty; even the least of his possessions must be respected as such. In the absence of Nenophar, who was locked in a tussle with the financial secretariats to try to lessen Bel-Tran's influence, Denes was running his estate himself.

His anger had made him hungry, so he ordered roast pork, milk and soft cheese to be brought to him at once. His appetite suddenly vanished when his steward came and announced that the Judge of the Porch wished to see him. Nevertheless, he put on a cheerful expression and invited the judge to share his meal.

Pazair sat down on the low dry-stone wall enclosing the pergola and watched Denes closely. 'Why did you employ Qadash's former steward, who had been found guilty of dishonesty?'

'The scribe who sees to employing people made a mistake. Qadash and I were sure that the miserable wretch had left the province.'

'He did leave, it's true, but only to take charge of your largest farm, near Khmun.'

'He must have used a false name. You may be certain he'll be dismissed first thing tomorrow.'

'That won't be necessary,' said Pazair. 'He's in prison.'

Denes smoothed his thin fringe of beard, putting a few stray hairs back in place. 'In prison? What has he done?'

'Did you not know that he was a go-between for stolen goods?'

'A go-between? How dreadful!' Denes seemed indignant.

'He was involved in an illegal traffic in amulets stored in chests,' specified Pazair.

'On my property? On my farm? That's incredible – insane! I do ask you for the greatest discretion, my dear Judge. My reputation shouldn't suffer because of that despicable fellow's crimes.'

'So you're one of his victims?'

'He's deceived me in the vilest way. He must know I never go to that estate – my business affairs keep me in Memphis, and I've no great fondness for the provinces. I dare to hope he will be punished very severely.'

'Had you no idea what your steward was doing?'

'None at all. I've acted in all good faith.'

'Did you know that treasure was hidden on that farm?'

Denes looked astounded. 'Treasure now, is it? What kind of treasure?'

'That's confidential. Do you know where your friend Qadash is?'

'Yes. He's here. He was suffering from exhaustion, so I invited him to stay.'

'If his health permits, may I see him?'

With much annoyance, Denes sent a servant to fetch the tooth-doctor.

Arms waving, and unable to stand still, Qadash launched into a series of involved explanations in which he defended himself for having employed the steward on his estate, while at the same time arguing that he had later dismissed him. He answered Pazair's questions only with disjointed phrases. Either he was losing his mind or he was playing a game.

Eventually Pazair interrupted Qadash and said, 'I think I understand what you are saying: that neither of you knew anything, and that the traffic in amulets was operating without your knowledge.'

Denes congratulated the judge on his conclusions. Qadash walked away without another word.

'You must forgive him,' said Denes. 'His age, you know, and he's been overworking . . .'

'My investigation is continuing,' said Pazair. 'The steward is only a pawn. I shall find out who devised the game and fixed its rules. You may be sure that I'll keep you informed.'

'I would be much obliged.'

'I should like to speak with your wife.'

'I don't know what time she'll return from the palace.'

'I'll come back this evening.'

'Is that really necessary?'

'Absolutely.'

When Pazair arrived that evening, he was shown into Nenophar's workshop. He found her, her face carefully painted, indulging in her favourite activity, making new clothes. She was sewing the sleeve of a long dress.

'I'm tired,' she said irritably. 'Being bothered in my own home like this is very disagreeable.'

'As you can see, I am sorry.' He went a little closer. 'Your work is truly remarkable.'

'Are you impressed by my talent for needlework?'

'I'm fascinated.'

Nenophar seemed bewildered. 'What is all this about?'

'Where do the fabrics you use come from?'

'That is no one's concern but mine.'

'I'm afraid it is.'

Outraged, she abandoned her work and got to her feet. 'I demand an explanation.'

'At your farm in Middle Egypt, among a number of suspicious items we found dresses, bedsheets and pieces of linen. I assume they belong to you.'

'Have you any proof of that?'

'Not formal proof, no.'

'In that case, spare me your assumptions, and leave here at once.'

'I am obliged to do so, but I must stress one point: I am not deceived.'

At last Panther had finished. It had taken her two weeks to assemble the ingredients: hairs from a sick man who had died the previous day, a few grains of barley stolen from a child's tomb before it was closed, some apple-pips, blood from a black dog, sour wine, donkey's urine and sawdust. The potion would work quickly and well. Now she must ensure that her rival, either willingly or by force, drank the mixture. As consumed with love as ever, but never again able to respond to a man's passion, Tapeni would bore Suti and he would soon leave her.

Panther heard a soft noise. Someone had just passed through the small garden and entered the little white house.

She put out the kitchen lamp and armed herself with a knife. So that she-devil Tapeni had dared to come and confront Panther under her own roof, no doubt intending to murder her. She heard the intruder go into the bedchamber, open a travelling-bag and begin throwing things into it.

Panther crept through the house to the bedchamber door.

Brandishing the knife, she hurled herself into the room.

'Suti!'

The young man spun round and saw her. Seeing the gleaming blade, he threw himself to one side. Panther dropped the knife.

'Have you gone mad?' He straightened up and seized her by the wrists. 'What the devil's that knife for?'

'To run her through.'

'Who are you talking about?'

'That creature you married.'

'Forget about her – and forget about me, too.'

Panther trembled. 'Suti . . . '

'As you can see, I'm leaving.'

'Where are you going?'

'On a secret mission.'

'You're lying! You're going back to her!'

He burst out laughing, let go of her, stuffed one last kilt into his bag, and threw it over his shoulder. 'Don't worry, she won't follow me.'

Panther grabbed her lover. 'You're frightening me. Tell me what's happened, please!'

'I'm regarded as a deserter and I must leave Memphis right away. If Asher gets his hands on me I'll be deported, and he'll make sure I don't come back.'

'Can't Pazair protect you?'

'I was careless and it's my own fault. If I succeed in doing what he has trusted me to do, I'll defeat Asher and come back.' He kissed her passionately.

'If you've lied to me,' she promised, 'I'll kill you.'

With the help of the temple priests, Kem investigated the most prestigious amulet workshops in Kebet, but found nothing. He left Thebes and took a boat to Memphis, where he carried out a similar investigation; it was equally disappointing.

It must mean, the big Nubian reflected, that the beautiful amulets being traded illegally did not come from a well-established workshop. So he questioned several informants, all of whom eyed Killer nervously. One of them, a dwarf of Syrian origin, agreed to talk, on condition that he received three sacks of barley and a donkey under three years old. Drafting a written request for the payment and following the proper procedure would have taken too long. So Kem paid for everything himself, and threatened to break the dwarf's ribs if he tried to lie. The dwarf said an illegal trade – he didn't know in what – had been operating for two years in the northern district of the city, near the naval boatyard.

For three days and nights, disguised as a water-carrier and with Killer at his side, Kem observed the comings and goings around the boatyard. After the yard closed in the evenings, strange workers slipped down an alleyway with no apparent way out, and re-emerged before dawn, carrying closed baskets which they handed to a boatman.

On the fourth night, the pair set off down the alleyway. It ended in a panel made from reeds, which were covered with dried mud so that the panel looked like a wall. Followed by Killer, Kem charged at it and broke through.

They found themselves in a stuffy, low-ceilinged work-shop where four craftsmen were working. Kem felled the nearest, Killer bit the second in the leg, and the third fled. The last, a short, pot-bellied, elderly man, stood rooted to the spot, hardly daring to breathe. In his hand was a magnificent lapis-lazuli Knot of Isis, which he dropped when Kem went towards him.

'Are you in charge?' demanded Kem.

The man nodded, too scared to speak.

Kem picked up the Knot of Isis. 'This is fine work – you're clearly no apprentice. Where did you learn your trade?'

'At . . . at the T-Temple of Ptah,' he stammered.

'Why did you leave?'

'I w-was expelled.'

'Why?'

The man hung his head. 'For theft.'

Kem looked around the workshop. Along the dried-mud walls were piled chests containing blocks of lapis-lazuli from the far-off mountainous regions. On a low table lay finished amulets; a nearby basket contained spoilt items and waste.

'Who's your employer?' asked Kem.

'I . . . I can't remember.'

'Come on, my brave fellow, lying is stupid. What's more, it infuriates my baboon – and he isn't called Killer for nothing, you know. I want the name of the man behind this illegal trade.'

'Will you protect me if I tell you?'

'You'll be safe in the thieves' prison.'

The fat man would be more than happy to leave Memphis, even to exchange it for the underworld. But he hesitated.

'I'm waiting,' said Kem grimly.

'Prison? Is there no way of avoiding it?'

'That depends on you, and above all on the name you give me.'

'He hasn't left any traces behind him, he'll deny everything, and my testimony won't be enough to convict him.'

'Don't bother yourself with the legal side of things.'

'Couldn't you just let me go?'

Hoping the Nubian would do nothing, the craftsman took a step towards the alleyway.

A huge, strong hand closed round his neck. 'The name – now!'

'It's Sheshi, Sheshi the inventor.'

Pazair and Kem walked along the canal, watching the cargo-boats. The sailors shouted to each other and sang, some leaving, others returning home. Everything spoke of Egypt's prosperity, happiness and peace.

And yet at night Pazair could not sleep: he sensed that tragedy was coming, though he could not identify the causes of the evil. He had told Neferet and, despite her natural optimism, she had had to admit that his fear was justified.

Pazair shook off his worries, and turned to Kem. 'You're right,' he said. 'The case against Sheshi would fail. He'd protest his innocence, and the word of a thief expelled from the temple would carry no weight.'

'But the man was telling the truth.'

'I don't doubt it.'

'The legal system,' grumbled the Nubian. 'What's the point of it?'

'Give me time. We now know of the bonds of friendship that link Denes to Qadash, and Qadash to Sheshi. Those three are definitely accomplices, and Sheshi – whose skill as an inventor must be very useful to them – is probably working for Asher as well. So we have four conspirators, responsible between them for quite a number of crimes. What we need now is for Suti to bring us proof of Asher's guilt. I'm convinced that Asher stole the sky-iron and that he's behind the traffic in precious things like lapis-lazuli, and perhaps even gold – his knowledge of Asian affairs would be a great advantage. Denes is an ambitious man, greedy for wealth and power; he's manipulating Qadash and Sheshi. And I'm not forgetting Nenophar, so skilled in handling the very kind of needle that killed Branir.'

'Four men and a woman. How can they threaten Ramses' reign?'

'That question torments me, but I cannot answer it. Why, if it was indeed the same people, did they loot a royal tomb? There are still so many uncertainties, Kem. Our work is far from complete.

'Despite my title,' Pazair went on, 'I shall continue to investigate alone. You're one of only three people I trust. I shall free you from all administrative work.'

'Yes, but . . . '

'What is it?'

'Be as careful as I am.'

'The only other people I trust are Suti and Neferet.'

'He's your blood brother, and she's your sister for eternity. If either betrays you, they will be damned on earth and in the afterlife.'

'Why are you so suspicious?'

'Because you're forgetting to ask one vital question: are there really only five conspirators, or are there more?'

At dead of night, her head covered with a shawl, she slipped silently into the warehouse where, in the name of her friends, she had arranged a meeting with the shadow-eater. She had been chosen, by the drawing of lots, to meet him and give him his instructions. Ordinarily, they would never have taken such a risk, but the urgency of the situation required both a meeting in person and the certainty that the orders would be understood perfectly. Dressed in a peasant-woman's coarse robe and papyrus sandals, and with her face thickly painted, she was sure she was unrecognizable and ran no risk of being identified.

The previous day, Denes had called an urgent meeting of his allies. The confiscation of the block of sky-iron was only a financial loss, but Pazair's discovery of the funerary items belonging to Pharaoh Khufu looked set to cause more serious difficulties. True, Pazair could neither identify the king, whose name had been carefully removed, nor understand that Ramses was obliged to keep silent about what was happening. Not one word could be spoken by the most powerful man in the world, who was locked in lonely solitude, unable to confess that he no longer possessed the symbols of government that gave his rule legitimacy.

Denes had advocated doing nothing – the judge's interference didn't frighten him – but the other conspirators had disagreed. Even if Pazair stood no chance of getting at the truth, he was causing them more and more problems in their various activities. Sheshi was the most vehement: he had just lost all his substantial future profits from his traffic in amulets. Determined, patient and thorough, the judge would eventually make a case, and one or more notables would be implicated, perhaps found guilty, or even imprisoned. If that happened, it would be a double blow. On one hand, the conspiracy would be severely weakened. On the other, Pazair's victims would publicly lose their integrity – which they would badly need on the day when Ramses abdicated.

The woman trembled when she heard someone say her name, then rejoiced. A delicious shiver ran though her, like the one she had felt when she stripped naked in front of the commander of the Great Sphinx's honour-guard at Giza. As she lured the commander towards her, she had made him drop his guard and opened the gates of death. It was her charms that had sealed their victory.

She knew nothing of the shadow-eater, except that he committed crimes to order, more for the pleasure of killing than for high fees. When she saw him, sitting there on a chest peeling an onion, she was both frightened and fascinated.

'You're late,' he said. 'The moon has passed the end of the port.'

'You must act again.'

'Who?'

'It will be a very delicate task.'

'A woman, a child?'

'A judge.'

'In Egypt, people don't murder judges.'

'You aren't to kill him, you're to cripple him.'

'Difficult.'

'What do you want?'

'Gold. And plenty of it.'

'You'll have it,' she promised.

'When?'

'Don't strike until you're certain of success. Everyone must be convinced that Pazair was the victim of an accident.'

'The Judge of the Porch himself? The amount of gold has just doubled.'

'We shan't tolerate failure.'

'Neither shall I. Pazair is well protected, so it's impossible to fix a specific time.'

'We can accept that. But the sooner the better.'

The shadow-eater got to his feet. 'There's just one more thing.'

'What?'

Quick as a snake, he twisted her arm, just short of breaking it, and forced her to turn away from him. 'I want an advance.'

'You wouldn't dare!'

'An advance in kind.'

He lifted up her dress.

She did not scream, but hissed, 'You're mad!'

'And you're careless. Your face doesn't interest me, and I don't want to know who you are. If you cooperate, it'll be better for both of us.'

When she felt his manhood between her thighs, she stopped resisting. Making love to a murderer was more exciting than her usual frolics. She'd never tell anyone about this. Their coupling was quick and rough, just the way she liked it.

'Your judge won't bother you any more,' promised the shadow-eater.

20

Shade was provided by palm-, fig- and carob trees. Sitting in the garden after her noon meal, and before resuming work, Neferet savoured the silence. It was soon broken by her monkey leaping around with little cries of joy as it brought a fruit to its mistress. Mischief did not quieten until Neferet sat down again; reassured, the monkey slipped under her chair and watched Brave's comings and goings.

It was said that the whole of Egypt was like a garden, where Pharaoh's benevolent shade enabled the trees to flourish, both in the joy of morning and in the peace of evening. Ramses himself often supervised the planting of olive- or persea-trees. He loved to walk in flower-filled gardens and gaze upon orchards. The temples enjoyed the shelter of tall trees in which the birds – messengers of the gods – built their nests. The sages said that a troubled soul is a tree withering in its heart's drought; a calm soul, on the contrary, bears fruit and spreads a gentle coolness around it.

Neferet planted a sycamore seedling in the centre of a small trench; a porous jar, which conserved moisture, protected the young plant's roots. As they grew, the fragile container would burst apart, and the fragments of pottery would mix with the earth, adding strength to the soil. Neferet took care to reinforce the border of dried mud, designed to hold in moisture after watering.

Brave started barking, announcing Pazair's imminent arrival; well before the judge crossed the threshold, and no matter time of day or night it was, the dog always sensed his master's approach. When he was away for a long time, Brave lost his appetite and no longer reacted to Mischief's provocation.

Forgetting the dignity of his office, the Judge of the Porch ran to his dog, which jumped up and decorated his clean kilt with two muddy footprints. The judge took it off and lay down on a mat, close to his wife.

'How gentle this sunshine is,' he said.

'You look exhausted.'

'I've had far more than the usual dose of troubles today.'

'Did you remember to take your copper-water?'

'I didn't have time to look after myself. My office wasn't empty for a single moment. Everyone in Egypt – from the footsoldier's widow to the scribe unable to gain advancement – wanted to see me.'

She lay down beside him. 'You aren't thinking clearly, Judge Pazair. Gaze upon your garden.'

'Suti's right. I'm trapped by this post. I want to go back to being a little village judge.'

'It isn't your destiny to go backwards. Has Suti left for Kebet?'

'He went this morning, with his weapons and his baggage. He promised me he'd return with Asher's head and a pile of gold.'

'Each day we must pray to Min, the protector of explorers, and Hathor, queen of the deserts. Our friendship will cross the space between us.'

'And what about your patients?' asked Pazair.

'A few of them are worrying me. I am waiting for some rare plants in order to make up my remedies, but the workshop at the central hospital has not responded to my orders.'

Pazair closed his eyes.

'There's something else worrying you, my darling, isn't there?' said Neferet.

'I can't hide anything from you. Well, yes, there is, and it concerns you.'

'Have I broken the law?'

'The position of principal doctor to the court has become vacant. As Judge of the Porch, I must examine the legal validity of the applications submitted to the council of specialists. I was obliged to accept the first one.'

'From whom?'

'Qadash. If he's chosen, the file Bel-Tran prepared in your favour will fall to the bottom of a rubbish pit.'

'Does he have any chance of success?'

'He presented a letter from Nebamon designating Qadash his preferred successor.'

'Is it a forgery?'

'Two witnesses have authenticated it and certified that Nebamon was sane when he wrote it. And who are those witnesses? Denes and Sheshi. Those villains aren't even hiding any longer!'

'My career doesn't matter. I'm happy simply to care for people – working as I do now is enough for me.'

'They'll try to stop you. And you'll be attacked in other ways, too.'

'Ah, but I'll have the best judge in Egypt to defend me.'

'Qadash . . . I've been wondering for a long time about his exact role, and now the veil has been torn down. What are the principal doctor's duties?'

'To treat Pharaoh, appoint doctors and remedy-makers to the official body based at the palace, to receive and check poisons and dangerous medicines, to issue directives regarding public health and ensure they are applied after obtaining the agreement of the tjaty and the king.'

Pazair shook his head worriedly. 'If Qadash had powers

like that . . . This is definitely the post he has been scheming for.'

'It isn't easy to influence the council of doctors who'll decide.'

'Don't deceive yourself. Denes will try to bribe them. Qadash is old, apparently respectable, has many years' experience, and – and Ramses suffers from only one notable ailment, toothache! This appointment is a phase of their plan. They must not succeed.'

'How can you stop them?'

'I don't know yet.'

'Are you afraid Qadash would harm Pharaoh's health?'

'No, that would be too risky.'

Mischief jumped on to Pazair's shoulder and pulled his hair. He yelped in pain and made a grab for her, but his hand closed on empty air. The monkey had already taken refuge under its mistress's chair.

'If that damned animal hadn't brought about our first meeting, I'd give it a good spanking.'

To gain forgiveness, Mischief climbed a date-palm and threw down some fruit, which Pazair caught in mid-air. Brave ran up and gulped it down.

When Pazair turned back to Neferet, she was looking sad.

'What's the matter?' he asked.

'I thought of a crazy plan.'

'What sort of plan?'

'I've given it up.'

'Tell me about it.'

'What's the use?' She nestled against him. 'I'd have liked . . . a child.'

'I think about it, too.'

'Is it what you want?'

'Yes, but until the light has been gained we'd be wrong to have a child.'

'I fought against that conclusion for a long time, but you're right.'

'Either I give up this investigation or we'll have to wait.'

'Forgetting Branir's murder would damn us as the vilest of people.'

He put his arm round her. 'Do you really need to keep that dress on when the air's so warm and gentle?'

The shadow-eater's task would not be easy. First, leaving his official post too often and for too long would draw attention to him. As he worked alone without accomplices, who might have denounced him at any time, and as he must get to know Pazair's habits and routine, he would have to be patient. Also, he had been ordered to turn the Judge of the Porch into an invalid, not to kill him, and to make the crime look like an accident, so that no investigation would be opened.

The execution of this plan presented enormous difficulties. So the shadow-eater had demanded three gold ingots, a fine fortune which would enable him to buy a farm in the Delta, and to set himself up and live a happy life there. In future he would kill only for pleasure, when the urge became irresistible, and would enjoy commanding an army of servants who were ready to satisfy his every whim.

As soon as he had the gold, he would set off on the hunt; he was excited at the idea of carrying out his masterpiece.

The oven had been heated until it was white-hot. Sheshi had arranged the moulds, into which the liquid metal would flow to form a large ingot. The temperature in the workshop was almost unbearable but Sheshi did not perspire, though Denes was bathed in sweat.

'I've got our friends' agreement,' said Denes.

'No regrets?'

'We have no choice.'

Denes took out of a fabric bag the gold mask and collar that had adorned the head and shoulders of Pharaoh Khufu's mummy. 'We can make two ingots out of these.'

'What about the third?'

'We'll buy it from Asher. His thefts of gold are expertly organized, but nothing escapes me.'

Sheshi gazed at the face of the man who had built the Great Pyramid. The features were stern and serene, extraordinarily beautiful. The goldsmith had created a feeling of eternal youth.

'This frightens me,' he confessed.

'It's only a funeral mask.'

'But the eyes . . . they're alive.'

'You're just imagining things. That judge has already cost us a fortune by seizing the block of sky-iron we wanted to sell to the Hittites and the gold scarab I was reserving for my tomb. Keeping the mask and collar has become too risky – besides, we need them to pay the shadow-eater. Hurry up.'

Sheshi obeyed Denes, as he always did. The sublime face and the collar disappeared into the furnace. Soon the molten gold would flow down a channel and fill the moulds.

'What about the gold cubit?' asked Sheshi.

Denes's face lit up. 'We could use it for the third ingot. So we needn't deal with Asher after all.'

Sheshi hesitated.

'It's better to get rid of it,' Denes went on. 'Let's keep only what's absolutely vital: the Testament of the Gods. Where it is, Pazair has no chance of finding it.'

Denes smirked when Khufu's royal cubit disappeared into the furnace. 'Before long, Sheshi, my fine fellow, you'll be one of the most important people in the kingdom. This evening the first part of the fee will be paid to the shadow-eater.'

The desert guard was a giant of a man. Two daggers with worn handles hung from the belt of his kilt. He never wore

sandals; he had walked so often on stones that even an acacia-
thorn could not pierce the thick soles of his feet.

'What is your name?' he demanded.

'Suti.'

'Where are you from?'

'Thebes.'

'Profession?'

'Water-carrier, linen-gatherer, pig-farmer, fisherman . . . '

An enormous short-haired dog with empty eyes sniffed the
young man. It weighed as much as a grown man, and its back
was covered with scars. Suti sensed that it was ready to spring
at any moment.

'Why do you want to be a miner?'

'I like adventure.'

'Do you also like thirst, scorching heat, horned vipers,
black scorpions, forced marches, and back-breaking work in
narrow, airless galleries?'

'Every trade has its disadvantages.'

'You're taking the wrong path, my lad.'

Suti smiled as foolishly as possible. The guard let him
pass.

In the queue waiting to sign on at the office, he cut a rather
fine figure. His confident air and impressive muscles
contrasted sharply with the sickly appearance of several of
the other men, who were clearly unfit for the job.

Two elderly miners asked him the same questions as the
guard, and he gave the same answers. He felt as though he
were being examined like a fine-bred animal.

'An expedition is being organized. Are you available?'

'Yes,' said Suti. 'Where's it going?'

'In our job, you do as you're told and you don't ask
questions. Half the new men fall by the wayside, and they
have to do whatever they can to get back to the valley – we
don't waste time on weaklings. We're leaving tonight, two
hours before dawn. Here's your equipment.'

Suti was given a cane, a mat and a rolled-up blanket. With a piece of string, he tied the blanket and the mat round the cane, which was vital in the desert. By banging it on the ground as you walked along, you could frighten snakes away.

'What about water?' he asked.

'You'll be given your ration. Don't forget the most precious thing.'

Suti hung round his neck the little leather bag into which the happy discoverer would slip gold, cornelian, lapis-lazuli or any other precious stones. The contents of the purse would belong to him, as well as his pay.

'It doesn't hold much,' he commented.

'Many purses stay empty, boy.'

'Only inadequate men's.'

'You've got a lot to say for yourself. The desert'll soon teach you to hold your tongue.'

More than two hundred men had assembled at the eastern gate of the city, close to the trail. Most were praying to Min and making three vows: to return home safe and sound, not to die of thirst, and to bring back precious stones in their leather bags. Amulets hung at their necks. The most educated of them had consulted star-watcher, and some had withdrawn from the journey because the omens were unfavourable. To unbelievers and miscreants, the old hands had passed on the usual message: 'We leave without God for the desert, we return with him into the valley.'

The leader of the expedition, Ephraim, was a tall, bearded man with immensely long arms. His body was covered with so much stiff black hair that he looked like a bear. When they saw him, several would-be miners changed their minds; people said he was brutal and cruel.

He reviewed his men, lingering over each volunteer. 'Are you the one called Suti?'

'I have that good fortune.'

'It seems you're an ambitious fellow.'

'I haven't come here to collect pebbles.'

'While you're waiting, you can carry my bag.' He passed an enormously heavy bag to Suti, who hoisted it on to his shoulder.

Ephraim grinned. 'Make the most of it. Soon you won't look so proud.'

The men shook themselves into wakefulness before sunrise and walked until mid-morning, travelling deep into a bare, arid landscape. Ephraim avoided the burning sand and kept to the paths, which were strewn with shards of rock as sharp as metal. The country fellows, ill prepared for this terrain, found their feet got cut to ribbons.

The first mountains took Suti by surprise. They seemed to form an impenetrable barrier, barring access to a secret land where the blocks of pure stone reserved for the gods' dwellings were formed. There a formidable energy was concentrated; the mountain gave birth to the rock, which was pregnant with precious minerals and did not unveil its riches except to patient, determined lovers. Fascinated, he laid down his burden.

A kick in the backside sent him tumbling into the sand.

'I didn't give you permission to rest,' said Ephraim sarcastically.

Suti got up.

'Clean my bag, and during the meal don't put it down on the ground. As punishment for disobeying me, you'll have no water.'

Suti wondered if he had been denounced, but then he saw that other volunteers were also being bullied. Ephraim liked to test his men by pushing them to the limit. A Nubian who made as if to raise his fist was promptly knocked unconscious and abandoned beside the track.

Late in the afternoon, they reached a sandstone quarry. Stone-cutters were removing blocks, which they marked with their team's special sign. Little grooves were cut out carefully along each vein, then round the desired block. The overseer used a mallet to insert wooden pegs into notches aligned with the aid of a rope, so as to detach the block from the mother rock without shattering it.

Ephraim hailed him. 'I'm taking a band of idle good-for-nothings to the mines. If you need a hand, just say so.'

'I wouldn't say no, but haven't they walked all day?'

'If they want to eat, they'll have to make themselves useful.'

'That's a bit irregular.'

'I'm the one who lays down the law.'

'Ten blocks need to be brought down from the top of the quarry. With thirty men, it wouldn't take long.'

Ephraim chose them, including Suti, from whom he retrieved his bag.

'Have some water and then start climbing.'

The overseer had built a slide but it had broken halfway down the slope, so the blocks had to be held back with ropes to that point, before they were freed and allowed to slide the rest of the way. A thick cable, held by five men on either side, was stretched horizontally in order to stop the blocks moving too fast. As soon as the slide was repaired, this would be unnecessary. But the overseer was behind schedule, and Ephraim's proposal would put that right.

The accident happened when the sixth block reached the cable too quickly. The men holding it back were tired, and could not slow it down. It hit the horizontal cable so hard that the workmen were flung aside, except for one middle-aged man, who fell on to the slide. He tried in vain to hold on to Suti's arm while two comrades hauled the young man backwards.

The unfortunate man's scream was soon stifled. The block crushed him, left the slide and shattered with a thunderous growl.

The overseer buried his face in his hands.

'Still, we've done half the work,' said Ephraim.

21

The ibex stag, whose chin was fringed with a short beard and whose two long, curved horns pointed to the sky, stood on an overhanging rock and gazed down at the miners making their way along beneath the burning sun. In the language of hieroglyphs, the ibex symbolized serene nobility acquired at the end of a life which had conformed to divine law.

'Look! Up there!' roared one of the miners. 'Kill it!'

'Shut up, you fool,' retorted Ephraim. 'That's the guardian of the mine. If we touch it, we'll all die.'

The stag scaled a near-vertical slope and, with a prodigious leap, disappeared on to the other side of the mountain.

Five days' forced march had exhausted the miners; only Ephraim seemed as fresh as at the outset. Suti was still strong, too; the inhuman splendour of the landscape renewed his strength. Neither Ephraim's brutality nor the exhausting conditions of the journey had dented his determination.

Having ordered the men to gather round, Ephraim climbed up on to a large rock, showing his authority over this band of good-for-nothings.

'The desert is immense,' he declared in his thunderous voice, 'and you're less than ants. You're forever complaining of being thirsty, like helpless old women. You aren't worthy of being miners and searching the bowels of the earth. Still, I've brought you here – the metals are worth more than you.

When you cut into the mountain, you hurt it; it'll try to take its revenge by swallowing you up. Too bad for you if you're careless. Set up camp now. Work begins tomorrow at dawn.'

The workmen put up the tents, beginning with Ephraim's, which was so heavy that carrying it had worn out five men. It was carefully unrolled, put up under Ephraim's watchful eye, and stood in splendour at the centre of the camp. The meal was prepared, the ground was dampened to lay the dust, and the men slaked their thirst with water which had been kept cool in goatskins. Fortunately, there was no shortage of it, because a well had been dug near the mine.

Suti was dozing, when someone kicked him hard in the ribs.

'Get up,' ordered Ephraim.

The young man swallowed his anger and obeyed.

'Most of the men here have something to be ashamed of. What about you?'

'That's my secret.'

'Talk.'

'Leave me alone.'

'I hate people who keep secrets.'

'I deserted from my compulsory work for the state.'

'Where?'

'In my village, near Thebes. They wanted to take me to Memphis to clean out canals. I chose to run away instead, and try my luck as a miner.'

'I don't like the look of you,' said Ephraim. 'I'm sure you're lying.'

'I want to make my fortune and nobody, not even you, is going to stop me.'

'You annoy me, little man. I'm going to put you in your place. We'll fight, bare-knuckled.'

Ephraim chose an arbiter, whose role would consist of disqualifying either man for biting; anything else was permitted.

Without warning, Ephraim charged Suti, seized him round

the chest, lifted him high, spun him round above his head and threw him. Suti hit the ground nearly ten paces away.

Grazed, and with a painful shoulder, the young man got up. Hands on hips, Ephraim looked at him contemptuously. The miners laughed.

Suti spat the sand out of his mouth. 'I'm ready for you now, so attack again if you're brave enough.'

Ephraim answered the challenge at once, but this time his long arms captured only empty air, as Suti dodged aside at the last moment. Suti regained some of his confidence. It seemed Ephraim knew only one hold, and was relying on his great strength to win. Even if the gods did not exist, Suti thanked them for having given him a turbulent childhood during which he had learnt to fight.

At least ten times, Suti avoided Ephraim's attacks. Ephraim got more and more angry, which tired him and made him stop thinking clearly. Suti could not afford to make a single mistake; if he got caught in a stranglehold, he'd be killed. Using all his speed and agility, he unbalanced Ephraim by hooking a foot through his leg, slid under the big man as he toppled, and used his opponent's own energy to trap him in a headlock. Ephraim crashed to the ground. Suti sat astride him and threatened to break his neck.

Ephraim punched the sand, accepting his defeat. 'All right, little man!'

'You deserve to die.'

'If you kill me, the desert guards will kill you.'

'I don't care. You won't be the first man I've sent to hell.'

Ephraim saw that he meant it. 'What do you want?'

'Swear that you won't torture the men any more.'

The miners were no longer laughing. They crowded round, hanging on every word.

'Hurry up, or I'll break your neck.'

'I swear, in the name of Min.'

'And before Hathor, Lady of the West. Say it.'

'Before Hathor, Lady of the West, I swear it.'

Suti relaxed his grip. Ephraim could not break an oath like that, sworn before so many witnesses. If he did, he would see his name destroyed for all eternity and would be condemned to utter destruction.

The miners shouted with joy. Two of them hoisted Suti on to their shoulders and carried him around in triumph.

When their excitement had abated somewhat, he spoke to them firmly.

'The leader here is Ephraim. He's the only one who knows the routes, the watering-places and the mines. Without him we'll never see the valley again, but if we obey him, and if he keeps his word, all will go well.'

Amazed, the bearded man laid a hand on Suti's shoulder. 'You're strong, little man, but intelligent, too.' He drew Suti aside. 'I've misjudged you.'

'I want to make my fortune.'

'We could be friends.'

'Perhaps, so long as it's useful to me.'

'It might be, little man.'

Women bearing offerings processed slowly into the palace of Princess Hattusa. Each wore a white dress held up by a strap which passed between her bare breasts, and an apron decorated with pearls, embroidered in the shape of a diamond. On their heads they wore wigs drawn into a horse-tail at the back, and they were so fresh and pretty that Denes felt his blood heating. When he was away from home he was always unfaithful to Nenophar with perfect and obligatory discretion. A scandal would discredit him, so he had no official mistress and was content with brief encounters which led nowhere. He did make love to his wife from time to time, of course, but in his eyes Nenophar's coldness justified his extra-marital adventures.

The steward of the harem came to see him in the garden.

Denes thought of asking for a girl, but decided against it: a harem was a centre of trade and business, where the ruling spirit was work, not debauchery.

In his capacity as a ship-owner, Denes had requested an official audience with Ramses' Hittite wife. She received him in a four-pillared hall, with walls painted bright yellow. The floor was decorated with a mosaic of green and red squares.

Hattusa was seated on an ebony chair, with gilded arms and feet. With her black eyes, very white skin and long, slender hands, she had the strange charm of Asian women. Denes kept on his guard.

'This is an unexpected visit,' she observed acidly.

'I am a transporter of goods, Princess, and you run a harem. No one will be surprised by our meeting.'

'And yet you considered it dangerous.'

'The situation has changed drastically. Pazair has become Judge of the Porch, and he is thwarting my activities.'

'In what way does that concern me?'

'My lady, surely you have not changed your mind?'

'Ramses has spurned me, and he humiliates my people. I want vengeance.'

Satisfied, Denes stroked his white fringe of beard. 'You shall have it, Princess. Our goals are still identical. The king is a tyrant – and an incompetent one, at that. He is chained to outdated traditions and has no vision of the future. Time is working in our favour, but some of my friends are getting impatient, so we have decided to undermine Ramses' popularity even more.'

'Will that be enough to bring him down?'

Denes was on edge, and knew he must not say too much. The Hittite was only a temporary ally, who would have to be discarded as quickly as possible after the king's fall. 'Trust us. Our plan cannot fail.'

'Be careful,' warned Hattusa. 'Ramses is an experienced warrior, skilful and brave.'

'He is bound hand and foot.'

A gleam of excitement shone in Hattusa's eyes. 'Should I not know more about this?'

'My lady, that would be pointless and inadvisable.'

Hattusa frowned. Her suppressed anger made her even more delectable. 'What do you propose to do?'

'To disrupt the whole of Egypt's trade. At Memphis I shall have no difficulty, but at Thebes I shall need your help. The people will grumble, and Pharaoh will be held responsible. The weakening of the country's trade will shake his throne.'

'How many consciences have to be bought?'

'Not many, but they are expensive. The principal scribes who control the movement of goods must make repeated "mistakes". The resulting investigations will be long and complicated, and the disruption will take several weeks to set up.'

'My trusted men will take action.'

Denes had little confidence in this plan's effectiveness. Although it was a fresh blow against the king, it would have only limited consequences. But he had stilled Hattusa's mistrust.

'I have something else to tell you in strict confidence,' he said in a low voice.

'I'm listening.'

He went closer and spoke even more quietly. 'In a few months' time, I shall possess a large quantity of sky-iron.'

The Hittite's eyes betrayed her interest. Used for magical ends, the rare metal would be a new weapon against Ramses. 'What is its price?'

'Three gold ingots at the time of the order, three on delivery.'

'When you leave the harem, they will be in your baggage.'

Denes bowed. His allies would never know about this transaction, and the princess would never receive the sky-iron. The thought of selling something he did not have and making such an enormous profit filled him with glee. Keeping the

173

princess waiting would be easy. If she got too impatient he would blame Sheshi – the inventor's servility had already been very useful.

Pazair and Neferet were dining with Bel-Tran and Silkis. The cook brought in a copper dish of grilled lamb chops, with delicious-looking fresh courgettes and peas, and laid it on the pedestal table in front of them. A serving-woman brought olives, radishes and a lettuce. Silkis prepared the seasoning herself, although she was wearing one of her best dresses and her most valuable earrings, discs decorated with rosettes and spirals.

'Thank you for accepting our invitation, my dear friends,' said Bel-Tran. 'To have both of you at our table is an honour.'

'There's no need for this formality,' protested the judge.

'I keep having a very strange dream,' Silkis said. 'I dreamt several times that I was drinking hot beer. I was so worried that I consulted the interpreter. His diagnosis frightened me. He said it means all my possessions are going to be stolen.'

'Don't worry so much,' advised Neferet. 'Dream-interpreters are often wrong.'

'May the gods hear you!'

'My wife is very worried,' said Bel-Tran. 'Couldn't you give her something to help?'

After the meal, while Neferet was prescribing calming herbal infusions for Silkis, Bel-Tran and Pazair strolled in the garden.

'I have so few opportunities to enjoy nature,' lamented Bel-Tran, 'because my work takes up more and more of my time. When I come home in the evening, my children are in bed. Not seeing them grow and not being able to play with them are painful sacrifices. Managing the granaries, my papyrus works, the Treasury secretariat . . . the days are just too short. Don't you feel the same way?'

'Yes, often. Being Judge of the Porch certainly isn't restful.'

'Are you making any progress in your investigation into General Asher?'

'It's moving on, little by little.'

'Something unexpected has happened, and I'm very worried about it. You know Princess Hattusa is a rather aggressive woman, and she hasn't forgiven Ramses for taking her away from her country.'

'She hardly bothers to hide her hostility.'

'Where will it lead? Opposing the king openly, or trying to conspire against him, would be suicidal. Nevertheless, she has just received a strange visit: from Denes.'

'Are you sure?'

'One of my colleagues thought he recognized him during a visit to the harem. He was so surprised that he checked, to make sure he wasn't mistaken.'

'Why is it so surprising for them to have met?'

'Hattusa has her own fleet of trading-ships. The harem is a state institution where a private ship-owner should have no role to play. If this was a friendly visit, what does it mean?'

Pazair thought for a moment. An alliance between the Hittite princess, the king's secondary wife, and one of the conspirators: Bel-Tran's revelation was certainly important. Could it be that Hattusa was the mastermind of the plot and Denes was her agent? The conclusion seemed too hasty. No one knew what they had talked about, though the mere fact that they had met indicated a meeting of interests, unlikely to be conducive to the kingdom's well-being.

'This collusion is suspicious,' emphasized Bel-Tran.

'Can we find out how far it goes?'

'I don't know. Are you thinking about preparations for an invasion from the north? It is true that Ramses has choked off the Hittites for the time being, but I doubt if they'll ever give up their dreams of expansion.'

'In that case, General Asher would be an essential link.'

The clearer the enemy's outline became, the more difficult

the battle promised to be and the more uncertain the future.

That same evening, a messenger from the palace brought Neferet a letter marked with the seal of Queen Tuya, Ramses' mother: she wished to consult Neferet as soon as possible. Although she lived in strict seclusion, the Mother of Pharaoh was still one of the most influential people at court. Her pride made her detest mediocrity and pettiness; she gave advice rather than orders, and watched over the greatness of the country with jealous care. Ramses both admired and loved her, and since the death of his adored wife, Nefertari, had made his mother his principal confidante. Some said that he never took a decision without first consulting her.

Tuya ruled over a large household and had a palace in each large town. The one in Memphis was made up of about twenty rooms and a vast four-pillared hall where she received important guests.

A steward led Neferet to the queen's bedchamber.

Now aged sixty, Tuya was thin with piercing eyes, a slender, straight nose, prominent cheekbones and a small, almost square chin. She wore the ritual wig of her office, shaped like a vulture, its wings encasing her face.

She said, 'I have heard much of you, Doctor Neferet. Tjaty Bagey, who is not inclined to pay idle compliments, says you have worked miracles.'

'Majesty, I could show you a long list of failures, too. A doctor who boasts of his or her success should change to another calling.'

'I am unwell and I need your skill – Nebamon's assistants are ignorant.'

'What is troubling you, Majesty?'

'My eyes. Also, I have strong, stabbing pains in my belly, my hearing is poor, and my neck is stiff.'

Neferet easily diagnosed that the stabbing pains were caused by abnormal secretions from the womb. She prescribed fumigation with terebinth resin mixed with high-quality oil.

The eye examination worried her more: the rims of the queen's eyes were reddened and sore; there were small, hard pustules on the insides of her eyelids; and the queen complained of pressure within her eyes and occasional dimness of sight.

The queen saw that the doctor was concerned. 'Be frank with me,' she ordered.

'Majesty, these are sicknesses I know and can cure. But the treatment will take a long time and will require you to be meticulous in its application.'

When she rose in the morning, the queen must wash her eyes with a solution based on hemp, which was very effective against pressure within the eye. The same solution, with the addition of honey and applied locally as an ointment, would soothe the belly pains. Another remedy, whose principal agent was black flint, would remove the infection from the rims of her eyes, as well as the malign humours. To get rid of the pustules, the patient must apply to her eyelids a lotion made from ladanum, galenite, tortoise-bile, yellow ochre and Nubian earth. Lastly, using the hollow quill of a vulture, she must put drops into her eyes. Aloes, chrysocolla, colocynth-flour, acacia-leaves, ebony-bark and cold water would be mixed, reduced to a paste, dried and then mixed with water. The resulting lotion must spend a night in the open air, receive the dew, and be filtered. Besides using it as drops, the queen must use it in compresses applied to the eye four times a day.

'How old and weak I am,' she remarked. 'Having to spend so much time on myself displeases me.'

'You are unwell, Majesty. But if you take the time to care for yourself, you will recover.'

'I think I must obey you, whatever it costs me. Accept this, with my thanks.' Tuya handed the doctor a magnificent collar of seven strings of cornelian and Nubian gold beads; the two clasps were shaped like lotus-flowers.

Neferet hesitated. 'Majesty, will you not at least wait to see if the treatment brings results?'

'I am feeling better already.'

Tuya fastened the collar round Neferet's neck, and stood back to judge its effect. 'You are very beautiful, Doctor.'

Neferet blushed.

'What is more, you are happy. Those close to me tell me that your husband is an exceptional judge.'

'Serving Ma'at is the whole meaning of his life.'

'Egypt needs people like you and him.'

Tuya called for her cup-bearer, who brought sweet beer and succulent fruit. The two women sat down on low chairs padded with comfortable cushions.

The queen went on, 'I have followed Judge Pazair's career and investigations for some time. I was amused at first, then intrigued, and in the end appalled. His deportation was unjust and abominable. Fortunately, he has won a first victory: his position as Judge of the Porch enables him to pursue the struggle with greater means. Appointing Kem commander of the city guards was an excellent move, and Tjaty Bagey was right to approve it.'

These few sentences were not spoken by chance, Neferet knew. When she reported them to Pazair, he would be transported with joy; through Tuya, Pharaoh's closest advisers were approving his conduct.

'Ever since the death of my husband and my son's accession to the throne, I have watched over the country's happiness. Ramses is a great king: he has dispelled the threat of war, enriched the temples, and fed his people. Egypt remains the beloved land of the gods. But I am worried, Neferet. Will you be my confidante?'

'If you think me worthy of your trust, Majesty.'

'Ramses is more and more preoccupied, sometimes absent-minded, as if he had suddenly aged. His character has changed. He seems to have lost interest in fighting, in resolving difficulty after difficulty, and making light of obstacles.'

'Could he be ill?'

'Apart from his toothache, he is still the most vigorous and tireless of men. But for the first time in his life he is wary of me, and I can no longer read his inner thoughts. That would not shock me if, as is his custom, he had told me his decision face to face. But he is wary of me, and I do not know why. Speak of it to Judge Pazair. I am afraid for Egypt, Neferet. So many murders in these last few months, so many enigmas unresolved, and the king distancing himself from me, his new taste for solitude . . . Pazair must continue his investigations.'

'Do you think, Majesty, that Pharaoh's reign is threatened?'

'He is greatly loved and respected.'

'But are there not rumours that good fortune is deserting him?'

'That always happens when a king has reigned for a long time. Ramses knows the solution: to celebrate a festival of regeneration, to strengthen his pact with the gods, and breathe joy back into the souls of his subjects. The rumours do not trouble me. But why has Pharaoh promulgated decrees restating his authority, which no one is challenging?'

'Could it be that an insidious evil is weakening his spirit?'

'If it were, the court would soon see its effects. No, his faculties are intact; and yet he has changed.'

Neferet sensed that she must not ask any more questions. It was for Pazair to weigh up these exceptional confidences and know how to make use of them.

Tuya changed the subject. 'I greatly appreciated your dignity when Nebamon died. He was worthless as a man, but he knew how to impose his personality. He showed rare injustice towards you, so I have decided to make recompense for what he did. He and I were in charge of the main hospital in Memphis, but he is dead, and I am not a doctor. Tomorrow a decree shall be published appointing you overseer of that hospital.'

22

Two servants emptied jars of lukewarm water over Pazair, who washed himself with a cake of natron. Afterwards, he brushed his teeth with a scented reed and rinsed with a mixture of alum and dill. He shaved with his favourite razor, which was shaped like a carpenter's chisel, and rubbed his neck with oil of wild mint to repel flies, mosquitoes and fleas. He rubbed the rest of his body with ointment based on natron and honey. If necessary, in the midday heat he would use a preparation made from carob and incense to prevent his sweat from smelling unpleasant.

As he finished his ablutions, the inevitable happened. He sneezed twice, five times, ten times. His cold had returned, his obstinate cold, again accompanied by coughing spasms, pains round his eyes, and buzzing in his ears. Admittedly it was his own fault: he was overworking, forgetting to take his medicine, and not getting enough sleep. But he certainly needed a new remedy.

Consulting Neferet wasn't easy, because she rose at six and left shortly afterwards for the hospital she now ran – he had hardly seen her for a week. Determined to do well in her new position, she was giving it her all, for she was now responsible for the largest centre of healing in Egypt. Queen Tuya's decree, approved immediately by the tjaty, had received the assent of all the doctors and remedy-makers at the hospital. The temporary administrator, who had been blocking the delivery of medicines to Neferet, had become a mere doctor's assistant, and now looked after bedridden invalids.

Neferet had told the scribes at the hospital that her vocation was healing, not administration, and had asked them to carry out the orders from the tjaty's office, which she had no intention of disputing. This had won most of them over to their new overseer, who worked closely with the different specialist doctors. Some patients who came to the hospital were very sick people whom town and country doctors had failed to cure, while others were well-off people who wanted treatment which would prevent the appearance or exacerbation of certain ailments. Neferet paid a great deal of attention to the workshop where remedies were prepared and dangerous, poisonous substances were handled.

Since the pain round his eyes was getting worse and he had been left to his own devices, Pazair decided to go to the only place where he would get some attention: the main hospital. The gardens laid out in front of it were delightful. There was no hint of the suffering so close by.

A friendly nurse greeted the visitor. 'How can I help you?'

'It's an emergency. I would like to consult the hospital overseer, Doctor Neferet.'

'I'm afraid that won't be possible today.'

'Not even for her husband?'

'You are the Judge of the Porch?'

'I'm afraid so.'

'Please follow me.'

The nurse led him through a series of bathing-chambers furnished with three stone basins, the first for total immersion, the second for sitting baths, and the third for the legs and feet. Other places were reserved for sleep cures. Small, well-ventilated rooms housed patients who were watched over constantly by the doctors.

Neferet was checking the preparation of a remedy, and noting the coagulation time of a substance by consulting a water-clock. Two experienced remedy-makers were assisting her.

Pazair waited until she had finished over before coming forward. 'May a patient have the benefit of your care?'

'Is it urgent?'

'An emergency.'

Barely keeping a straight face, she led him into a consulting-room. The judge sneezed loudly, at least ten times.

'Hmm, you weren't joking. Any difficulty in breathing?'

'I've had a whistling noise in my chest ever since you stopped taking care of me.'

'What about your ears?'

'The left one's blocked.'

'Are you feverish?'

'A little.'

'Lie down on the stone bench. I must listen to your heart.'

'You already know what it says.'

'We are in a respectable place, Judge Pazair. I must ask you to behave with proper decorum.'

While she sounded his heart, the Judge of the Porch remained silent.

'You were right to tell me. A new course of treatment is needed.'

In the workshop, Neferet used a dowsing-wand to choose the appropriate remedy. It twitched in her hand when she passed it over a sturdy plant with broad, five-lobed leaves of pale green, and red berries.

'Bryony,' she said. 'It's a mortal poison, but used very much diluted it will eliminate the congestion and clear your breathing-passages.'

'Are you absolutely sure?'

'I'd stake my position on it.'

'Then give me some quickly. My scribes must be cursing me for being away so long.'

There was unheard-of uproar in the judge's offices. Scribes who were usually calm, who spoke quietly and never gesticulated, were shouting at each other, unsure what to do. Some said it was best to wait, in the judge's absence; others advocated exercising firmness – so long as they didn't have exercise it themselves; a third group demanded that the city guards be summoned. Broken tablets and torn papyri lay strewn across the floor.

Silence fell when Pazair arrived.

He looked around in astonishment. 'Have you been attacked?'

'In a manner of speaking,' replied an old scribe, aghast. 'We could not hold back the fury. Now she has invaded your office.'

Intrigued, Pazair crossed the huge room where the scribes worked and went into his own office. He found Panther kneeling on a mat, searching through the archives.

'Whatever has got into you?' he asked

'I want to know where you've hidden Suti.'

'Get up and leave my office.'

'Not until I know.'

'I shall not use force, but I shall summon Kem.'

That threat carried the day. She obeyed.

'We'll discuss this outside,' said Pazair.

She stalked out in front of him, watched with great interest by the scribes.

'Clear up this mess and get back to work,' he ordered them.

Pazair and Panther walked quickly and turned into a narrow, busy street. On a market day like this, buyers thronged around the peasants selling fruit and vegetables, in a great din of haggling. The judge and the Libyan escaped

183

from the tide of humanity and took refuge in a deserted, silent alleyway.

'I want to know where Suti's hiding,' she insisted, on the verge of tears. 'Since he left, I can't think of anything but him. I forget to put on my perfume and paint my face. I've lost all sense of time, I just wander round the streets.'

'He isn't hiding. He's on a delicate and dangerous mission.'

'With another woman.'

'Alone, and without help from anyone – man or woman.'

'But he's married!'

'He thought the marriage necessary to his investigation.'

'I love him, Judge Pazair, I'm dying of love for him. Can you understand that?'

Pazair smiled. 'Better than you think.'

'Where is he?'

'I can't tell you that, Panther. If I did, I'd put him in danger.'

'You wouldn't – I swear it! I'd never, never tell another soul.'

Moved, and convinced of her love and sincerity, Pazair yielded. 'He has enlisted in a party of miners which left from Kebet.'

Glowing with happiness, Panther kissed him on the cheek. 'I shall never forget your help. If I have to kill him, you'll be the first person to know.'

The rumour spread through all the provinces, from north to south. At Pi-Ramses, Pharaoh's royal capital in the Delta, at Memphis and at Thebes, it quickly infected all levels of government and deeply troubled the officials responsible for carrying out the tjaty's instructions.

Before he could read the report by General Asher that had sparked the rumours, Pazair had to resolve a housing problem which was tearing a family apart: two cousins had bought the same piece of land from a dishonest seller. Pazair dealt with the case quickly – he ruled that the seller must repay twice his profit – and then turned to Asher's report on the state of the Egyptian army.

The general considered the situation in Asia unstable because of the constant cuts in the Egyptian forces that kept the peace there, and said the small princedoms would eagerly unite under the banner of the elusive Libyan warlord Adafi. The troops' weapons were of poor quality, because since the victory over the Hittites no one had paid any attention to improving them. As for the state of the barracks, even in the interior of the country things were bad: neglected horses, damaged chariots which had not been repaired, lack of discipline, poorly trained officers. In the event of an invasion, would Egypt be capable of repelling it?

The impact of such a report would, Pazair knew, be strong and long lasting. He wondered what Asher was hoping to achieve by it. If the future proved Asher right, he would be seen as a clear-sighted prophet and would occupy a position of great strength, the position of a possible saviour of the country. And if Ramses gave him credit for analysing the problem correctly, Asher would insist that his demands be met; his influence would be strengthened accordingly.

Pazair thought of Suti. What arid track was he on at this hour of the day, hunting for virtually impossible evidence against the murderer who was trying to dictate the country's military strategy?

He summoned Kem, and said, 'Can you carry out a rapid investigation into the main barracks in Memphis?'

'In what respect?'

'The troops' morale, the state of their equipment, the health of both men and horses.'

'Easily, so long as I have an official reason.'

The judge suggested a plausible one: the search for a chariot which had knocked down several people and must bear signs of the accident. 'Do it quickly,' he urged.

As soon as Kem had left, Pazair hurried to the official residence of Bel-Tran, who was getting to grips with the inventory of grain harvests. The two men climbed up to the terrace of the building, away from indiscreet ears.

'Have you read Asher's report?' asked Pazair.

'It's horrifying.'

'Assuming it's accurate.'

'Do you think it isn't?'

'I suspect him of exaggerating the situation for his own benefit.'

'Is there any evidence of that?'

'We must gather it as quickly as possible.'

'Asher will be punished.'

'Perhaps not. If Ramses agrees with him, Asher will be have a free hand and will be seen as the saviour of Egypt. If that happens, no one will dare criticize him.'

Bel-Tran nodded his agreement.

'You wanted to help me,' said Pazair, 'and the time has come.'

'What do you need?'

'Information about our troops serving abroad, and on how much has been spent on weapons and military equipment over the last few years.'

'It won't be easy, but I'll try.'

On his return to his office, Pazair wrote a long letter to Kani, the High Priest of Karnak, asking him about the state of the troops stationed in the Theban region and of their equipment. The letter was written in a code based on the term 'medicinal plant', Kani's speciality, and entrusted to a reliable messenger.

'There's nothing much to report,' said Kem.

'A little more detail, please,' said Pazair.

'The barracks is calm, and the buildings and equipment are in good repair. I examined fifty chariots, and found that the officers keep them in excellent condition, as they do their horses.'

'What do they think of Asher's report?'

'They take it seriously, but they think it concerns all the barracks except theirs. By gaining their trust, I was able to inspect the one that lies furthest south of the city.'

'And what did you find?'

'Exctly the same thing: nothing to report. They also think Asher's criticism is well-founded – for other people.'

Pazair thanked Kem, and hurried off to see Bel-Tran. They met in the courtyard in front of the Temple of Ptah, where many people were chatting, indifferent to the priests' comings and goings.

'On the first point,' said Bel-Tran, 'I got conflicting information, because Asher is keeping to himself almost all information on the troops in Asia. Officially, the number of troops has been cut and there has been unrest again; but a scribe of the recruits assured me that the list of men in service hasn't changed. On the second point, it was easy to find out the truth, because the army records are kept at the Treasury. Spending has been the same for several years, and no lack of equipment has been reported.'

'So Asher lied.'

'His report is more subtle than that. He presents the facts in an alarmist manner, without actually stating too much. Many senior officers support him, and a number of courtiers are afraid of Hittite plots. They see Asher as a hero because he's giving people a much-needed jolt.'

Brave was curled up asleep at his master's feet. Pazair was sitting beside the pool, whose surface was covered with lotus-flowers. A breeze gently ruffled the dog's coat and the judge's hair. Neferet was consulting a medical papyrus which Mischief persisted in rolling up, despite her mistress's reprimands. The last glimmers of daylight bathed the garden ın golden light; tits, robins and swallows were singing their evening songs.

'Our army in in an excellent state,' said Pazair. 'Asher's report is a web of lies, which he hopes will make the civilian authorities panic and will weaken the troops' morale. If he succeeds, that will make it easier for him to take control.'

'Why doesn't Ramses censure him?' asked Neferet.

'He trusts him, because of his past feats of arms.'

'Can anything be done about it?'

'I must give my findings to Tjaty Bagey, who'll pass them on to Pharaoh. They'll be countersigned not only by Kem but by Kani, whose answer I've just received. Both at Thebes and at Memphis, our military strength is intact. The tjaty will extend the checks to the whole country and then take action against Asher.'

'Then perhaps this is the end for Asher.'

'Let's not take that for granted. He'll protest, proclaim his good faith and his love for the country, will accuse his subordinates of having given him false information. But he'll be stopped in his tracks. And I'm hoping to take my advantage further.'

'How?'

'By confronting him.'

General Asher was supervising the elite chariot troops' exercise in the desert. There were two men in each chariot; the officer fired his bow at a moving target, while his assistant handled the reins, driving at top speed. Any man who was clumsy was expelled from the corps.

When Pazair arrived, two footsoldiers asked him to wait and not to venture on to the practice area: a stray arrow might hit an incautious passer-by.

At last Asher, covered in dust, gave the signal to rest, and walked unhurriedly over to Pazair.

'You don't belong here, Judge,' he said.

'There is no part of Egypt where I don't belong,' retorted Pazair.

Asher's ratlike face tightened with annoyance, and he scratched the scar that ran down his chest from shoulder to navel. 'I'm going to wash and change. Come with me.'

Asher and Pazair went to the bath-house for senior officers. While two soldiers poured warm water over the general's body, the judge opened his attack.

'I'm contesting your report.'

'On what grounds?'

'That much of it is inaccurate.'

'You aren't a soldier – your opinion's worthless.'

'It is a matter of facts, not opinions.'

'I refute them.'

'Without knowing what they are?''

'I can easily guess. You walked around two or three barracks, and were shown a few brand-new chariots and a handful of soldiers who are happy with their lot. You're ignorant and incompetent, and you were duped.'

'Is that how you would describe the commander of Memphis's city guards and the High Priest of Karnak?'

The question put the general in an awkward position. He dismissed the soldiers and dried himself.

'They're new to their posts, and as inexperienced as you are.'

'That's a feeble argument.'

'What are you looking for now, Judge Pazair?'

'Still the same treasure: the truth. Your report is false, and I have sent my comments and objections to the tjaty.'

'You dared—'

'It was not daring, it was a duty.'

Asher stamped his foot in anger. 'That was a stupid thing to do! You'll get your fingers burnt.'

'That is for Tjaty Bagey to judge.'

'I'm the expert!'

'Our military strength is not in decline, and you know it perfectly well.'

The general's jerky movements, as he donned his kilt, betrayed his tension. 'Listen to me, Pazair. What matters is the spirit of my report – the details are unimportant.'

'What does that mean?'

'A good general must foresee the future in order to ensure the defence of the country.'

'Does that justify making alarmist, unfounded claims?'

'You don't understand.'

'Is there perhaps a link with Sheshi's activities?'

'Leave him out of it.'

'I'd like to question him.'

'You can't. He's in hiding.'

'On your orders?'

'On my orders.'

'I'm afraid I must insist.'

Asher's voice became unctuous. 'If I wanted to get the attention of the king, the tjaty and the court by pointing out our weaknesses, it was with the aim of removing them and getting a final agreement for the making of a new weapon which will render us invincible.'

'Your naivety surprises me, General.'

Asher's eyes narrowed like a cat's. 'What are you insinuating?'

'Your famous weapon is no doubt an unbreakable sword made of sky-iron.'

'Swords, spears, daggers – Sheshi's working on the project day and night. I shall demand that he be given back the block kept in the Temple of Ptah.'

'So it belonged to him, then?'

'The important thing is that he uses it.'

'Some lies can deceive even the most sceptical people.'

'What do you mean?'

'Sky-iron isn't unbreakable.'

'You're mad!'

'Sheshi's lying, either to you or to himself. The priests at Karnak will confirm what I say. The ritual use of sky-iron made you dream, mistakenly. You wanted to acquire a weapon of such power that even the highest authority in Egypt would have to fall in with your wishes. But you've failed.'

The ratlike face displayed utter bafflement. Was Asher, wondered Pazair, realizing that he had been fooled by his own accomplice?

As soon as the judge had left the bath-house, the general picked up a terracotta jar of warm water and smashed it against a wall.

23

Suti unrolled his mat and spread it out on a flat stone. Wearily, he lay down on his back and gazed up at the stars. The desert, the mountains, the rocks, the mine, the stiflingly hot galleries where you had to crawl on your belly, scraping off your skin . . . Most of the men were grumbling and already regretting an adventure which was turning out to be more exhausting than lucrative. But Suti was in his element. Sometimes he was so absorbed by the landscape that he even forgot Asher. He, who loved the pleasures of the town, had no difficulty in forming a bond with this hostile region, as if he had always lived here.

In the sand to his left, he heard a characteristic swishing. A horned viper passed close to the mat, leaving an undulating trail behind it. On the first night Suti had played the snake's little game and had been afraid of it, but now he was used to it. He knew instinctively that he wouldn't be bitten; scorpions and snakes did not frighten him. An accepted guest in their domain, he respected their customs and worried less about them than about the blood-drinking sand-tick, from which some of the miners were suffering badly. Its bite was painful, and the flesh became sore and infected. Ephraim kept sand-ticks away by sprinkling himself with a lotion made from marigolds. Suti was simply lucky: the ticks weren't interested in him.

Despite an exhausting day, the young man could not sleep. He got up, and walked slowly towards a dry riverbed which was bathed in moonlight. Moving about alone at night in the desert was mad. Fearsome gods and fantastical animals were on the prowl, devouring unwary wanderers, whose bodies were never found. If anyone wanted to get rid of him, this was the perfect time and place.

A faint sound put him on the alert. At the bottom of the hollow, where the water bubbled during the stormy rains, an antelope with lyre-shaped horns was scraping away determinedly at the sand with its front hooves, looking for an underground spring. Another antelope came to join it; this one had very long horns, scarcely curved at all, and white fur. The two animals were the incarnation of the god Set, whose inexhaustible energy they possessed. They were not mistaken: soon they were lapping up the precious water, which welled up between two round stones. They were followed by a hare and an ostrich. Fascinated, Suti sat down. The animals' nobility and happiness were a secret sight whose memory he would cherish for all eternity.

He heard someone coming and looked round. It was Ephraim.

The big man laid a hand on Suti's shoulder. 'You love the desert, little man. But it's a vice and if you go on feeding it you'll eventually see the falcon-headed, lion-bodied monster, which no hunter can pierce with arrows or catch with a noose. Then it'll be too late for you. The monster will seize you in its claws and carry you off into the darkness.'

'Why do you hate Egyptians?'

'I'm of Hittite descent, and I'll never accept the Egyptians as my masters. Here, on these desert tracks, I'm the one who's master.'

'How long have you been leading teams of miners?'

'Five years.'

'Haven't you made your fortune yet?'

'You ask too many questions,' growled Ephraim.

'If you've failed, what hope have I got?'

'Who says I've failed?'

Suti smiled. 'That's reassuring.'

'Don't be too quick to rejoice.'

'But if you're rich, why go on sweating and slaving?'

'I hate valleys, fields and the Nile. Even if I was made of gold, I wouldn't leave my mines.'

'Made of gold . . . I like that expression. Up to now, you've had us explore worked-out mines.'

'You're observant, little man. What better training could there be? When the serious work begins, the toughest men will be ready to search the belly of the mountain.'

'The sooner the better.'

'You're in a mighty hurry.'

'Why wait?'

'Hundreds of men have set out on the gold road, but almost all of them have failed.'

'Aren't the seams of ore marked?'

'The maps belong to the temples and never leave there. And anyone who tries to steal gold is immediately arrested by the desert patrols.'

'Can't one evade them?'

'Their dogs are everywhere.'

'But you've got the map in your head, haven't you?'

The bearded man sat down next to Suti. 'Who told you that?'

'No one, don't worry. But you're not a man to keep valuable information anywhere else.'

Ephraim picked up a pebble and crushed it between his fingers. 'If you try to deceive me, I'll kill you.'

'How many times do I have to tell you that all I want is to get rich? I want an enormous estate, horses, chariots, servants, a pine-forest, a—'

'A pine-forest? There aren't any in Egypt.'

'Who's talking about Egypt? I can't stay in this damned country. I want to settle in Asia, in a princedom Pharaoh's army won't enter.'

'You're beginning to interest me, boy. You're a criminal, aren't you?'

Suti didn't answer.

'The guards are looking for you, and you're hoping to escape by hiding among the miners. But those guards are stubborn. They won't rest till they've hunted you down.'

'This time they won't take me alive.'

'Have you been in prison?'

'I'll never let them lock me up again.'

'Which judge is after you?'

'Pazair, the Judge of the Porch.'

Ephraim whistled admiringly. 'You're big game! When that judge dies, a lot of people like you will throw a gigantic party.'

'He never gives up.'

'Perhaps fate will be against him.'

'My purse is empty; I'm in a hurry.'

'I like you, little man, but I'm not taking any risks. Tomorrow we'll be digging for the real thing, and then we'll see what you're made of.'

Ephraim divided his men into two teams. The first, larger one was set to collecting copper, which was vital for making tools, especially stone-cutters' chisels. Broken up and washed, the metal was smelted on the site of extraction in rudimentary furnaces, then poured into moulds. Sinai and the deserts provided large quantities of copper, which still had, however, to be imported from Syria and western Asia, as the communities of builders were so fond of it. The army used it, too, blending it with tin to produce strong blades.

The second team, to which Suti belonged, was made up of only ten determined men. Everyone knew that the real difficulties were just beginning. In front of them was the entrance to a gallery, a hell-mouth opening on to depths which might conceal treasure. Round their necks the miners strung their leather purses, which would be filled to bursting if they struck lucky. They wore only leather kilts and covered their bodies with sand.

Who would go first? That was the best position, but also the most dangerous. Suti was pushed forward. He turned round and struck out. A general tussle followed. Ephraim interrupted it, picking up a small fighter by the hair and making him cry out in pain.

'You,' he ordered, 'take the lead. You'll need a torch.'

The men formed a line. The passageway was narrow and very steep, and the miners bent double, looking for footholds. Their eyes scanned the walls, searching for the glint of a precious metal whose nature Ephraim hadn't specified. The leader moved too fast and raised a cloud of dust; the second, half-choked, pushed him in the back. Caught off balance, he lost his footing and tumbled down the slope to a level area below, where the miners were able to stand straight.

'He's passed out,' said one of his comrades.

'So much the better,' retorted another.

After getting their breath back, in the stifling atmosphere, they went on into the belly of the mine.

'There! Gold!'

The discoverer was immediately joined by two envious competitors, who knocked him to the ground.

'Fool! It was just a shiny stone.'

Suti sensed menace at every step: the men behind him intended to get rid of him. With the sure instinct of a wild animal, he ducked at the very moment they attacked him, trying to smash his skull with a stone. The first attacker fell head over heels, and Suti broke his ribs with a kick.

'I'll kill the next one,' he swore. 'Have you gone mad? If we go on like this, none of us will get out alive. Either we kill each other now or we share everything.'

The able-bodied men chose the second solution.

The miners crawled on into another passageway. Feeling ill, two gave up. The torch, which was made of rags soaked in sesame oil, was handed to Suti, who had no hesitation in taking the lead.

Even further down, in the darkness, he saw a flash of light. His mouth watering, he speeded up, and at last touched the treasure.

'Copper! It's only copper.'

Suti was determined to make Ephraim tell the truth about his ill-gotten gains. As he squeezed back out of the gallery, he was instantly astonished by the abnormal silence hanging over the site. The miners had been drawn up into two rows, under the watchful eyes of ten desert guards and their enormous dogs. Their leader was none other than the big man who had questioned Suti before he signed on.

'Here are the others,' said Ephraim.

Suti and his comrades were made to stand in a line, including the wounded; the dogs growled, ready to bite. Each guard held a ring to which were attached nine leather thongs, enabling him to strike hard and fast.

'We're in pursuit of a deserter,' said the big man. 'He ran from work duty, and a complaint has been lodged against him. I believe he's hiding among you fellows. The rules of the game are simple. If he gives himself up, or you denounce him, the matter will be settled. But if you keep quiet we'll question you all, using the punishment ring – no one will be spared. We'll repeat the process as many times as necessary.'

Suti's eyes met Ephraim's. The Hittite would not try to deceive the guards: betraying Suti would consolidate his reputation with the forces of law and order.

'Have a little courage, men,' said Ephraim. 'The runaway has gambled and lost. We miners aren't a rabble of layabouts.'

197

No one stepped forward.

Ephraim went closer to his men. Suti had no chance of escape. The miners themselves would turn against him.

The dogs barked and strained at the leash. The guards waited calmly for their prey.

Ephraim grabbed the diminutive fighter again, and threw him at the feet of the guards' commander. 'Here's your deserter.'

Suti felt the weight of the giant's gaze on him. For a moment, he thought he'd challenge Ephraim's denunciation. But the suspect, under the threat of the dogs, was already babbling a confession.

'I still like you, little man.'

'You deceived me,' said Suti angrily.

'I put you to the test. Anyone who can get out of that abandoned mine can get out of any kind of trouble.'

'You should have warned me.'

'The test wouldn't have been conclusive. Now I know what you're made of.'

'The guards will be back for me before long.'

'I know, so we aren't staying here. As soon as I have all the copper the overseer at Kebet wants, I shall send three-quarters of the men back to the valley with it.'

'And then?'

'And then, with the men I've have chosen, we shall carry out an expedition which hasn't been authorized by the temple.'

'If you don't go back with your miners, the guards will be after you, too.'

'If I succeed, it'll be too late. This will be my last exploration.'

'Won't there be too many of us?'

'On the gold road you need bearers, for part of the journey. Usually, little man, I go back alone.'

*

Tjaty Bagey received Pazair in his office, just before he was due to go home for lunch. He sent away his secretary, and dipped his swollen feet in a stone basin of luke-warm salt water. Although Neferet's treatment meant his illness was no worse, the tjaty had not given up his wife's fat-laden cooking and was continuing to overload his liver.

Pazair was growing used to Bagey's coldness. The tjaty's long, stern, unattractive face and questioning eyes showed clearly that he was not interested in making people warm to him. On the walls of his office hung maps of the provinces, some of which he had drawn himself when he was a map-maker.

'You have set me no easy task, Judge Pazair. Ordinarily, a Judge of the Porch is content to fulfil his many duties without investigating in the field.'

'The seriousness of the case required it.'

'Shall I add that military matters are not within your remit?'

'The trial did not clear General Asher of all suspicion; I am in charge of pursuing the case. It is the man himself who interests me.'

'Why dwell on his report about the state of our troops?'

'Because it is a lie, as is proved by the irrefutable testimonies of the head of the Memphis guards and the High Priest of Karnak. When I convene a new trial, this document will add weight to the case. The general is still making a mockery of the truth.'

'Convene a new trial? Is that really what you intend to do?'

'Asher is a murderer. Suti, unlike the general, did not lie.'

'But Suti is in difficulty with the law.'

Pazair had been worried that the tjaty would raise that point.

Bagey had not raised his voice, but he seemed annoyed. 'Asher has lodged a complaint against him, and the charge is a serious one: desertion.'

'That charge cannot be substantiated,' objected the judge. 'Suti was taken on by the Memphis guards before he received the document – Kem's registers are quite clear on that point. That means that Suti the former soldier belongs to a state body, and that there has been no interruption of his career and no desertion.'

Bagey made notes on a clay tablet. 'I suppose you can prove your case?'

'Yes, I can.'

'What do you really think of Asher's report?'

'That it is intended to create confusion in order to make the general seem like the country's saviour.'

'Suppose he is telling the truth?'

'My first inquiries indicate precisely the opposite. I admit they've been limited in time and scope, but you, Tjaty, have the ability to reduce the general's arguments to nothing.'

The tjaty reflected.

Suddenly, Pazair was seized by a terrible doubt. Was Bagey in league with Asher? Was the image of the unbending, honest, incorruptible tjaty merely an illusion? If it was, the Judge of the Porch's career was about to come to an abrupt end, under some administrative pretext. At least he wouldn't have long to wait. Bagey's reply would tell him what to expect.

'Excellent work,' declared Bagey. 'Every day you justify your appointment and you surprise me. I was wrong to favour age in designating senior judges. However, I console myself by assuming that you are an exception. Your analysis of Asher's report is very worrying, and the support of Commander Kem and the High Priest of Karnak, even though both were only recently appointed, gives it a great deal of weight. Moreover, you stood firm in the face of my doubts. I shall therefore challenge the accuracy of the report and order a detailed inventory of our available weapons.'

Pazair waited until he was safely home and in Neferet's arms before he wept with joy.

General Asher sat down on the shaft of a chariot. The barracks was asleep, the sentries dozing. What had a country as powerful as Egypt to fear, united round its king and solidly built on ancestral values which not even the strongest winds had shaken?

Asher had lied, betrayed and murdered in order to become a powerful and respected man. He wanted to seal an alliance with the Hittites and the Asian princes, to create an empire of which Ramses himself would not have dared dream. The illusion had been shattered, because of one piece of ill fortune. He had been deceived for months: Sheshi had used him.

The great General Asher! Soon he would be a helpless puppet, unable to withstand Judge Pazair's repeated attacks. He had not even had the pleasure of having Suti locked up. Complaint rejected and report refused by the tjaty. The re-examination would lead to Asher's condemnation, and he would be sent to prison for damaging the troops' morale. When Bagey took hold of a matter, he became as fierce and stubborn as a hound gripping a bone between its teeth.

Why had Sheshi encouraged him to write that report? Dazzled by the idea of becoming a national hero, acquiring the stature of a statesman, gaining the people's loyalty, Asher had lost touch with reality. Through deceiving others, he had eventually deceived himself. Like Sheshi, he believed in the extinction of Ramses' kingdom, the mixing of the races, the overthrow of the traditions inherited from the age of the pyramids. But he had forgotten the existence of archaic men like Tjaty Bagey and Judge Pazair, servants of Ma'at, lovers of the truth.

Asher had suffered from being written off as a soldier of no account, whose future was already marked out, and who lacked ambition. The instructors had been very wrong about him. Classified in a category from which he could not escape, the general could no longer bear the army. He would either control it or destroy it. The discovery of Asia, of its princes skilled in trickery and lies, of its clans' constantly changing alliances, had prompted him to conspire and form bonds with Adafi, the leader of the rebellion.

A plaything in the hands of a trickster: his future glory was toppling into ridicule. But his false friends did not know that the wounded animal still had unsuspected resources. Ridiculous in his own eyes, Asher would rehabilitate himself by dragging down his allies with him.

Why had evil taken hold of him? He could have been content with serving Pharaoh, loving his country, and following in the footsteps of the generals who had been satisfied with carrying out their duty. But the taste for intrigue had wormed its way into him like a sickness, coupled with the desire to gain control of what properly belonged to other people.

Asher could not stand people who stepped out of their proper station, like Suti or Pazair. They diminished him and prevented him from blossoming. Some built, others destroyed; if he belonged to the latter category, were the gods not responsible for that? No one could alter their will.

As a man was born, so he died.

24

Eyes half-closed, tiny ears quivering, nostrils just above the surface of the water, the hippopotamus yawned. When another male bumped into him, he growled. These two huge crocodile-killers led the two main herds that shared the Nile south of Memphis. They loved swimming in deep water, where despite their bulk – each one weighed more than two chariots – they stopped looking ungainly and became almost graceful. They hated being disturbed when they were sleeping or resting, and were liable to open their jaws almost flat and then run the intruder through with canine teeth nearly a cubit long. Easily roused to anger, they yawned to frighten the adversary. Usually, they climbed up on to the riverbank at night and fed on fresh grass, which it took them a whole day to digest. During the day they enjoyed the sun on a sandy bank, far from human habitation, often going back into the water to protect their delicate skin.

The two battle-scarred males faced each other, baring their teeth. Then, abandoning their mutual hostility, they swam side by side to the bank. There madness overtook them, and they ravaged the crops in the fields, smashed the trees in the orchards, and spread panic among the farmers. A small child who did not dodge aside quickly enough was trampled and killed.

Twice, three times, the male hippos began again, while the

females protected their young against crocodile attacks. Several village headmen appealed to the Memphis guards for help. Kem arrived and organized the hunt. The two males were killed, but other calamities struck the countryside: marauding flocks of sparrows, a plague of house-mice and field-mice, mysterious deaths of cattle, colonies of worms in the grain reserves – not to mention hordes of scribes fiercely determined to check the tax declarations. To fend off the bad luck, many farmers wore a fragment of cornelian on a necklace; the flame it contained defeated the harmful attacking forces.

Nevertheless, rumours spread apace. The red hippopotamus was becoming destructive because Pharaoh's protective magic was weakening. A poor annual flood was predicted, which surely proved that the king's power over nature was exhausted, and that he must renew his alliance with the gods by celebrating a festival of regeneration.

The weapons inspections and checks ordered by the tjaty took their course, but Pazair was still worried, because there had been no news from Suti. He had written to Suti in code, telling him that Asher's position was becoming untenable and that there was no point in taking big risks. In a few days, Suti's mission might even have become unnecessary.

Something else worried him, too. According to Kem, Panther had disappeared. She had left during the night, without telling her neighbours where she was going, and none of Kem's informants had spotted her in Memphis. Was it possible that, unhappy and deeply hurt, she had returned to Libya?

The festival of Imhotep, model of the sages and patron of scribes, gave the judge a rest day, which he devoted to treating his cold and cough with solutions of bryony and to thinking about his problems. Seated on a folding stool, he admired a large flower arrangement Neferet had created, binding together palm-leaf fibres, persea-leaves and masses of lotus-petals. Winding the carefully concealed cord required great dexterity. It was clear that Brave appreciated this work of art: he stood on his hind legs, put his paws on the table and tried to eat the lotus-flowers. Pazair called him off a dozen times, before presenting him with something more attractive in the form of a bone.

A storm was threatening. Heavy dark clouds, coming from the north, would soon block out the sun. Animals and people were becoming anxious, insects began to bite. The cleaning-woman was running about in all directions, and the cook had broken a jar. Everyone both longed for and feared the rain. It would be torrential, damaging the humblest houses and, in the areas close to the desert, forming torrents of mud and stones.

Despite the heavy demands of her work at the hospital, Neferet ruled her household with a smile and never raised her voice. The servants adored her, while they feared Pazair, whose stern appearance concealed shyness. True, he found the gardener rather lazy, the cleaning woman too slow and the cook greedy, but they all took pleasure in their work, so he held his tongue.

With a light brush, Pazair himself groomed Way-Finder, who found the stifling heat very trying. Cool water and fresh fodder cheered the donkey, who flopped down in the shade of a sycamore. Covered in sweat, Pazair felt in need of a wash. He crossed the garden, where the dates were ripening, walked along the wall separating it from the street, passed the poultry-yard, where the geese were honking, and entered the big house – he was at last beginning to get used to it.

The sound of voices indicated that the bathing-room was occupied. A young servant-girl, standing on a low wall, was pouring the contents of a water-jar on to Neferet's golden body. The lukewarm water slid over her silken skin, then ran away along a pipe whose opening was in the limestone paving covering the floor.

The judge sent away the girl and took her place.

'What an honour,' said Neferet, smiling. 'The Judge of the Porch in person. Would he be willing to massage me?'

'He is your most devoted servant.'

They went into the massage-room.

Pazair adored Neferet's slender waist, her sun-kissed sensuality, her firm, high breasts, her softly curved hips, her slender hands and feet. More in love with her every day, he could not decide whether to gaze at her without touching her or to drag her into a whirlpool of caresses.

She stretched out, face down, on a stone bench covered with a mat, while Pazair undressed and then selected aromatic oils; some of the phials and vases were made of glass in different colours, others of alabaster. He spread a little oil on his wife's back, and gently rubbed it in from her bottom to the nape of her neck. Neferet considered a daily massage very important. It eased tension, eased muscle spasms, calmed the nerves, and improved the circulation of energy into the organs, which were all linked to the tree of life where spinal marrow was formed, and also maintained balance and good health.

Pazair picked up a box in the shape of a naked girl swimming, pushing in front of her a duck with jointed wings; its body served as a container. Pazair scooped up some ontment, this time scented with jasmine, and smoothed it over Neferet's neck.

The shiver his touch produced did not escape him. His lips followed his fingers; Neferet rolled over and welcomed her lover.

The storm had still not broken.

Pazair and Neferet ate lunch in the garden, much to the delight of Brave, who careered round the little rectangular tables, made of reeds and papyrus stems, on which a servant-girl had set the cups, dishes and jars. The judge had tried in vain to train the dog not to beg during meals, but Brave had detected an ally in Neferet – anyway, how could his sensitive nose resist such delicious food?

'I'm feeling hopeful,' said Pazair.

'That's unusual for you.'

'Asher must not escape us. A murderer and a traitor . . . How can anyone soil himself like that? I never thought I'd have to fight against absolute evil.'

'You may encounter worse things than Asher.'

'Now you're being pessimistic.'

'I'd love simply to be happy, but I can feel that our happiness is being threatened.'

'Because of the investigation?'

'You're becoming more and more exposed. Do you really think Asher will let himself be struck down without fighting back?'

'I'm convinced he's only a minor player, not the leader of the conspiracy. He was deceived about the sky-iron – his accomplices lied to him.'

'He might have been play-acting.'

'No, I'm sure he wasn't.'

Neferet took her husband's hand. This simple contact was all they needed to communicate with each other. Neither the monkey nor the dog disturbed them, respecting the beauty of a moment when two people achieved a unity above and beyond themselves.

The cook shattered this paradise.

'It's happened again,' she complained. 'The chambermaid has filched the medallion of fish I was going to use to garnish your meal.'

Reluctantly, Neferet got up and went to investigate. The guilty servant, who had deprived the judge of his favourite delicacy, had hidden, well aware of the enormity of her crime. The cook called her in vain, then began to search the house.

Her scream frightened Brave, who hid under a table. Pazair ran to see what the matter was.

He found the cook crying as she bent over the chamber-maid, who lay like a broken doll on the paved floor of the reception-chamber.

Neferet was already examining her. 'She's paralysed,' she said.

When the shadow-eater saw Judge Pazair come out of the house, he cursed his bad luck. He had prepared his attack with minute attention to detail, using all the information about Pazair's tastes that he had got from a talkative servant-girl. He had disguised himself as a fish-seller and had sold the cook a fine grey mullet and a little medallion with pink, appetising flesh.

To make the medallion, he had used the liver of a puffer-fish, which inflated itself with air when a predator threatened it. As well as the bones and the head, the liver contained a deadly poison. The shadow-eater had used only a tiny dose, so as to produce incurable paralysis.

A stupid, greedy girl had cost him certain success. He would have to try again and again, until he succeeded.

'We'll care for her at the hospital,' said Neferet, 'but there's no hope of improvement.'

'Do you know what caused it?' asked Pazair, in great distress.

'I would wager it was a fish.'

'Why?

'Because our cook bought a grey mullet and a medallion from a travelling fish-seller, who had both fresh and prepared fish. The medallion must have been made from poisonous fish.'

'That means the crime was premeditated.'

'The dose was calculated to cripple, not to kill. And you

were the chosen victim. Nobody would murder a judge, would they? But they could stop him thinking and acting.'

Trembling, Neferet took refuge in Pazair's arms. She imagined him powerless, his eyes glazed, foam around his lips, his limbs motionless. Even like that, she would love him till death.

'He'll try again,' said Pazair. 'Did the cook give you a description of him?'

'Only a very vague one. An ordinary middle-aged man, not the sort you'd remember.'

'Then it wasn't Denes or Qadash. It might have been Sheshi, perhaps, or a killer in their pay. He made a big mistake in letting us know he exists. I shall set Kem on his trail.'

The council of doctors and remedy-makers charged with appointing the kingdom's new principal doctor received the first candidates to be approved by the law. They were an eye specialist, a doctor from Elephantine, Nebamon's former right-hand man, and Qadash.

Like his colleagues, Qadash answered questions about his methods, presented the discoveries he had made during his career, and disclosed his failures and their causes. He was questioned at length about his plans.

The votes were split, and no candidate achieved the required majority. A supporter of Qadash annoyed the council with his biased advocacy, and was sternly warned against following past practice: nobody would accept the sort of vote-fixing Nebamon had encouraged. The supporter admitted defeat.

A second round of voting brought the same result. The kingdom would therefore have to remain without a principal doctor.

'General Asher? Here?' asked Denes in surprise.

His steward confirmed that the general had arrived at the gates.

'Tell him— No, let him come in. But not here, in the stable.'

Denes took the time to do his hair and perfume his skin. He cut off two long white hairs, which spoiled the neatness of his narrow fringe of beard. It was very annoying to have to talk to that hidebound old soldier, but Asher might still be useful – notably as a scapegoat.

He found the general admiring a magnificent grey horse.

'A fine beast,' said Asher. 'Is it for sale?'

'Everything's for sale, General, that's the law of life. The world is divided into two categories: those who can buy, and the rest.'

'Spare me your homespun reasoning. Where is your friend Sheshi?'

'How should I know?'

'He's your most faithful ally.'

'I have dozens.'

'He's supposed to be working on making new weapons, under my supervision, but he hasn't been to the workshop for three days.'

'I am sorry, but your problems don't interest me very much.'

Asher barred Denes's way. 'You thought I was a fool who'd be easy to control, and Sheshi pushed me into a mantrap. Why?'

'Your imagination's running away with you.'

'If everything's for sale, sell me Sheshi. Name your price.'

Denes hesitated. One day he'd grow tired of Sheshi's servility, but this was not the time to get rid of him. He had another role in mind for his best supporter.

He said, 'You're asking a great deal, General.'

'Are you refusing?'

'There are the bonds of friendship to consider.'

'I've been stupid, but you don't know what I'm really capable of. You were wrong to make a fool of me.'

*

Qadash gesticulated wildly. His white hair standing on end, all the little veins on his nose straining fit to burst, he called upon the gods of sky, earth and the world between to bear witness to his misfortune.

'Calm down,' said Denes, embarrassed. 'Be like Sheshi.'

The inventor was sitting, sipping a sweet drink, on the floor in the darkest corner of the dining-chamber where the three men had eaten. The atmosphere was sinister. Nenophar was still trying to undermine Bel-Tran at court, but she was making scant progress and was getting more and more angry about it.

'Calm down? How do you explain your failure to have me made principal doctor?'

'It's merely a temporary setback.'

'But you bought the same doctors Nebamon did.'

'A simple misunderstanding. You can rely on me to remind them of our contract. At the next vote there'll be no unpleasant surprises.'

'I'm going to be principal doctor – you promised! Once I'm appointed, we'll control all the drugs and poisons. We must have control of the country's health – it's essential.'

'It will fall into our hands, as will the other organs of power.'

Qadash hitched up the shawl wound round his body, covering his cat-skin corslet. 'Why hasn't the shadow-eater done something?'

'He needs more time.'

'Time, always time! I'm an old man, and I want to make the most of my new advantages.'

'Being impatient won't help us.'

'Sheshi,' said Qadash, 'what do you think? Oughtn't we to hurry?'

'Sheshi must stay in hiding,' explained Denes.

Qadash lost his temper. 'I thought we held the reins!'

'We do, but Asher's position is getting weaker. Judge

Pazair challenged his report, and the tjaty is following up Pazair's findings.'

'That man Pazair again! When will we be rid of him?'

'The shadow-eater's dealing with that. But we've no need to hurry. People are grumbling more every day about Ramses.'

Sheshi took a sip of his drink.

'I'm tired,' confessed Qadash. 'You and I are already rich. Why do we need more?'

Denes pursed his lips. 'I don't quite understand you.'

'We could simply give up.'

'It's too late.'

'Denes is right,' said Sheshi.

Qadash rounded on him. 'Have you ever thought about being yourself, just once?'

'Denes commands, and I obey.'

'And supposing he leads you to ruin?'

'I believe in a new country, which only we are capable of building.'

'Those are Denes's words, not your own.'

'Are you saying you disagree with us?'

'Pah!' Qadash turned away sulkily.

'I grant you,' Denes said, 'that it's annoying to have supreme power within our grasp, and yet to have to wait. But you must admit that we're avoiding taking unnecessary risks and the mesh we've woven is indestructible.'

'Will Asher hunt me for long?' asked Sheshi anxiously.

'You're out of his reach – he's at bay.'

'But he's stubborn and vicious,' objected Qadash. 'Didn't he come to cause you trouble, even threaten you? Asher won't go down alone. He'll drag us down with him.'

'That is certainly what he intends to do,' agreed Sheshi, 'but he's deluding himself again. Don't forget, he doesn't hold a single key. By seeing himself as Egypt's saviour, he's doomed himself.'

'But you encouraged him, didn't you?' said Qadash.

'He was becoming a problem.'

'At least with him Judge Pazair has a bone to gnaw,' laughed Denes. 'There'll be a fight to the death between those two, and we must encourage them. The more ferocious the fight, the more blinded the judge will be.'

'But what if the general tries force against you?' asked Qadash. 'He already suspects that you're hiding Sheshi.'

'Can you imagine him attacking my house at the head of an army?'

Taking offence, Qadash grew sullen.

'We're like gods,' Denes assured him. 'We've created a river and no dam can stem its flow.'

Neferet was brushing the dog, while Pazair was reading a scribe's report littered with errors. Suddenly, his attention was caught by a bizarre sight. Ten paces away from him, on the rim of the lotus-pool, a magpie was attacking another bird, stabbing with its beak.

He put down the papyrus, and went and chased the magpie away. He found that its prey was a swallow, its wings spread out and its head covered in blood. The magpie had pecked out one of its eyes and torn open its head; spasms still racked its lacerated body. Pazair was horror-struck: the swallow was one of the forms Pharaoh's soul assumed when it rose up to heaven.

'Neferet, come quickly!'

She ran up. Like Pazair, she revered the beautiful bird, which bore two names, 'Greatness' and 'Stability'. Its joyful dances in the gold and orange light of the sunset made the heart sing.

Neferet knelt and picked up the wounded bird. In her warm, gentle hands it relaxed, glad to have found refuge.

'We can't save it,' she said sadly.

'I shouldn't have interfered.' Pazair was angry with

himself for his thoughtlessness. Man ought not to interfere in nature's cruel game, or step between life and death.

The bird's claws sank into Neferet's hands, clinging to her as though to the branch of a tree. Despite the pain, she did not put it down.

Pazair was inconsolable: he had committed a crime against the spirit. He was unworthy to be a judge, because he had inflicted pointless suffering on a swallow, tearing it away from its destiny.

'Wouldn't it be better to kill it? If necessary, I—'

'You couldn't do it.'

'I'm responsible for its death-agonies. How can anyone ever trust me again?'

25

Princess Hattusa was dreaming of another world. She, who had been given to Egypt to seal the peace with the Hittites, was nothing but a deserted woman.

The wealth of her harem did not console her. She had hoped for love, for Pharaoh's warm affection, but instead had to live a lonelier and more frightening life than that of a recluse. The more her life was diluted in the waters of the Nile, the more she hated Egypt.

When would she again see Hattusa, the great Hittite capital after which she was named? It lay on a high plateau, at the far edge of an inhospitable landscape made up of ravines, gorges and steep mountains beyond arid plains – the terrain protected the city from attack. The city was a fortress, built from enormous blocks of stone, and it loomed over enclosed hillsides and valleys, a symbol of the pride and savagery of the first Hittites, who had been warriors and conquerors. Its ramparts followed the contours of the landscape, adapting themselves to the rocky peaks and spurs. By their very presence they repulsed invaders. As a child, the princess had run through the steep alleyways, stolen cups of honey placed on rocks to placate the demons, played ball with boys who vied with each other in skill and power.

In those days, she had not counted the hours.

Of all the foreign princesses who had come to live at the

Egyptian court as tokens of alliance and in respect for treaties, not one had ever returned to her own country. Only the Hittite army could deliver Princess Hattusa from her gilded prison. She knew very well that neither her father nor her family had given up their plans to seize the Delta and the Nile valley, to turn Egypt into a colony of slaves and a gigantic grain-store. She must eat away at the country's foundations, undermine it from inside, weaken Ramses and impose herself as regent. Many women had reigned in the past, and it was a woman who had inspired the war of liberation from the Hyksos invaders in the north of the country. Hattusa had no other choice: by freeing herself, she would offer her people the most wonderful victories.

Denes had not realized that in offering her the sky-iron he was strengthening her belief and her powers. Among the Hittites, anyone who owned sky-iron obtained the favour of the gods. There was no better way of communicating with them than through this treasure from the depths of space. As soon as she had the block in her possession, Hattusa would have it made into amulets, necklaces, bracelets and rings. She would dress herself in sky-iron, would look like the daughter of the fire-stones that tore through the clouds.

Denes was a pretentious idiot, but he would be useful. Disrupting Egypt's trade was a severe blow to Ramses' prestige; but there was another, even more effective, way to open up the road to conquest.

Hattusa was preparing to fight the decisive battle. She must persuade one man, just one, in order to split Egypt apart and thus open a breach into which the Hittites would pour.

At noon, the Temple of Amon in Karnak was dozing. Of the three offertory rituals that the High Priest celebrated in the king's name, the mid-morning ritual was the shortest. It consisted simply of venerating the closed innermost shrine containing the divine statue, which had been brought back to life at the dawn ceremony, and ensuring that the invisible power made fertile the immense stone vessel that guaranteed the world's harmony.

Kani the gardener, though he was now High Priest of the Temple of Amon and the third most important official in the country after Pharaoh and the tjaty, had lost none of his peasant ways. Some of the haughtier scribes, who had been educated at the best schools in the country, looked down on his lined skin and calloused hands, but he ignored them and ruled the men with the same care he gave to his plants. And, despite the heavy demands of the daily rituals and administration, he allowed no one else to take charge of the garden where he grew medicinal plants.

To everyone's surprise, Kani had gained the support of the whole priesthood, which was notoriously difficult to charm. He had no time for acquired privileges, and was determined that the temple's estates should be prosperous and the divine service maintained in respect of the Rule. Since he knew no method of achieving this but hard work and the love of a job well done, that was the method he applied. His words, which could be somewhat earthy, often shocked scribes accustomed to more delicacy, but he never spared himself when it came to work, and knew how to impose his will. There had been no serious opposition to him. Despite all the gloomy predictions, Karnak obeyed him and Ramses' courtiers never failed to commend him on his excellent choice.

That was all nonsense, in Hattusa's eyes.

The king, the supreme tactician, had avoided appointing someone with a strong personality who might have clashed with him. Ever since the reign of Akhenaton, relations between Pharaoh and the High Priest of Amon had been tense. Karnak was too wealthy, too powerful, too big; the god of victories reigned there. True, the king appointed the High Priest, but once in his post the latter always tried to extend his power. The day a schism appeared between a High Priest, master of the South, and a king reduced to reigning only over the North, Egypt would be doomed.

Kani's appointment was her opportunity to achieve just that. A man of the people, a peasant, would soon grow intoxicated by luxury and wealth. Having become king of a temple, he would aspire to govern the provinces of Middle Egypt, then the whole country. He did not know it yet, but Hattusa was certain of it. It was up to her to reveal Kani to himself, to arouse in him an all-consuming ambition, to seal an alliance against Ramses. No lever could be more effective than the High Priest of Amon.

Hattusa had dressed simply, without a necklace or jewels; austerity suited the immense pillared hall where the High Priest had agreed to receive her. No one would have been able to distinguish Kani from the other priests, had he not been wearing the gold ring that was the emblem of his office. With his shaven head and broad chest, he was far from elegant. The princess congratulated herself on her appearance: he must dislike coquetry.

'Shall we walk?' he suggested.

'This place is magnificent.'

'It either crushes us or raises us up.'

'Ramses' builders and craftsmen are geniuses.'

'They express the will of Pharaoh, as do you and I.'

'I am only his secondary wife, part of his diplomacy.'

'You symbolize peace with the Hittites.'

'I am not fulfilled by being a symbol.'

'Do you wish to withdraw into the temple? The priestesses of Amon would welcome you gladly. Since the death of Nefertari, the Great Royal Wife, they feel they have lost a mother.'

'I have other, more ambitious plans,' said Hattusa.

'Do they concern me?'

'To the highest degree.'

'As you can see, I am surprised.'

'When Egypt's destiny hangs in the balance, surely the High Priest of Karnak should not remain indifferent?'

'That destiny is in Ramses' hands.'

'Even if he holds you in contempt?'

'I did not receive that impression.'

'Because you do not know him – his duplicity has deceived many people. To him, the office of High Priest of Amon is an inconvenience, and he sees no solution, in the short term, except to oust the holder and occupy it himself.'

'But he does so already,' Kani pointed out. 'Pharaoh is the sole intermediary between the gods and his people.'

'I am not concerned with the worship of the gods. Ramses is a tyrant, and your powers hinder him.'

'What are you suggesting?'

'That Thebes and its High Priest should refuse to accept this dictatorship.'

'To oppose Pharaoh is to deny life.'

'You come from a modest background; I am a princess. Let us be allies. We shall have the ear of both the people and the court. We shall create another Egypt.'

'Setting South and North against each other would break the country's backbone and cause paralysis. If Pharaoh no longer links the Two Lands, misery, poverty and invasion will be our lot.'

'It is Ramses who is leading us to that disaster, and only you and I can avert it. If you help me, you'll become very rich.'

'Lift up your head, Princess, and look around you,' said Kani. 'There is no wealth in the world greater than to gaze upon the gods, who live for ever in these stones.'

'You are Egypt's last hope. If you do not act, Ramses will lead the country to ruin.'

'You are a disappointed woman, bent on vengeance. Unhappiness oppresses you, and you wish to ruin your adopted land. To divide Egypt, break its backbone, turn it into a Hittite province . . . Is that what you secretly want?'

'What if it is?'

'That would be high treason, Princess. The judges would demand the death penalty.'

'You are missing your chance to save Egypt.'

'At the heart of this temple neither chance nor mischance exists, only the service of the gods.'

'You are wrong.'

'If it is wrong to be loyal to Pharaoh, this world no longer deserves to exist.'

Hattusa had failed. Her lip trembled. 'Will you denounce me?'

'The temple loves silence. Silence the voice of destruction within yourself, and you will know peace.'

The swallow clung to life. Neferet had settled it in a basket lined with straw, safe from cats and other predators. She dripped a little water into its damaged beak. Unable to feed itself, let alone fly, the bird was becoming used to her presence, and was unalarmed when she took its basket out into the garden so that it might feel the sun's warmth.

Pazair was still angry with himself for his stupid interference.

'Why don't you question Nenophar again?' asked Neferet. 'Serious suspicions have fallen on her.'

'She's the official steward of fabrics, and an excellent needlewoman, I know, but I can't see her murdering Branir in cold blood. She's haughty, loud, sure of herself, full of her own importance—'

'Or perhaps just an accomplished actress?'

'I agree. And she's also physically strong.'

'Didn't the murderer attack Branir from behind?'

'Yes, that's right.'

'Then accuracy mattered more than strength – plus having a

good knowledge of the body, so as to strike in the right place.'

'Nebamon is still the best suspect.'

'Before he died he told me the truth. He wasn't guilty.'

'If I summon Nenophar before a court, she'll deny the charge and will be acquitted. All I have is some worrying clues, not proof. Questioning her again would bear no fruit. She'd protest her innocence, call upon her many relations and friends to support her, and submit a complaint of harassment. I need something new.'

'Have you told Kem about the attempted poisoning?'

'He and Killer are watching me day and night – they take it in turns to sleep.'

'Can't he send guards to protect you?'

'I've already suggested that, but he doesn't trust them.'

'You won't stop him protecting you, will you?' asked Neferet anxiously.

'Sometimes it's highly inconvenient.'

'Judge of the Porch, your duties take precedence over your convenience.'

'Do you think I'm behaving like an old man?'

She considered for a moment. 'That's a matter which ought to be examined carefully. We'll see, tonight, if—'

He caught her in his arms, lifted her and carried her indoors. 'This old man will marry you as many times as he has to. Why wait until tonight?'

The Judge of the Porch held his seal over the papyrus. Since the early morning, the seal had given authorization to a huge number of documents relating to the proper conduct of agricultural works, controls on property revenues, and the delivery of goods. Pazair read quickly and could get the gist of a report in a few seconds.

This one shocked him. 'Five days' delay for a delivery of fresh fruit?'

'That's correct,' said a scribe, nodding.

'It's unacceptable. I refuse to approve this. Have you set a fine?'

'I sent the necessary documentation to my colleague in Thebes.'

'What was his reply?'

'It hasn't arrived yet.'

'Why not?'

'They're overwhelmed by similar delays.'

'This chaos has been going on for over a week, and nobody told me!'

The scribe began to stammer an excuse. 'There were more important inquir—'

'More important? Dozens of villages are at risk of running out of fresh food. It seems unimportant to you only because of the size of your belly!'

Thoroughly discomfited, the scribe laid a pile of papyri on the judge's mat. 'There have been other delays, too, in the delivery of other goods. We've just had warning of a very alarming one: no fresh vegetables from Middle Egypt will reach the Memphis barracks for ten days.'

Pazair blanched. 'Can you imagine the soldiers' reaction? To the docks, quickly!'

Kem himself drove the chariot alongside the canal that ran parallel to the Nile, with its warehouses and granaries, and drew up at the docks where goods arrived. The instant the chariot stopped, Pazair leapt out and ran to the office where fresh produce was registered.

Inside, a small boy was fanning two sleepy scribes.

'What are our stocks of fruit and vegetables?' demanded Pazair.

'Who are you?' asked one of the scribes.

'The Judge of the Porch.'

The two men jumped to their feet in horror, and bowed very low.

'Forgive us, Judge,' said the scribe. 'For several days we've had no work at all, because the deliveries have been disrupted.'

'Where are the boats being delayed?'

'Nowhere. They arrive at Memphis, but not with the right cargoes. Today, the largest fruit-boat was carrying stones. What can we do?'

'Is it still at the quayside?'

'It is leaving again soon, bound for Thebes.'

Pazair and Kem, accompanied by Killer, crossed a naval boatyard, and reached the port, where a seagoing vessel was about to leave for Cyprus. On the fruit-boat, the sails were being hoisted. The judge stepped on to the gangplank.

'Just a moment,' said Kem, holding him back by the arm.

'We must hurry.'

'I have a bad feeling.'

The baboon was sitting up very straight, its nostrils drawn in.

'I'll go first,' said Kem firmly.

When they got aboard, he saw why Killer was upset. Among the cases on deck was a cage, and behind its wooden bars a panther was pacing up and down. The animal, which a sailor told them had been captured in the Nubian desert, was magnificent.

'Where's the captain?' asked Pazair.

A man of around fifty, with a low brow and a heavy frame, left the tiller and came towards them. 'I'm about to cast off my moorings,' he shouted. 'Get off my boat.'

'City guards,' said Kem. 'I'm acting on orders from the Judge of the Porch, here present.'

The captain lowered his voice. 'All my documents are in order, although the dock offices won't accept my load of stones.'

'Weren't they expecting vegetables?'

'Yes, but I was requisitioned.'

'Requisitioned?' Pazair was astonished. 'By which secretariat?'

'I have to obey the scribes. I don't want any trouble.'

'Show me your ship's records.'

While Pazair was examining them, Kem had a chest opened. It did indeed contain stones destined for the temple sculptors.

The records noted a big cargo of fresh fruit, which had been loaded on the eastern bank of Thebes, requisitioned in the middle of the river by naval scribes, and unloaded at Thebes west. The boat had then sailed north, to the quarries of Gebel el-Silsila, where it had taken on a cargo of chests of stone ordered by – Karnak! In accordance with its first instructions, the boat had headed for Memphis, where the captain had been refused permission to unload the stones because they were not the cargo specified.

Deeply suspicious, Kem examined the contents of several other chests. All were filled with blocks of stone.

The shadow-eater had been following Pazair since the morning. The presence of Kem and Killer complicated a task which was already extremely difficult. He must devise a new plan and wait for a moment when their vigilance slackened.

Ah! Here was an opportunity: the panther.

Aboard the cargo-boat, Pazair was deep in discussion with the captain, while Kem and Killer were inspecting the hold. A group of sailors were going aboard, taking rations for the crew. The shadow-eater tagged on to them, got aboard and hid behind the mainmast. As soon as he was sure he had not been spotted, he crawled towards the cage.

One by one, he pulled out four of the five bars imprisoning the animal. As if it realized his intention, the panther froze, ready to spring for freedom.

Pazair was getting furious. 'Where is the seal of the river guards?' he asked the captain for the third time.

'They forgot to put it on, they—'

'Do not leave Memphis.'

'But I've got to. I have to deliver these stones.'

'I am taking away your ship's journal to examine it in detail.' The judge headed for the gangplank.

As he passed the cage, the shadow-eater removed the fifth bar and lay down flat on the deck.

At the sound of Pazair's footsteps, the panther sprang out of the cage and crouched, snarling, at the top of the gangplank. Fascinated and afraid, Pazair gazed deep into its eyes. He saw no hatred there: it would attack him simply because he was an obstacle in its way.

A ferocious howl made the whole crew jump. Killer shot out of the hold and leapt between the panther and the judge. Mouth gaping, eyes bright red, hair on end, arms swinging like a prize-fighter's, the baboon defied its opponent.

In the grasslands, even a hungry panther abandoned its kill when a group of baboons threatened it, but this one defiantly bared its teeth and unsheathed its claws. The baboon jumped up and down excitedly.

Dagger in hand, Kem stepped to Killer's side. He would not leave his best officer to fight alone.

At that, the panther retreated and slunk back into its cage. Kem went slowly forward and, keeping his eyes firmly on it, replaced the bars one by one.

'Over there!' shouted a sailor. 'There's a man running away!'

The shadow-eater had escaped from the boat by sliding down a mooring-rope on to the quay, and was disappearing round the corner of a dockside building.

'Can you describe him?' Pazair asked the sailor.

'Sorry, no. All I saw was the vague shape of a man running away.'

Pazair thanked Killer by placing his hand in the powerful,

velvety paw. The baboon had calmed down now; there was pride in its eyes.

'Somebody tried to kill you again,' said Kem.

'I don't think so. I think they wanted me to be badly wounded. You'd have dragged me out of the panther's claws, but in what state?'

'As commander of the city guards, I'd like to lock you up in your house.'

Pazair smiled. 'As Judge of the Porch, I'd set myself free on the grounds of unlawful arrest. Still, the fact that our enemies are acting like this proves that we're moving in the right direction.'

'I'm afraid for you.'

'I must go forward. What else can I do?'

Kem took something out of his pouch. 'This will help you.' It was the stopper from a jar. 'There are ten like this in the lower hold: the captain's wine reserve. The inscriptions identify the owner of the cargo.'

The hieroglyphics were hastily scrawled but readable. They said, '*Harem of Princess Hattusa*'.

26

The captain of the cargo-boat confessed, without having to be asked, that he was indeed working for Princess Hattusa. Not content either with the material evidence or with this declaration, Pazair continued his investigation in more depth.

Kem questioned the regional commanders of the river guards. It seemed that none of them had given the order to requisition a consignment of fruit and vegetables at Thebes, which was why the official seal was not on the ship's journal.

Pazair summoned the captain again. 'You lied to me.'

'I was afraid.'

'Of whom?'

'Of the law, of you, and especially of her.'

'Princess Hattusa?'

'I've been in her service for two years. She's generous, but very demanding. She ordered me to do what I did.'

'Do you realize that you have disrupted the delivery of fresh food?'

'If I hadn't obeyed I'd have been dismissed. And I wasn't the only one – others did the same.'

Two scribes each took down the captain's statement and Pazair read both copies, making sure they were identical. The captain agreed that they were accurate.

Tense and anxious, the judge sent a message to Bel-Tran, asking for a meeting.

They met in the potters' district, where craftsmen with skilful hands and agile feet made a thousand and one vessels, from tiny ointment vases to large jars for holding dried meat. Many pupils watched closely as a master-potter worked, before taking their own turn at the wheel.

'I need your help again,' said Pazair.

'My position isn't easy,' said Bel-Tran. 'Nenophar's waging a veritable war against me. She's trying to form a group of courtiers to demand my dismissal, and some of them have the tjaty's ear.'

'Bagey will judge the case on its merits.'

'Yes, but I have to spend my evenings checking the accounting scrolls, so that no one can find even the slightest irregularity in my work.'

'What weapons is Nenophar using?'

'Lies and insinuations. I know how powerful they can be, but all I can do in response is work harder.'

Pazair smiled. 'I've just uncovered some facts which may help you.'

'What are they?'

'There's been disruption of the trade in fresh foodstuffs.'

'Was it simply an administrative error?'

'No, it was deliberate.'

'But if the people don't get the food they need,' said Bel-Tran, aghast, 'they may stop working, or perhaps even riot!'

'Don't worry, I've identified the culprit.'

'Who is it?'

'Princess Hattusa.'

Bel-Tran adjusted his kilt. 'Are you sure?'

'My file contains proof and written statements.'

'This time she's gone too far. But attacking her would call the king into question.'

'Would Ramses let his people go hungry?'

'The question is meaningless. But would he let his wife, symbol of peace with the Hittites, be convicted?'

'She has committed a serious crime. If high-born people can evade the law, Egypt will become a land of compromises, privileges and lies. I shall not suppress the matter, but without an official complaint from the Treasury the princess will block the case.'

Bel-Tran did not hesitate for long. 'It may cost me my career, but you shall have your complaint.'

Ten times that day, Neferet moistened the swallow's beak. The bird turned its head towards the light; the doctor stroked it and spoke to it, desperate to save its life.

Pazair returned late, exhausted. 'Is it still alive?'

'It seems in less pain.'

'Is there any hope at all?'

'In all honesty, no. Its beak is still closed, and it's gently slipping away. We've become friends.' She looked at him more closely. 'Why are you so worried?'

'Princess Hattusa is trying to starve Memphis and the villages in the region.'

'That's absurd! How could she possibly succeed?'

'Through corruption, by playing on the government's inertia. But it is indeed absurd: there are too many levels of control. She must have lost her mind. The Treasury is lodging a complaint, through Bel-Tran, and I'm leaving for Thebes to lay charges against the princess.'

'Aren't you forgetting Branir, Asher and the conspirators?'

'Perhaps not, if Hattusa is Denes's ally.'

'Bringing a case against the most famous general in Egypt, then against a royal wife . . . You're no ordinary judge, Pazair!'

'And you're no ordinary woman. Do you approve of what I'm doing?'

'Yes, but it may be dangerous. What will you do to protect yourself?'

'Nothing. I must question her, and present the charges.

Then I shall pass the matter to the tjaty; he wouldn't accept a slapdash case.'

'I love you, Pazair.'

They kissed.

Neferet, though, was still anxious. 'Your enemies have tried poison and then a wild panther. What will they try next?'

'I don't know, but don't worry. Kem and I will be travelling on a boat belonging to the river guards.'

Before dinner, he paid a visit to the swallow. To his great surprise, it raised its head. The injured eye had scarred over, and the little body quivered with more energy.

Amazed, Pazair dared not move. Neferet took some straw and laid it under the bird's feet, to serve as a perch. The swallow gripped it.

Suddenly, with stunning energy, it beat its wings and took flight.

Instantly, from all corners of the sky, came a dozen of its fellows; one of them kissed it, like a mother rediscovering her child. Then a second, a third and the whole flight, mad with joy. The community of swallows danced above Neferet and Pazair, who could not hold back their tears.

'Look! They're reunited,' breathed Pazair.

'You were right to tear it away from death. Now it's living among its own kind. What does it care for tomorrow?'

The sky was a radiant blue, the sun reigning over all.

At the prow of the boat, Pazair gazed admiringly at his country. He thanked the gods for allowing him to be born on this magic soil, in this land of contrasts between cultivated fields and desert. Beneath the crowns of the palm-trees flowed the benevolent waters of the irrigation channels, and peaceful villages of white houses sheltered in the trees' shade. The golden corn gleamed, the green of the palm-groves charmed the eye. Wheat, linen and fruit were born out of the black earth, which had been cultivated by generations of peasants. Acacias and sycamores vied in beauty with tamarisks and perseas; on the banks of the Nile, far from the landing-stages, papyrus and reeds throve. In the desert sand, plants sprang up at the first sign of rain, and the depths preserved the sky-water for weeks on end, in springs which could be detected with a dowsing-rod. The Delta and its fertile expanses, the valley with the sacred river cutting its way between the arid mountains and the barren plateaux, enchanted the soul and put man in his rightful place in creation, after animals, minerals and plants, according to the sages' teachings. Only the human race, in its vanity and madness, tried from time to time to distort life; that was why the goddess Ma'at had offered it law, so that the twisted staff might be made straight.

'I think you're wrong to do this,' said Kem.

'Surely you don't think the princess is innocent?' asked Pazair.

'You'll get your fingers burnt.'

'My case is watertight.'

'Perhaps, but what will it be worth in the face of a royal wife's denials? I wonder if you aren't actually helping the rabble trying to destroy you. Can you imagine how angry Hattusa will be? Even Bagey won't be able to protect you.'

'She is not above the law.'

'A fine thought – and a laughable one.'

'We shall see.'

'Where do you get such confidence from?'

'From my wife's eyes, and just recently from the flight of a swallow.'

Without warning, a fierce wind sprang up, and unexpected whirlpools churned the Nile's waters. At the prow of the boat, the man who sounded the river with a long staff could no longer do so. The sudden storm took the sailors by surprise, and they were slow to reduce sail: the yards broke, the mainmast twisted, and the rudder stopped responding to the tiller. Steering an erratic course, the boat hit a sandbank. They dropped the stern anchor, a heavy stone block which would hold the the vessel steady in the strong current. People were running about on deck; Kem re-established calm with his powerful voice. With the captain, he assessed the damage and gave orders to proceed with repairs.

Shaken about and soaked, Pazair felt useless. Kem took him into the cabin, while two experienced sailors dived to check the condition of the hull. As luck would have it, it had not suffered too badly; as soon as the Nile's anger was stilled, they could resume their journey.

'The crew are worried,' said the big Nubian. 'Before we left, the captain forgot to repaint the magic eyes on either side of the prow. His forgetfulness might cause a shipwreck, because the boat is blind.'

Pazair took his writing-materials from his travelling-bag. He prepared some very black, almost indelible ink, and restored the protective eyes with his own steady hand.

Alerted by the captain of Princess Hattusa's fruit and vegetable boat, five bodyguards from her harem, stationed a day's march to the north of Thebes, waited for the boat carrying Judge Pazair to pass by. Their mission was simple: to stop it by any means necessary. If they succeeded, they would each receive a parcel of land, two cows, a donkey, ten sacks of wheat and five jars of wine.

They were delighted by the storm, for it meant that a shipwreck and death by drowning were thoroughly plausible. For a judge, being absorbed by the Nile would be a fine end. The legend ran that those who drowned gained direct access to paradise, if they were godly men.

On board their fast skiff, the five attackers were planning to take advantage of the weather and the sky laden with black clouds to approach their prey, which was still immobilized near the sandbank. They stopped a little way from it, threw themselves into the water, swam to the boat and climbed on to the deck with ease. Their leader, armed with a mallet, felled the guard on watch. The other river guards were asleep on their mats, rolled up in their blankets, so all that remained was to force open the cabin door, seize the judge and drown him. They would be innocent; it was the Nile that would kill him. Barefoot, moving soundlessly, they halted before the closed door. Two watched the sailors, three would take care of Pazair.

A black shape leapt from the roof of the cabin and landed on the leader's shoulders. He howled with pain as the baboon's teeth sank into him. Flinging open the light wooden door of the cabin, Kem charged at the intruders, a dagger in either hand, and mortally wounded two of them. The two others, terrified, tried in vain to escape, but the guards, now awake and alert, pinned them to the deck.

Killer did not slacken his grip until Kem gave the order. By then, the leader of the raiding-party was drenched in blood and almost unconsicous.

'Who sent you?' demanded Kem.

The wounded man said nothing.

'If you refuse to speak, my baboon will interrogate you.'

'Princess Hattusa,' he gasped.

As before, Pazair was amazed by the harem. Canals, maintained to perfection, served vast gardens where the great ladies of Thebes liked to walk, coming to take the air in the shade and show off their latest dresses. There was abundant water, flower in harmonious colours were planted everywhere, and bands of female musicians practised the pieces they would play at forthcoming banquets. Hard work went on in the weaving and pottery workshops, but in surroundings that were both comfortable and relaxing. Experts in enamel and rare woods started on their masterpieces at sunrise, while bearers loaded jars of scented oil on to a trading-ship.

In accordance with tradition, Princess Hattusa's harem was a little town where exceptionally talented craft workers took the necessary time to experience beauty in their hearts and hands, so as to pass it on in flawless objects and products.

Pazair could have strolled for hours on end through this ordered world, where no work seemed burdensome, could have wandered along the sandy paths, conversed with the gardeners as they weeded, sampled the fruit while talking to the elderly widows who had chosen to live here. But, alas, in his capacity as Judge of the Porch he had requested an audience with the princess.

The head steward showed him into the reception-hall, where Princess Hattusa sat in state, flanked by two scribes.

Pazair bowed.

'I am extremely busy,' said Hattusa, 'so please be brief.'

'I should like to speak with you privately.'

'The official nature of your action forbids it.'

'On the contrary, I think it demands it.' Pazair unrolled a papyrus. 'Do you wish your scribes to register the charges?'

With an irritated wave of her hand, the princess dismissed them.

'Are you aware of what you are saying?'' she said when they had gone.

'Princess Hattusa, I accuse you of stealing foodstuffs and of arranging an attempt on my life.'

The beautiful dark eyes flamed. 'How dare you!'

'I have proof, witness statements and written depositions. I therefore consider you guilty. Before arranging your trial, I call on you to explain your actions.'

'No one has ever spoken to me like this!'

'No royal wife has ever committed such crimes.'

'Ramses will destroy you.'

'Pharaoh is the son and servant of Ma'at. Since truth gives

life to my words, he will not stifle them. Your rank cannot keep your crimes secret.'

Hattusa stood up and walked away from her throne. 'You hate me because I am a Hittite.'

'You know perfectly well that that is not so. No resentment guides my steps, even though you ordered my death.'

'To stop your boat and prevent you from arriving in Thebes – that's what I told them to do.'

'Then they misunderstood you.'

'No one in Egypt would ever take the risk of killing a judge. The court will reject your theory and regard your witnesses as liars.'

'That defence is skilful, but how can you justify the theft of food?'

'If your so-called proof is as convincing as your allegations, my good faith will be obvious to all.'

'Princess, be good enough to read this document.'

Hattusa read the papyrus. Her face fell, and her long hands clenched. 'I shall deny it.'

'The witnesses go into great detail, and the facts are overwhelming.'

She defied him, magnificent as ever. 'I am the wife of Pharaoh.'

'Your word has no more worth than that of the humblest peasant. Your position makes your actions even more inexcusable.'

'I shall prevent you from holding a trial.'

'Tjaty Bagey will preside over it.'

She sank down on to one of the steps before the throne. 'Why do you want to ruin me?'

'What are you hoping to achieve, Princess?'

'Do you really want to know, Judge of Egypt?'

Nervously, Pazair met her passionate gaze.

'I hate your country, I hate its king, its glory and its power. Seeing the Egyptians starving to death, the children moaning, the animals dying, would be my greatest happiness. By keeping me prisoner in this false paradise, Ramses thought my rage would ebb away, but all it does is grow. I have suffered injustice, and I will no longer endure it. May Egypt die, may it be invaded by my people, or by one of the barbarian tribes. I shall be the greatest supporter of Pharaoh's enemies. And believe me, Judge Pazair, their numbers are growing every day.'

'Denes the ship-owner, for example?'

The princess anger was suddenly stilled. 'I have not said so.'

'You fell into a trap, didn't you?'

'I told you the truth – that famous truth which Egypt loves so much.'

27

As usual, the reception had been a dazzling success. Nenophar had paraded in a sumptuous dress, delightedly accepting her guests' eager compliments. Denes had concluded several advantageous agreements, and was pleased with the continued growth of a shipping business which compelled the admiration of everyone who mattered in Egypt. No one knew that he held supreme power in his hands. Free of impatience, though edgy, he was growing more and more excited about the future: anyone who had criticized him would be cast down lower than the ground, and those who had supported him would be rewarded. Time was on his side.

When the last guests had left, Nenophar said she was tired and withdrew to her apartments. Denes went out into the orchard, to check that no fruit had been stolen.

A woman suddenly emerged from the darkness.

'Princess Hattusa!' he exclaimed. 'What are you doing in Memphis?'

'You are never to speak my name again. I am still awaiting your delivery.'

'I don't understand.'

'The sky-iron.'

'I beg you to be patient, my lady.'

'That's impossible. I need it immediately.'

'Why?'

'You have led me into madness.'

'No one will trace things back to you.'

'Judge Pazair already has.'

'He is just trying to intimidate you.'

'He has laid charges against me, and intends to make me appear before a court, as the accused.'

'That's merely an idle boast,' said Denes scornfully.

'You do not know him.'

'He has no evidence.'

'On the contrary, he has not only evidence but witnesses' statements and depositions.'

'Ramses will intervene.'

'Pazair is entrusting the case to Tjaty Bagey; the king must submit to the law. I shall be convicted, Denes, stripped of all my lands and, at best, shut away in some provincial palace. The penalty may even be heavier.'

'That is indeed worrying.'

'I want the sky-iron.'

'I haven't got it yet.'

'By tomorrow at the latest. Otherwise . . .'

'Otherwise?'

'I shall denounce you to Judge Pazair. He suspects you, but does not know that you were behind the thefts of food. The jurors will believe me: I know how to be convincing.'

'It will take longer than a day to get it.'

'In two days' time the moon will be full and the sky-iron will make my magic effective. Tomorrow evening, Denes, or you will be destroyed with me.'

Watched with astonishment by Mischief, Brave took a bath. The dog first dipped a cautious paw into the lotus-pool to check that the water was to his liking.

Today was the servants' rest day, and Neferet went herself to lift the water-jar from the bottom of the well. Her mouth was like a lotus-bud, her breasts like love-apples; Pazair watched her go to and fro, placing flowers on an offering-table in memory of Branir, feeding the animals, raising her eyes to the swallows that, every evening, flew in circles over their home. Among them was the survivor, its wings spread wide.

Neferet checked the sycamore fruit; they were a pretty shade of yellow at the moment, but would become red as they ripened. In May she would open them on the tree to empty them of the insects that had chosen to live inside them. The sweet, fleshy fruit would then be edible.

'I have re-read the Hattusa case,' said Pazair, 'and my scribes have checked that it is properly formulated. I can send it to the tjaty with my findings.'

'The princess may not be afraid of him.'

'True, but she knows how determined I am.'

'What will she do?'

'It doesn't matter. It is up to Bagey to conduct the trial, and nothing she does will stop him doing so.'

'Even if Pharaoh asks you to withdraw the case?'

'He can dismiss me, but I'll never give up. If I did, my heart would be tainted for ever – even you couldn't cleanse it.'

Neferet came and sat down on a mat beside her husband's chair. 'Kem told me there was a third attempt on your life.'

'Yes, but this time they were Hattusa's men and they hoped to kill me by drowning me. Previously it was one man on his own and he wanted to cripple me.'

'Has Kem identified him yet?'

'Not yet. The fellow seems particularly cunning and skilful, and Kem's informants are saying nothing. But enough of that. What has the council of doctors decided?'

'The election has been delayed and new candidates have been invited to put themselves forward. Qadash is continuing with his application and is paying endless visits to the members of the council.' She leant her head against him. 'Whatever happens, we shall have known happiness.'

*

Pazair set his seal on the judgement of a provincial court, sentencing a village headman to twenty strokes of the rod and a heavy fine, for slanderous denunciation. The headman would probably appeal; if his conviction was confirmed, the punishment would be doubled.

Shortly before noon, the judge received a visit from the lady Tapeni. Small and slender, with jet-black hair, she knew how to use her charms and had persuaded hard-headed scribes to let her into the Judge of the Porch's office.

'What can I do for you?' he asked.

'You know very well.'

'I'm afraid I don't.'

'I want to know the hiding-place of your friend Suti, who is also my husband.'

Pazair had not expected this. It seemed that Tapeni, as well as Panther, was far from indifferent to the adventurer's fate.

'He has left Memphis.'

'Why?'

'He's on an official mission.'

'And of course you will not tell me the nature of his mission.'

'That is prohibited.'

'Is it dangerous?' asked Tapeni.

'He trusts in his good luck.'

'Suti had better come back. I am not the kind of woman who lets herself be forgotten and abandoned.' Her voice contained as much menace as tenderness.

Pazair tried an experiment. 'Have any great ladies been causing you problems recently?'

'Given my position, they're always demanding the finest fabrics.'

'Nothing more serious?'

'I don't understand.'

'The lady Nenophar, for example. Has she by any chance demanded your silence?'

Tapeni looked troubled. 'I told Suti about her, because she's a superb needlewoman.'

'She isn't the only one in Memphis. Why did you throw her name into the ring?'

'Your questions are annoying me.'

'I regret that, but they are extremely important.'

'Why?'

'I am investigating a serious crime.'

A strange smile floated about Tapeni's lips. 'Is Nenophar involved?'

'What exactly do you know?'

'You have no right to keep me here.' Quick as a flash, she made for the door. 'I may know a great deal, Judge Pazair, but why should I trust you with my secrets?'

Running a good hospital afforded little respite. As soon as one patient was cured, another replaced him and the battle began again. Neferet never tired of treating the sick; relieving suffering gave her endless joy. The staff helped her unflaggingly, and the scribes ensured that the hospital was properly run, so she was able to devote herself to her art, improving old remedies and trying to find new ones. Her work was full of variety: she might have to operate to remove a malignant growth, or set a broken limb, or comfort patients who were incurably sick. Some of her team of doctors were experienced, some were beginners. They obeyed her gladly, and she never so much as had to raise her voice to them.

Today had been particularly demanding. Neferet had saved a forty-year-old man, who was suffering from a blockage in his intestines. Tired, she was drinking some cool water when Qadash burst into the room where the doctors washed and changed.

He said loudly, 'I want to see the list of drugs the hospital possesses.'

'Why?'

'I am a candidate for the post of principal doctor, and I need that list.'

'What do you intend to do with it?'

'I must know all the drugs used in the country.'

'Why? As a tooth-doctor, you use only specific remedies.'

'Give me that list at once.'

'There's no reason why you should see it. You don't work at this hospital.'

'You don't understand, Neferet. I must prove my skills. Without a list of the drugs, my application will be incomplete.'

'Only the kingdom's principal doctor could compel me to give it to you.'

'I am the future principal doctor.'

'Nebamon has not yet been replaced, so far as I know.'

'Do as I say – you won't regret it.'

'Certainly not.'

'If I have to, I'll break down the door of your workshop.'

'You would be severely punished.'

'Do not resist me any longer. Very soon I shall be your superior. If you refuse to cooperate, I shall dismiss you from your post.'

Several doctors, alerted by the raised voices, came to Neferet's support.

'Your mob doesn't impress me,' sneered Qadash.

'Get out of here,' ordered a young doctor.

'You are ill advised to speak to me in that tone of voice.'

'And your behaviour is unworthy of a doctor.'

'This is an emergency,' declared Qadash.

'Only from your point of view,' Neferet corrected him.

'The post of principal doctor must be given to a man of experience. All of you here like me. Why do we have to argue like this? We all work with the same wish to serve others.'

Qadash pleaded his cause with emotion and conviction. He pointed to his long career, his devotion to the sick, his wish to be useful to the country without being hampered by ridiculous administrative procedures.

But Neferet stood firm. If Qadash wanted the list of poisons and drugs, he must justify its use. Until Nebamon's successor had been appointed, she would guard it closely.

The head of Asher's general staff was very sorry, but his superior was absent.

Pazair persisted. 'This is not a courtesy visit. I must question him.'

'The general has left the barracks.'

'When?'

'Yesterday evening.'

'Where was he going?'

'I don't know.'

'Don't the regulations require him to inform you as to his movements?'

'Yes.'

'Then why did he not do so?'

'I cannot tell, Judge.'

'This is thoroughly unsatisfactory.'

'Search the barracks if you wish.'

Pazair questioned two other officers, but learnt nothing more. According to several witnesses, the general had left by chariot, heading south. Suspecting a ruse, the judge then went to the Foreign Affairs secretariat: no troops had been sent to Asia.

Pazair asked Kem to find the general as quickly as possible. The commander soon confirmed that he had gone south, but could not be more precise. Asher had been careful to cover his tracks.

The tjaty was annoyed. 'Are you not exaggerating, Judge Pazair?'

'I have been trying to find Asher for a week.'

'Have you been to the barracks?'

'There is no trace of him there.'

'What about the Foreign Affairs secretariat?'

'It has not sent him on a mission – unless it is a secret one.'

'In that case I would have been informed, and I have not been.'

'Then we can reach only one conclusion: the general has disappeared.'

'That is outrageous. His office forbids such dereliction of duty.'

'He has tried to escape the net that was closing around him.'

'Have your constant attacks worn him down?'

'To my mind, he was afraid you would take action against him.'

'That means the law would have convicted him.'

'His friends have probably deserted him.'

'Why should they do that?' asked Bagey.

'Asher realized he was being used.'

'But for a soldier to run away!'

'He is a coward and a murderer.'

'If your accusations are correct, why did he not head for Asia and join his real allies there?'

'He may have only pretended to go towards the South.'

'I shall give the order to close the borders. Asher will not leave Egypt.'

If he had no help, Asher would not escape the net. And no one would dare help a disgraced general and disobey an order made by the tjaty.

Pazair ought to have been delighted by this formidable victory. The general could not justify his desertion; betrayed by traitors, he would betray them in turn during his second trial. He had probably tried to take revenge on Denes and Sheshi and then, when he failed, had chosen to run away.

'I shall send the provincial governors a decree ordering

Asher's immediate arrest. Have Kem pass it on to the guards' commanders in all the cities.'

The system for sending urgent messages was so efficient that Asher would be sought everywhere in less than four days.

'Your work is not yet done,' continued the tjaty. 'If the general is indeed only a cat's-paw, you must trace the head of the plot.'

'That is indeed what I intend to do,' confirmed Pazair, whose thoughts were turning to Suti.

Denes took Princess Hattusa to the secret forge where Sheshi was working. Located in a working-class district, it was hidden behind an open-air kitchen run by some of Denes's employees. Sheshi was experimenting with combinations of metals, and testing the effects of vegetable acids on copper and iron.

The heat in the forge was unbearable. Hattusa took off her cloak and hood.

'My friend, you have a royal visitor,' announced Denes delightedly.

Sheshi did not look up. He was concentrating on a delicate operation, a solder incorporating gold, silver and copper.

'This is to be the hilt of a dagger,' he explained. 'It will belong to the future king, when the tyrant has gone.'

With one foot, Sheshi pumped regularly on a pair of bellows, to bring the fire to white heat. He handled the metal with bronze pincers, and had to work very quickly, for the pincers melted at the same temperature as the gold.

Hattusa was impatient. 'I'm not interested in your experiments. I want the sky-iron I paid for.'

'You paid for only part of it,' said Denes.

'Deliver it to me, and you shall have the balance.'

'So you're still in a hurry?'

'Don't be insolent! Show me what is due to me.'

'You will have to wait.'

'That is enough, Denes! Have you lied to me?'

'Not altogether.'

'Does the sky-iron not belong to you?'

'I shall soon get it back.'

'You have made a fool of me!'

'No, Princess, you're mistaken there. It was a simple matter of anticipation. We are working together for Ramses' ruin, isn't that the important thing?'

'You are nothing but a thief.'

'It is pointless to be angry. We have no choice but to go on working together.' Denes's expression betrayed his contempt.

'You are wrong, Denes. I shall do without your help.'

'It would be most unwise to break our agreement.'

'Open that door and let me leave.'

'Will you keep silent about what you know?'

'I shall act in my own interests.'

'I require your word.'

'Stand aside.'

As Denes did not move, Hattusa pushed him out of the way. In fury, he pushed her back and she fell against the red-hot pincers, which Sheshi had laid on a stone. She screamed, stumbled, and fell into the hearth. Her dress caught fire instantly.

Neither Denes nor Sheshi went to her aid, Sheshi awaiting instructions from his master. When Denes opened the door and fled, Sheshi followed him. The forge burst into flames.

28

Before presiding over the court's ordinary session, to be held in front of the porch of the Temple of Ptah, Pazair had written a coded message to Suti: *'Asher is lost. Take no further risks. Come back immediately.'*

The judge entrusted the document to a messenger vouched for by Kem; as soon as the man reached Kebet, he would hand it to the desert guards, who were in charge of passing messages to the miners.

The court was judging a series of minor offences, from the non-payment of a debt to an unjustified absence from work. The guilty parties admitted they were at fault, and the jurors were lenient. Among the latter was Denes.

At the end of the hearing, he approached the judge. 'I am not your enemy, Pazair.'

'I am not your friend.'

'Precisely. You should be wary of those who claim to be your friends.'

'What are you insinuating?'

'Your trust is sometimes misplaced. Suti, for example, certainly doesn't deserve it. He sold me information about your investigation and about you yourself, in exchange for money.'

'My office forbids me to hit you, but I might forget myself and do it.'

'One day you'll be grateful to me.'

*

As soon as she arrived at the hospital, Neferet was asked for help by several doctors who had been toiling since the middle of the night, trying to save the life of a woman who had been badly burnt. The fire had occurred in a working-class district where an unauthorised furnace had caught fire. The unfortunate victim must have been careless; her chances of survival were non-existent.

The doctor in charge had treated the injured flesh by applying black mud and the cattle-dung, heated and crushed into fermented beer. Neferet reduced some grilled barley and colocynth to powder, mixed them with dried acacia-resin, and soaked the mixture in oil; then she made greasy poultices which she applied to the burns. She treated the least serious of the burns with yellow ochre crushed in sycamore-sap, colocynth and honey.

'That will ease the pain,' she said.

'How can we feed her?' asked an assistant.

'We can't at the moment.'

'We must give her water.'

'Slide a reed between her lips and feed copper-water through it, one drop at a time. Watch her all the time. If anything at all happens, however minor, let me know.'

'What about the poultices?'

'Change them every three hours. Tomorrow we'll use a mixture of wax, cooked beef-fat, papyrus and carob. Make sure there is a supply of very fine bandages in her room.'

'Do you hold out any hope, then?'

'To be honest, no.' Neferet turned to the hospital's head steward, who was waiting to talk to her. 'Do we know who she is? We must inform her family.'

The steward had been afraid Neferet would say that. He led her into an empty room nearby.

'I'm afraid, Doctor, there may be complications. Our patient is no ordinary person.'

'What is her name?'

He showed her a magnificent silver bracelet. On the inside was engraved the owner's name, which the flames had not erased: '*Hattusa, wife of Ramses*'.

A hot wind from Nubia set everyone's nerves on edge. It whipped up the desert sand, covering the houses with it. People conscientiously blocked up every aperture, but a fine yellow dust got in everywhere and obliged the housewives to clean constantly. Many people complained of breathing difficulties, causing the doctors a great deal of work. Pazair was not spared. A course of drops soothed his sore eyes, but he struggled against all-consuming fatigue. Kem, on the other hand, seemed as impervious to the heat and wind as Killer was.

The two men and the baboon were taking the air in the shade of a sycamore, near the lotus-pool. Brave, at first hesitant, had eventually settled at his master's feet, but he did not take his eyes off Killer for a second.

'There's still no news of Asher,' said Kem.

'He won't be able to get out of the country,' said Pazair.

'He can go to earth for weeks, but if he does his supporters will drift away and someone will probably denounce him. The tjaty's orders are quite clear. Why do you think Asher's done this?'

'Because he knew that this time he'd lose his case.'

'So his allies deserted him?'

'They didn't need him any more.'

'What conclusion have you come to?'

'That there is no military conspiracy, no attempted invasion.'

'But Princess Hattusa came to Memphis.'

'Like Asher, she's been eliminated because the conspirators don't need her any more. What have you found out about the fire?'

'The forge didn't belong to anyone, but the open-air kitchen was run by employees of Denes.'

'That's very interesting,' said Pazair.

'There's nothing to incriminate him explicitly.'

'No, but at each step we come up against him. And the fire was a serious crime.'

'People were seen running away, but the witnesses differ as to how many and have given only vague descriptions.'

'A forge . . . Sheshi must have been working there.'

'Could he have lured Hattusa there to kill her?'

'I can't believe that anyone would burn a woman alive. Unless, of course, we are dealing with monsters.'

'If we are, we'd better prepare ourselves for some tough battles.'

'I assume it's no use asking you to lift the protective measures around me?'

'Even if I weren't commander of the guards, and even if you gave me orders to the contrary, I'd maintain the watch over you.'

Pazair would never decipher the mystery of Kem. Cold, distant, always in control of himself, he disapproved of the judge's actions but helped him without a second thought. The Nubian would never have any confidant but Killer; damaged physically, he was even more damaged in his soul. To him, justice was only an illusion. But Pazair believed in it, and Kem trusted Pazair.

'Have you told the tjaty about the fire?' asked Kem.

'Yes, I've sent him a detailed report. Hattusa hadn't told anyone she was coming to Memphis, it seems. Neferet is watching over her day and night.'

On the fifth day, Neferet ground colocynth, yellow ochre and copper particles to an oily paste and applied it to Hattusa's burns, which she bandaged with infinite gentleness. Despite the pain, Hattusa tried to resist.

On the sixth day, the look in the princess's eyes changed. She seemed to emerge from a long sleep.

'Hold firm. You are in the main hospital at Memphis. The most difficult stage is over. Now each hour that passes brings you closer to healing.'

The once-beautiful Hittite was horribly disfigured. No matter what ointments and lotions she used, her superb skin would never be more than a series of pinkish scars.

Hattusa raised a hand and gripped Neferet's wrist.

'Princess, yours is a sickness I know and can cure,' she promised.

Neferet had at last consented to rest for a while. She had fought fiercely to save Hattusa, with her own hands preparing the bandages and remedies which, little by little, were healing the appalling burns.

Pazair lay beside his wife and watched her as she slept. His love for her grew and blossomed like the crown of a palm-tree. Each dawn brought a new colour, undreamt-of and sublime; Neferet had the gift of making life smile and lighting up the darkest night. If Pazair was went on fighting with undimmed enthusiasm, it was only so that he might continue to charm her and prove to her that she had not made a mistake in marrying him. Beyond his weaknesses blazed the certainty of a union which not time nor custom nor ordeals could ever wear away.

A ray of sunshine lit up the bedroom and touched Neferet's face. She stirred gently.

'Hattusa is saved,' she murmured.

'You've been neglecting me, for the benefit of your patient.'

She snuggled up to him. 'She was young, and so beautiful. How will she ever be able to accept what has happened to her?'

'Has there been any word from Ramses?'

251

'Yes, through the palace's head steward. As soon as she's well enough to be moved, she'll be taken there to be cared for.'

'Unless her confession means that she's denied such a privileged position.'

Troubled by those words, Neferet sat up in bed. 'Hasn't she been punished enough?'

'Forgive me, but I must question her.'

'She hasn't yet said a single word.'

'As soon as she's well enough to speak, let me know.'

Hattusa drank her barley broth and carob-juice. Her life-force was returning, but her gaze was still vacant, as if she were lost in a nightmare.

'How did it happen?' asked Neferet.

'He pushed me. I wanted to leave the forge, and he stopped me.'

The words came slowly and painfully. Neferet dared not ask her patient any more questions.

'The bronze tongs . . . they burnt my dress, a flame flared up, I fell against the forge, the fire caught me.' The voice became strident. 'They ran away, they abandoned me!'

Wild-eyed, Hattusa tried to regain the past and wipe away the tragedy that had destroyed her beauty and her youth. She slumped back, exhausted and defeated.

Suddenly, she sat up straight again and screamed her pain. 'They ran away, curse them, Denes and Sheshi!'

Neferet quickly administered a calming draught, and stayed with the princess until she fell asleep.

As she was leaving the hospital, the head steward of the Mother of Pharaoh's house approached her and said, 'Her Majesty wishes to see you immediately.'

Neferet was invited to take her place in a chair carried by bearers. The men hurried.

Tuya received her without ceremony.

When the greetings were over, Neferet asked, 'How is your health, Majesty?'

'Thanks to your treatment, it is excellent. Have you been informed of the decision taken by the council of doctors?'

'No.'

'The situation is becoming intolerable, so the kingdom's principal doctor will be appointed next week. A single name must emerge from the council's deliberations.'

'That is surely a necessity?'

'Qadash's only rivals will be puppets, because he has been able to deter all his worthy opponents. The former friends of Nebamon, the weak and the undecided will vote for him.' The queen's anger accentuated her natural gravity.

'I refuse to accept that as inevitable,' she went on. 'Qadash is incompetent, wholly unworthy to hold such an important office. I have always been concerned with the people's health. Measures must be taken to improve their well-being, to promote cleanliness so that epidemics are prevented. This man Qadash makes a mockery of such things. He wants power and glory, nothing else. He is worse than Nebamon. You must help me.'

'But how, Majesty?'

'By standing against him.'

Neferet gave Pazair permission to enter the room where Princess Hattusa was resting. Her face and limbs were still heavily bandaged – even her eyes were covered by very fine linen. To prevent gangrene and infection, the doctor had treated the wounds with a lotion reserved for the most serious cases. Copper particles, chrysocolla, fresh terebinth resin, cumin, natron, asafoetida, wax, cinnamon, bryony, oil and honey had been finely crushed and reduced to an oily mass.

'May I speak with you, Princess?' asked Pazair.

'Who are you?'

'Judge Pazair.

253

'Who permitted you to—'

'Doctor Neferet, my wife.'

'She's my enemy, too.'

'My request was official. I am investigating the fire.'

'The fire . . .'

'I want to identify the culprits.'

'What culprits?'

'Didn't you mention the names Denes and Sheshi?'

'No, you're mistaken.'

'Why did you go to the forge?'

'Do you really want to know?'

'If you will consent to tell me.'

'I went there to get sky-iron to use in magic against Ramses.'

'You ought to have been more wary of Sheshi.'

'I was alone.'

'How do you explain—'

'It was an accident, Judge Pazair, a simple accident.'

'Why are you lying?'

'I hate Egypt, its civilization and its values.'

'So much that you will not even testify against the men who did this to you?'

'Whoever tries to destroy Ramses has my sympathy. Your country rejects the only truth: war. Only war excites the passions and reveals human nature. My people were wrong to make peace with you, and I'm paying for that mistake. I wanted to awaken the Hittites, show them the right way . . . Now I shall be shut away in one of those palaces I loathe. But others will succeed, I'm convinced of that. And you won't even have the pleasure of putting me on trial. You aren't cruel enough to torture a sick woman still further.'

'Denes and Sheshi are criminals. They would laugh at your ideals.'

'My mind is made up. Not one word shall I say.'

*

As Judge of the Porch, Pazair ratified Neferet's candidacy for the post of principal doctor of the kingdom of Egypt. She had all the necessary qualifications and experience. Moreover, her position as director of the hospital, the official support of the king's mother, and the warm encouragement of many of her colleagues, gave substantial weight to her application.

She dreaded this unsought-for ordeal – Qadash would used the vilest methods to deter her. All she wanted was to heal; she certainly did not want honours and responsibilities.

Pazair could not comfort her. He himself was shaken by Hattusa's madness, knowing that she was doomed to the most desperate loneliness. Her testimony would have brought about the conviction of Denes and Sheshi, but once again they had escaped punishment.

He felt as though he had come up against an insurmountable wall. An evil spirit was protecting the conspirators and guaranteeing their impunity. Knowing that Asher had vanished, and being assured that no military conspiracy threatened Egypt, ought to have reassured him, but a dull anguish persisted. He could not understand the motive for so many crimes and the contemptuous assurance of a man like Denes, whom apparently no blow could shake. Did Denes and his acolytes have some secret weapon, beyond the judge's reach?

Aware of each other's distress, Pazair and Neferet each thought of the other before themselves. As they made love, they saw the birth of a new dawn.

29

When the All-Seeing Ones and their dogs returned from dangerous areas in the eastern desert, they allowed themselves a day's rest before setting off again on patrol. They used the time to bind up their wounds, have a massage and go to the ale-house, where meek, welcoming girls sold them their bodies for a night. The guards exchanged information they had gathered during raids and took to prison any sand-travellers and other raiders they had captured.

The big guard who oversaw the recruitment of miners attended to his dogs, then went to see the scribe in charge of messages.

'Anything for my lot?'

'Ten or so.'

The guard read the names on the scrolls. 'Well, well, there's one for Suti. He's a strange fellow. He doesn't seem like a miner.'

'That's nothing to do with me,' retorted the scribe. 'Sign here to acknowledge receipt.'

The guard distributed the messages himself; he always asked the recipients about the people who had written to them. Three miners were missing from the roll-call, two old hands, who were working in a copper mine, and Suti. The guard checked, and found that Ephraim's expedition had returned to Kebet the previous evening, so he went to the ale-house, visited the inns, and inspected the encampments. No luck: the mining-office informed him that Ephraim, Suti and five other men had failed to report to the scribe charged with noting down all comings and goings.

He set a thorough search in motion. Still nothing: the seven men had disappeared. Others before them had tried to make off with precious stones, but they had all been caught and severely punished. Why had an experienced man like Ephraim embarked on such a mad venture?

Forgetting their rest and relaxation, the All-Seeing Ones got organized at once. They had the souls of hunters, and nothing pleased them more than worthy game. The big guard would lead the search.

With the agreement of the messages scribe, and because of the circumstances, the guard opened the letter to Suti. The hieroglyphs, though individually readable, meant nothing when taken together. Clearly, it was in code. So he was right: Suti was not a miner like the others. But what master did Suti serve?

The seven men had taken a difficult route, leading south-east. All equally strong, they walked at a regular pace, ate little, and took long stops at the water-sources, whose locations only Ephraim knew. He had demanded absolute obedience, and permitted no questions about their destination. At the end of their journey, he said, a fortune awaited them.

'Over there – a guard!' The miner pointed towards a strange, motionless form.

'Keep going, fool,' ordered Ephraim. 'That's just a wool-tree.'

Twice the height of a man, the tree had bluish, grooved bark; its broad, green and pink leaves were reminiscent of the material used to make winter cloaks. The fugitives used the wood to light a fire and cook a gazelle they had killed that morning. Ephraim knew that the wool-tree's sap was not poisonous. He gathered some leaves, kneaded them, ground them to powder and shared them with his companions.

'A good purgative,' he commented, 'and a very effective remedy for venereal disease. When you're rich, you'll be able to afford gorgeous women.'

'Yes, but it won't be in Egypt,' mourned a miner.

'Asian women are warm and yielding. They'll soon make you forget your provincial girls.'

Their bellies full and their thirst slaked, the little band resumed their journey.

One of the miners was bitten on the ankle by a sand viper, and died in agonizing convulsions.

'Idiot,' muttered Ephraim. 'The desert doesn't forgive carelessness.'

The dead man's best friend said furiously, 'You're leading us all to our deaths. No one can escape those creatures.'

'I can, and so can those who tread where I do.'

'I want to know where we're going.'

'A loose-tongued man like you would talk to the wind and betray us.'

'Tell me.'

'Do you want me to break your head?'

The miner looked around: the endless desert was full of death-traps. He gave up, and collected his equipment.

'If attempts like ours have failed,' said Ephraim, 'it wasn't by chance. It was because a spy infiltrated the group, and managed to let the guards know about his movements. I've taken special precautions, but I can't be certain there isn't an informer among us.'

'Whom do you suspect?'

'You and everyone else – any one of you could have been bought. If there is a spy, he'll give himself away sooner or later. And I shall enjoy that.'

*

The All-Seeing Ones began their search from the last known position of Ephraim and his group, and calculated how far they could have travelled if they were moving fast. Messengers alerted their colleagues in the north and south regarding these dangerous criminals and their quest for valuable metals. As ever, the manhunt would be crowned with complete success.

Ephraim knew the tracks, water-sources and mines as well as the guards did, and might well guess what the guards would do. So the big guard, who was to lead the patrol, abandoned the usual plan, and trusted to his instinct. In Ephraim's place, he would have tried to reach the area full of abandoned mines. There was no water, the heat was unbearable, there were snakes everywhere, and there were no mines there . . . Who would venture into that hell? In fact, it was an admirable hiding-place, and perhaps more than that, assuming the seams were not completely exhausted. As regulations demanded, the big guard took two experienced men and four dogs with him. By cutting across the usual routes, he could intercept the fugitives in the hilly area where a few wool-trees grew.

Kem was bound hand and foot. He longed to set off on the trail of General Asher, who had still not been found, but he had to stay in Memphis to protect Pazair. None of his men would be vigilant enough.

He could tell from Killer's edginess that danger was not far away. After two failures, the shadow-eater would have to take extra care so as not to be spotted. Now that the element of surprise had been lost, arranging an accident would be far more difficult, but he would surely try to take strong, decisive action.

Keeping Pazair safe had become the main goal of Kem's life. To him, the judge embodied an impossible form of life which must be preserved at all costs. Never, in all the long years when Kem had suffered so much, had he met anyone like this. He would never admit to Pazair how much he admired him, for fear of feeding that creeping, unctuous beast called vanity, which was so swift to rot hearts.

Killer awoke. Kem gave him some dried meat and sweet beer, then leant back against the low wall of the terrace from which they kept watch on the judge's house. Now it was his turn to sleep, while the baboon stood guard.

The shadow-eater cursed his bad luck. He had been wrong to accept this job; it was outside his special expertise, which was killing quickly and leaving no trace. For a moment he felt like giving up, but if he did his employers would denounce him, and his word would carry no weight against theirs. Moreover, he had set himself a challenge. Up till now, his career had not been marred by a single failure; he took extraordinary pleasure in the fact that his finest victim would be a judge.

Unfortunately, Pazair was guarded closely and efficiently. Kem and Killer were worthy opponents, and it would be extremely difficult to beat their vigilance. Since the panther episode, Kem had never been more than a pace away from the judge, and he had strengthened that protection by using several of his best men.

The shadow-eater's patience was infinite. He could wait for the smallest chink in the armour, the slightest slip in alertness. As he was walking through the market at Memphis, where sellers were displaying exotic products from Nubia, an idea came to him. An idea which might well eliminate his opponent's main line of defence.

'It's late, my darling,' said Neferet.

A dozen unrolled papyri lay in front of Pazair, who was seated on the floor, flanked by two tall pedestal lamps. 'After reading these scrolls, I'm not tired any more.'

'What are they?'

'Denes's accounts.'

'Where did you get them?'

'From the Treasury.'

'You didn't steal them, did you?' she asked with a smile.

'I made an official request to Bel-Tran, and he responded at once by giving me these.'

'What have you discovered?'

'A number of irregularities. Denes has failed to pay certain duties, and seems to have cheated over the tax on his revenues.'

'What penalty does he face, apart from a fine?'

'With the help of my comments, Bel-Tran will be able to ruffle Denes's financial peace.'

'Denes again – you're becoming obsessed with him.'

'Why, why, why is he so sure of himself? I must somehow find a way of piercing his shell.'

Neferet sighed, and changed the subject. 'Any news of Suti?'

'No. He should have sent me a message through the desert guards.'

'He must have been prevented from doing so.'

'Yes . . . he must have.'

His hesitation surprised Neferet. 'What do you think has happened?'

'Nothing.'

'The truth, Judge Pazair!'

'During the last court session, Denes alleged that Suti had betrayed me.'

'And you're letting yourself wonder if it's true?'

'May Suti forgive me.'

'Two in the right-hand gallery, the others in the left,' ordered Ephraim. 'Suti and I will take the middle one.'

The miners were uneasy.

'They're in very bad condition,' said one of them. 'The

props are half rotten, and if they collapse we won't get out alive.'

'I brought you to this hell because the desert guards think it's worked-out. No water and only worked-out mines, that's what they say in Kebet. I've shown you the ancient well; you can find the treasure in these galleries yourselves.'

'Too risky,' decided one miner. 'I'm not going in.'

Ephraim went over to him. 'Us inside, you on your own outside? I don't like the idea of that.'

'Too bad.'

Ephraim's fist smashed down on the man's skull with such incredible force that he crumpled to the ground.

One of his colleagues bent over him, then straightened up, his eyes wide. 'You've killed him!'

'One suspect the less. Let's get into the galleries.'

Suti went ahead of Ephraim.

'Go carefully, little man. Feel the beams above your head.'

Suti crawled along the red, stony ground. The slope was gentle, but the ceiling very low. Ephraim held the torch.

A white gleam sprang out of the darkness. Suti reached out and felt it. The metal was soft and cool.

'It's silver – gold-bearing silver!'

Ephraim passed him some tools. 'A whole seam of it, little man. Get it out without damaging it.'

Under the pale silver gleamed gold. The precious silver was used to cover the flagged floors of certain temple rooms and sacred objects which stood on the floor, so as to preserve their purity. Indeed, the dawn was made up of silver stones which radiated the original light from the dawn of creation.

'Is there any gold further down?' asked Suti.

'Not here, little man. This mine's only a first step.'

The four dogs guided the three desert guards. For two hours, they had detected a human presence in the area around the abandoned mines. The guards kept their satisfaction in check; without a word, they readied their bows and arrows.

Flat on their bellies at the top of a hill, their tongues lolling out, the dogs watched the miners removing several big chunks of pure silver from the galleries. A veritable fortune.

When the thieves assembled to celebrate their triumph, the guards fired their arrows and released the dogs. Two miners were brought down by arrows, and a third by the dogs. Suti took refuge in a deep gallery, and was soon followed by Ephraim, who had strangled a dog with one hand, and by the last survivor from his team.

'Go deeper!' roared Ephraim.

'We'll suffocate,' objected Suti.

'Do as you're told.'

Ephraim led the way. Seizing a stone, he broke through the ceiling of the gallery at its end. Heedless of the dust and fragments of stone which fell on him, he created a chimney in the crumbling rock. Feet braced against the walls, he dragged up Suti, who helped his companion. The three men managed to get out of the mine and, once outside, gulped in the fresh air greedily.

'We can't stay here – the guards won't give up this easily. We'll have to walk for at least two days, without water.'

The big guard stroked the dogs, while his men dug trenches for the bodies. The first part of the operation had been a success: they had killed most of the fugitives and recovered a large quantity of silver. But three men were still on the run.

The guards conferred. Their leader decided to go on alone, with the strongest dog and some food and water, while the other two took the silver back to Kebet. The fugitives had no chance. Knowing they were being hunted by men armed with bows and arrows and by a ferocious hound, they would have to force their pace. There was no water within a three-day march. Heading south, they would inevitably run into a guard patrol.

The patrol-leader and his dog would take no risks, and would be content to bring down their quarry by cutting off all lines of retreat. Once more, the All-Seeing Ones would have defeated the criminals.

On the morning of the second day, the three fugitives licked up the dew that had collected on the stones along the way. The surviving miner wore round his neck his leather purse, which contained fragments of silver, and clutched it constantly. He was the first to break. His legs buckled, and he fell to his knees on the scree.

'Don't leave me,' he begged.

Suti turned and went back.

'If you try to help him,' warned Ephraim, 'you'll both die. Follow me, little man.'

If he carried the miner on his back, Suti would soon be left behind. They would become lost in this torrid desert, where only Ephraim knew the way.

His chest on fire, his lips cracked, the young man followed Ephraim.

The dog wagged its tail eagerly when it found the miner's body. The guard praised the dog, and turned the body over with his foot. The man had not been dead for long. He was still clutching his leather purse, so tightly that the guard had to cut his hands off to recover the silver.

The guard sat down, worked out the value of the silver, gave his dog food and water, and then had some himself. Used to interminable marches, neither of them felt the sun's bite. They were careful to rest regularly, and wasted no energy at all.

Now it was two against two, and the distance between guard and thieves was getting smaller all the time.

He turned round. Several times he had had the feeling he

was being followed; but the dog was pulling in the direction of his quarry, and did not signal anything amiss.

He cleaned his dagger in the sand, moistened his lips, and resumed the hunt.

'Just one more effort, little man. There's a seep-well near the mine.'

'Are you sure it won't have run dry?'

Ephraim did not reply. So much suffering must not be in vain.

A circle of stones marked the site of the well. Ephraim dug with his bare hands, and Suti soon joined him. At first there was nothing but sand and pebbles; then softer, almost damp earth; finally, a sort of mud, wet fingers – and water, water rising up from the underground Nile.

The guard and his dog watched. An hour ago they had caught up with the fugitives, but they had kept their distance. They heard the pair sing out, saw them gulp down water, congratulate themselves, then head for the abandoned mine, which was not shown on any map.

Ephraim had played his game astutely. He had not confided in anyone at all, keeping strictly to himself a secret he must have extracted from an old miner.

The guard checked his bow and arrows, took a swig of water and prepared to end the hunt.

'This is where the gold is, little man, in the last seam in a forgotten gallery. Enough gold to enable two good friends to live out happy lives in Asia.'

'Are there any other places like this?'

'A few.'

'Why don't we mine them?'

'There's no time. We've got to get away – and so has our employer.'

'Who is he?'

'The man who's waiting for us here at the mine. The three of us will get the gold out and transport it on sleds to the sea. Then a boat will take us to a desert area where chariots are hidden.'

'Have you stolen a lot of gold for him?'

'He won't like it if you ask questions. Look, there he is.'

A small man with thick legs and a ratlike face came towards them. Despite the burning sun, Suti's blood ran cold.

'The guards are hot on our heels,' said Ephraim. 'Let's dig the gold out and get away from here.'

'You've brought me an very unexpected companion,' said General Asher in astonishment.

With his last shreds of strength, Suti fled towards the desert. He had no chance of beating Ephraim and Asher – the latter was armed with a sword. First he must escape from them, then he would have to think.

A guard and his dog barred his way. Suti recognized the big man who oversaw the recruitment of miners. The guard drew his bow; one word from him and the dog would go for Suti's throat.

'Not a step further, my lad.'

'Thank be to the gods that you're here!'

'You can pray to the gods before you die.'

'Don't shoot the wrong man. I'm on an official mission.'

'On whose orders?'

'Judge Pazair's. I had to prove that General Asher was mixed up in smuggling precious metals. And now I've got that proof. The two of us can arrest him.'

'You're a brave lad, but you're out of luck. I work for General Asher.'

30

Neferet lifted the double lid of her face-paint box, which was divided into compartments decorated with red flowers. It contained pots of lotion, ointment, face- and eye-paint, pumice stone and perfumes. While the household, including the monkey and the dog, was still asleep, she liked to make herself beautiful, then walk barefoot in the dew to hear the first song of the tits and the hoopoes.

The dawn was her time, the time when life was reborn, the awakening of a nature whose every sound was filled with the divine word. The sun had just overcome the darkness, after a long and perilous battle; its triumph nourished creation, its light was transformed into joy, making the birds dance in the sky and the fish jump in the river.

Neferet treasured the happiness the gods had granted her, which she must give them in return. It did not belong to her, but passed through her like a flow of energy, coming from and returning to the source. Anyone who tried to take possession of the otherworld's gifts condemned themself to drying out like a dead branch.

Kneeling before the lakeside offering-table, the young woman laid a lotus-flower on it. It embodied the new day, in which eternity would be accomplished in a moment. The entire garden was meditating, the leaves of the trees bowing beneath the morning breeze.

When Brave licked her hand, Neferet knew that the sacred rite was at an end. The dog was hungry.

'Thank you for seeing me before you go to the hospital,' said Silkis. 'The pain is unbearable – it kept me awake all last night.'

'Lean your head back.' Neferet examined her patient's left eye.

Silkis was so anxious that she could not keep still.

'This is a sickness I know and can cure,' said Neferet. 'Your eyelashes are so tightly curled that they're touching the eye and irritating it.'

'Is it serious?'

'No, only painful. Would you like me to deal with it immediately?'

'If it doesn't hurt too much.'

'It's a simple procedure.'

'Nebamon hurt me terribly when he altered my body.'

'This will be far less severe than that.'

'I trust you.'

'Stay seated, and relax.'

Eye complaints were so common that Neferet always kept her private store of remedies stocked with plenty of ingredients, even rare ones like bat's blood, which she mixed with frankincense to produce a sticky lotion. This she spread over the offending eyelashes, after drawing them out straight. As they dried, she held them rigid and was able to pull them easily out by the roots. To stop them growing back, she applied a second lotion consisting of chrysocolla and galenite.

'There you are,' she said. 'All better.'

Silkis smiled with relief. 'You have such a gentle touch – I didn't feel anything at all.'

'I'm glad to hear it.'

'Will I need any other treatment?'

'No, the cure's permanent.'

'I do wish you could cure my husband. His skin condition worries me a lot – he's so busy that he never thinks about his health. I hardly see him any more. He leaves early in the morning and comes back late in the evening, laden with papyri which he reads half the night.'

'Perhaps this overwork will be over soon.'

'I'm afraid it won't. At the palace they all praise his skill, and at the Treasury they can't manage without him.'

'That's rather good news, isn't it?'

'At first sight, yes, but for our family life, which he and I value so much . . . The future frightens me. People are talking about Bel-Tran as a future director of the Double House. Egypt's finances in his hands – what a crushing responsibility!'

'Aren't you proud of him?'

'I'm afraid the distance between us will grow even greater, but what can I do? I admire him so much.'

Every day, the fishermen laid out their catch before Mentmose, who was now overseer of Delta fisheries in a little town near to the coast. Fat, heavy and slow, Mentmose was sinking deeper into boredom every day. He hated his miserable official house, loathed having to deal with the fishermen and fish-sellers, and flew into a rage over the most insignificant detail. How could he get out of this dead-end town? He never saw a single courtier any more.

When he saw Denes appear at the end of the quay, he thought he was hallucinating. Forgetting all about the fishermen, he stared at the ship-owner's massive form, his square face, his fringe of fine white beard. It really was him, one of the wealthiest, most influential men in Memphis.

'Get out of here,' Mentmose ordered a fisherman who wanted him to authorize the sale of the fish.

Denes observed the scene with an ironic smile. 'You're a

long way from the Memphis city guards' operations, my friend.'

'Are you laughing at my misfortune?'

'Not at all. I'd like to lighten your burden.'

During his career Mentmose had lied a great deal. When it came to trickery, dissimulation and setting snares, he considered himself an expert, but he had to admit that the ship-owner ran him close.

'Who sent you, Denes?' he asked.

'No one – it was my own idea. Tell me, would you like to get your revenge?'

'Revenge . . .' said Mentmose in a high voice.

'Afer all, we have a common enemy.'

'Pazair, Judge Pazair!'

'An inconvenient individual,' observed Denes. 'His position as Judge of the Porch hasn't cooled his ardour in the least.'

Mentomose clenched his fists in fury. 'Replacing me with that damned Nubian, who's even more savage than his baboon!'

'You're right: it was unjust and stupid. Shall we rectify the error?'

'What are you planning to do?'

'To tarnish Pazair's reputation.'

'But he's beyond reproach, isn't he?'

'He only seems so, my friend. Every man has his weaknesses, and if not we'll invent some. Do you recognize this?' Denes held out his right hand, in the palm of which lay a seal-ring. 'He uses it to authorize documents.'

'Did you steal it?'

'I had it made. It's a copy of one I was given by a scribe on his staff. We'll use it on a rather compromising document, to put an end to Judge Pazair's career and restore you to your rightful position.'

The air was laden with a strong smell of fish, but to Mentmose it smelt very sweet.

*

Pazair placed the ebony box between Neferet and himself. He slid open the drawer, and took out the varnished terracotta playing pieces, which he placed on the thirty bone squares. Neferet made the first move. The rule was to move a pawn of the darkness towards the light, trying not to let it fall into one of the traps laid in its path, and passing through numerous doors.

Pazair made a mistake on his third move.

'You aren't paying attention,' said Neferet.

'I still haven't heard from Suti.'

'Is that really so surprising?'

'Yes, I'm afraid it is.'

'How could he possibly get in touch with you from the middle of the desert?'

The judge's mood did not lighten.

'Are you daring to think he really has betrayed you?'

'He should at least give me a sign that he's alive.'

'Are you thinking the worst?'

Pazair got to his feet, forgetting the game.

'You're wrong,' said Neferet. 'Suti's alive.'

The rumour had all the effect of a thunderclap: after being a principal official of the Treasury and overseer of granaries, Bel-Tran had been appointed director of the Double House, in charge not only of the country's money but also of its trade, and answerable only to the tjaty and Pharaoh. It was his job to receive and draw up registers of minerals and precious materials, the tools destined for the temple workshops and for specialist craftsmen, sarcophagi, ointments, fabrics, amulets and ritual objects. He would pay peasants for their harvests and set taxes, assisted by a large number of scribes.

Once the surprise was over, nobody challenged his appointment. Many court officials had recommended Bel-Tran to the tjaty. Although his rise to power was too rapid for certain people's tastes, and although he had a difficult personality and a marked tendency towards authoritarianism, he was remarkably skilled and efficient. He had proved that in the way he had reorganized the secretariats, producing greater efficiency and better control of expenditure. Beside him, the former overseer cut a poor figure: soft and slow, he had become bogged down in routine, with a foolish obstinacy which had discouraged his remaining supporters.

Once appointed to this coveted post as a reward for his tireless work, Bel-Tran made no secret of his intention to leave the well-trodden pathways and give the Double House more prestige and authority. Ordinarily impervious to choruses of praise, Tjaty Bagey had been impressed by the sheer number of people who had spoken in Bel-Tran's favour.

Bel-Tran's huge new offices were right in the heart of Memphis. At the entrance, two guards checked all visitors. Neferet explained who she was, and waited until her summons was confirmed. She walked past an enclosure for animals and a poultry-yard where accounting-scribes received taxes paid in kind. A stairway led to granaries which were emptied and re-filled according to contributions. An army of scribes, seated on daises, occupied one floor of the building. The head produce-receiver kept a permanent watch on the entrance to the shops where the peasants deposited fruit and vegetables.

Neferet went into another building and passed through a chamber where senior scribes were drawing up lawsuits. A secretary showed her into a vast hall with six pillars, where Bel-Tran received important visitors. The new director of the Double House was issuing instructions to three scribes; he spoke quickly, darting from one idea to another, dealing with several different matters at the same time.

As soon as he had finished he dismissed them and turned to her. 'Thank you for coming, Doctor.'

'Your health is now a concern of the state.'

'It mustn't hinder my work.' He showed her his left leg, on which there was a red patch a hand-span across, edged with white spots.

'Your liver is overtaxed and your kidneys aren't working properly. You must rub the red patch with a lotion made of acacia-flowers and egg-whites, and several times a day you must drink ten drops of aloe-juice, as well as your usual remedies. Be patient, and treat yourself regularly.'

'I confess I often forget.'

'This condition may become serious if you don't take care.'

'I do wish I could deal with everything, but I can't. I hardly ever even get the chance to see my son. I'd love to see him more often, make him understand that he'll be my heir, make him aware of what his responsibilities will be.'

'Silkis complains that you're never at home.'

'My dear, sweet Silkis! She understands how important my work is. And how is Pazair?'

'The tjaty has just summoned him, no doubt to speak to him about the arrest of General Asher.'

'I admire your husband enormously. In my opinion, he was predestined for greatness; there is a strength of will in him which cannot be diverted from its path by anything or anyone.'

When Pazair arrived, Bagey was engrossed in a legal scroll concerning free travel on ferries for people of slender means. Shoulders rounded, back bent, the tjaty was clearly feeling the weight of his years. He did not raise his head, merely said, 'I expected you earlier.'

Pazair was surprised at such curtness.

'Sit down, Judge. I must finish this work.'

Pazair, who thought he had won Bagey's friendship, was suddenly the object of cold anger, and had no idea why.

'The Judge of the Porch's behaviour must be beyond reproach,' the tjaty went on in a hoarse voice.

Pazair nodded. 'I have myself fought in the past to ensure that the office was not tainted by any irregularities.'

'And now you occupy that office.'

'Are you accusing me of something?'

'Worse than that, Pazair. How can you possibly justify what you have done?'

'What am I accused of?'

'At least be honest and admit what you have done.'

'Am I to be condemned yet again without proper grounds?'

The tjaty rose angrily to his feet. 'You forget to whom you are speaking.'

'I abhor injustice, wherever it comes from.'

Bagey snatched up a wooden tablet covered in hieroglyphs, and thrust it in front of Pazair. 'Do you recognize this seal?'

'Of course – it's mine.'

'Read the tablet.'

'It concerns the delivery of best-quality fish to a store-house in Memphis.'

'A delivery you yourself ordered. But that storehouse does not exist. You diverted the fish from its proper destination, the city market. The boxes were found in outbuildings at your house.'

'The investigation was remarkably prompt.'

'You were denounced.'

'By whom?'

'The letter was anonymous but all the details were accurate. In Kem's absence, the checks were carried out by one of his subordinates.'

'Who is a former colleague of Mentmose, no doubt.'

Bagey looked embarrassed. 'That's correct.'

'Did it not occur to you that someone was trying to deceive you?'

'Of course it did. All the signs point in that direction: the fact that Mentmose is in now employed in the fisheries, that the checks were made by a man loyal to him, his longing for revenge . . . But that does not change the fact that your seal has been used on a compromising document.' The look in the tjaty's eyes had changed; Pazair saw that he hoped to be shown that the truth was very different.

'I have conclusive proof of my innocence.'

'Nothing would please me more.'

'I always take one or two simple precautions,' explained Pazair. 'I learnt a lot from my previous ordeal – I'm less stupid than I used to be. Every bearer of a seal ought to take precautions. I suspected that some day my enemies would use mine, so on all official documents I place a small red dot after the ninth and twenty-first words, and beneath my seal I draw a tiny five-pointed star, almost drowned in the ink but visible if you look very closely. Please examine this tablet, and check whether those signs are there.'

The tjaty stood up, went to a window and held the tablet in the sunlight.

'They are not there,' he said.

Bagey left nothing to chance. He himself checked a large number of the documents signed by Pazair, and found that every one all had the red dots and the little star. Rather than share this secret, he advised the Judge of the Porch to alter his mark and not to speak of it to anyone.

On the tjaty's orders, Kem questioned the guard who had received the denunciation but omitted to inform his commander. The man soon broke, and confessed that he had been bribed and had had an assurance from Mentmose that Judge Pazair would be found guilty. Kem instantly sent a detachment of five footsoldiers to the coast. They brought Mentmose back to Memphis in a very short time.

'I am receiving you in private,' said Pazair, 'in order to spare you a trial.'

'I'm innocent,' protested Mentmose hotly. 'I've been slandered.'

'Your accomplice has confessed.'

Mentmose's bald head turned pink. With great difficulty, he contained his rising anger. He, who had held so many destinies in the palm of his hand, had no influence over this judge. So he became unctuous. 'The weight of misfortune overwhelms me, and evil tongues are attacking me. How can I defend myself?'

'Give up and admit your guilt.'

Mentmose was having difficulty breathing. 'What fate have you in store for me?'

'You aren't worthy of any position of authority. The poison flowing through your veins rots everything you touch. I am sending you far away from Egypt, to Byblos in Canaan. You will be one of a team of men maintaining our ships.'

'Working with my hands?'

'Is there any greater happiness?'

Mentmose's nasal voice filled with anger. 'I'm not the only one responsible. It was Denes who prompted me to do it.'

'How can I believe you? Lying was always your favourite pastime.'

'Don't say I didn't warn you.'

'Strange that you should suddenly show goodness.'

Mentmose sniggered. 'Goodness? It's nothing of the sort, Judge Pazair. It's delight in seeing you struck by lightning, drowned in the Nile's flood, buried beneath a hail of stones. Good fortune will desert you, and you'll have more and more enemies.'

'Your boat leaves in an hour. Don't be late.'

31

'Get up,' ordered Ephraim.

Suti struggled to his feet. He was naked, with a wooden collar round his neck and his arms tied behind him at the elbows. Ephraim dragged him forward by a rope bound tightly round his waist.

'A spy, a filthy spy! I was wrong about you, little man.'

'Why did you join the team of miners?' asked General Asher softly.

Suti's lips were dry, his body covered in bruises from punches and kicks, his hair full of sand and blood, but he still defied his enemy. His eyes were lit by a flame of intense hatred.

'Let me teach him a lesson,' said the guard.

'Later,' said Asher. 'His resistance amuses me. You were hoping to catch me red-handed, and prove that I'm the head of a gold-smuggling ring, weren't you? Well, you're right. A senior officer's pay wasn't enough for me. I can't change Egypt's government, so I decided to make the most of my fortune.'

'Are we heading back north?' asked Ephraim.

'Certainly not. The army's waiting for us at the edge of the Delta. We'll go south, skirt Elephantine and fork off towards the western desert, where we'll join Adafi.'

With chariots, food and water, thought Suti, Asher would probably succeed.

'I have the map of the wells,' said Asher. 'Have you loaded the gold?'

Ephraim smiled. 'This time the mine really is worked out. But what about the spy? Shouldn't we get rid of him?'

'No. Instead, we'll conduct an interesting experiment: how long will he survive, walking all day, on only two mouthfuls of water? Suti's very strong, and the results will be useful when we are training the Libyan troops.'

'All the same, I'd like to question him again,' persisted the guard.

'Be patient. He won't be stubborn for much longer.'

Aggression. An aggression which was part of his body, imprinted on each muscle, in each step. Because of it, Suti would fight until his heart refused to speak in his limbs. Held prisoner by the three plotters, he'd had no chance of escape. At the very moment when he had Asher in his grasp at last, his victory had been transformed into disaster. There was no way of letting Pazair know what he'd discovered. All his efforts had been in vain, and he'd die far from his friend, from Memphis, the Nile, the gardens and the women.

Dying was stupid. Suti didn't want to go back under the earth, to talk to jackal-headed Anubis, to confront Osiris and the scales of judgment. He wanted to fall in love, fight his enemies, gallop in the desert wind, get richer than the richest noble in all Egypt, just for the fun of it. But the collar felt heavier and heavier.

He walked on, dragged by a rope attached to the back of Asher's chariot. It pulled tight as soon as he moved his legs, and tore at the flesh of his hips, his back and his belly. The chariot went slowly, because it could not leave the narrow track in case it sank into the sand, but to Suti it seemed to go faster and faster, forcing him to use up his very last resources. He was close to giving up, but somewhere he found new energy to keep himself alive. One more step, and then another.

And the day passed, dragging its way through his battered body.

The chariot halted. Suti stood for a long time, motionless, as if he no longer knew how to sit down. Then his knees bent, and he sank down, backside resting on his heels.

'Are you thirsty, little man?' Sarcastically, Ephraim swung a water-skin under his nose. 'You're as strong as a wild animal, but you won't last more than three days. I've got a bet with the guard, and I hate losing.'

He gave Suti a drink. The cool water moistened Suti's lips and spread through his entire being.

The guard aimed a kick at him, knocking him down in the sand. 'My friends are going to rest; I'm standing watch, and I'm going to interrogate you.'

'We've got a bet on,' objected Ephraim. 'You mustn't damage him.'

Suti stayed stretched out on his back, his eyes closed. Ephraim went away, and the guard walked round his prisoner.

'Tomorrow, you'll die, but before then you'll talk. I've broken tougher miners than you.'

Suti barely heard the sound of the man's footsteps in the sand.

'You told us about your mission,' the guard went on, 'but I want to be absolutely sure. How were you keeping in contact with Judge Pazair?'

Suti smiled faintly. 'He'll come and find me. All three of you will be convicted.'

The guard sat down by Suti's head. 'You're alone, and you haven't managed to get word to the judge. No one's coming to find you, no one's going to help you.'

'Thinking that will be your last mistake.'

'The sun's making you mad.'

'The more treacherous you are, the more you lose touch with reality.'

The guard hit him. 'Don't annoy me any more, or I'll give you to my dog as a toy.'

The sun was low in the sky to the west, and the heat began to ease. It would soon be dark.

'Don't go to sleep just yet,' said the guard. 'Until you talk, my dagger will be at your throat.'

'I've told you everything.'

'No you haven't. Why did you run head first into our ambush?'

'Because I'm a fool.'

The guard stabbed his dagger into the ground beside Suti's head. 'All right, then, my lad, sleep if you can. Tomorrow will be your last day.'

Despite his exhaustion, Suti could not even doze. Out of the corner of his eye, he saw the guard run his finger over the point of his dagger, then the blade. When the man lay down, he put it beside him. Suti knew he would use it before dawn. As soon as he sensed Suti weakening, he'd cut his throat, only too happy to rid himself of a dead weight. He'd have no difficulty justifying himself to General Asher.

Suti gritted his teeth. He wasn't going to die in a surprise attack. When the guard attacked him, he'd spit in his face.

The moon, the sovereign warrior, pointed its curved knife at the summit of the sky. Suti begged it to come down and kill him, to cut short his suffering. He might not be very devout, but couldn't the gods grant him this one little favour?

The only reason he was still alive was his love of of the desert. In sympathy with the power of desolation, aridity and solitude, he breathed according to its rhythm. The ocean of sand and stone was becoming his ally. Instead of exhausting him, it gave him back his strength. This winding-sheet, sunburnt and windswept, pleased him more than any noble's tomb.

The guard sat nearby, watching for the prisoner to weaken.

As soon as Suti closed his eyes, the killer would slip into his sleep, like the raptor death, and steal his soul. Nourished by the sun, his thirst slaked by the moon, Suti would hold firm.

Suddenly, the guard gave a choked shout. He waved his arms like a wounded bird, tried to stand up, and fell backwards.

Emerging from the night, the goddess of death appeared.

Suti's head cleared for a moment, and he knew he must be dying. He was passing through the fearsome space between the worlds, where monstrous creatures attacked the dead.

'Help me,' commanded the goddess. 'We must turn the body over.'

Suti rolled on to his side. 'Panther! But how—'

'Later. We must hurry. I have to recover the dagger I stuck in his neck.'

The Libyan helped her lover struggle to his feet, and they pushed the body over, she with her hands, he with his feet. Panther pulled out the weapon, cut Suti's bonds, took off the wooden collar and held him close.

'It's so good to feel you,' she murmured. 'It was Pazair who really saved you. He told me that you'd left from Kebet, with the miners. I found out that you'd disappeared, and I followed the guards – they were boasting that they'd soon find you. But before long the only one left was this one. We Libyans know how to survive without difficulty in this hell. Come, you must drink some water.'

She led him behind a sand-dune, from where she had watched the camp and the chariots without being seen. Incredibly, she had carried all through the desert two big water-skins, which she had filled at each watering-place, a sack of dried meat, a bow and some arrows.

'What about Asher and Ephraim?' asked Suti.

'They're asleep in the chariots, along with an enormous dog. It would be useless trying to attack them.'

Suti was close to fainting, but Panther covered him with kisses.

'No,' he croaked, 'not now.'

She helped him to lie down, lay beside him, and began to caress him. Despite his extreme weakness, she was delighted to find his virility stirring.

'I love you, Suti, and I'm going to save you.'

A frightened shriek tore Neferet from her sleep. Pazair moved, but did not wake. She put on a robe and went out into the garden.

She found a servant-girl, who had brought fresh milk, standing by the stone threshold in tears. She had dropped her pots, and the contents were spread out all over the ground.

'There,' she whimpered, pointing at threshold.

Neferet crouched down. She saw the shattered fragments of red vases, which had borne the name of Judge Pazair, painted with a brush in black ink, followed by incomprehensible magic incantations.

'The evil eye!' cried the servant. 'We must leave this house at once.'

'The power of Ma'at is more powerful than the power of darkness, isn't it?' said Neferet, taking the girl by the shoulders.

'But the judge's life will be shattered like the vases.'

'Do you think he doesn't know how to defend himself? Watch these fragments for a minute – I'm going to the workshop.'

Neferet returned with a pot of glue, of the sort used by vase-menders. With the servant's help, she spread out all the pieces of the puzzle and, without hurrying, fitted them back together. Before gluing them in place, she removed the inscriptions.

'You are to give these vases to the washerman,' she told the girl. 'As they hold the water which washes away the soiling, they will themselves be purified.'

The servant kissed Neferet's hands. 'Judge Pazair is very lucky. Ma'at protects him well.'

'Will you bring us some fresh milk?'

'I'll go and milk my best cow straight away,' said the girl, and she ran off.

The peasant drove a post twice his own height into the soft earth, and attached a long, flexible pole to the top. To the thicker end he attached a clay counterweight, and to the thinner end a rope holding a pottery jar. Hundreds of times every day, he would slowly pull the rope so that the jar dipped into the canal water, then slacken his grip so that the counterweight raised the pot to the level of the pole, then rotate the pole and empty the jar's contents on to his plot of land. In an hour, he could transfer enough water to irrigate all his crops. By means of this system, water was carried to high ground which the Nile flood did not reach.

He had barely started work when he heard a deep, most unusual sound, almost like an animal roaring. Clutching the rope, he listened hard. The roar grew louder. He grew more worried. He abandoned his watering, climbed a nearby hillock and looked around.

Stupefied, he saw a raging flood racing towards him, laying waste everything in its path. Upstream, the built-up canal bank had been breached; men and animals were drowning, struggling in vain against the muddy torrent.

Pazair was the first official to arrive on the scene. Ten dead, half a herd of cattle lost, fifteen watering-machines destroyed: the toll was heavy. Already, workmen were rebuilding the bank, helped by army artificers; but the water reserves had been lost. The state, in the person of the Judge of the Porch, who had assembled the population in the square of the nearest village, undertook to compensate and feed them. But everyone wanted to know who was responsible for the incident; so Pazair questioned – at great length – the two local officials in charge of maintaining the canals, reservoirs and dams. He could find no fault with their work: regular inspections had been carried out according to regulations, and had shown nothing amiss. The judge exonerated them at a public audience.

Everyone named the only possible culprit: the evil eye. A curse had fallen upon the dam, before reaching the village, then the province, and then the entire country.

Pharaoh was no longer exercising his protective role. If he did not celebrate his festival of regeneration within the year, what would become of Egypt? The people still trusted him. Their voices and their demands would reach the village headmen, town mayors, provincial governors, court dignitaries, and Ramses himself. Everyone knew that the king travelled a lot, and there was nothing he did not know about his subjects' aspirations. Faced with difficulty, sometimes lost in the turmoil, he had always taken the right path.

The shadow-eater had at last seen a way out of the stalemate. To get close enough to Pazair to cause an 'accident', he must first eliminate the judge's protectors. The most dangerous was not Kem but Killer, whose canine teeth were longer than a panther's, and who could bring down any wild animal. However, the shadow-eater had unearthed the right adversary, albeit at a high price.

Killer would not be able to hold out against another male baboon which was larger and more powerfully built. The shadow-eater had found one, chained it, muzzled it, and left it unfed for two days while he waited for the right moment. That moment came at midday, when Kem fed Killer. At the far end of the terrace from which the Nubian was watching Pazair's house, the judge was dining alone with his wife. Killer picked up a piece of beef and began to eat it.

The shadow-eater unchained his baboon and carefully removed its muzzle. Attracted by the smell of the meat, it climbed silently along the white housefront and stood up in front of its fellow baboon. Ears red with anger, eyes bloodshot, buttocks flushing purple, the attacker showed its teeth, ready to bite. Killer abandoned his meal and did likewise. The attempt at intimidation had failed; each recognized the same desire to fight in the other's eyes. Not a sound had been made.

By the time Kem's instinct told him to turn round, it was too late. The two baboons roared, and charged in to attack.

It was impossible to separate them or strike down the enemy; the baboons formed a single mass, constantly moving, rolling to right and left. With incredible ferocity, they tore at each other, screaming and howling.

The battle did not last long. The shapeless mass grew still. Kem did not dare go near.

Very slowly, an arm emerged and pushed away the loser's corpse.

'Killer!' Kem ran to him and supported him as he collapsed, covered in blood. He had succeeded in ripping out the attacker's throat, though it had cost him deep wounds.

The shadow-eater spat with rage and slunk away.

Killer stared fixedly at Nefetet while she cleaned his wounds, before spreading Nile mud over them.

'Is he in much pain?' asked Kem anxiously.

'Few humans would be so brave.'

'Can you save him?'

'Oh yes, certainly. His heart is as strong as a rock, but he'll have to accept bandages and must stay relatively still for a few days.'

'He'll do it if I tell him to.'

'For the next week, he mustn't eat too much. And if there's any problem at all, let me know at once.'

Killer laid a paw on the doctor's hand. Eternal gratitude filled his eyes.

*

The council of doctors was meeting for the tenth time.

In Qadash's favour were his age, reputation, experience, and ability as a tooth-doctor – Pharaoh much appreciated this last. On the other hand, Neferet had exceptional healing powers, demonstrated her skill daily at the hospital, was admired by many other doctors, and had the support of Queen Tuya.

'My dear colleagues,' said the oldest council member, 'the situation is becoming scandalous.'

'Well, let us elect Qadash, then,' cut in Nebamon's former assistant. 'He would be a sound, safe choice.'

'What have you against Neferet?'

'She's too young.'

'Ordinarily I'd agree with you,' said another doctor, 'but she runs the hospital remarkably well and efficiently.'

'The office of principal doctor demands a representative, level-headed man,' persisted Nebamon's man, 'not a young woman, however gifted she may be.'

'I think you're wrong. She has plenty of energy and stamina, whereas Qadash hasn't any longer.'

'Speaking like that about our esteemed colleague is insulting.'

'Esteemed? Not by everyone, by any means! Don't forget, he was mixed up in illegal trafficking, and was found out by Judge Pazair.'

'Who, I remind you, is Neferet's husband.'

The argument grew more and more acrimonious, and the tone more and more shrill.

'My dear colleagues,' protested the oldest council member, 'have a little dignity!'

'Let us put an end to this, and proclaim Qadash's election.'

'Never! It must be Neferet – no one else.'

Despite all the promises, the situation ended as it had begun. One firm decision was taken: at the council's next meeting, the kingdom's new principal doctor would be appointed.

*

Bel-Tran had brought his son to visit his country estate. The little boy played with the papyri, jumped over the folding stools, and broke a scribe's brush.

'That's enough,' said his father sternly. 'You must respect those things – you'll use them yourself when you're a senior official.'

'I want to be like you and order other people about, but not do any work.'

'Unless you work, and work hard, you won't even be a field scribe.'

'I'd rather be rich and own lots of land.'

Pazair's arrival interrupted the conversation. Bel-Tran handed his son over to a servant, who took him to the stable-yard; he was learning to ride.

'You look worried, my friend,' said Bel-Tran.

'I still don't know what's happened to Suti.'

'What about Asher?'

'There's been no trace of him in Egypt, and the border posts haven't reported anything.'

'That's strange.'

'And then there's Denes. What did you make of his accounts?'

'They're full of irregularities – indeed, they're full of intentional "mistakes" and malpractice.'

'Enough, taken together, to incriminate him?'

'You're nearing your goal, Pazair.'

It was a warm night. Brave, who had been pelting round and and round the lotus-pool, fell asleep at his master's feet. Exhausted after a long day at the hospital, Neferet had dozed off. The judge was drawing up the charge-sheet by the light of two lamps.

Asher had condemned himself by his flight, giving irrefutable substance to the charges laid against him at his previous trial. Denes had committed fraud, theft and bribery. Sheshi led a group of smugglers. Qadash, though only an accomplice, could not be unaware of these activities. Many precise points and damning statements, both written and oral, would be presented to the jurors.

The four men would find their reputations destroyed, and would be sentenced to punishments of varying severity. The judge would have liked to destroy the whole conspiracy, but he still had to find Suti and continue his quest for the truth: along the path that led to Branir's murderer.

32

The ostrich halted, sensing danger. It flapped its wings frantically but of course could not take off, so it executed a little dance hailing the rising sun, and then hurtled off into the dunes.

Suti tried in vain to draw his bow. His muscles hurt, and he was still too weak to do much. Panther massaged him, and rubbed his limbs with ointment from a phial which hung from her belt.

'How many times have you been unfaithful to me?' she asked.

Suti gave an exasperated sigh.

'If you don't tell me, I'll leave you here – and don't forget that I've got the water and food.'

'All that effort, and it comes down to this.'

'When you want the truth, there's nothing you can't do. Judge Pazair convinced me of that.'

Her words made Suti feel a bit better, but he knew that Ephraim and Asher would soon find the dead guard and set off in search of their prisoner.

'We must get away from here as quickly as possible,' he said.

'Answer me first.' The dagger-blade stroked Suti's chest. 'If you've betrayed me, I'll turn you into a eunuch.'

'You know about my marriage to Tapeni.'

'I shall strangle her with my bare hands. Any others?'

'Of course not.'

'Not even at Kebet, that town of every luxury?'

'I signed on as a miner, and after that I was in the desert.'

'At Kebet, nobody stays chaste.'

'Well, I did.'

'I ought to have killed you the moment I found you.'

'Quiet!' hissed Suti. 'Look.' He pointed.

Ephraim had discovered the guard's body. He loosed the dog. It sniffed the wind, but would not leave its master. Ephraim conferred with Asher. After a while, they got into their chariots and drove off. It seemed that escaping from Egypt with the gold was more important than hunting down their prisoner. Now that the guard was dead, there were only two of them to share the spoils.

'They've gone,' said Panther.

'Let's follow them.'

'Have you lost your mind?'

'I'm not going to let Asher get away.'

'Aren't you forgetting the state you're in?'

'Thanks to you, it's improving by the hour. Walking will help me get better.'

Panther shook her head. 'I'm in love with a madman.'

Seated on the terrace of his house, Pazair gazed eastwards. Unable to sleep, he had left the bedchamber in order to immerse himself in the starry night. The sky was so clear that he could make out the shapes of the pyramids at Giza, draped in a dark blue tinged with the first blood of the dawn. Anchored in a thousand years of peace, built of stone, love and truth, Egypt lay spread out in the mystery of the day that was about to be born. Pazair was no longer the Judge of the Porch, not even a judge at all; he tried to forget himself, to become absorbed into the immensity where the impossible marriage between the invisible and the visible was celebrated, in communion with the spirits of the ancestors, whose presence remained tangible in every murmur of its earth.

Barefoot and silent, Neferet appeared beside him.

'It's very early – you should still be asleep,' he said.

'This is my favourite time of day. In a few moments, gold will illuminate the fringe of the mountains and the Nile will come back to life.' She stroked his hair. 'What's troubling you?'

How could he admit to her that he, the judge who was so sure of his truths, was in the grip of doubt? People thought him unshakeable, impervious to events, whereas the least of them marked him, sometimes like a wound. Pazair could not accept the existence of evil and had not become inured to crime. Time had not wiped away the death of Branir, which he had been unable to avenge.

'I want to give up, Neferet.'

'You're exhausted, otherwise you wouldn't say that.'

'I agree with Kem: justice, if it even exists, cannot be applied.'

'Are you afraid you may fail?'

'My cases are solid, my accusations well founded, my arguments irrefutable. But Denes, or one of his acolytes, can still use a legal weapon and destroy what I have patiently built up. If that happens, what would be the point of going on?'

'This feeling will pass.'

'The ideal of Egypt is sublime, but it doesn't stop men like Asher existing.'

'But you put a stop to his activities, didn't you?'

'After him there'll be another, and then another . . . Is it worth caring any more?' He took her hands tenderly. 'I'm unworthy of my office.'

'Pointless words are an insult to Ma'at.'

'Would a true judge doubt the law?'

'The only thing you doubt is yourself.'

The young sun bathed them in light which was at once fierce and caressing.

'It is our life that's in the balance, Neferet.'

'We aren't fighting for ourselves,' she said. 'We're fighting so the light that unites us can grow. To deviate from that path would be a crime.'

'You're stronger than I am.'

She smiled in amusement. 'Tomorrow you'll agree with me.'

United, they experienced the rebirth of the day.

Pazair was due to see the tjaty, but he kept sneezing and complained of a sharp pain in the back of his neck. Neferet calmly gave him a drink made from the willow-tree's leaves and bark, a remedy she often used to combat fever and several other illnesses.*

The medicine worked quickly. Pazair was breathing more easily and looking much better by the time he was shown into Bagey's office.

'Tjaty,' he said, 'here is the complete file regarding General Asher, Denes the ship-owner, Sheshi the inventor, and Qadash the tooth-doctor. As Judge of the Porch, I ask you to hold a public trial: the charges are high treason, damage to the kingdom's security, attempted murder, perjury and fraud. Certain points are well established, others are still somewhat vague. The charges are, nevertheless, such that I feel there is no point in waiting any longer.'

'This is an exceptionally serious matter.'

'I am aware of that.'

'The accused are persons of considerable standing.'

'That makes their crimes all the more abhorrent.'

*Willow contains the substance that forms the essential component of aspirin, which was thus 'invented' and used more than four thousand years ago.

'You are right,' said Bagey. 'Even though Asher has not yet been found, I shall open the trial after the Festival of Opet.'*

'Suti is still missing, too.'

'I share your anxiety about him, so I have ordered a division of footsoldiers to search the desert around Kebet, together with special desert guards. Now tell me, in your findings do you identify Branir's murderer?'

'No, Tjaty,' said Pazair despondently. 'I have failed. I cannot be certain.'

'I want his name.'

'I shall never give up the investigation.'

'And there's another point. Neferet's candidacy for the post of principal doctor is awkward. Those with sharp minds will not fail to point out that Qadash's conviction would free the way for her, your wife, to be appointed, and they will try to discredit her.'

'I have thought of that.'

'What does Neferet herself think?'

'That if Qadash is guilty he must be punished.'

'You must not fail. Neither Denes nor Sheshi is an easy target, and I fear the possibility of a reversal of the situation, of the kind Asher specializes in. The traitors have a particular talent for justifying their crimes.'

'I shall place my hopes in your court. Therein, falsehood will be destroyed.'

Bagey laid a hand on the copper heart he wore round his neck. The gesture signified that he was placing the awareness of his duty before everything.

The conspirators had gathered at the abandoned farm where they met in emergencies. Denes, usually so confident and sure of himself, seemed worried.

---

*The hippopotamus-goddess, who symbolized fertility, both spiritual and material.

'We must act at once,' he said. 'Pazair has handed his files to Bagey.'

'Is that just a rumour, or do you know it for a fact?'

'The matter has been lodged with the tjaty's court and will be heard after the Festival of Opet. It's good that Asher's implicated, but I don't want my own reputation compromised.'

'I thought the shadow-eater was supposed to incapacitate Pazair?'

'He's had a run of bad luck, but he won't give up.'

'That's all very well, but it hasn't prevented you from being charged.'

'We're the masters of the game – don't forget that. All we have to do is use a little of our power.'

'Without coming out into the open?'

'That won't be necessary. A simple letter will do it.'

Denes's plan was accepted.

'To avoid any more problems like this,' he added, 'I suggest we bring forward one of the phases of our plan: the replacement of the tjaty. That way, it won't matter what Pazair does in future.'

'Isn't it a bit too soon to do that?'

'You must face the facts: the time has become propitious.'

Watched in astonishment by Asher and Ephraim, the dog leapt out of the chariot and charged up a small hillock covered in scree.

'Since his master's death,' said Ephraim, 'it's as if he has gone mad.'

'We don't need him,' said the general. 'I'm sure now that we've escaped the patrols. The way is open.'

The dog raced about with foam-flecked lips. It seemed to fly from rock to rock, paying no heed to the sharp flints. Suti forced Panther to lie down flat in the sand and drew his bow. When the dog was within bowshot, it halted.

Man and animal stared defiantly into each other's eyes.

Well aware that he must not miss his target, Suti waited for the attack; he did not like the idea of killing a dog. Suddenly, the animal gave a howl of despair and crouched down in the manner of a sphinx. Suti laid his bow aside and went towards it. Submissively, the dog let itself be stroked. There was exhaustion and anguish in its eyes. It had been freed from a cruel master, but would it be accepted by a new one?

'Come,' said Suti, and the dog's tail wagged joyfully. Suti realized he had a new ally.

Qadash staggered drunkenly into the ale-house. The forthcoming trial terrified him, despite Denes's assurances and the solid foundations of the conspiracy. He was afraid that he would be unable to stand up to Judge Pazair and that, if he was found guilty, the post of principal doctor would be lost to him for ever. So he felt an irresistible urge to dull his senses; wine had not given enough relief, so he was planning to relax his nerves in the lap of a prostitute.

Sababu was once again running the largest establishment in Memphis, and maintaining its good reputation. Her girls recited poems, danced and played music before offering their erotic skills to an elegant, wealthy clientele.

Qadash bumped into the door-keeper, pushed aside a flute-player and charged at a very young Nubian servant-girl, who was carrying a dish of pastries. He threw her on to a pile of cushions and tried to rape her. The girl's cries of distress alerted Sababu, who beat him away with a hearty punch.

'I want her,' he demanded.

'This little one is only a servant.'

'I want her all the same.'

'Leave this house at once.'

The girl took refuge in Sababu's arms.

'I'll pay whatever I have to.'

'Keep your money – just go.'

'I'll have her, I swear I will.'

295

Qadash did not go far from the ale-house. Crouching in the shadows, he kept watch as the employees left. A little after dawn, the Nubian girl and other young serving-wenches came out of the ale-house and set off home.

Qadash followed his prey. As soon as he saw a deserted alleyway, he seized her by the waist and clamped a hand over her mouth. The girl struggled, but he was half crazed and far too strong for her to fight off. He tore off her dress, threw himself on her, and raped her.

'My dear colleagues,' announced the oldest member of the doctors' council, 'we can defer the appointment of the kingdom's principal doctor no longer. Since no other candidates have presented themselves, we must choose between Neferet and Qadash. We shall continue our deliberations until the decision has been taken.'

This line of action received general approval. Each member of the council spoke, sometimes calmly, sometimes vehemently. Qadash's supporters were virulently against Neferet. She, they said, was taking advantage of her husband's position to have Qadash found guilty, thus clearing the path for herself. Slandering a well-reputed doctor and soiling his reputation were scandalous tactics, which ought to disqualify her.

A retired doctor added that Ramses was suffering more and more often from toothache, and he would like to have an experienced tooth-doctor at hand. Should they not think first and foremost of Pharaoh, on whom the country's prosperity depended? No one opposed the argument.

After four hours of debate, the votes were cast.

'Qadash will be the next principal doctor,' announced the oldest council member.

Two wasps buzzed round Suti and attacked the dog, which was chewing a piece of dried meat. The young man watched them, hoping to spot their nest buried in the ground nearby.

'My luck has returned,' he said. 'Get undressed.'

Panther was glad of the invitation. When she was naked, she rubbed herself against Suti.

He shook his head. 'We'll make love later.'

'Then why . . . ?'

'Every single bit of my body must be covered. I'm going to dig up part of the nest and put it in a water-skin.'

'If you're stung, you'll die. Those wasps are ferocious.'

'I intend to live until I'm very old.'

'To sleep with other women?'

'Cover my head.'

As soon as he had located the nest, Suti began to dig. The wasps' stings did not penetrate the fabric, despite the fury of their attacks. Suti thrust a good portion of the buzzing horde into the water-skin.

'What are you going to do with it?' asked Panther.

'That's a military secret.'

'Stop laughing at me.'

'Trust me.

She laid her hand on his chest.

'Asher mustn't get away,' he said.

'Don't worry, I know the desert.'

'If we lose his trail . . . '

She knelt down and stroked the tops of his thighs, so diabolically slowly that Suti was unable to resist her. Between a nest of maddened wasps and a dozing hound, they revelled in their youth with an insatiable passion.

Neferet was very upset.

The young Nubian girl had been weeping ever since her admission to the hospital. Wounded in her soul as well as her flesh, she clung to the doctor as though she were drowning. The savage who had raped and deflowered her had fled, but several people had given fairly good descriptions. However, only the victim's direct testimony could lead to a formal accusation.

Neferet treated the girl's internal injuries and gave her remedies to calm her. Eventually the girl began to shake less violently, and she accepted a drink of water.

'Would you like to talk to me?' asked Neferet.

The child's lost gaze fixed on her protector. 'Will I get better?'

'I promise you will.'

'There are vultures in my head, they're devouring my belly . . . I don't want a child by that vile monster.'

'You won't have one.'

'But suppose I'm pregnant?'

'I will carry out the abortion myself.'

The little Nubian burst into tears again. 'He was old,' she revealed between sobs, 'and he stank of wine. When he attacked me in the ale-house, I noticed he had red hands, prominent cheekbones and a big nose, covered in purple veins. He was a demon, a real demon with white hair.'

'Do you know his name?'

'No, but Sababu does.'

It was the first time Neferet had ventured into a house of pleasure. The wall-paintings and perfumes were heady and suggestive, for they had to create an atmosphere conducive to the abandonment of good sense. The courtesans must be able easily to seduce visitors in search of love.

Neferet was not kept waiting, for she had treated Sababu in Thebes.

'I'm happy to welcome you,' said Sababu, 'but aren't you worried about what people will say?'

'Not in the least.'

'You've cured me, Neferet. Since I've been following your treatment to the letter, my rheumatism has almost disappeared. But you look tense, worried . . . Does this place offend you?'

'No, it's nothing like that. I've bad news for you, I'm afraid. One of your servant-girls has been raped savagely.'

'I thought that crime no longer existed in Egypt.'

'She's a little Nubian girl, whom I have been treating at the hospital. Her body will recover, but it may never forget. She gave me a description of the attacker, and said you know his name.'

'If I tell you, will I have to give evidence at the trial?'

'Of course.'

'In this business, discretion has to be my only religion.'

'As you wish.' Neferet turned away.

'No, wait. Please try to understand, Neferet. If I give evidence, people will realize that I am in an illegal situation.'

'All that matters to me is the look in that little girl's eyes.'

Sababu bit her lip. 'Will your husband help me keep this house?'

'I can't promise that.'

'The criminal's name is Qadash. He almost assaulted the child right in here. He was drunk – and very violent.'

Sombre and withdrawn, Pazair paced up and down. 'I don't know how to tell you the bad news, Neferet.'

'Is it that bad?'

'Yes. It's an injustice, a monstrous injustice.'

'I must speak to you about a monster, too. You must arrest him at once.'

He went to her and took her face in his hands. 'You've been crying.'

'This is very serious, Pazair. I've begun the investigation; now you must finish it.'

'Qadash has been elected principal doctor of the kingdom. I have just been officially informed.'

'Qadash is a criminal of the vilest kind: he has raped a young virgin.'

33

Ephraim and Asher rested before skirting Elephantine and crossing the southern border. They found a cave big enough to hide the chariot, and spent a peaceful night there. The general knew where the garrisons were, and how to slip through the holes in the net. He was looking forward to enjoying his wealth in Libya with his friend Adafi, and to training sand-travellers to attack Egypt. The future was rosy; it was a good time to plan an invasion of the Delta and the acquisition of the best lands in the north-west.

Asher lived only to take his revenge on Egypt. By forcing him to flee, Judge Pazair had created an enemy whose cunning and obstinacy would be more destructive than an entire army.

Eventually the general fell asleep, while his accomplice stood guard.

The water-skin of wasps clutched in one hand, Suti climbed on to the rock that overhung the entrance to the cave. He edged forward with difficulty, taking care not to knock down any pebbles and betray his presence. Panther watched anxiously. Would he be quick enough to extract the nest without being stung, skilful enough to throw it into the cave? He would not get a second chance.

Reaching the edge of the overhang, he concentrated. Flat

on his belly, he held his breath and listened intently. Not a sound. High in the sky, a falcon was circling. Suti took out the stopper, swung his arm like a pendulum, and flung the water-skin into his enemies' lair.

An infuriated buzzing filled the calm air of the desert. Ephraim came staggering and lurching out of the cave, surrounded by enraged wasps which he tried in vain to wave them away. Stung a hundred times, he crumpled, clutched his throat, and suffocated to death.

Asher had reacted more quickly: he dived under the chariot and kept very still. When the wasps had gone, he emerged from the cave, sword in hand.

In front of him were Suti, Panther and the dog.

'Three against one?' sneered the general. 'Very brave!'

'What would a coward like you know about bravery?' retorted Suti.

'I have a great deal of gold. Aren't you two interested?'

'I'm going to kill you, Asher, and then I shall take it all.'

'You're dreaming. That dog has lost all his fierceness, and you haven't got a weapon.'

'Wrong again, General,' said Suti, and Panther picked up the bow and arrows and handed them to him.

Asher retreated, his ratlike face tensing. 'If you kill me, you'll get lost in the desert.'

'Panther's an excellent guide, and I'm getting used to the place. We'll survive, you can be sure of that.'

'It is wrong for a human being to raise his hand against another human being: that is our law. You wouldn't dare kill me.'

'You no longer count as a human being.'

'Vengence taints the soul. If you make yourself guilty of murder, you'll be condemned by the gods.'

'You don't believe that any more than I do. If they exist, they'll be grateful to me for having killed the most poisonous snake in Egypt.'

'The load on this chariot is only a small part of my treasure. Why don't you come with me? I can make you richer than a Theban noble.'

'Come with you where?'

'To Adafi's lands, in Libya.'

'He'd kill me.'

'I shall introduce you as my most faithful friend.'

Panther was behind Suti. He heard her coming closer. Libya, her country! Wouldn't General Asher's proposition seduce her? To take Suti to her homeland, have him all to herself, live in luxury . . . How could she resist all those temptations? But he did not turn round. Traitors prefer to strike from behind.

Panther handed him an arrow.

'You're wrong,' Asher hissed. 'We were born to understand each other. You're an adventurer, like me; Egypt suffocates us – we need broader horizons.'

'I saw you torture an Egyptian, a defenceless man, to death. You showed him no mercy.'

'I wanted him to tell me the truth – I knew he was planning to denounce me. You'd have done what I did.'

Suti drew his bow and fired. The arrow found its mark between the general's eyes.

Panther flung her arms round her lover's neck. 'I love you – and we're rich!'

Kem arrested Qadash at his home, at midday. He read him the charge-sheet and bound his hands. The tooth-doctor protested only feebly; his head felt heavy and his vision was blurred.

He was taken immediately to Judge Pazair.

'Do you confess your guilt?' asked the judge.

'Of course not.'

'Witnesses have identified you.'

'I went to Sababu's ale-house, met some disagreeable girls and left almost at once. I didn't like any of them.'

'Sababu's statement is very different.'

'Who will believe that old prostitute?'

'You raped a young Nubian girl, a servant in Sababu's house.'

'That's slander! That liar wouldn't dare say such a thing to my face.'

'Your judges will decide.'

'You surely don't intend to—'

'The trial will take place tomorrow.'

'I want to go home.'

'I shall not allow you to go free in the meantime: you might attack another child. Kem will ensure your safety at the guard-post.'

'My . . . safety?'

'That entire district of the city wishes to kill you.'

Qadash clung to the judge. 'You have a duty to protect me!'

'That is, alas, true.'

Nenophar went to the weaving-shed with the firm intention of obtaining the best fabrics, as usual, and making her rivals white with rage. She looked forward to many enjoyable hours making elaborate dresses which she would wear with incomparable elegance.

Tapeni irritated her, with her mutinous eyes and her air of superiority; but she knew her craft to perfection and procured flawless fabrics. Thanks to her, Nenophar was always ahead of fashion.

Tapeni wore a curious smile.

'I want some finest-quality linen,' demanded Nenophar.

'That will be difficult.'

'I beg your pardon?'

'To tell you the truth, it won't be possible.'

'What has got into you, Tapeni?'

'You're very rich, and I'm not.'

'I've always paid you, haven't I?'

'I want more now.'

'A price increase in the middle of the year? That is hardly correct, but I'll agree.'

'It isn't fabric that I want to sell you.'

'Then what is it?'

'Your husband is a well-known man, a very well-known man.'

'Denes?'

'He must be above reproach.'

'What are you insinuating?'

'High society is cruel. If one of its members is found guilty of immorality, he soon loses his influence – and even his fortune.'

'Just what do you mean by that?'

'Don't lose your temper, Nenophar. If you're reasonable and generous, your position won't be threatened. All you have to do is buy my silence.'

'What do you know that is so compromising?'

'Denes is unfaithful to you.'

Nenophar thought the roof of the workshop had fallen on her head. If Tapeni had proof of what she was alleging, and if she spread the story throughout the Theban nobility, Nenophar would become a laughing-stock and would never dare reappear at court or at any social event.

'You . . . you're making it up!'

'No, I'm not. I know everything.'

Nenophar did not argue. Her spotless reputation was her most precious possession. 'What do you want in exchange for your silence?'

'The revenues from one of your farms and, as soon as possible, a fine house in Memphis.'

'That's outrageous!'

'Can you imagine yourself as a scorned wife, with the name of Denes's mistress on everyone's lips?'

Nenophar closed her eyes in panic.

Tapeni felt a savage joy. Sharing Denes's bed just once – he was a dull and selfish lover – had opened the road to riches. Soon she would be a great lady.

Qadash was in a rage. Certain that Denes would already have smoothed the way, he demanded to be freed immediately. Now that he was sober again, he kept boasting about his new appointment in an effort to get out of his cell.

'Calm down,' ordered Kem.

'Show some respect, my friend! Do you know whom you are speaking to?'

'To a rapist.'

'There's no need to use that word.'

'It is the simple and horrible truth, Qadash.'

'If you don't let me go, you'll be in serious trouble.'

Kem smiled. 'I'm just about to unlock the cell door.'

'At last! You aren't stupid – and you'll find that I can be grateful.'

Just as Qadash took a breath of air in the street, the Nubian gripped him by the shoulder.

'Good news, Qadash: Judge Pazair has been able to assemble the jurors more quickly than he expected. I'm taking you to court.'

When Qadash saw Denes among the jury, he knew he was saved. A sombre, tense atmosphere reigned over the porch in front of the Temple of Ptah, where Pazair had convened the court. A large crowd, alerted by word of mouth, was eager to attend the trial. The guards kept them outside the wooden building, which comprised a roof and thin pillars; inside were the witnesses and the jurors, six men and six women of varying ages and social situations.

Pazair, wearing an old-style kilt and short wig, seemed to be in the grip of intense emotion. After placing the

305

proceedings under the protection of Ma'at, he read out the charges.

'Qadash the tooth-doctor, principal doctor of the kingdom, residing at Memphis, is accused of having raped a young Nubian girl, who works as a servant in the house of the lady Sababu, yesterday morning at dawn. The victim, who is in hospital, does not wish to appear and will be represented by Doctor Neferet.'

Qadash was relieved. He could not have hoped for better. He was confronting his judges, whereas the servant was running away from them. He knew three members of the jury besides Denes, and they were all influential people who would plead in his favour. Not only would he emerge from the court completely exonerated but he would attack Sababu and obtain compensation.

'Do you acknowledge the facts?' asked Pazair.

'I deny them.'

'Let the lady Sababu give her testimony.'

All eyes fell on the famous owner of the best-known alehouse in Egypt. Some had thought she was dead, others in prison. A little too heavily made-up, but with her head held proudly high, she stepped forward with confidence.

'I remind you,' said Pazair, 'that false testimony is subject to serious punishment.'

'Qadash the tooth-doctor was drunk. He forced open my door and threw himself at the youngest of my Nubian servant-girls, whose only task is to offer pastries and drinks to the clients. If I had not intervened and had him thrown out, he would have done violence to the child.'

'Are you certain of that?'

'Do you consider an erect penis sufficient proof?'

A murmur ran through the assembled throng. The coarse language shocked the jury.

Qadash asked and was given permission to speak.

'This person runs an illegal business,' he said. 'Every day

she soils the good name of Memphis. Why do the city guards and the courts not deal with this prostitute?'

'We are not here to try Sababu, we are here to try you. Moreover, your morality did not prevent you from going to her ale-house and attacking a little girl.'

'It was just a moment of madness – everyone's felt that that at some time.'

'Was the Nubian child raped in your ale-house?' Pazair asked Sababu.

'No.'

'What happened after this first attack?'

'I calmed the child down and she went back to work. At dawn she left, as usual, to go home.'

Sababu was followed by Neferet, who described the girl's physical state after the rape. She did not spare the assembly any of the details, and they were horrified by such savagery.

Qadash broke in again. 'I do not question my excellent colleague's observations, and I deplore this young girl's misfortune, but how am I involved?'

'I would remind you,' Pazair declared solemnly, 'that the only punishment applicable to rape is the pain of death. Doctor Neferet, have you firm proof that Qadash is the guilty party?'

'He exactly fits the victim's description of her attacker.'

'And I would remind the court,' cut in Qadash, 'that Doctor Neferet tried to obtain the post of principal doctor. She failed, and must now feel a certain resentment. Moreover, it is not up to her to carry out an investigation. Has Judge Pazair recorded the girl's own statement?'

That argument carried weight.

The Judge of the Porch called two river boatmen who had seen the tooth-doctor run away after the crime. They both identified him as the rapist.

'I was drunk,' he protested. 'I must have fallen asleep there. Is that reason to accuse me of such an appalling crime, for which, if I was a juror myself, I would apply the law without hesitation?'

Qadash's defence made a good impression. The girl had been raped, the tooth-doctor had indeed been in the vicinity, and had tried to attack her earlier that night: taken together, the evidence tended to mark him out as the rapist, but, out of respect for the rule of Ma'at, Judge Pazair could not venture beyond a strong presumption. His links with Neferet weakened her testimony, on which Qadash had succeeded in throwing suspicion.

However, the Judge of the Porch asked her to speak again in the girl's name, before giving his conclusions and presiding over the jury's deliberations.

A trembling hand slipped into Neferet's.

'Come with me,' begged the Nubian girl, clinging to the doctor. 'I will speak, but not alone.'

Hesitating, stumbling over each word, she spoke of the violence she had suffered, the terrible pain, the despair. When her deposition was over, a heavy silence fell over the porch.

His throat dry, the judge asked her the decisive question. 'Do you see, anywhere in the court, the man who raped you?'

The girl pointed to Qadash. 'That's him.'

The deliberations did not last long. The jurors applied the ancient law, which was such a strong deterrent that no rapes had been committed in Egypt for many years. Because of his eminent position in his profession and his office of principal doctor, Qadash would not enjoy the benefit of any extenuating circumstances. The jury unanimously sentenced him to death.

34

'I shall appeal,' declared Qadash.

'I have already set things in motion,' said Pazair. 'Beyond the court of the porch, there is only the tjaty's court.'

'He will overturn this unjust verdict.'

'Have no illusions. Bagey will confirm the sentence if your victim confirms her accusations, which have been duly registered.'

'She wouldn't dare!'

'Don't deceive yourself.'

The tooth-doctor did not seem unduly shaken. 'Do you really think I'll be punished? Poor judge! You'll soon sing a different song.'

Qadash laughed darkly as Pazair left the cell.

It was the end of September, the second month of a mediocre annual flood, and Egypt was fervently celebrating the festival of the goddess Opet, symbol of fertility and generosity. For the twenty or so days while the floodwaters receded, leaving behind the fertile silt, the people haunted the riverbanks, where travelling vendors sold melons and watermelons, grapes, pomegranates, bread, cakes, grilled poultry and beer. Open-air kitchens served good, cheap meals, while female musicians and professional dancing-girls delighted the ear and the eye. Everyone knew that the temples were celebrating the rebirth of the creative energy; it had been exhausted in the course of a long year during which the gods had made the earth fertile. To prevent them leaving the world of men, they must be offered the joy and gratitude of an entire land, in which no one died of hunger or thirst. The Nile would thus retain its original power, which it drew from the ocean of energy in which the universe was bathed.

At the height of the celebrations, Kani, High Priest of Amon, opened the innermost shrine in the temple; it contained the statue of the god, whose true form was for ever inaccessible. Covered with a veil, it was placed in a gilded wooden boat carried by twenty-four shaven-headed priests dressed in long linen robes. Amon emerged from the temple accompanied by his wife, Mut, the divine mother, and their son, Khonsu, who traversed the celestial spaces in the form of the moon. Two processions left for the temple at Luxor, one travelling by river and the other by land.

Dozens of vessels escorted the divine trinity's enormous, gold-covered boat, while girls playing tambourines, sistra and flutes hailed its progress towards the southern shrine. Pazair, as Judge of the Porch, had been invited to the ceremony that took place in the great courtyard of the temple of Luxor. Outside, everyone was celebrating, but behind the temple's high walls all was silence and contemplation.

Kani offered flowers to the divine trinity and poured a libation in their honour. Then the ranks of courtiers parted to allow the Pharaoh of Egypt to pass through, and all bowed in unison. The king's innate nobility and seriousness impressed Pazair deeply. A man of medium height, very robust, with a hooked nose, broad forehead, and red hair hidden beneath the Blue Crown, he did not so much as glance at anyone, but gazed intently at the statue of Amon, the image of the creation mystery that Pharaoh embodied.

Kani read out a text singing of the many forms of the god, who could take form in the wind, in stone or in the ram with curled horns, without being reduced to any of these manifestations. Then the High Priest withdrew, leaving the king to cross the threshold of the covered shrine alone.

The food at the feast given by Pharaoh to celebrate the Festival of Opet included fifteen thousand loaves, two thousand cakes, a hundred baskets of dried meat, two hundred of fresh vegetables, seventy jars of wine and five hundred of beer, and fruit in profusion. More than a hundred floral arrangements decorated the tables where the revellers extolled the merits of Ramses' government and of Egyptian peace.

Pazair and Neferet received the warmest congratulations from the members of the court, the judge by reason of his courage in the Qadash affair, and Neferet because she had just been appointed – by unanimous vote of the council – the kingdom's principal doctor, following the rapist's dismissal. People tried to forget the flight of General Asher, who was still being hunted, and the murder of Branir, which was still unsolved, as were the mysterious deaths of the honour-guard. The judge remained impervious to these demonstrations of friendship; Neferet, whose charm and beauty enchanted the most cynical observers, paid them no more heed than he did. She could not forget the terrified face of a little girl whose wounds would never heal.

Kem, as commander of the city guards, was in charge of security at the feast. Flanked by Killer, he watched everyone who went near the judge, ready to take instant action if he or Killer sensed the slightest danger.

'You are the couple of the year,' declared Denes. 'Convicting a leading citizen like Qadash is a remarkable achievement, which honours our legal system. And seeing a woman as outstanding as Neferet rising to lead our doctors shows that our medical system, too, is excellent.'

Pazair smiled slightly. 'Don't be too lavish with your compliments.'

'You both have the ability to overcome any and all ordeals.'

Neferet had been looking around. 'I cannot see the lady Nenophar,' she said in surprise.

'She isn't well,' said Denes.

'Permit me to wish her a speedy recovery.'

'She will much appreciate your kind words. Now, may I deprive you of your husband for a few moments?'

Denes led Pazair into the shade of a canopy where cool beer and grape-juice were being served.

'My friend Qadash is a fine man. Becoming principal doctor turned his head, and that's why he got drunk and behaved so deplorably.'

'Not a single juror pleaded for mercy,' Pazair reminded him. 'You yourself kept silent and voted for the death penalty.'

'The law is explicit, but it takes account of remorse.'

'Qadash has shown none.'

'Is he not in deep despair?'

'Quite the contrary: he boasts and swaggers and issues threats.'

'He really has lost his head.'

'He's convinced that he'll escape the supreme penalty.'

'Has the date of his execution been set?'

'The tjaty's court has rejected his appeal and confirmed the sentence. In three days, Kem will give the poison to the condemned man.'

'Didn't you use the word "threats"?'

'If he were driven to suicide, Qadash would not sink into the abyss alone. He has promised me a confession before taking the poison.'

'Poor Qadash,' said Denes. 'To climb so high and sink so low . . . How can one not feel sadness and regret in the face of his fall? Soften his last hours, I beg you.'

'Kem is no torturer. Qadash is being treated properly.'

'Only a miracle can save him.'
'Who would pardon such a crime?'
'I shall see you presently, Judge Pazair.'

The council of doctors received Neferet. Her opponents asked her a thousand questions about abstruse details in the most varied fields. She made hardly any mistakes, and her election was confirmed.

Since Nebamon's death, many files relating to public health had remained in suspense. Neferet asked for a transitional period during which she could train her successor at the hospital. Her new duties seemed so overwhelmingly heavy that she wanted to run away, to take refuge in a post as a country doctor, to stay with the sick and appreciate every moment of their recovery. Nothing had prepared her to head a body of experienced doctors and influential courtiers, and an army of scribes overseeing the making and distribution of remedies, or to take decisions ensuring the population's health and well-being. Before, she had taken care of a village; now it was a kingdom so powerful that it forced the admiration of its enemies as well as its allies. Neferet dreamt of leaving with Pazair, hiding in a little house in Upper Egypt, at the edge of the farmed area, facing the Peak of the West, and savouring the wisdom of mornings and evenings there.

She would have liked to confide in Pazair, but when he returned from his office he wore an expression of utter dismay.

'Read this decree,' he said, handing her a fine-quality papyrus, marked with Pharaoh's seal. 'Please read it aloud.'

She did so. '"*I, Ramses, desire that heaven and earth should be joyful. May those who were in hiding emerge, may no man suffer by reason of his past faults, may the prisoners be freed, may the troublemakers be pacified, may the people sing and dance in the streets.*" An amnesty?'

'A general amnesty.'

'Isn't that highly unusual?'

'I know of no other example.'

'Why has Pharaoh decided to do this?'

'I don't know.'

'But it means Qadash will go free.'

'A general amnesty,' repeated Pazair, still shocked. 'Qadash's crime is wiped away, General Asher is no longer to be hunted down, the murders are forgotten, the case against Denes has been abandoned.'

'Aren't you being too gloomy?'

'This is failure, Neferet. Total, final failure.'

'Why don't you appeal to the tjaty?'

Kem opened the cell door.

Qadash seemed unworried. 'Are you freeing me?'

'How do you know that?'

'It was inevitable. A good man always triumphs.'

'You are benefiting from a general amnesty.'

Qadash recoiled from the fury in the Nubian's eyes. 'Don't lay a hand on me, Kem! You wouldn't benefit from any amnesty.'

'When you appear before Osiris, he will close your mouth. Demons armed with knives will slice open your flesh for all eternity.'

'Keep your childish stories to yourself. You have treated me with contempt, and insulted me. It's a pity . . . You missed your chance, like your friend Pazair. Make the most of your position; you won't command the guards for much longer.'

Tjaty Bagey was late. His legs and feet were swollen, and his shoulders bowed; and because of his exhausted state he had agreed to be brought to his office in a chair, by bearers. Just as they did every day, crowds of senior officials wished to speak with him, present him with difficulties they had come up against, and learn his opinion.

Although Pazair did not have an appointment, the tjaty received him first.

The judge could not contain his anger. 'This amnesty is unacceptable.'

'Be careful what you say, Judge of the Porch. The decree emanates from Pharaoh himself.'

'I cannot believe that.'

'It is, however, the truth.'

'Have you seen the king?'

'He dictated the text to me himself.'

'And what did you say?'

'I made him aware of my astonishment and incomprehension,' said Bagey.

'But could not sway him?'

'Ramses would brook no discussion.'

'It is appalling that a monster like Qadash should escape punishment!'

'The amnesty is a general one, Judge Pazair.'

'I refuse to apply it.'

'You must obey, as must I.'

'How can one condone such injustice?'

'I am old, you are young. My career is drawing to a close, yours is just beginning. Whatever my opinion may be, I am obliged to remain silent. You must not do anything foolish.'

'My mind is made up – I don't care what the consequences will be.'

'Qadash has been freed, and his trial cancelled.'

'Will Asher be given his job back, too?'

'His crime has been wiped out. If he can provide a plausible explanation, he will.'

'So only Branir's murderer escapes the pardon, because he hasn't been identified.'

'I am as bitter as you, but Ramses must surely not have acted lightly.'

'His motives do not matter to me.'

'He who rebels against Pharaoh rebels against life.'

'You are right, Tjaty Bagey. For that reason, I cannot continue my work any longer. You will have my resignation this very day. From now on, consider me no longer Judge of the Porch.'

'Think about this, Pazair.'

'In my place, would you have done otherwise?'

Bagey did not reply.

'There is one last favour I should like to ask of you,' said Pazair.

'As long as I am tjaty, my door will be open to you.'

'Free access would be contrary to the justice you and I love with all our hearts. I would ask you to keep Kem at the head of the city guards.'

'I have every intention of doing so.'

'And what will happen about Neferet?'

'Qadash will invoke his previous election and begin court proceedings to regain his title of principal doctor.'

'He need not trouble himself: Neferet has no wish to fight him. She and I are going to leave Memphis.'

'This is a terrible mess,' said Bagey wearily.

Pazair imagined Denes making merry with his friends. Pharaoh's astonishing decree had given them back their utterly unhoped-for purity. All they had to do was keep from making any more stupid mistakes, and they would remain respectable citizens and be able to continue their conspiracy, whose nature was still a mystery and, for Pazair, out of reach for ever. General Asher would soon reappear and no doubt produce an explanation to justify his absence. But what role had Suti played and where was he, assuming he was still alive?

Broken, sick at heart, the judge looked up and saw ten swallows fly overhead. A second group joined the first, then a third, then several others. A hundred birds brushed past him giving cries of joy, all along his way. Were they thanking him for saving one of their kind? Passers-by were moved by the sight. Everyone knew the proverb: 'He who has the swallow's favour has also the king's.' Swift, graceful, light of heart, the birds with their bluish, softly rustling wings accompanied Pazair to the door of his house.

Neferet was seated beside the lotus-pond where the tits were playing. She wore only a short, transparent dress, which left her breasts bare. As he approached, Pazair was enveloped by sweet scents.

'We have just received some fresh ingredients,' she explained, 'and I'm preparing the ointments and perfumed oils for us to use in the coming months. If you didn't have any in the mornings, I fear you'd be angry with me.' Her voice was full of humour.

Pazair kissed his wife on the neck, took off his kilt, and sat down on the grass. At Neferet's feet were stone vases. They contained frankincense, a translucent brown resin from incense trees; myrrh, stuck together in little red masses, gathered in the land of Punt; green galbanum gum resin imported from Persia; dark ladanum resin bought in Greece and Minoa. Phials contained several flower-essences. Neferet would use olive-oil, honey and wine to create subtle mixtures.

'I have resigned,' said Pazair. 'At least I no longer have anything to fear, since I no longer have any power.'

'What is the tjaty's opinion?'

'The only worthwhile one: a royal decree cannot be challenged.'

'As soon as Qadash reclaims his post as principal doctor, we'll leave Memphis. He'll have the law on his side, won't he?'

'I'm afraid so.'

'Don't be sad, my love. Our destiny is in God's hands, not in our own. It is his wishes that are being accomplished, not

317

our desires. We can build our own happiness. I'm glad. To live with you under the shelter of a hundred-year-old palm-tree, to heal humble folk, to take the time to love each other – what destiny could be better than that?'

'How can we forget Branir? And Suti . . . I can't stop thinking about him. My heart is on fire, and I balk like a donkey.'

'Whatever happens, don't ever change.'

'I shan't be able to give you a big house and such beautiful dresses any more.'

'I shall do very well without them. In fact, I might as well take this one off right away.'

Neferet slipped the straps down over her shoulders. Naked, she lay down beside Pazair. Their bodies understood each other perfectly; their lips united in such a passionate ardour that they shivered, despite the warmth of the sunset. Neferet's satin skin was a paradise in which only pleasure had the force of law. Pazair lost himself in it, intoxicated, communing with the wave that bore them away.

'More wine!' bellowed Qadash.

The servant hurried to obey.

Since his return, Qadash had been celebrating with two young Syrian lads – he would never touch a girl again. Before his misadventure, he had felt only a moderate taste for boys, but from now on he would be content with handsome foreign ones, whom he would denounce to the guards once he had tired of them.

In the evening, he would go to the conspirators' meeting summoned by Denes. Their anonymous letter to Ramses had had the results they had predicted. Caught in their net, the king had had to yield to their demands and proclaim a general amnesty in which Denes's case was wiped out along with the others. There was only one dark cloud on the horizon: the inevitable return of General Asher, who was now of no use to them whatever. But Denes would know how to get rid of him.

The shadow-eater entered Qadash's estate through the garden. He walked on the stone borders so as to leave no trace of his progress along the sandy path, and slunk stealthily off towards the kitchen. Crouching under the window, he listened to the two servants' conversation.

'I'm taking them a third pitcher of wine.'

'Should I open a fourth?'

'You'd better. The old fellow and the two young ones drink more than a thirsty regiment. I'm going, otherwise he'll fly into a rage.'

The wine-steward removed the stopper from a jar originating from the town of Imau, in the Delta and bearing the label 'Fifth year of Ramses'. A fine red wine, which lingered on the palate and banished inhibitions. His work done, the man left the kitchen and went outside to relieve himself against one of the garden walls.

The shadow-eater took advantage of the moment to fulfil his mission. Into the jar, he poured a poison based on plant extracts and snake-venom. Writhing in convulsions, Qadash would suffocate and die, together with his two foreign lovers, who would probably be accused of the crime. No one would have any interest in making this sordid story public.

After a death-agony lasting several minutes, Qadash gave up his soul to the god of hell. At that moment Denes was enjoying the caresses of a beautiful Nubian girl with plump buttocks and heavy breasts. He would never see her again, but intended to enjoy her with his customary brutality. To him, women were little more than beasts created for men's satisfaction.

Denes would miss his friend Qadash. Denes had treated him extremely well, even obtaining him the post of principal doctor, which had been promised to him since the beginning of the conspiracy. Unfortunately, though, the tooth-doctor had got old. On the verge of senility, making one mistake after another, he had become dangerous. By threatening to confess everything to Judge Pazair, Qadash had condemned himself to death: at Denes's suggestion, the conspirators had asked the shadow-eater to see to him. True, they regretted losing control of the post of principal doctor, but Judge Pazair's swift resignation had surpassed their wildest dreams. No one now would oppose their success.

The final stages were approaching: first they would seize the post of tjaty, then they would take supreme power.

35

A strong wind swept through the burial-ground at Memphis, where Pazair and Neferet were wending their way towards Branir's house of eternity. Before leaving the great city for the South, they wanted to pay homage to their dead master and assure him that, despite their slender means, they would keep trying to identify the murderer until their last breath.

Neferet was wearing the beaded amethyst belt Pazair had given her. Feeling the cold, the former Judge of the Porch had wrapped himself in a shawl and a woollen cloak. They met the conscientious old priest charged with the upkeep of the tomb and its garden; he received the proper fee from Memphis for seeing that the tomb was kept in perfect condition and for renewing the offerings.

In the shade of a palm-tree, the dead man's soul, in the form of a bird, came to slake its thirst in a pool of cool water after drawing the energy of resurrection from the light. Each day, it walked in the grounds of the shrine to breathe in the scents of the flowers.

Pazair and Neferet shared bread and wine in memory of their master, linking him to their meal, whose echo resounded in the invisible world.

'Be patient,' urged Bel-Tran. 'I can't bear to see you leave Memphis.'

'All Neferet and I want,' said Pazair, 'is to live a simple, calm life.'

'But neither of you has given your full measure,' argued Silkis.

'Opposing destiny is mere vanity.'

For their last evening in Memphis, Pazair and Neferet had accepted an invitation from Bel-Tran and Silkis. Bel-Tran, who was suffering from an attack of urticaria, had been persuaded by Neferet to let her treat his swollen liver and to adopt a healthier way of life. His leg-wound was weeping more and more frequently.

'Drink more water,' advised the doctor, 'and insist that your next doctor gives you something to ensure that your kidneys work properly – they don't at the moment.'

'One day perhaps I'll have time to take care of myself. The Treasury is drowning me in demands which must be dealt with immediately – but I mustn't lose sight of the overall picture.'

Bel-Tran's son and daughter came running in. The boy accused his sister of stealing the brush with which he was learning to draw beautiful hieroglyphs in order to become as rich as his father. The little red-haired girl, furious at the accusation, however right it might be, promptly slapped him and he burst into tears. Ever the attentive mother, Silkis took the children away and tried to put an end to the quarrel.

'You see,' said Bel-Tran, 'we badly need a judge!'

Pazair smiled. 'That investigation would be much too difficult for me.'

'You seem detached, almost pleased,' observed Bel-Tran in surprise.

'That's only how I seem; without Neferet, I'd have given up and despaired. This amnesty has ruined all my hopes of seeing justice triumph.'

'And I'm not looking forward to finding myself up against Denes again – which I'm bound to do without you as Judge of the Porch.'

'Trust Tjaty Bagey. He won't appoint anyone who cannot do the job.'

'There are rumours that he's preparing to leave office to enjoy a well-deserved retirement.'

'The king's decision has shaken him as much as me, and he's hardly in glowing health. But why has Ramses done this?'

'Perhaps he believes in the virtues of clemency.'

'It's done nothing to strengthen his popularity,' said Pazair. 'The people fear that his magical power is weakening and that, little by little, he's losing contact with the heavens. Giving criminals their freedom is not worthy of a king.'

'And yet his reign has been exemplary until now.'

'Can you understand his decision, and do you accept it?'

'Pharaoh sees further than we do.'

'That's what I thought, before the amnesty.'

'Return to work,' said Bel-Tran earnestly. 'Egypt needs you, and you, too, Neferet.'

'I'm afraid I'm as stubborn as my husband,' said Neferet.

'Will nothing persuade you to change your minds?'

'Only the re-establishment of justice.'

Bel-Tran himself refilled the cups with cool wine.

'After we've gone,' Pazair asked him, 'would you be good enough to carry on the search for Suti? Kem will help.'

'I'll approach the authorities straight away. But wouldn't it be better if you stayed in Memphis and worked with me? Neferet's reputation is so firmly established that she'll never lack for patients.'

'My financial skills are very limited,' confessed Pazair. 'You'd soon find me incompetent and a hindrance.'

'What are your plans, Doctor?'

. 'To settle in a village on the west bank of Thebes.'

Silkis, who had put the children to bed, came back into the room just in time to hear Neferet's answer.

She said, 'Give up the idea, I beg you! You can't just abandon your patients.'

323

'Memphis is bursting with excellent doctors.'

'Yes, but you're my doctor, and I don't want to change.'

'Between ourselves,' said Bel-Tran gravely, 'there must be no material difficulties. Whatever your needs may be, Silkis and I promise to meet them.'

'We're deeply grateful,' said Pazair, 'but I can no longer occupy a high post in the law. My ideals have been destroyed, and all I want is to enter into silence. The earth and animals don't tell lies; and I hope that Neferet's love will make the darkness less impenetrable.'

The solemnity of his words put an end to the discussion. The two couples talked about the beauty of the garden, the delicacy of the flowers and the excellent food, forgetting the difficulties that lay ahead.

'How are you feeling, my darling?' Denes asked Nenophar, who was reclining on a pile of cushions.

'Very well.'

'What did the doctor find?'

'Nothing, because I'm not ill.'

'I don't understand.'

'Do you know the fable of the lion and the rat? The lion caught the rat and was about to eat it. The rat begged for mercy: it was so small that it wouldn't nearly satisfy the lion's appetite, whereas if the lion let it live it might one day help him out of a sticky situation. The lion let it go. A few weeks later, hunters captured the lion and trussed him up in a net. The rat gnawed through the mesh, freed the lion and climbed up into its mane, and the two of them escaped.'

'Every schoolboy knows that story.'

'You should have remembered it before you slept with Tapeni.'

Denes's square face suddenly looked strained. 'Whatever are you talking about?'

Nenophar rose haughtily to her feet, full of icy anger.

'Because she was your mistress, that slut is behaving like the rat in the fable. But she's also the hunter. She's the only one who can free you from the net she's caught you in: blackmail. That's what we're facing – and all because of your infidelity.'

'You're exaggerating.'

'No, my loving husband. Respectability is a very expensive possession. Your mistress's tongue is hanging out so far that she may very well ruin our reputation.'

'I'll make her keep quiet.'

'You underestimate her. It would be better to give her what she wants, or we'll both be made to look ridiculous.'

Denes paced nervously up and down the room.

Nenophar went on, 'You seem to forget, my dear, that adultery is a serious offence, a vice punishable by law.'

'This was only a minor aberration.'

'Really? How often has it been repeated?'

'You're imagining things.'

'A noble lady on your arm for social occasions, and young girls in your bed the rest of the time. It's too much, Denes. I want a divorce.'

'You're mad!'

'On the contrary, I'm completely sane. I shall keep this house, my personal fortune, the inheritance I brought with me and my lands. Because of your disgraceful behaviour, the court will sentence you to pay me a food pension, and you'll be fined as well.'

Denes clenched his teeth. 'That isn't funny.'

'Your future is likely to be difficult, my darling.'

'You have no right to destroy our life like this. After all, we've spent our best years together.'

'Surely you aren't suddenly having tender feelings?'

'We've been partners for a long time.'

'You're the one who's dissolved the partnership. Divorce is the only solution.'

'Can you imagine the scandal?'

'Better that than ridicule. Besides, you'll be affected by it but I shan't. I shall be seen, quite rightly, as a victim.'

'This course of action is crazy. Accept my sincere apologies, and let us continue to put on a good front.'

'You betrayed me, Denes.'

'I didn't mean to, you know that. We're bound together, my dear. If you ruin me, you'll ruin yourself, too. Our affairs are so intermingled that a clean break is impossible.'

'I know them better than you do. You spend your time posturing, I spend mine working.'

'You forget that I'm destined for great things. Don't you want to share them?'

'Be more specific.'

'This is only a passing storm, my dear – every couple goes through them.'

'I thought I was sheltered from such intemperate behaviour.'

'Let's declare a truce, and not act too hastily – that would be damaging, because a rat like that woman Tapeni would be only too happy to undermine what we've built up so patiently.'

'Well, you'll have to deal with her.'

'I was going to ask if I might.'

Way-Finder had already climbed aboard the boat for Thebes; he was munching fresh fodder and gazing at the river. Mischief had escaped from her mistress and climbed to the top of the mast. Brave, who was more reserved and rather uneasy at the prospect of a long crossing, pressed against Pazair's legs. The dog did not care for rolling and pitching, though he would follow his master on to even the stormiest of seas.

The move had been arranged quickly. Pazair had left the official house and its furniture for his successor, though Bagey had so far refused to appoint one, preferring to perform the office himself until some suitable candidates could be found. This was the old tjaty's way of showing his regard for Pazair, who, in his eyes, had lost none of his merit.

The judge carried the mat he had had since the beginning of his career, and Neferet her medical equipment. All around them were chests full of with jars and pots. Their companions on the voyage were some loud-voiced merchants, who were practising boasting about the wares they hoped to sell in the great market at Thebes.

For Pazair there was only one disappointment: Kem had not come to say goodbye. He supposed the Nubian disapproved of what they were doing.

'Neferet, Neferet! Don't go!' called a woman's voice.

The doctor turned round.

A breathless Silkis caught her arm. 'It's Qadash. He's dead!'

'What happened?'

'Something horrible. Come over here.'

Pazair led Way-Finder off the boat and called Mischief. Seeing her mistress walking away, the monkey jumped down on to the quayside. Brave retraced his steps with relief.

'Qadash and his two young foreign lovers have been murdered, poisoned, and a servant told Kem, who's gone to the scene of the crime, and one of his men told Bel-Tran – and here I am,' said Silkis all in one breath. 'Everything's in chaos, Neferet, but the vote making you principal doctor has the force of law again. And you can go on caring for me.'

'Are you sure that—'

'Bel-Tran says your appointment can't be called into question. You're staying in Memphis.'

'We no longer have a house, we—'

'My husband's already found you another one.'

Neferet took Pazair's hand hesitantly.

'You have no choice,' he said.

Brave barked in a most unusual way, signifying not anger

but a kind of stunned joy. That was his way of welcoming the arrival of a two-masted boat from Elephantine.

In the prow stood a long-haired young man and a beautiful woman.

'Suti!' yelled Pazair.

The feast given by Bel-Tran and Silkis was improvised but lavish. It celebrated both Neferet's restoration to her post and Suti's safe return.

The hero held the stage, describing his exploits, which everyone wanted to hear about in detail. He told of how he had joined the miners, of the journey through the burning hell of the desert, the All-Seeing One's betrayal, his encounter with Asher, Asher's departure for an unknown destination, and his own miraculous escape thanks to Panther. The Libyan girl grew almost intoxicated with laughter, but she never once took her eyes off her lover.

As promised, Bel-Tran had given Pazair the use of a house, a small one in the northern part of the city, until Neferet was allocated an official residence. The couple were happy to welcome Suti and Panther, who could stay as long as they wanted.

When they got home, the Libyan collapsed on to her bed and fell asleep instantly, and Neferet withdrew into her bed-chamber. The two men climbed up to the roof terrace.

'The wind's cool,' said Suti pensively. 'Some nights in the desert it was icy.'

'I waited and waited for a message from you.'

'It was impossible to get one to you, and if you sent me one it didn't reach me. But never mind that. Did my ears deceive me or did I really hear during dinner that Neferet is now the kingdom's principal doctor and that you've resigned as Judge of the Porch?'

'Your hearing is as good as ever.'

'Were you forced out?'

'No, not at all. I left of my own accord.'

'Why? Have you despaired of this world?'

'Ramses has decreed a general amnesty.'

'So every murderer will be exonerated.'

'It could not be put better.'

'Your beautiful legal system is in tatters,' said Suti sardonically.

'No one understands the king's decision.'

'All that matters is the result.'

'I have a confession to make.'

'A serious one?'

'I doubted you. I thought you'd sold me out.'

Suti stiffened, ready to strike. 'I'm going to break your head, Pazair.'

'And I deserve it – but so do you.'

'Why?'

'Because you lied to me.'

'This is the first chance we've had to talk freely. I was hardly going to tell the truth to that fellow Bel-Tran and his simpering wife. I might have known I couldn't deceive you.'

'I don't believe you abandoned the hunt for Asher. Your story was true until you met him, but after that I don't believe it.'

'Asher and his henchmen tortured me, with the intention of slowly burning me alive. But the desert became my ally, and Panther was my good spirit. And the thought of our friendship saved me when my courage almost failed.'

'Once you were able to move freely, you followed the general's trail. What was his plan?'

'To reach Libya via the South.'

'That was shrewd. Did he have any accomplices?'

'The dishonest All-Seeing One and an experienced miner.'

'What happened to them? Are they dead?'

'The desert is cruel,' said Suti.

'What was Asher looking for in those desolate places?'

'Gold. He was planning to enjoy the fortune he had amassed, and do it in safety in the land of his friend Adafi.'

'You killed him, didn't you?'

'His cowardice and weakness were unlimited.'

'Was Panther a witness?'

'More than that. She sentenced him, by handing me the arrow I fired.'

'Did you bury him?'

'The sand is quite good enough for his coffin.'

'You gave him no chance at all, did you?'

'He didn't deserve one.'

'So the celebrated general won't benefit from the amnesty . . .'

'Asher had already been judged. I merely carried out the sentence that ought to have been pronounced, and did it according to the law of the desert.'

'That's a rather brutal way of looking at it.'

'I feel lighter. In my dreams, the face of the man Asher tortured and murdered looks peaceful at last.'

'What became of the gold?'

Suti smiled. 'Spoils of war.'

'Aren't you worried that there'll be an investigation?'

'It won't be you who carries it out.'

'No, it will be Kem. He's an honest man and can't be bought bought or used. Besides, he lost his nose because he was falsely accused of stealing gold.'

'But he's your man, isn't he?'

Pazair shook his head. 'I'm nothing any more.'

'But I am. I'm rich. Letting a chance like that pass me by would have been stupid.'

'Gold is reserved for the gods.'

'They can spare some – they've got plenty.'

'You're embarking on a very dangerous adventure.'

'The most difficult part is behind me.'

'Will you leave Egypt?'

'I don't intend to, and I want to help you.'

'I'm now merely a little country judge with no power, just like I was before.'

'You can't mean you're giving up your quest?'

'I no longer have any means of continuing it.'

'Are you going to trample all your ideals underfoot? Can you really forget Branir's murder?'

'Denes's trial was about to begin. It would have been a decisive step towards the truth.'

'The charges laid out in your file have been erased, but what about the others?'

'What do you mean?'

Suti grinned. 'My friend Sababu keeps a private – very private – journal. I'm sure it contains some interesting details, and you might find just what you need in it.'

'I'll bear it in mind,' said Pazair. 'But now, my brother, what about you? Before Neferet is locked up in meetings and administration, get her to examine you. Your health must have been affected by what you've been through.'

'I was indeed planning to ask her.'

'What about Panther?'

'She's a daughter of the Libyan desert, and as indestructible as a scorpion. May the gods grant that she leaves me soon!'

'But love—'

'—wears out faster than copper, and anyway I prefer gold.'

'If you gave it back to the Temple at Kebet, you'd get a reward.'

'You're joking! It would be a pittance compared to what I've got in my chariot, and Panther wants to be very rich. To have followed the gold road and come back victorious . . . could anything be more amazing?'

'But let's change the subject,' Suti went on. 'Your punishment for doubting me is going to be very severe.'

Pazair smiled. 'I'm ready.'

'You and I are going to disappear for two days and go fishing in the Delta. I want to see some water, swim, roll in lush fields of green grass, go boating in the marshes.'

'But Neferet's being installed as—'

'I know her: she'll let you go.'

'Will Panther?'

'If you're with me, she'll trust me. She'll help Neferet to prepare for the ceremony – she's very skilful at dressing hair and preparing wigs. And we'll come back with some enormous fish.'

36

Doctors and remedy-makers practising in every field of medicine gathered to witness Neferet's instalment as principal doctor. They were admitted to the great open-air courtyard of the Temple of Sekhmet, the goddess who caused illnesses while also revealing the remedies that would cure them. Tjaty Bagey presided over the ceremony; everyone noticed how tired he looked. That a woman should fill the highest post in medicine did not shock the Egyptians, even if her male colleagues did allow themselves a few criticisms relating to her lack of physical strength and of authority.

Panther had worked with great skill. Not only had she dressed Neferet's hair but she had also attended to her clothes. The young doctor wore a long linen robe of immaculate whiteness, with a broad necklace of cornelians, lapis-lazuli bracelets at her wrists and ankles, and a striped wig. Her regal bearing made a strong impression on the audience, despite her gentle eyes and the delicate beauty of her slender body.

The most senior member of the doctors' council draped Neferet in a panther-skin to signify that her duty, like that of the priest charged with giving life to the royal mummy during the resurrection rites, was to instil a constant flow of energy into the immense body that was Egypt. Then he handed her the principal doctor's seal, which gave her authority over all the doctors in the kingdom, and the writing-desk on which she would draw up decrees concerning public health before submitting them to the tjaty.

The official speech was brief; it set out Neferet's duties and called upon her to respect the will of the gods in order to preserve the happiness of mankind. When his wife took the oath, Judge Pazair hid his face and wept.

Despite suffering pain so excruciating that only Kem could understand it, Killer had recovered all his strength. Thanks to Neferet's treatment, he would suffer no lasting consequences from his wounds. He had got his normal appetite back, and had resumed his guard patrols.

Pazair stroked Killer and made much of him. 'I shall never forget that I owe him my life,' he told Kem.

'Don't spoil him too much or he'll get soft, and that would be dangerous for him. Anything to report?'

'No. Now that I've resigned, I'm not at risk any more.'

'How do you see your future?'

'An appointment to an outlying district, I hope, where I can serve humble people to the best of my ability. If a difficult case arises, I'll let you know.'

'Do you still believe in the law?'

'To prove you right breaks my heart in two.'

'I want to resign, too.'

'No, stay in your post, I beg you. At least you can arrest criminals and guarantee the citizens' safety.'

'Yes – until the next amnesty. Nothing surprises me any more, but I'm very sorry about you.'

'There's not much we can do in this situation – in fact, our room for action is pathetic – but let's do the right thing. My greatest fear, Kem, was that I might not get your agreement.'

'I cursed the fact that I was delayed at Qadash's house, instead of greeting you on the quayside.'

'What are your conclusions about his death?'

'A triple poisoning. But whose idea was it? The two

youngsters were sons of a travelling actor. The funeral ceremonies took place most discreetly, without anyone present apart from the specialist priests. It's the most sordid affair I've ever had to deal with. The bodies won't rest in Egypt; they've been handed over to the Libyans, because Qadash was of Libyan origin.'

'Could it have been murder, committed by a fourth person?' asked Pazair.

'Are you thinking of the man who kept attacking you?'

'During the Festival of Opet, Denes asked me about Qadash. I didn't hide the fact that Qadash had promised me to confess before he was executed.'

'Hmmm,' said Kem thoughtfully. 'It's more than possible that Denes wanted to get rid of an dangerous witness.'

'But why use so much violence?'

'Extremely powerful interests must be involved. Of course, Denes would have used the services of a creature of the shadows. I'll keep trying to identify him. Now that Killer's fully recovered, we shall resume our inquiries.'

'There's one thing that puzzles me: Qadash seemed absolutely certain that he wouldn't be executed.'

'He probably believed Denes would buy him his freedom.'

'Yes, probably, but . . . He behaved with such arrogance, as if he knew there was going to be an amnesty.'

'Someone might have been indiscreet,' said Kem.

'I'd have got wind of it.'

'Don't deceive yourself – you'd have been the last to know. The court knows how unbending you are and knew that Denes's trial would have had tremendous repercussions.'

Pazair rejected the horrible suspicion that tormented him: collusion between Ramses and Denes, corruption at the very pinnacle of state, the beloved land of the gods delivered up to squalid appetites.

Kem saw that the judge was troubled, and said, 'We need facts – nothing but facts will enlighten us. So I'm planning to go back over a trail which will lead us to your attacker. His confession will be full of interest.'

'Then it's your turn to be careful,' said Pazair.

The man with the limp was one of the best sellers in the secret market at Memphis. He stood on a disused quay as cargo-boats arrived, laden with produce of every kind. The guards kept one eye on these practices; the taxation scribes levied the taxes without rancour. The man with the limp could have retired long ago to his house by the river – he was sixty – but he enjoyed conducting long negotiations and fooling gullible people. His latest victim had been a scribe from the Treasury, who fancied himself knowledgeable about ebony. Flattering his vanity, the man with the limp had sold him a piece of furniture made from ordinary dark wood at the price of ebony, which had been imitated very cleverly.

Another fine deal was in prospect: a man who had recently come into a lot of money wanted to acquire a collection of Nubian shields belonging to one of the most warlike tribes. A tinge of danger, while one was well protected in a city house, was a delicious sensation, which merited spending serious money. In league with some excellent craftsmen, the dealer had ordered counterfeit shields, much more impressive than the real ones. He would damage them himself so that they bore the traces of furious 'battles'.

His warehouse was full of similar marvels, which he produced sparingly and with consummate skill. Only the biggest prey interested him, people whose stupidity and self-importance he found irresistible. As he drew back the bolt on the warehouse door, he laughed aloud at the thought of the next day.

An animal hide, black and covered in hair, fell on to his shoulders as he pushed the door open. Entangled in the disgusting pelt, the man gave a shout, fell over, and called for help.

'Don't make so much noise,' ordered Kem, allowing him a little air.

'Oh, it's you, Commander. What's got into you?'

'Do you recognize this hide?'

The dealer peered at it. 'No.'

'Don't lie.'

'I'm honesty itself.'

'You're one of my best informants,' conceded the Nubian, 'but it's the dealer I'm questioning. You recently sold a large male baboon. Who bought it?'

'I don't trade in animals.'

'A fine big creature like this ought to have been enlisted in the city guards. Only a scoundrel like you could have arranged to have it smuggled here.'

'Do you really think I'd do something like that?'

'I know how greedy you are.'

'I didn't do it.'

'You're making Killer angry,' warned Kem.

'But I don't know anything.'

'Perhaps you'll find him more persuasive than me.'

The dealer looked at Killer, and gave up. 'I heard that an enormous baboon had been captured near Elephantine. Yes, his sale would make someone a lot of money, but it wasn't my sort of deal. On the other hand, I could arrange the transport . . . '

'At a fat profit, I expect.'

'Bribes and expenses, mainly.'

'Don't try to make me feel sorry for you. I'm interested in only one thing: who bought the baboon?'

'It's very delicate . . . '

Killer stared fixedly at him, scratching the ground with an impatient paw.

'Do you promise to keep my name out of it?'

'Is Killer loose-tongued?'

'No one must know that I told you. Go and see Short-Thighs.'

*

The man certainly deserved his nickname. He had a large head, a hairy body and legs which were too short, but thick and sturdy. Since childhood, he had carried huge numbers of chests and boxes; now that he had become his own boss, he ruled over a hundred small producers, whose fruit and vegetables he sold. Alongside these official activities, Short-Thighs dabbled in assorted illegal trades, some more profitable than others.

The sight of Kem and Killer gave him no pleasure at all.

'Everything's fully in order here,' he said.

'You don't like the guards much, do you?' said Kem.

'No – and less than ever since you've been in charge.'

'Why? Have you got a guilty conscience?'

'Ask your questions.'

'Are you in such a hurry to talk?'

'Your baboon will force me to, so we might as well get it over with.'

'Actually, it's a baboon I want to talk to you about.'

'I hate the monsters.'

'And yet you bought one from the man with the limp.'

Short-Thighs looked uncomfortable, and pretended to arrange his packing-cases. 'I had an order for one.'

'From whom?'

'A strange fellow.'

'What's his name?'

'I don't know.'

'Describe him.'

'I can't.'

'How surprising,' said Kem sarcastically.

'Yes, it is,' retorted Short-Thighs, 'because I'm usually pretty observant. But the man who ordered the baboon was a sort of shadow, with no substance or distinguishing features. He wore a wig pulled down low over his forehead, almost covering his eyes, and a tunic which hid the shape of his body.

I wouldn't recognise him, especially as our meeting was only brief – he didn't even haggle over the price.'

'What was his voice like?'

'Peculiar. I think he was disguising it. He probably fruit-stones between his cheeks and his jaw.'

'Have you seen him again since then?'

'No.'

The trail ended there. The murderer's mission had no doubt ended with the fall of Pazair and the death of Qadash.

Sababu was pinning up her coiled hair. 'This is a most unexpected visit, Judge Pazair,' she said with amusement. 'Please allow me to finish doing my hair. Do you really need my services so early in the morning?'

'Not your services, no; I need to talk to you.'

The place was ostentatiously luxurious, filled with costly perfumes which made the head spin. Pazair looked for a window, but in vain.

'Does your wife know what you're doing?'

'I hide nothing from her.'

'So much the better. She's an exceptional person and an excellent doctor.'

'You keep a private journal, don't you?'

'In what capacity are you questioning me? You're no longer Judge of the Porch.'

'A small judge without any pretensions. You're quite free not to answer.'

'Who told you about my journal?'

'Suti. He thinks it may contain evidence against Denes.'

'Suti . . . a wonderful boy and a splendid lover. For his sake I'll make a small gesture.' The voluptuous Sababu stood up and disappeared for a few moments behind a hanging. She reappeared carrying a papyrus.

'Here's the scroll in which I've noted my best clients' foibles, their perversions and the desires they don't dare admit to. Reading through it again, it's disappointing. Taken as a whole, the nobility of this country are healthy. They make love in natural ways, without physical or mental cruelty. There's nothing here of use to you, Judge. This past deserves only oblivion.' She tore the papyrus into shreds. 'You didn't try to stop me. Suppose I was lying?'

'I trust you.'

Sababu looked at the judge seriously. 'I can't help you, or love you, and I'm sorry for that. Make Neferet happy, think only of her happiness, and you'll live the most beautiful of lives.'

Panther slid back up Suti's naked body, more supple than a papyrus-stalk dancing in the wind. She stopped, kissed him, and resumed her inexorable progress towards her lover's lips. Tired of being passive, he put an end to her tender exploration, and threw her on to her side. Their legs intertwined, they embraced each other with the turbulence of a Nile flood, and shared a blazing pleasure at the very same moment. Both knew that they were bound together by this perfect desire and its accomplishment, but neither would admit it.

Panther was so passionate that a single bout was not enough for her; she easily reawakened Suti's ardour with intimate caresses. The young man called her his 'Libyan she-cat', evoking the goddess of love, who had left and gone into the western desert in the form of a lioness and returned, soft and seductive, in the form of a cat, domesticated but never completely tamed. Panther's slightest movement aroused passion, shimmering and painful; she played Suti like a lyre, making him resound in harmony with her own sensuality.

'I shall take you into town for our midday meal,' said Suti. 'A Hellene has just opened a tavern where he serves vine-leaves stuffed with meat, and white wine from his country.'

'When are we going to fetch the gold?'

'As soon as I'm fully fit again.'

'You seem virtually recovered to me.'

'Making love to you is easier, if no less exhausting, than walking for several days in the desert. I'm not strong enough yet.'

'I'm going with you – you couldn't do it on your own.'

'Who can we sell it to without being denounced?'

'The Libyans? They'd certainly buy it.'

'Never. Let's try to find someone in Memphis. If we can't, we'll have to stay in Thebes and look for an outlet. It'll be risky.'

'And exciting! Wealth has to be earned.'

'Tell me, Panther, what did you feel when you killed the guard?'

'Fear that I might miss.'

'Had you killed anyone before?'

'I wanted to save you, and I did. I'll kill you, too, if you ever try to leave me again.'

Suti sampled the atmosphere of Memphis with astonishment. It disconcerted him, felt almost foreign, after his long spell in the desert. At the heart of the Sycamore district, a colourful crowd was milling around the Temple of Hathor to hear a crier announce the dates of the next festival. Recruits were heading towards the military area to receive their equipment. Merchants were driving donkeys and chariots towards the storehouses, where they would obtain their allocations of cereals and fresh produce. At the 'Good Journey' port, boats were manoeuvring as they prepared to unload, the sailors loudly singing the traditional homecoming songs.

The Greek had opened his tavern in a narrow street in the southern district, not far from Judge Pazair's first office. As Panther and Suti were walking along it, they heard someone screaming in fear.

A chariot, drawn by a maddened horse, was thundering

along the tiny street. Its terrified driver had let go of the reins. The left wheel hit the front of a house, the chariot lurched, and the driver was thrown out on to the ground. Some other passers-by managed to stop the horse.

Suti ran up and bent over the victim.

It was a woman – the lady Nenophar! Her head was covered in blood, and she was not breathing.

Initial treatment was given at the scene, then Nenophar was taken to the hospital. She had multiple bruises, a triple fracture of the left leg, a broken rib, and a deep wound on her neck. Her survival was something of a miracle. Neferet and two other doctors operated on her immediately. Thanks to her robust constitution, Nenophar would live, but she would walk on crutches for the rest of her life.

As soon as she was able to speak, Kem was given permission to question her, together with Pazair.

'The judge is accompanying me as a witness,' explained Kem. 'I think it advisable to have a magistrate present at our interview.'

'Why?'

'Because I cannot establish the cause of the accident.'

'The horse simply lost its head – I couldn't control it.'

'Do you usually drive a chariot?' asked Pazair.

'Of course not.'

'Then what happened?'

'I got in first, and a servant was supposed to get in and take the reins. But something – a stone, probably – hit the mare. She neighed, reared and bolted.'

'That sounds as though someone tried to kill you.'

Nenophar turned her bandaged head, and let her eyes wander. 'That isn't very likely.'

'I suspect your husband.'

'That's a hateful thing to say!'

'Am I wrong? Behind his apparently honourable nature,

342

there hides a vain, vile creature, concerned only with his own interests.'

Nenophar seemed shaken.

Pazair widened the breach. 'Other suspicions attach to you yourself.'

'To me?'

'Branir was stabbed with a mother-of-pearl needle. You use a needle exactly like that one, and with remarkable skill.'

Nenophar sat bolt upright, white-faced. 'That's horrible. How dare you accuse me of such a thing!'

'At the trial that was cancelled because of the amnesty, you would have been incriminated in an illegal trade in fabrics, dresses and sheets. One crime may well have led to another.'

'Why are you attacking me like this?'

'Because your husband is at the centre of a criminal conspiracy. Who better than you to be his accomplice?'

A sad smile twisted Nenophar's lips. 'You've been misinformed, Judge. Before the accident, I was intending to get a divorce.'

'Have you changed your mind?'

'It was Denes who, through me, was the target. I shan't desert him in the midst of the storm.'

'Forgive my brutality. I wish you a speedy recovery.'

The two men sat down on a stone bench. Killer was calm, so they knew they were not being watched.

'What do you think?' asked Pazair.

'A notable case of chronic, incurable stupidity,' said Kem. 'She simply cannot understand that her husband tried to get rid of her because the divorce would have reduced him to penury – it's Nenophar who has all the money. Denes didn't realize that he held a winning hand whatever the outcome of the murder attempt. Either Nenophar would die in the accident or she'd become his loyal ally again. Difficult to find a more idiotic woman of her social standing.'

'Short and to the point,' commented Pazair, 'but persuasive. One fact, I feel, has been established: she is not Branir's murderer.'

37

In the depths of a winter which was proving colder than usual, Ramses celebrated the festivals of the resurrection of Osiris. After the fertility of the Nile, which was seen by all, came the fecundity of the spirit, gaining victory over death; in each shrine lamps were lit, so that the eternal light of rebirth might shine forth.

The king went to Saqqara. For an entire day, he meditated before the Step Pyramid, then before the statue of its builder, his illustrious predecessor Pharaoh Djoser.

The single open gate in the curtain-wall could be passed through only by the soul of the dead pharaoh or by the reigning king, during his festival of regeneration, in the presence of the gods of heaven and earth.

Ramses called upon his ancestors, who had become stars in the heavens, to inspire him and show him how to escape from the dark chasm into which his invisible enemies had cast him. The majesty of the place, consecrated to the radiant silence of transfigured life, restored his serenity; it filled his gaze with the play of light, bringing to life the giant stone staircase at the centre of the immense burial-ground.

At sunset, the answer was born in his heart.

Kem was not a man who enjoyed working in an office, so he questioned Suti as they walked along beside the Nile.

'You had an extraordinary adventure. To get out of the desert alive is no mean feat.'

'My good luck protects me better than any god could.'

'She's a fickle friend – don't make too many demands on her.'

'Caution bores me.'

'Ephraim was an unmitigated scoundrel. His death can't have grieved you much.'

'He fled with Asher.'

'Despite intensive searches by the desert patrols, they still haven't been found.'

'I saw how clever they were at avoiding the guards as they moved about.'

'You're a magician,' said Kem.

'Is that a compliment or a criticism?'

'Escaping from Asher's claws was an almost supernatural achievement. Why did he let you go?'

'I don't know – I can't understand it.'

'He ought to have killed you, you must admit. Another strange point: what did he hope to achieve by hiding in a mining area?'

'When you arrest him, he can tell you,' said Suti.

'Gold is the supreme wealth, the inaccessible dream. Like you, Asher cared nothing for the gods; all he wanted was wealth. Ephraim knew about the abandoned mines, and told him where they were. By acquiring all that gold, the general made sure he need not fear the future.'

'Perhaps. He didn't confide in me.'

'Didn't you want to follow him?'

'I was injured, at the end of my strength.'

'I believe you killed him. You hated him enough to try anything.'

'He was too strong for me in the state I was in.'

'I've been in a situation like that myself. The will can dictate to even the most exhausted body.'

'When Asher comes back, he'll benefit from the amnesty, won't he?'

'He isn't going to come back. The vultures and the rodents have eaten his flesh, and the wind will disperse his bones. Where have you hidden the gold?'

'All I've got is my good luck.'

'Stealing it is an unforgivable crime. No one has ever succeeded in keeping gold stolen from the belly of the mountains. Give it back, before your good luck deserts you.'

'You've become a real guards commander,' said Suti sarcastically.

'I like order. A country is happy and prosperous when people and things are in their proper places. The place for gold is inside the temple. Take your hoard back to Kebet, and I'll say not a word about it. If you don't, you can consider me your enemy.'

Neferet refused to live in the house that had belonged to Nebamon, beause it was impregnated with too many harmful vibrations. She preferred to wait until the government allocated her another house, and was content with modest lodgings, where she got what sleep she could at night.

On the very first day after her installation, the various councils concerned with the country's health all requested audiences, eager to show their dedication to their work. Neferet calmed their anxieties and restrained their impatience; before dealing with future promotions, she must attend to the needs of the people. So she summoned the officials in charge of distributing water and of ensuring that no village went short; then she examined the list of hospitals and remedy-stores, noting that some provinces lacked necessary facilities. The division of specialist and general doctors between the South and the North was unsatisfactory. Finally, among the most urgent matters, she must respond to the foreign countries that were asking for Egyptian doctors to treat illustrious patients.

She was beginning to grasp the full extent of her task. To this was added the polite hostility of the doctors who had been caring for Ramses since Nebamon's death. They all boasted of their abilities and claimed that the king was pleased with their treatment.

Walking in the streets refreshed her. So few people knew her face, particularly in the areas near the palace, that she could stroll at her ease, after a day of stressful conversations in which everyone she spoke to put her to the test.

When Suti fell into step beside her, she was astonished.

'I must speak with you alone,' he said.

'Without Pazair?'

'For the moment, yes.'

'What are you afraid of?'

'My suspicions are too vague and so terrible . . . He'd get carried away for all the wrong reasons. I'd rather talk to you first; you shall be the judge.'

'Is it about Panther?'

'How did you guess?'

'She occupies a certain place in your life . . . and you seem very much in love.'

'Don't deceive yourself. Our understanding is a purely sensual one. But Panther . . . ' He hesitated.

Neferet, who liked to walk quickly, slowed her pace.

'Remember the circumstances of Branir's murder,' he went on, after a few moments.

'A mother-of-pearl needle was plunged into his neck, with such accuracy that it killed him instantly.'

'Panther killed the guard exactly like that, using a dagger. And he was a huge man.'

'It's just coincidence.'

'I hope so, Neferet, I hope so with all my heart.'

'Don't torture yourself any more. Branir's soul is so close

to me, so alive, that your accusation, if there were any truth in it, would have awoken an immediate certainty within me. Panther is innocent.'

Neferet and Pazair hid nothing from each other. Since the moment when love had united them, a complicity reigned which daily life could not wear down and which no arguments ever shattered. When the judge came to bed, late that night, she woke up and told him of Suti's anxieties.

'He felt guilty at the idea of living with the woman who might have assassinated Branir,' she said.

'How did he get this mad idea?'

'From a nightmare.'

'It's absurd. Panther didn't even know Branir.'

'Someone might have used her dangerous gifts.'

'She killed the guard out of love; reassure Suti about that, will you?'

'You seem sure of yourself.'

'I am sure of her, and of him.'

'So am I.'

The visit by Ramses' mother threw the order of the audiences into disarray. Governors of provinces, who had come to request health equipment, bowed as Tuya passed by.

She kissed Neferet. 'Here you are, in your proper place.'

'I miss my village in Upper Egypt.'

'No regrets, no remorse: they are futile. All that matters is your mission, in the service of the country.'

'How is your health, Majesty?'

'Excellent.'

'I must give you a routine examination.'

'Only to reassure yourself.'

Despite the queen's age and previous infections, her sight was satisfactory. Nevertheless, Neferet asked her to continue following the treatment strictly.

'Your work will not be easy,' said the queen. 'Nebamon had the art of putting off urgent matters and burying files, and he surrounded himself with loyal supporters who never questioned anything he did. They are weak, narrow-minded, hidebound people, and they will oppose any changes you wish to make. Inertia is difficult to combat, but do not lose heart.'

'How is Pharaoh?'

'He is away in the North, inspecting the garrisons there. I have a feeling that he is preoccupied with General Asher's disappearance.'

'Can you share his thoughts once more, Majesty?'

'Unfortunately, no. If I could, I would have asked him the reason for that contemptible amnesty of which our people disapprove so much. Ramses is tired, and his power is wearing out. The High Priests of Iunu, Memphis and Thebes will lose no time in arranging the festival of regeneration that everyone rightly believes is necessary.'

'The country will rejoice.'

'Ramses will once again be filled with the fire that enabled him to defeat his most formidable enemies. Do not hesitate to ask me for help; our relationship now has an official nature.'

Such encouragement increased Neferet's energy tenfold.

After the weavers had left, Tapeni inspected the workshop. Her practised eye could detect even the smallest theft; neither a tool nor a piece of cloth must disappear from her domain, on pain of immediate punishment. Only the utmost strictness could ensure constant quality in the work.

A man came in.

'Denes!' she exclaimed. 'What do you want?'

He closed the door behind him. His massive frame advanced slowly, his expression grim.

'Why are you here?' she asked. 'You said we ought not to see each other again.'

'That's right.'

'You made a mistake. I'm not a woman you can use and then abandon.'

'You made another mistake. I'm not a man to be blackmailed.'

'Either you give in or I'll ruin your reputation.'

'My wife's just had a serious accident. If it weren't for the gods' mercy, she'd be dead.'

'That changes nothing in the agreements I made with her.'

'No agreements have been made.'

With one hand, Denes seized Tapeni by the throat and flattened her against a wall. 'If you go on bothering me, you'll have an accident, too. Your disgusting methods won't work with me. Don't try to make use of my wife, and forget all about our little affair. Be content with your craft if you want to live until you're old. Goodbye.'

Freed from his ruthless grip, Tapeni gulped in air.

Suti checked that he was not being followed. Since Kem's interrogation, he feared he might be being watched. The Nubian's warning must not be taken lightly: even Pazair would not be able to protect his friend if Kem proved him guilty.

Fortunately, his suspicions about Panther had been dispelled, but the two of them must leave Memphis without Kem's knowledge. Making the best use of their fabulous wealth would be a delicate enterprise, and they could not do it alone, so Suti contacted a few dubious characters, mostly established dealers in stolen goods. He did not tell them about the gold, of course, but merely said it would be a sizeable transaction, and that he would need to transport the material a long way.

Short-Thighs struck him as useful. The dealer asked no questions, and agreed to provide Suti with strong donkeys, dried meat and water-skins, at a place of his choosing. Bringing the gold back from the cave to the great city, hiding it, buying a luxurious house and leading a grand life would entail taking a lot of risks, but Suti thoroughly enjoyed playing on his luck. He was sure it would not desert him just when he was about to become rich.

In three days' time, he and Panther would take a boat to Elephantine. Armed with the wooden tablet on which Short-Thighs had written his instructions, they would collect the donkeys and supplies in a village where nobody knew them. Then they would retrieve part of the gold from its hiding-place, and come back to Memphis in the hope of trading it in a parallel market which Greeks, Libyans and Syrians were trying to establish. The gold's market value was so high, and it was so rarely available, that Suti was sure to find a buyer.

He was risking life imprisonment, if not death. But when he owned the finest estate in all Egypt, he would organize magnificent parties at which the guests of honour would be Pazair and Neferet. He would burn his wealth like straw, so that a fire of joy rose to the heavens, where the non-existent gods would laugh with him.

The tjaty's voice was hoarse, his face drawn. 'Judge Pazair,' he said, 'I have summoned you here to address your recent conduct.'

'What have I done wrong?'

'Your opposition to the amnesty is too open. You never miss an opportunity to declare it.'

'To keep silent would be dishonest.'

'What you are doing is extremely foolish.'

'But you yourself, Tjaty, made your opposition known to the king.'

'I am an old tjaty, you are a young judge.'

'How could Pharaoh be offended by the opinion of an insignificant district judge?'

'You used to be Judge of the Porch. Keep your thoughts to yourself.'

'Will my next appointment depend on my silence?'

'You are intelligent enough to answer that question yourself,' said Bagey. 'A judge who challenges the law is not fit to practise.'

'If that is so, I renounce my office.'

'But your work is your whole reason for living.'

'The wound will never heal, I know, but better that than hypocrisy.'

'You are being too unyielding.'

Pazair smiled. 'Coming from you, that is a compliment.'

'I detest pomposity, but I believe this country needs you.'

'By remaining faithful to my ideal, I hope to be in harmony with the Egypt of the pyramids, the Peak of the West and the undying suns. That Egypt did not recognize the amnesty. If I'm wrong, justice will follow its course without me.'

'Hello, Suti.'

The young man put down his cup of cool beer. 'Tapeni!'

'It's taken me a long time to find you. This tavern is a bit sordid, but you seem to like it.'

'How are you?'

'I've been rather lonely since you left.'

'A pretty woman needn't ever be lonely.'

'Have you lost your memory? You're my husband.'

'When I left your house, our divorce was consummated.'

'You're wrong, darling. I regard your escape as a mere . . . absence for a while.'

'Our marriage took place because it was necessary for my investigation. The amnesty put an end to it.'

'I take our marriage seriously.'

'Stop joking, Tapeni.'

'You're the husband I've always dreamt of.'

'Oh, really, I—'

'I order you to get rid of your Libyan whore and return to our matrimonial home.'

'That's crazy.'

'I don't want to lose everything. Do as I say, or you'll regret it.'

Suti shrugged, and emptied his cup in a single draught.

Brave was romping about in front of Pazair and Neferet. The dog looked at the canal water, but kept well away from it. The little green monkey clung to her mistress's shoulder.

'Bagey disagrees with my decision,' said Pazair, 'but I shall hold to it.'

'Where will you work? In the provinces?'

'Nowhere. I'm not a judge any more, because I oppose an unjust decision.'

'If only we'd been able to go to Thebes,' sighed Neferet.

'Your colleagues would have brought you back.'

'My position isn't as strong as it looks. A few influential members of the court are unhappy at having a woman as principal doctor. If I make even a tiny mistake, they'll demand my resignation.'

'I'm going to fulfil an old dream, and become a gardener. In our future home, my work will be useful.'

'Pazair . . . '

'We'll live together in utter happiness. You'll work for the health of Egypt, and I'll care for the flowers and trees.'

Pazair's eyes did not deceive him. He had indeed received a summons from the principal judge in the sacred town of Iunu, to the north of Memphis. Iunu had no trade or agricultural importance to speak of, and consisted only of temples built around an immense obelisk, a petrified ray of sunlight.

'I'm being offered a post as a judge dealing with religious affairs,' he told Neferet. 'Nothing ever happens in Iunu, so I won't exactly be overworked. Usually the tjaty sends elderly or frail judges there.'

'Bagey has intervened in your favour,' she said. 'At least you'll keep your title.'

'He's getting me away from civil matters – very shrewd of him.'

'Don't refuse the offer.'

'If anyone tries to impose constraints on me, however small, or if they try to make me accept the amnesty, my stay in Iunu will be a short one.'

Iunu was home to the writers of the sacred texts, rituals and mythological tales designed to pass on the wisdom of the ancients. Within the temples, which were surrounded by high walls, a modest number of priests celebrated the cult of energy in the form of light.

Pazair found a silent town, without merchants or market-stalls. In the small white houses lived the priests and also craftsmen whose job was to create or maintain ritual objects. The commotion of the outside world did not reach them.

Pazair reported to the office of the principal judge, where a white-haired old scribe greeted him with obvious annoyance. After examining the summons, he withdrew.

The place was calm, almost sleepy, so unlike the bustle of Memphis that Pazair could scarcely believe men worked here.

Two guards armed with clubs suddenly entered the room. 'Judge Pazair?'

'What do you want?'

'Follow us.'

'Why?'

'Orders from above.'

'I refuse.'

'There's no point trying to resist. We'll use force if we have to.'

Pazair realized that he had fallen into a trap. Anyone who defied Ramses paid the price. He was going to be given not a post as a judge but a place in the burial-ground of oblivion.

38

Flanked by the two guards, Pazair was taken to the door of an oblong building adjoining the curtain-wall of the Temple of Ra.

The door opened to reveal an old, shaven-headed priest with lined skin and black eyes, dressed in a panther skin.

'Judge Pazair?' he said.

'Detaining me like this is illegal.'

'Instead of talking nonsense, come in, wash your hands and feet, and pray.'

Surprised, Pazair obeyed. The two guards took up positions outside, and the door closed again.

'Where am I?' asked the judge.

'In the House of Life at Iunu.'

The judge was astounded. It was here, in a place forbidden to outsiders, that the sages of past times had composed the pyramid texts, which revealed the changes of the soul and the process of rebirth. The people knew that the most famous mages had been trained in this mysterious school; only a few were called to it, and they never knew the day or the hour when the call would come.

'Purify yourself.'

Nervously, Pazair did so.

'My name is Hairless,' said the priest. 'I guard this door and keep out all harmful elements.'

'But I was summoned—'

'Don't bother me with useless words.' Hairless had an authority which made Pazair's protests stick in his throat. 'Take off your kilt and put on this white robe.'

Pazair felt he was being transported into another world, where there were no landmarks. Light entered the House of Life only through narrow slits near the tops of the stone walls, which were plain and without inscription.

'I am also called "the Slaughterman",' said Hairless, 'because I behead the enemies of Osiris. Here are kept the annals of the gods, the books of knowledge, and the rituals of the mysteries. You may never speak to anyone of what you will see and hear. Destiny strikes down the loose-tongued.'

Hairless led Pazair down a long passageway which ended in a sandy courtyard. In the centre, a mound of sand housed a mummy of Osiris, the receptacle of life in its most secret aspect. Called the Divine Stone, it was spread with precious ointments and covered with a ram's skin.

'Within it, the energy that creates Egypt dies and is reborn,' explained Hairless.

All round the courtyard were libraries and workshops for the craftsmen who were allowed to work in the enclosure.

'What do you see, Pazair?'

'A mound of sand.'

'This is how life takes form. Energy springs from the ocean where the worlds are contained as seeds; it materializes in the form of a mound. Seek the highest, most vital element, and you will approach the very beginning.' He pointed to a closed door. 'We shall enter that chamber, and you shall appear before your judge.'

The judge was seated on a gilded wooden throne; he wore a curled wig which covered his ears, and a long tunic. On his chest was a broad knot; in his right hand, he held a sceptre of command; in his left, a long cane. Behind him was a set of golden scales. This formidable man was charged with the

357

secrets of the House of Life and the distribution of offerings, and was guardian of the primordial stone.

He surveyed Pazair for a moment or two, then said, 'You claim to be an honest judge.'

'I try to be.'

'Why do you refuse to apply the amnesty decreed by Pharaoh?'

'Because it is unjust.'

'In this enclosed place, before these scales, far from the eyes of outsiders, do you dare to maintain that opinion?'

'I do.'

'I can do no more for you.'

Hairless seized Pazair by the shoulder and dragged him out of the chamber.

So, thought Pazair, all those fine words were merely part of the trap. The priests' goal was to break his resistance. Persuasion had failed, so now they would use violence.

'Enter here.' Hairless knocked on a bronze door.

A single lamp lit the small, windowless room. Two channels, hollowed out of the thick walls, brought in vital air.

A man sat on a gilded throne, looking at Pazair. A man with red hair, a broad forehead and a hooked nose. On his wrists were gold and lapis-lazuli bracelets, the upper parts of which were decorated with the heads of two wild ducks. The favourite jewellery of King Ramses.

'You are . . .' Pazair dared not speak the word – 'Pharaoh' – that burnt on his lips.

'And you are Pazair, who resigned from his post as Judge of the Porch and has openly criticized my amnesty decree.' The king's voice was full of anger and reproach.

Pazair's heart raced. Face to face with the most powerful ruler on earth, he could think of nothing to say.

'Well, answer me. Have I been told lies about you?'

'No, Majesty.'

The judge realized that he had forgotten to kneel. He dropped to his knees on the ground.

358

'Get up. Since you defy your king, at least behave like a warrior.'

Nettled, Pazair stood up. 'I shall not recant.'

'Why do you oppose the amnesty?'

'Exonerating guilty men and freeing criminals are insults to the gods and marks of contempt for human suffering. If you follow this dangerous road, you will end by accusing the victims.'

'Do you claim to be infallible?'

'No, Majesty. I have made many mistakes – but not to the detriment of innocent people.'

'And are you incorruptible?'

'My soul is not for sale.'

'Disrespect for the throne is itself a crime,' Pharaoh pointed out.

'I respect the Rule of Ma'at.'

'Do you think you know it better than I, who am her son?'

'The amnesty is a grave injustice, and upsets the country's balance.'

'Do you think you can speak to your king like this, and live?'

'If I die, I shall at least have had the pleasure of telling you my true thoughts.'

Ramses' tone changed. Instead of being angry, his words were slow and serious. 'Since your arrival in Memphis, I have been watching you. Branir was a wise man, who never acted lightly. He chose you because of your integrity; his other pupil was Neferet, who is today the kingdom's principal doctor.'

'She has succeeded, I have failed.'

'You have succeeded equally, for you are the only honest judge in Egypt.'

Pazair was speechless.

'Despite much opposition, including my own, your opinion has not changed. You have held your own against the King of Egypt, in the name of justice. You are my last hope. I am alone,

359

Pazair, caught in an appalling dilemma. Will you help me, or do you prefer your quiet life?'

Pazair bowed low. 'I am your servant, Majesty.'

'Are those the words of a courtier, or do you mean what you say?'

'My actions will answer for me.'

'For that reason, I am placing the future of Egypt in your hands.'

'I . . . I don't understand.'

'We are in a safe place here, and no one will hear what I am about to reveal to you. Think hard, Pazair; you can still draw back. When I have spoken, you will be charged with the most difficult mission ever entrusted to a judge.'

'The vocation Branir awakened in me cannot be stifled.'

'Judge Pazair, I appoint you tjaty of Egypt.'

'But, Majesty, Tjaty Ba—'

'Bagey is old and tired. Several times in the last few months he has asked me to replace him. Your refusal to accept the amnesty enabled me to find his successor, despite the advice of those close to me, who had other men in mind.'

'Why can Bagey not undertake the task you wish to entrust to me?'

'On one hand, he is no longer strong and energetic enough to carry out the investigation; on the other, there would be gossip among the members of his government, who have been in place too long. If the slightest hint of the truth should filter through, the country would fall into the hands of demons from the darkness. Soon you will be the most important person in the kingdom after Pharaoh, but you will be alone, friendless and without support. Do not confide in anyone. Get rid of many of the existing ministers and surround yourself with new men, but do not trust them.'

'Majesty, you spoke of an investigation . . . ?'

'This is the truth, Pazair. The sacred insignia of kingship, which legitimize the reign of each pharaoh, were housed within the Great Pyramid. The pyramid was broken into and violated, and the insignia were stolen. Without them, I cannot celebrate the festival of regeneration that the High Priests are rightly demanding in the name of our people. In less than a year, when the Nile flood is reborn, I shall be compelled to abdicate, to the benefit of a thief and a criminal who is lurking in the shadows.'

'So the amnesty decree was forced on you.'

'For the first time, I was obliged to act contrary to justice. I faced threats that the theft from the pyramid would be revealed and my downfall brought about.'

'Why did the enemy not do that a long time ago?'

'Because he is not ready; seizing the throne cannot be done hastily. The moment of my abdication will be the most favourable one, and the usurper will accede to power peacefully. I agreed to the demands of the anonymous message, in order to see who, if anyone, who would dare stand against the amnesty. Apart from Bagey and yourself, no one has challenged it. The old tjaty has more than earned his rest. You, as his successor, will identify the criminals, or else we shall fall together.'

Pazair thought back over his investigation, right from the crucial moment when he had been the grain of sand that disrupted the evil machine, by refusing to authorize the transfer of a member of the honour-guard.

Ramses went on, 'Never has Egypt seen such a wave of murders. I am convinced that they are linked to this monstrous conspiracy. Why were the honour-guard killed? Because the Sphinx is near the Great Pyramid, and the soldiers were blocking the looters' way. They had to get rid of them in order to enter the pyramid without being seen.'

'How did they get in?'

'By an underground passageway which I thought had been sealed. You must inspect it – there may still be clues there. For a long time I have believed General Asher to be at the centre of the plot.'

'No, Majesty, he only seemed to be.'

'If we still cannot find him, it is because he is in Libya, uniting the tribes against Egypt.'

'Asher is dead.'

'Have you proof of that?'

'My friend Suti told me.'

'Did he kill him?'

Pazair hesitated.

'You are my tjaty. There must be no shadows between us: the truth shall be our bond.'

'Yes, Suti killed him. Suti hated Asher because he saw the general torturing and killing an Egyptian soldier.'

'For a long time I believed in Asher's good faith, but I was mistaken.'

'If Denes's trial had taken place, his guilt would have been proved.'

'That upstart ship-owner!'

'He and his friends Qadash and Sheshi made a formidable trio. Qadash wanted to be principal doctor, while Sheshi said he was working on a way of making unbreakable weapons. Sheshi and Denes were probably responsible for Princess Hattusa's accident.'

'Are those three the only ones in the plot, or are there others?'

'I do not know.'

'Find out.'

'I have been wandering in the dark, Majesty. Now I must know everything. What are the sacred objects that were stolen from the Great Pyramid?'

'The first is a small adze made of sky-iron, used to open the mummy's mouth during the resurrection ritual.'

'It is safe, Majesty. It is in the hands of the High Priest of the Temple of Ptah, in Memphis.'

'And some lapis-lazuli amulets.'

'Sheshi was smuggling amulets. I am sure they are safe at Karnak, with the High Priest.'

'A gold scarab.'

'Kani has that, too!' Pazair felt a mad hope for a moment: had he saved the pyramid's treasures without realizing it?

'The looters,' Ramses went on, 'tore off Khufu's gold mask and collar.'

Those words instantly dashed Pazair's hopes. He could not answer.

'If they have behaved like the profaners of the past, we shall never recover them, nor the gold cubit dedicated to Ma'at. They will have melted them down and turned them into gold bars which they will have sold abroad.'

Pazair was close to tears. How could people be vile enough to destroy such beauty?

He asked, 'If some of the items have been saved and the rest destroyed, what have our enemies still got?'

'The most vital thing of all,' replied Ramses, 'the Testament of the Gods. My goldsmiths have the skill to make another cubit, but the Testament is unique, passed on from pharaoh to pharaoh. During the festival of regeneration, I shall have to show it to the gods, to the High Priests, to the Friends of Pharaoh and to the people of Egypt. Such is the will of the rule of kings; it was so yesterday and will be so tomorrow, and I shall submit to it.

'In the months we have left before the festival, our enemies will not be idle. They will try to weaken me, to corrupt and undermine my power. It is up to you to find the strength to thwart their plans. If you fail, I fear that the civilization of our fathers will be destroyed. Murderers bold enough to desecrate our most sacred shrine clearly have only contempt for the fundamental values by which we live. With so much at stake, my person does not matter. My throne, though, is the symbol of a thousand-year-old dynasty and of the traditions upon which this country is built. I love Egypt as you do, beyond life, beyond time. It is her light that they wish to extinguish. You must save it, Tjaty Pazair.'

39

For a whole night Pazair meditated, seated on the ground before a statue of Thoth, which depicted him in the form of a baboon crowned with the moon's disc. The temple lay silent; on the roof, the star-watchers were at work. Still in shock from his conversation with Pharaoh, he treasured these few last hours of peace before his enthronement, before crossing the threshold of a new life he had never wished for.

He thought of the happy moment when Neferet, Brave, Way-Finder, Mischief and he had prepared to embark for Thebes, of peaceful days in a little village in Upper Egypt, of his wife's gentle sweetness, the regular cycle of the seasons, far from affairs of state and human ambition. But that was now no more than a fading dream, far out of reach.

Two priests led Pazair to the House of Life, where he was greeted by Hairless. The future tjaty knelt down on a mat; Hairless placed a wooden rule on his head, then offered him water and bread.

'Drink and eat,' he ordered. 'Be vigilant in all circumstances, or this food and water will become bitter. May pain be transformed into joy by your actions.'

Washed, shaven and perfumed, Pazair put on an old-fashioned kilt, a linen robe, and a short wig. The priests guided him to the royal palace, around which huge crowds had gathered in response to the announcement the previous evening that a new tjaty had been appointed.

Calm now, and indifferent to the clamour, Pazair entered the great audience chamber where Pharaoh sat upon his throne, wearing the White and Red Crowns fitted together to symbolize the union of Upper and Lower Egypt. On either side of the king sat the Friends of Pharaoh, including Bagey and Bel-Tran. Many courtiers and dignitaries were gathered between the pillars of the hall; among them, Pazair immediately made out the kingdom's principal doctor. At once serious and smiling, Neferet did not take her eyes off him for a moment.

Pazair remained standing, facing the king. In front of him, the bearer of the Rule unrolled the papyrus on which the spirit of the laws was written.

'I, Ramses, Pharaoh of Egypt, appoint Pazair tjaty, servant of the law, and support of the country. In truth, it is not a favour which I grant you, for your office is neither sweet nor agreeable, but more bitter than bile. Act in accordance with the Rule, no matter what subject you are dealing with; give justice to all, no matter what their condition. Act so that you are respected because of your wisdom and your calm words. When you give orders, take care to persuade; offend no one, and reject violence. Do not take refuge in silence, confront difficulties, do not bow your head before senior officials. May your way of judging be transparent, without dissimulation, and may everyone perceive that it is right; the water and the wind will carry your words and your acts to the people. May none accuse you of having been unjust towards them by failing to listen. Never act according to your preferences; judge those you know in the same way as those you do not know, do not seek to be liked or disliked, do not show favour to anyone, but do not be excessively rigorous or intransigent. Punish rebels, the arrogant and the loose-tongued, for they sow trouble and destruction. Your only

365

refuge is the Rule of Ma'at, which has not altered since the time of the gods and which will still endure when mankind has ceased to exist. Your only way of life is righteousness.'

Bagey bowed before Pharaoh, laid his hand upon the copper heart he wore at his throat, and began to take it off to return it to the king.

'Keep that symbol,' decreed Ramses. 'You have shown yourself worthy of it for so many years that you have acquired the right to bear it with you into the afterlife. For now, live a happy and peaceful old age, but do not forget to counsel your successor.'

The former tjaty and the new one embraced, then Pharaoh bestowed on Pazair a superb new copper heart, made in the royal workshops.

'You are the master of justice,' proclaimed Ramses. 'Watch over the happiness of Egypt and her people. You are the copper that protects the gold, the tjaty protecting Pharaoh. Act in accordance with my orders, but be neither weak nor servile, and have the skill to extend my thoughts. Each day, you shall give me an account of your work.'

The members of the court hailed the new tjaty with deference.

The provincial leaders, governors of estates, scribes, judges, craftsmen, and the men and women of Egypt all sang the praises of the new tjaty. At the state's expense, feasts in his honour were held everywhere, offering the best food and beer.

What destiny could be more enviable than the tjaty's? Servants hurried to satisfy his every whim, he travelled in a cedar-wood boat, the dishes served at his table were succulent, he drank rare wines while musicians played charming airs, the keeper of his vines brought him purple grapes, his steward brought poultry grilled and flavoured with herbs, and fish with delicate flesh. The tjaty sat on ebony-wood seats and slept in a gilded wooden bed with a comfortable mattress; and masseurs soothed away his tiredness.

But all that luxury was just an illusion. The work would be 'more bitter than bile', as the enthronement ritual had stated.

Neferet was principal doctor, Kani was High Priest of Karkak, Kem was commander of the guards . . . The gods had chosen to favour the just, by permitting them to offer their lives to Egypt. The heavens ought to have been bright and people's hearts filled with celebration, but Pazair was sombre and tormented.

In less than a year, would the gods' beloved land be covered in darkness?

Neferet put her arms round Pazair and hugged him. He had told her every word of his conversation with Ramses; united in the secret, they shared its weight. They gazed up into the lapis-blue sky, where the soul of Branir shone among the stars.

Pazair had accepted the house, garden and lands with which Pharaoh endowed his tjaty. Guards handpicked by Kem were posted at the entrance to the vast, walled estate, and others kept it under permanent watch from neighbouring houses. No one could get near without showing a safe-conduct pass or a properly drawn-up summons. Situated not far from the royal palace, the estate formed an island of greenery where five hundred trees flourished, including seventy sycamores, thirty perseas, a hundred and seventy date-palms, a hundred doum-palms, ten fig-trees, nine willows and ten tamarisks. Rare species, imported from Nubia and Asia, were represented by just one example of each. A shimmering vine provided wine reserved for the tjaty. Neferet's monkey was enchanted, imagining a thousand and one climbs and just as many feasts.

Twenty gardeners tended the estate; the cultivated part was divided into squares criss-crossed by irrigation channels. A procession of water-carriers watered lettuces, leeks, onions and cucumbers, which were grown on terraces.

In the centre of the garden was a well. A gently sloping ramp gave access to a hut, sheltered from the wind, where the tjaty might enjoy the winter sun. On the opposite side was a rectangular bathing-pool, with another hut beside it, in the shade of the tallest trees; the hut gave shelter from the north wind in winter.

Pazair had refused to part with the mat he had used as a provincial judge, although there was enough fine furniture in the house to satisfy the most demanding tastes. Neferet was reassured by the many brushes and brooms, concerned as she was to keep such a large house clean.

'The bathing-room is splendid,' said Pazair.

'The barber is waiting for you; he will be at your service every morning.'

'So will your hairdresser.'

'Shall we manage to escape, from time to time?'

He took her in his arms. 'Less than a year, Neferet. We have less than a year to save Ramses.'

Denes disliked having to mark time. Still, he once again had the unconditional support of his wife, who had been bedridden for a long time and would be frail for the rest of her life. By avoiding a divorce, he had both safeguarded his wealth and neutralized Tapeni's threats. But with Pazair's unexpected appointment as tjaty the horizon had grown suddenly dark. Cracks had appeared in the fabric of the conspirators' plot; nevertheless, they were certain to succeed, because they had the Testament of the Gods.

Sheshi was nervous and advised proceeding with the utmost caution. After losing the post of principal doctor and failing to gain that of tjaty, the plotters must stay in the shadows and make use of their infallible weapon, time. The High Priests of the most important temples had just announced the date of the king's festival of regeneration, the first day of the new year, in the month of July, when the star Sopdet's appearance in the crablike group of stars announced the Nile flood. On the eve of his abdication, Ramses would know the name of his successor and hand over power to him in plain sight of the whole country.

'Has the king confided in Pazair?' asked Denes.

'Of course not,' said Sheshi. 'He cannot tell anyone at all – if he confides in even one person, he weakens himself. Pazair's no more virtuous than any other man. He'd immediately gather a group of supporters and move against the king.'

'Why did Ramses choose him?'

'Because the little judge is cunning and ambitious. He must have tricked Ramses into thinking him a man of integrity.'

'You're right. The king's making an enormous mistake.'

'But we must be wary of Pazair – we've seen how dangerous he can be.'

'Having so much power will soon corrupt him. If he weren't stupid, he'd have joined us.'

'Too late. He's playing his own game.'

'We must make sure he gets no chance at all to incriminate us.'

'Let's pay him homage and shower him with gifts. Then he'll think we fully accept him as tjaty.'

Suti waited patiently for the explosion of anger to end. Panther had broken crockery and stools, torn up clothes, and even trampled an expensive wig underfoot. The little house was in a state of utter chaos, but the Libyan still showed no signs of calming down.

'I won't!' she said.

'Be patient for just a little while.'

'You said we'd be leaving tomorrow.'

369

'Pazair wasn't about to be appointed tjaty when I said that,' retorted Suti.

'I don't care.'

'Well I do.'

'Why do you want to wait? He's already forgotten all about you. Let's leave, as we agreed.'

'There's no hurry.'

'I want to get our gold back.'

'It won't run away.'

'Yesterday, all you talked about was our journey.'

'I must see Pazair and find out what his plans are.'

'Pazair, Pazair, always Pazair! Are we never going to be rid of him?'

'Be quiet.'

'I'm not your slave.'

'Tapeni's ordered me to send you away.'

'You dared see that she-devil again!'

'She tracked me down in a tavern. She regards herself as my legal wife.'

'Stupid woman.'

'The tjaty's protection will be useful.'

Pazair's first guest was his predecessor. Despite his bent back and the pains in his legs, Bagey walked without a stick. The two men went out into the garden and sat down in the hut by the pool.

'You throughly deserve your promotion,' said Bagey. 'I could not have dreamt of a better tjaty.'

'I shall try to continue your work as you would have done yourself.'

'My last year was difficult and disappointing. It was time for me to go, and fortunately the king listened to me. Your youth will not be a handicap for long; the office soon brings a man to maturity.'

'What advice would you give me?'

'Ignore gossip, keep your distance from courtiers, study each case in depth, and always be extremely thorough in everything you do. I'll introduce you to my closest colleagues, and you shall test their skills.'

The sun broke through the clouds and bathed the hut in light. Seeing that Bagey was uncomfortable, Pazair put up a palm-frond shade.

'Do you like this house?' asked Bagey.

'I haven't yet had time to explore it.'

'It was too big for me, and the garden was nothing but trouble. I prefer my quarters in town.'

'I shan't be able to do the work without your help. Will you stay at my side and advise me?'

'That is my duty. All the same, give me some time to attend to my son.'

'Is he having difficulties?'

'His employer isn't happy with him. I'm worried that he may be dismissed, and my wife is anxious.'

'If there's anything I can do . . .'

'No, I cannot accept any help from you: giving me or my family special treatment would be a serious offence. Shall we set to work?'

Pazair and Suti embraced.

Suti looked around. 'I like your estate. I want one just like it, and I shall use it to stage unforgettable parties.'

'Would you like to be tjaty?'

'Certainly not! Work disagrees with me. Why did you accept such an heavy burden?'

'It was made impossible for me to refuse.'

'I'm hugely rich now. Escape from all this, and we'll enjoy life to the full.'

Pazair shook his head. 'I can't.'

'Don't you trust me?'

'Pharaoh has entrusted a vital mission to me.'

'Well, don't end up as one of those stuffy senior officials full of their own importance.'

'Are you criticizing me for becoming tjaty?'

'Are you criticizing the way I made my fortune?'

'Won't you stay here and work with me?'

'Letting this chance pass me by would be a crime.'

'If you commit a real crime, I shan't be able to protect you.'

'Then our friendship's finished,' said Suti.

'No. You're my friend and you always will be.'

'A friend doesn't issue threats.'

'I want to stop you making a disastrous mistake,' said Pazair. 'Kem won't give up, and he'll be merciless.'

'We're evenly matched.'

'Don't provoke him, Suti.'

'Don't tell me how to behave.'

'Stay here – please. If you knew the real importance of my work, you wouldn't hesitate for a moment.'

'Defending the law? What fanciful nonsense! If I'd respected it, Asher would still be alive.'

'I didn't testify against you,' Pazair reminded him.

'You're tense and worried. What are you hiding from me?'

'We've dismantled one plot, but that was only the first stage. Let's go on together.'

'I prefer my gold.'

'Give it back to the temple.'

'Will you inform on me?'

Pazair did not reply.

'The role of tjaty eclipses that of friend, doesn't it?'

'Don't go back to the desert, Suti.'

'It's a beautiful and hostile world. When you're disillusioned with power, you'll join me there.'

'I don't want power. I want to safeguard our country, ourselves, our faith.'

'Good luck, Tjaty. I'm taking the gold road again.'

The young man left the beautiful garden without a backward glance. He hadn't mentioned Tapeni's demands, but what did that matter?

Before Suti had crossed the threshold of his home, four guards surrounded him and bound his hands behind his back.

Alerted by the sounds of the struggle, Panther rushed out with a knife in her hand, and tried to free him. She wounded one guard and knocked over another, but was eventually overcome and bound.

The guards immediately took the pair to the court, where they were accused of flagrant adultery. Tapeni was jubilant: this was a far better result than she'd hoped for. The adultery was made worse by their having resisted the guards. Tapeni's testimony – she spoke of having been been seduced and then deserted pleased the judges, whereas Panther insulted them, and Suti's arguments seemed unconvincing.

Tapeni asked the jury to be lenient, so Panther was sentenced only to immediate expulsion from Egypt, and Suti to a year's imprisonment, at the end of which he would have to get a job and earn the compensation he owed his rejected wife.

40

Pazair looked at the Sphinx. The giant statue's eyes gazed at the rising sun, confident of its victory over the forces of destruction, won after a hard fight in the underworld. The watchful guardian of the plateau where the pyramids of Khufu, Khafra and Menkaura stood, it took part in the eternal struggle on which the survival of humanity depended.

The tjaty ordered a team of quarrymen to move the great stele that stood between the Sphinx's paws. This revealed a sealed vase and a flagstone with a ring. Two men lifted the flagstone, revealing the entrance to a narrow, low-ceilinged passageway.

Armed with a torch, the tjaty entered first. Not far from the entrance, his foot struck a dolerite cup. He picked it up and, stooping, continued on his way. A wall blocked his path. By the light of the flame he noticed that several stones had been worked free; a complete row pivoted. On the other side was the basement chamber of the Great Pyramid.

The tjaty walked along the route that the thieves had taken several times, then examined the cup. The dolerite, one of the hardest forms of granite and very difficult to work, bore traces of a very oily substance.

Intrigued, Pazair left the pyramid and took the cup to the workshop at the Temple of Ptah, where the specialists identified the substance as stone-oil,* whose use was forbidden in Egypt. As it burnt, the oil dirtied the walls of tombs and clogged up the craftsmen's lungs.

The tjaty demanded a swift investigation of the miners of the western desert and of the secretariat in charge of wicks and lamp-oils. Then, for the first time, he entered the audience chamber where his principal colleagues had gathered.

The tjaty was Pharaoh's overseer of works, the leader of the teams of craftsmen and trade bodies, charged with putting every man in his rightful place by teaching him his duties and ensuring his well-being. He was also in charge of the archives and the country's government, the most senior scribe, the head of the army, and guarantor of civil peace and security. As such, the tjaty must speak clearly, weigh his thoughts, calm people's passions, remain unmoved when storms raged, and see that justice was done in matters both great and small.

His official garb consisted of a long, starched apron made from thick fabric and reaching up to the chest; two straps, passing behind the neck, held it up. On his kilt, which had a panel at the front, was a panther skin, a reminder that the first citizen of the empire, after Pharaoh, must act with speed. A heavy wig hid his hair, and a broad collar covered the upper part of his torso.

Wearing sandals with straps and carrying a sceptre in his right hand, Pazair walked between two rows of scribes, climbed the steps leading to a dais where a high-backed chair stood, then turned to face his subordinates. At his feet was a piece of red cloth, on which were laid forty staffs of command designed to punish the guilty. When the tjaty hung a figurine of Ma'at on his thin gold chain, the audience began.

Pazair said, 'Pharaoh has clearly set out the duties of the tjaty, which have not varied since the day when our

*Petroleum.

forefathers built this country. We live by the same truth as Pharaoh, and shall together continue to hand down justice without differentiating between rich and poor. Our glory lies in spreading justice across the land, so that men breathed it in and it drives evil from their bodies. Let us protect the weak from the strong, refuse to listen to flatterers, oppose disorder and brutality. Each of you owes it to himself to be an example; anyone who derives personal profit from his office will lose his title and his post. No one will gain my trust by way of fine words; only by fine deeds.'

The brevity of the speech, the rigorous nature of its content, and the calmness of the new tjaty's voice, surprised the officials. Those who had been planning to take advantage of his youth and inexperience to lengthen their rest periods abandoned their plans immediately; those who had hoped to profit from Bagey's departure were disappointed.

Everyone wondered what the tjaty's first public order would be, because it would set the tone of his administration. Some of his predecessors had been preoccupied first and foremost with the army, some with irrigation, others with taxes.

'Bring me the scribe in charge of honey production.'

An icy wind blew over the desert around Khargeh oasis. The old bee-keeper sentenced to life imprisonment thought of his hives, large jars where the bees built their combs. He had harvested the honey without protection, for he was not afraid of them and could always tell if they were getting angry. The bee was one of Pharaoh's symbols, a tireless worker, an alchemist capable of creating edible gold. The old bee-keeper had harvested a hundred types of honey, from the reddest to the most transparent, until the day when an envious scribe had accused him of theft. Stealing honey, whose transport was overseen by the guards, was a serious crime. Never again would he pour it into little vessels, sealed with wax and numbered, never again would he hear the buzzing of the swarm, his favourite music. When the sun had wept, a few tears had been transformed into bees as they hit the ground. Born out of divine light, they had built nature. But Ra's light now illuminated only the emaciated body of a prisoner, who cooked revolting meals for his comrades in misfortune.

There was a commotion near the prison gates. Abandoning his ovens, he followed the other prisoners.

A veritable expedition was approaching: fifty soldiers, chariots, horses and carts. Were the Libyans attacking? He rubbed his eyes and made out Egyptian footsoldiers. The prison guards bowed before a man who walked, without hesitation, towards the kitchen.

Astounded, the old man recognized Pazair. 'You . . . you survived!'

'You gave me good advice.'

'Why have you come back?'

'I haven't forgotten my promise.'

'Run away, quickly! They'll lock you up again.'

'Don't worry, I am the one who gives the guards their orders.'

'Does that mean you've become a judge again?'

'Pharaoh has appointed me tjaty.'

'Don't make fun of an old man.'

Two soldiers brought over a fat scribe with a double chin.

'Do you recognize him?' asked Pazair.

'That's him!' exclaimed the bee-keeper. 'That's the liar who got me convicted!'

'I propose an exchange: he'll take your place in prison, and you'll take his as head of the secretariat of honey supplies.'

The old bee-keeper fainted clean away. The tjaty caught him as he fell.

The report was clear and concise: Pazair congratulated the scribe. Stone-oil, which was found in large quantities in the western desert, was of enormous interest to the Libyans. They had tried several times to extract it for commercial purposes, but Pharaoh's army had intervened. Egyptian scholars considered stone-oil a harmful and dangerous product.

Only one specialist, at court, was in charge of studying it, in order to identify its properties. He alone had access to the stock kept in a state warehouse, under military control. When he read the man's name, the tjaty thanked the gods and went immediately to the royal palace.

'Majesty,' said Pazair, 'I explored the underground passage leading from the Sphinx to the chamber beneath the Great Pyramid.'

'Have the entrance sealed for ever,' ordered Ramses.

'The stonemasons are already at work.'

'What clues did you find?'

'A dolerite cup in which stone-oil had been burnt to provide light.'

'Who could have procured the oil?'

'Only the specialist charged with studying it.'

'What is his name?'

'Sheshi the inventor, slave and scapegoat of Denes.'

'Do you know where to find him?'

'He's hiding at Denes's house, according to Kem.'

'Do they have accomplices or are they the core of the conspiracy?'

'I shall find out, Majesty.'

Tapeni prevented the tjaty's chariot from pulling away.

'I want to speak to you,' she said.

The officer whose job was to drive the vehicle and ensure Pazair's safety raised his whip, but the tjaty restrained him and asked, 'Is it very urgent?'

Tapeni smiled. 'You will be glad to hear what I have to say.'

378

He got down from the chariot. 'Be brief.'

'You're the embodiment of justice, are you not? Well, you'll be proud of me. A deceived, abused woman who has been dragged through the mud is a victim, isn't she?'

'Indeed.'

'My husband deserted me, and the court punished him.'

'Your husband . . .'

'Yes, your friend Suti. His Libyan whore has been deported, and he's been sentenced to a year in prison. Actually, it's a very light sentence, and a mild imprisonment: the court sent him to Tjaru in Nubia, where he'll serve in the garrison. The place is not very welcoming, apparently, but Suti will have the privilege of helping defend his country against the barbarians. When he comes back, he'll enlist in a body of messengers and will pay me a pension in food.'

'You were going to separate amicably.'

'I changed my mind; I love him, as it happens, and I won't tolerate being abandoned. If you intervened in his favour, you'd be violating the rule of Ma'at, and I'd make sure he knew it.' Her smile was menacing.

'Suti will serve his sentence,' agreed the tjaty, hiding his anger. 'But on his return—'

'If he attacks me, he'll be accused of attempted murder and sent to a much harsher prison. He's my slave – for ever. I am his future.'

'The investigation into Branir's murder is not closed.'

'It's up to you to find the murderer.'

'That is my dearest wish. You told me once that you knew important secrets.'

'That was just boasting.'

'Or was it carelessness? You're an excellent needle-woman, are you not?'

Tapeni looked wary. 'In my trade, that's essential.'

'Perhaps, but I can't help wondering whether the murderer isn't very close to me at this precise moment.'

The pretty brunette could not meet the tjaty's eyes. She turned on her heel and walked rapidly away.

Pazair ought to have gone to see Kem, but he chose instead to check the truth of Tapeni's words. So he went to his office and had the account of the trial brought to him, together with the judgement concerning Suti. The documents confirmed the facts. The tjaty was in the worst of positions. How could he help his friend without betraying the law of which he was the guarantor?

Sombre, indifferent to the gathering storm, he went out again and climbed back into his chariot. With Kem's help, he must work out a plan of action.

Neferet had taken a few minutes from her overcrowded schedule to treat Silkis's indigestion. Despite her youth, Bel-Tran's wife put on weight quickly as soon as greed grew stronger than her wish to be slender.

'I think a two-day fast is necessary,' said Neferet.

'I thought I was going to die,' said Silkis. 'I could hardly breathe for the waves of nausea.'

'They relieve your stomach.'

'I'm so tired – but I'm ashamed to say that to you. All I do is care for my children and my husband.'

'How is Bel-Tran?'

'He's delighted to be working under Pazair – he admires him so much. With their respective qualities, the two of them will ensure the country's prosperity. But he spends so much time working . . . I miss him and I get lonely. Don't you?'

'Well, the answer is to see each other every day and talk freely.'

'Forgive me for asking, but . . . wouldn't you like to have a child?'

'Not before we've caught Branir's murderer. We made a vow before the gods, and we shall keep it.'

*

A dark veil covered Memphis. Thick clouds hung over the city because there was no wind, and all the dogs were howling. The light had got so dim that Denes lit several lamps. His wife had taken a soothing draught and was asleep. All Nenophar's famous energy had faded, to be replaced by a permanent lassitude. Now docile and submissive, she would cause him no more trouble.

He went out into the garden, and joined Sheshi in the workshop where the inventor spent his time sharpening the blades of knives and swords; it helped him work off his nervous tension.

Denes handed him a cup of beer. 'Rest for a while.'

'Is there any news of Pazair?'

'He's busy with the honey harvest. His speech impressed the senior scribes, but that was only words, after all. The factions will soon start tearing each other apart, and he won't have the stature to survive.'

'You're an optimist.'

'Patience is a valuable quality. If Qadash had understood that, he'd still be alive today. While the new tjaty works and works, we'll enjoy life and look forward to the pleasures of absolute power.'

'All I want is to live to be a few months older,' said Sheshi.

'You're discreet, efficient and tireless, and you're going to be an outstanding statesman. Thanks to you, Egyptian knowledge will take a gigantic leap forward.'

'Stone-oil, drugs, metals . . . this country doesn't make proper use of its resources. By developing methods and skills Ramses has disdained, we'll rid ourselves of tradition.'

All at once, Sheshi's excitment died. 'There's someone outside,' he said.

'I didn't hear anything.'

'I'm going to check.'

'It's probably a gardener.'

'They don't come anywhere near the workshop.' Sheshi

381

stared suspiciously at Denes. 'Have you called on the services of the shadow-eater?'

The ship-owner's face hardened. 'It was Qadash who stepped out of line, not you.'

A flash of lightning zig-zagged across the sky, and the thunder rolled. Sheshi went out of the workshop, took a few steps towards the house, then turned and ran back inside. Denes had never seen him look so pale, and his teeth were chattering.

'It's a ghost!' he quavered.

'Calm down.'

'I saw it – a shape blacker than the night, with a flame instead of a face!'

'Pull yourself together and come with me.'

Reluctantly, Sheshi agreed.

The left wing of the house was on fire.

'Water, quickly!' Denes rushed forward, but a black shape seemed to spring out of the flames, and it barred his way.

The ship-owner recoiled. 'Who are you?'

The ghost was brandishing a torch.

Recovering a little of his courage, Sheshi seized a dagger from the workshop and bore down on the strange figure. It went badly for him, for the spectre thrust the torch into his face. Flesh sizzling, Sheshi howled and fell to his knees, trying to force away the instrument of his torture. The creature picked up the dagger he had dropped, and cut his throat.

Horrified, Denes ran towards the house.

The ghost's voice stopped him in his tracks. 'Do you still want to know who I am?'

He turned round. It was a human being, not a demon from the otherworld, who was threatening him. Curiosity replaced fear.

'Look, Denes. Look at your work and Sheshi's.'

It was so dark that he had to go closer.

In the distance, he heard shouts. People had started to notice the fire.

The ghost unveiled itself. The fine-featured face was no more than a mass of scars.

'Don't you recognize me?'

'Princess Hattusa!'

'You destroyed me, and now I'm destroying you.'

'You murdered Sheshi!'

'I punished my torturer. A killer's crime seizes him and takes possession of him.' She thrust her dagger deep into the flames, as though her hand was impervious to them. 'You won't run away, Denes.'

She advanced on him, the blade glowing red.

He could have charged at her and knocked her over, but her madness frightened him: the guards could have the job of arresting her.

Lightning tore across the sky, thunder rolled over the house, and a tongue of fire leapt out of the wall, which crumbled and set fire to Denes's clothing. He staggered, and rolled on the ground to put out the flames.

He did not see the figure bearing down on him, the ghost with the dead face.

41

The caravan advanced slowly; Kem watched it as far as the border. Hattusa, seated in the back of a chariot, was as inert as a soulless statue. When he had come upon her at the scene of the crime, she had offered no resistance. Servants, who had run up to put out the fire, had seen her dragging the bodies of Sheshi and Denes into the flames. Torrential rain had fallen on Memphis, putting out the flames and washing the blood from the princess's hands.

She had not answered any of the questions put to her by the tjaty, who was so overwhelmed that his voice shook. As soon as he reported the facts to Ramses, the king had ordered the embalmers to give the bodies of the two conspirators a cursory preparation, then bury them somewhere remote, far from a burial-ground, without any rites. Through Hattusa, evil had struck down the men of darkness.

With the tjaty's agreement, the king had decided to send the princess back to her own country. However, even the announcement of her liberation, which she had so longed for, did not produce a reaction. Broken, her gaze empty, Hattusa wandered in worlds which were inaccessible to anyone but herself.

The official document that Kem handed to a Hittite officer spoke of an untreatable illness, and the necessary return of the princess to her family. The honour of the Hittite emperor was safe, and no diplomatic incident would trouble the peace that had been so dearly bought.

Under Pazair's watchful eye, workmen searched the remains of Denes's house, and gathered together their meagre finds. Ramses himself examined them. It was thought that this was the king's way of showing his interest in the tragic deaths of the ship-owner and the inventor, whereas he was in fact searching for a trace of the Testament of the Gods.

In vain: the disappointment was a cruel one.

'Are all the conspirators dead?' he asked Pazair.

'I do not know, Majesty.'

'Whom do you suspect?'

'Denes seemed to me to be their leader. He tried to make use of General Asher and Princess Hattusa, in order to establish links with foreign powers. No doubt he envisaged a change of policy, based on trade.'

'Sacrificing the spirit of Egypt to an all-pervading greed . . . What a pernicious plan! Did his wife help him?'

'No, Majesty. She does not even realize that her husband tried to kill her. Her servants saved her, and she has left Memphis and is living with her parents in the north of the Delta. According to the doctors who examined her, she has lost her reason.'

'Neither she nor Denes had the necessary stature to attack the throne.'

'Supposing that he did indeed hold the Testament at his house, would it not have been burnt in the fire? If no one – neither you nor your enemies – can produce it at the festival of regeneration, what will happen?'

A glimmer of hope showed in Ramses' eyes. He said, 'As tjaty, you will bring together the country's authorities and explain the situation to them; then you will address the people. As for me, I shall celebrate an era of renewed births, marked by the drawing up of a new pact with the gods.

Perhaps I shall fail, for the process is long and difficult; but at least a man of darkness will not take power. Let us hope you are right, Pazair, and that Denes was the instigator of the conspiracy.'

As they did every evening, the swallows were dancing over the garden where Pazair and Neferet met after a day of hard work. The birds flew low over their heads, giving shrill, joyful cries, swooping round at top speed, describing enormous curves in the blue winter sky.

Brave and Mischief had called a truce. The dog was sleeping at his master's feet, the little green monkey under her mistress's chair.

The tjaty was suffering from a cold and breathing difficulties, and been examined thoroughly by the principal doctor.

'My poor health ought to bar me from being tjaty,' he said.

'It's a gift from the gods,' said Neferet, 'because it makes you think, instead of rushing in blindly like a ram with more enthusiasm than good sense. Besides, it doesn't diminish your energy at all.'

'You look worried.'

'In a week's time, I shall present the council of doctors with the measures to be taken to improve public health. Some measures will be unpopular, but I believe they are vital. It will be a hard-fought battle.'

'The date of the festival of regeneration has been proclaimed throughout the land,' said Pazair. 'At the time of the next flood, Ramses will be reborn.'

'Have any other conspirators shown themselves since the deaths of Denes and Sheshi?'

'No.'

'Then the Testament of the Gods must have been destroyed in the fire.'

'That seems more and more likely.'

'And yet you still have doubts.'

'To keep such a valuable thing in his house seems senseless to me. But then Denes was so over-confident that he thought he was invulnerable.'

'And what about Suti?'

'The judgement was correctly handed down; there were no procedural irregularities.'

'What can be done?'

'I can see no legal solution.'

'If you organize his escape,' said Neferet, 'make it a masterstroke.'

'You read my thoughts too well. This time Kem won't help me. If the tjaty did something like that, Ramses would be tarnished and the prestige of Egypt with him. But Suti's my friend, and we swore to help each other, no matter what.'

'Let's think about it together. At least let him know you aren't abandoning him.'

Alone and weaponless, with several days' walking ahead of her, and only one water-skin and a few dried fish to sustain her, Panther had little chance of survival. The Egyptian guards had left her at the border with Libya, ordering her to go back to her country and never to return to the land of the Pharaohs, on pain of heavy punishment.

At best, she would be spotted by a band of rapacious sand-travellers and raped. They'd keep her alive only until the first lines appeared on her face.

The beautiful Libyan turned her back on the land of her birth.

She would never abandon Suti. It would be a long and dangerous journey from the north-western Delta to the Nubian fort where her lover was locked away. She would have to take bad roads, find water and food, escape wandering brigands. But she was determined that Tapeni would not emerge victorious from their long-distance battle.

*

'Soldier Suti?'

The young man did not answer the officer.

'A year's disciplinary regime in my fortress. The judges gave you a fine present, my lad. You must show yourself worthy of it. On your knees.'

Suti stared him straight in the eyes.

'A stubborn one – I like that. Don't you like this place?'

The prisoner looked around. The banks of the turbulent Nile, the desert, sun-scorched hills, an intensely blue sky, a pelican catching fish, a crocodile lazing on a rock.

'Tjaru isn't altogether lacking in charm. Your presence is an insult to it.'

'A joker, too,' said the officer. 'And the son of a rich family, I suppose?'

'You cannot imagine how rich.'

'You impress me.'

'That's only a beginning.'

'On your knees. When you address the commander of this fortress, you will be polite.'

Two soldiers hit Suti on the back, knocking him face down on the ground.

'That's better,' said the officer. 'But you aren't here to rest, my lad. First thing tomorrow, you'll stand guard at our most forward position – unarmed, of course. If a Nubian tribe attacks, you'll warn us. Their tortures are so agonizing that the victim's screams can be heard a long way away.'

Rejected by Pazair, separated for ever from Panther, forgotten by everyone, Suti would not get out of Tjaru alive, unless hatred gave him the strength he needed.

His gold awaited him, and so did Tapeni.

Bak was eighteen years old. The son and grandson of army officers, he was rather small, but hard-working and courageous. He had black hair, finely drawn features, and a strong, musical voice. After wavering between becoming a soldier or a scribe, he had entered the archives secretariat, just before Pazair's appointment. To the most recent arrival fell the most thankless tasks, notably the filing of scrolls used by the tjaty when studying a case. That was why Bak had the ones concerning stone-oil; now that Sheshi was dead, they were no longer of interest.

Meticulously, he arranged them in a wooden box which the tjaty would seal himself, and which would be reopened only on his orders. It should have been quick to do, but Bak took care to examine each papyrus. It was just as well he did. One of them was missing the tjaty's annotation, so he could not have read it. The detail seemed unimportant, since the matter was filed for no further action; nevertheless, the young scribe noted it down and handed the note to his superior, so that it might follow the proper administrative path.

Pazair insisted on reading all the remarks, observations and criticisms written by his subordinates, no matter what how junior, so he found Bak's note.

Towards the end of the morning, he summoned the young scribe and asked him, 'What did you notice that was unusual?'

'Your seal is missing from a report by a Treasury employee who was dismissed.'

'Show me.'

Indeed, Pazair found a document he had not read. No doubt a scribe from his own office had omitted to include it in the case of papyri relating to stone-oil.

'One grain of sand in a device,' thought the tjaty, thinking of a little provincial judge who, simply through his concern that a job should be done well, had detected a cancer aiming to destroy Egypt.

'From tomorrow, you will take charge of the archives and inform me directly of any anomalies. We shall meet each day, at the start of the morning.'

After he left the tjaty's office, Bak ran towards the street. Once in the open air, he gave a shout of joy.

'This conversation seems rather formal,' remarked Bel-Tran easily. 'We could have had it over the midday meal at my house.'

'Without wishing to stand on ceremony,' said Pazair, 'I think we must both submit to the dignity of our respective offices.'

'You're the tjaty, and I'm director of the White House and in charge of the country's trade and money. According to the order of precedence, I must obey you. Have I read your mind right?'

'Like this, we shall work in harmony.'

Bel-Tran had put on weight, and his round face was becoming positively moonlike. Despite the skill of his weaving-women, his kilt was always too tight.

Pazair went on, 'You're a specialist in trade and finance, and I'm not. Your advice will be most welcome.'

'Advice or instructions?'

'The economy must not come before the art of governing, for men don't live on material possessions alone. Egypt's greatness is born of its vision of the world, not from its economic power.'

Bel-Tran's lips pursed, but he did not answer.

'One minor matter worries me. Have you been involved at all with a dangerous product, stone-oil?'

'Who's accusing me?'

'That's putting it too strongly. A report by a scribe you dismissed implicates you.'

'What is his complaint?'

'That, for a short period, you lifted the ban on exploiting stone-oil in a clearly designated area of the western desert and authorized a trade from which you deducted a large commission. It was a brief but extremely lucrative operation.

There was nothing illegal, in fact, because you had the agreement of the specialist concerned, Sheshi. But Sheshi was a criminal, involved in a conspiracy against the state.'

'What are you insinuating?'

'That connection makes me uneasy. I'm sure it's just an unfortunate coincidence, but as a friend I'd like an explanation.'

Bel-Tran got to his feet. His expression was transformed so completely that Pazair was speechless. The warm, friendly face was replaced by one full of hatred and arrogance. The voice, usually quiet but measured, was brimming with anger and violence.

'An explanation as a friend? What naivety! How long it's taken you to understand, my dear Pazair, tjaty of straw! Qadash, Sheshi and Denes my accomplices? Rather my devoted servants, whether or not they realized it. If I supported you against them, it was only because of Denes's stupid ambition – he wanted to be director of the White House and control the country's finances. I was the only one fit to be director. It should have been a simple step from there to seizing the post of tjaty, but you stole it from me. The whole government recognized me as the most suitable candidate, the members of the court all suggested me when Pharaoh consulted them, and yet it was you, an obscure, disgraced judge, whom the king chose. A clever manoeuvre, my dear fellow; you surprised me.'

'You're mistaken.'

'Not about myself, Pazair. The past doesn't interest me. Either you play your own game and lose everything, or else you obey me and become very rich, without having the cares of a power you are not competent to wield.'

'I am the tjaty of Egypt.'

'You're nothing, because Pharaoh is finished.'

'Does that mean you've got the Testament of the Gods?'

A sneer of satisfaction twisted Bel-Tran's face. 'So

Ramses did confide in you. How stupid of him. He really isn't worthy to reign any more. But enough of this talk, my dear friend. Are you with me or against me?'

'I've never been so disgusted in all my life.'

'I'm not interested in your emotions.'

'How can you bear your own hypocrisy?'

'It's a more useful weapon than your ridiculous honesty.'

'Don't you know that greed is the most deadly of all evils and that it will deprive you of a tomb?'

Bel-Tran burst out laughing. 'Your morality is that of a backward child. Gods, temples, houses of eternity, rituals – all that stupid, outworn stuff. You have no understanding at all of the new world we're entering. I have great plans, Pazair. Even before driving Ramses out, I shall put them into practice. Open your eyes, see the future!'

'Give back the things you stole from the Great Pyramid.'

'Gold is a rare and extremely valuable metal. Why should it be frozen into ritual objects which only a dead man can see? My people melted them down. I have enough money to buy a lot of consciences.'

'I can have you arrested within the hour.'

'No, you can't. With one gesture I shall bring Ramses down, and you with him. But I shall do it at my chosen time, and according to the plan. Imprisoning or killing me wouldn't stop it. You and your king are bound hand and foot. Give up following a man who's more dead than alive, and place yourself at my service. I shall grant you one last chance, Pazair. Take it.'

'I shall fight you to my last breath.'

'In less than a year your name will be obliterated from the annals. Make the most of your pretty wife, because soon everything will crumble around you. Your universe is worm-eaten – I've eaten away the posts that supported it. Too bad for you, tjaty of Egypt. You'll regret underestimating me.'

*

Pharaoh and his tjaty spoke in the secret room of the House of Life in Memphis, far from prying eyes and ears.

Pazair revealed the truth to Ramses.

'Bel-Tran the papyrus-maker,' said Ramses, 'the man in charge of distributing the great texts, the man responsible for the country's money and trade . . . I knew he was ambitious and acquisitive, but I never imagined that he was a traitor, a destroyer.'

'He has had time to weave his web, to create a network of accomplices in all classes of society, to poison the government.'

'Will you dismiss him immediately?'

'No, Majesty. Evil has at last shown its face. We must now try to work out what his plan is, so that we can fight it.'

'But he has the Testament of the Gods.'

'He probably isn't working alone, so killing him would not ensure our victory.'

'Nine months, Pazair; we have nine months left, the length of a pregnancy. Go to war, identify Bel-Tran's allies, dismantle his fortresses, disarm the soldiers of darkness.'

'Majesty, we should remember the words of the old sage Ptah-hotep: "Great is the Rule, lasting its effectiveness; it has not been disrupted since the time of Osiris. Iniquity is capable of gaining possession of the many, but evil will never bring its undertakings to fruition. Have no part in any plot against the human race, for God punishes such actions."'

'He lived in the time of the great pyramids and was a tjaty, like you. Let us hope he was right.'

'His words have endured through time.'

'It is not my throne that is at stake, but tomorrow's civilization. Either treason will bear it away, or justice will be done.'

From Branir's tomb, Pazair and Neferet gazed out over the huge burial-ground at Saqqara, which was overlooked by the

Step Pyramid of Pharaoh Djoser. The priests of the *ka*, servants of the immortal soul, tended the gardens of the tombs and laid offerings on the stone tables of the shrines, which were open to pilgrims. Stone-cutters were restoring an ancient pyramid, while others were excavating a tomb. The city of the dead lived a life of serenity.

'What have you decided?' Neferet asked Pazair.

'To fight. To fight to the end.'

'We shall find Branir's murderer.'

'He has already been punished, don't you think? Denes, Sheshi and Qadash died in horrible circumstances, and the law of the desert sentenced General Asher.'

'The murderer is still at large,' she said. 'When our master's soul at last knows peace, a new star will appear.'

She laid her head gently on Pazair's shoulder. Nourished by her strength and love, the Egyptian judge would fight a battle which was lost before it began, in the hope that the happiness of the divine land would not disappear from the memory of the Nile, from granite and from light.